Caroline Graham was born in W___ ___kshire in the
1930s. She was educated a_ _____ High School
for Girls and later at t__ _____ __y. She has
served in the WRN_ ___ _____ __ ___ __eau and,
during the 19__ ___ _____.

She starte_ ___ _____ __ ___ __king first as a
freelance jou_____ ___ ___C and Radio London.
She then swi_____ __ _____iting plays for radio and
television after ___ ___ing to Suffolk in 1975. Her first
novel, *Fire Dance*, was published in 1982, followed by
The Envy of the Stranger in 1984, which has been
dramatised for Radio Four. She received resounding
critical acclaim for her first Barnaby novel, *The
Killings at Badger's Drift*, which is available as a
Headline paperback. Caroline Graham also writes
books for children.

Also by Caroline Graham

The Killings at Badger's Drift
The Envy of the Stranger
Fire Dance

BMX Star Rider
BMX'ers Battle it Out

Death of a Hollow Man

Caroline Graham

HEADLINE

First published in Great Britain in 1989
by Century Hutchinson Ltd

First published in paperback in 1990
by HEADLINE BOOK PUBLISHING

10 9 8 7 6 5 4

ISBN 0 7472 3350 0

Printed and bound in Great Britain by
Cox & Wyman Ltd, Reading, Berkshire

HEADLINE BOOK PUBLISHING
A division of Hodder Headline PLC
338 Euston Road
London NW1 3BH

To Beryl Arnold
With Love

Acknowledgement

The author gratefully acknowledges permission
from London Management to quote from *Amadeus*
by Peter Shaffer.

Contents

AMADEUS

by

PETER SHAFFER

THE VENTICELLI:	CLIVE EVERARD
	DONALD EVERARD
VALET TO SALIERI:	DAVID SMY
COOK TO SALIERI:	JOYCE BARNABY
ANTONIO SALIERI:	ESSLYN CARMICHAEL
TERESA SALIERI:	ROSA CRAWLEY
JOHANN KILIAN VON STRACK:	VICTOR LACEY
COUNT ORSINI-ROSENBERG:	JAMES BAKER
BARON VAN SWIETEN:	BILL LAST
CONSTANZE WEBER:	KITTY CARMICHAEL
WOLFGANG AMADEUS MOZART:	NICHOLAS BRADLEY
MAJOR-DOMO:	ANTHONY CHALLIS
JOSEPH II, EMPEROR OF AUSTRIA:	BORIS KENT
KATHERINA CAVALIERI:	SARAH PITT KEIGHLEY
CITIZENS OF VIENNA:	KENNY BADEL,
	KEVIN LATIMER,
	NOEL ARMSTRONG,
	ALAN
	HUGHES, LUCY
	MITCHELL, GUY
	CATCHPOLE,
	PHOEBE GLOVER
DESIGN:	AVERY PHILLIPS
LIGHTING:	TIM YOUNG
WARDROBE:	JOYCE BARNABY
STAGE MANAGER:	COLIN SMY
ASSISTANT STAGE MANAGER	DIERDRE TIBBS

DIRECTED BY HAROLD WINSTANLEY

CURTAIN RAISER

'You can't cut your throat without any blood.'

'Absolutely. People expect it.'

'I disagree. There wasn't any blood in the West End production.'

'Oh, Scofield,' murmured Esslyn dismissively. 'So mannered.'

The Causton Amateur Dramatic Society were taking a break during a rehearsal of *Amadeus*. The production was fairly well advanced. The Venticelli were finally picking up their cues, the fireplace for the palace at Schönbrunn was promised for the weekend and Constanze seemed at long last to be almost on the point of starting to learn at least one or two of her lines, whilst remaining rather hazy as to the order in which they came. But the sticky question as to how Salieri should most effectively cut his throat had yet to be solved. Tim Young, the only member of the company to shave the old-fashioned way, had promised to bring his razor along that very evening. So far there was no sign of him.

'You ... um ... you can get things, can't you? That make blood? I remember at the RSC –'

'Well of course you can get things, Dierdre,' snapped Harold Winstanley. (He always reacted very abrasively to any mention of the RSC.) 'I don't think there are many people present who are unaware of the fact that you can *get* things. It's just that I do try to be a tiny bit inventive ... move away from the usual hackneyed routine. *Comprenez?*' He gazed at the assembled company, inviting them to admire his superhuman patience in the face of such witless suggestion. 'And talking of routine – isn't it time we had our coffee?'

'Oh yes, sorry.' Dierdre Tibbs, who had been sitting

on the stage hugging her corduroyed knees in a rather girlish way, scrambled to her feet.

'Chop chop then.'

'If you think Scofield was mannered,' said Donald Everard, picking up Esslyn's put-down, 'how about Simon Callow?'

'How *about* Simon Callow?' shrilled his twin.

Dierdre left them happily rubbishing their betters and made her way up the aisle towards the clubroom. Dierdre was supposed to be the assistant director. She had been general dogsbody on dozens of productions until a few weeks ago when, fortified by a couple of sweet Martinis, she had shyly asked the committee to consider her promotion. To her delight they had voted, not quite unanimously, in her favour. But the delight was short lived for it seemed that her role vis-à-vis the present state of play at the Latimer was to be no different from that at any time previously. For Harold would brook no discussion (his own phrase) on points of production, and her few tentative suggestions had either been ignored or shot down in flames.

In the clubroom she took the mugs from their hooks and placed them very carefully on the tray to avoid clinkage, then turned on a thin thread of water and filled the kettle. Harold, quick to describe himself as a one-man think tank, found the slightest sound disturbing to his creative flow.

Of course as a director, Dierdre admitted sadly to herself, he had the edge. Twenty years earlier he had acted at Filey, produced a summer season at Minehead and appeared in a Number One Tour (Original West End Cast!) of *Spider's Web*. You couldn't argue with that sort of experience. One or two of them tried, of course. Especially newcomers who still had opinions of their own and hadn't sussed the pecking order. Not that there were many of these. The CADS were extremely selective. And Nicholas, who was playing Mozart whilst darkly awaiting the results of an audition from the Central School of Speech and Drama. He argued sometimes. Esslyn didn't argue. Just listened attentively to everything Harold said then went his own unsparkling way. Harold consoled himself for this intransigence by directing everyone else to within an inch of their lives.

Dierdre spooned cheap powdered coffee and dried milk into the mugs and poured on boiling water. One or two little white beads bobbed to the surface and she pushed them down nervously with the back of a spoon, at the same time trying to remember who took sugar and who was sweet enough. Best take the packet and ask. She went cautiously back down the aisle, balancing her heavy tray. Esslyn had got on to Ian McKellen.

'So – quite against my better judgement – I allowed myself to be dragged along to this one-man effort. Nothing but showing off from start to finish.'

'But,' said Nicholas, his grey eyes innocently wide, 'I thought that's what acting was.'

The Everards, poisonous lick spittles to the company's leading man, cried: 'But I know exactly what Esslyn means.'

'So do I. McKellen has always left me stone cold.'

Dierdre slipped in her question about the sugar.

'Heavens you should know that by now, poppet,' said Rosa Crawley. 'Just a *morceau* for me.' She dragged the words out huskily. She was playing Mrs Salieri and had never had such a modest role, but in *Amadeus* it was the only mature feminine role on offer. Obviously servants and senior citizens were beneath her notice. 'You've been keeping us sustained through so many rehearsals,' she continued, 'I don't know how you do it.' There was a spatter of mechanical agreement in Dierdre's direction and Rosa trapped a small sigh. She knew that to be gracious to bit players and stage management was the sign of a real star. She just wished Dierdre would be a bit more responsive. She accepted her chipped mug with a radiant smile. 'Thank you, darling.'

Dierdre parted her lips slightly in response. Really, she was thinking, with a waistline like a baleen whale even one *morceau* was one too many. To add to her annoyance

Rosa was wearing the long fur coat she (Dierdre) had bought from Oxfam for *The Cherry Orchard*. It had walked after the last-night party and wardrobe had never been able to clap hands on it again.

'Oh my God!' Harold glared into his mug, blue glazed with H.W. (DIR) on the side in red nail varnish. 'Not those bloody awful ferret droppings again. Can't somebody produce some real milk? *Please?* Is that too much to ask?'

Dierdre handed out the rest of the mugs, following up with the sugar bag, avoiding Harold's eye. If real milk was wanted let someone with a car bring it. She had enough stuff to lug to rehearsals as it was.

'I'm a bit worried about the idea of a razor at all,' said Mozart's Constanze, returning to the point at issue. 'I don't want a fatherless child.' She made a face into her mug before leaning back against her husband's knee. Esslyn smiled and glanced round at the others as if asking them to excuse his wife's foolishness. Then he drew the nail of his index finger delicately across her throat, murmuring, 'A biological impossibility, surely?'

'One of the problems about a lot of blood,' said Joyce Barnaby, wardrobe mistress/keeper of the cakes/singing noises off, 'is getting Esslyn's shirt washed and ironed for the next night. I hope we're going to have more than one.'

'*Molto costoso*, my darling,' cried Harold. 'You all seem to think I'm made of money. The principal's costumes cost a bomb to hire as it is. All very well for Peter Shaffer to ask for ten servants all in eighteenth-century costume . . .'

Joyce sat back placidly in her seat, picked up Katherina Cavalieri's braided skirt and continued turning up the hem. At least once during the rehearsals of any production Harold railed about how much they were spending, but somehow, when things were urgently needed, the money was always there. Joyce had wondered more than once if it came out of his own pocket. He did not seem to be a wealthy man (he ran a modest import/export business) but threw himself so completely into the theatre, heart,

14

body, mind and spirit, that none of them would have been surprised if he had thrown his profits in as well.

'I don't envy Sarah the weight of that skirt,' Rosa husked across at Joyce. 'I remember when I was playing Ranyevskaia –'

'Will my padding be ready soon, Joyce?' asked the second Mrs Carmichael, collecting many a grateful glance by this intercession. When Rosa started on her Ranyevskaia everyone ran for cover. Or her Mrs Alving. Or even, come to that, her Fairy Carabosse.

'And the music,' asked Nicholas. 'When are we having the music?'

'When I get a forty-eight-hour day,' came back Harold, whippet quick. 'Unless' – he positively twinkled at the absurdity of the idea – 'you want to do it yourself.'

'OK.'

'What?'

'I don't mind. I know all the pieces. It's just a question of –'

'It's not just a question of anything, Nicholas. The stamp of any director worth his salt must be on every single aspect of his production. Once you start handing over bits here and pieces there for any Tom, Dick and Harry to do as they like with you might as well abdicate.' It was an indication of Harold's standing within the company that the verb struck no one present as inappropriate. 'And rather than worry about your padding, Kitty, I should start worrying about your lines. I want them spot on by Tuesday. D.L.P. Got that?'

'I'll try, Harold.' Kitty's voice just hinted at a lisp. Her Ds were nearly Ts. This pretty affectation plus her tumble of fair curls, smooth peachy complexion and exaggerated cupid's bow created an air of childlike charm so appealing that people hardly noticed how at variance it was with the sharp gleam in her azure eyes. As she spoke her delicious bosom rose and fell a shade more rapidly as if indicating an increased willingness to please.

Harold regarded her sternly. It was always a complete mystery to him when anyone connected with the CADS

15

declined to commit their every waking moment to whatever happened to be the current production. In deed whilst at the theatre and in thought whilst absent. Avery had once said that, had it been within his power, Harold would have ordered them to dream about the Latimer. And Kitty of all people, Harold was now thinking, had enough time on her hands. He wondered what she found to do all day, then realized he had wondered aloud. Kitty demurely lowered her glance as if the question had been faintly naughty.

Dierdre started to reclaim the mugs. Several still held coffee but no one insisted on their divine right to full rations. She looked elsewhere when collecting Kitty's, for Esslyn had now stopped caressing his wife's throat and had slipped his fingers into the neck of her drawstring blouse where they dabbled almost absentmindedly. Rosa Crawley also looked elsewhere at this evidence of her one-time husband's insensitivity and coloured up, an ugly crimson. Harold, oblivious as always to off-stage dramas, called across to his designer: 'Where on earth *is* Tim?'

'I don't know.'

'Well, you should know. You live with him.'

'Living with someone,' riposted Avery, 'doesn't give you psychic powers. I left him filling in the Faber order and he said he'd only be half an hour. So your guess is as good as mine.' Although he spoke stoutly Avery was, in fact, consumed with anxious fears. He couldn't bear not to know where Tim was and what he was doing and who he was doing it with. Each second spent in ignorance of this vital information seemed like a year to him. 'And don't expect me to stay late,' he added. 'I've got a *daube* in the oven.'

'*Daubes* pay for a long simmer,' suggested wardrobe. Fortunately Tom Barnaby was not present or he might well have choked to hear the casual way in which his wife, whose culinary disasters went from strength to strength, claimed kinship with a man whose cooking was legendary. Every member of the CADS had angled and wangled and hinted and nudged their way towards a possible invitation to dine chez Avery. Those who succeeded ate at humbler tables for weeks afterwards, re-creating their triumphs, and doling out gastronomic recollections a crumb at a time to make them last.

Now Avery replied crisply: 'Long simmers, Joycey darling, must stop at precisely the right moment. The line between a wonderful, cohesive stew with every single item still quite separate yet relating perfectly to the whole, and a great sloppy mess, is a very narrow one indeed.'

'Bit like a theatrical production really,' murmured Nicholas, lobbing a subversively winning smile across at his director. Catching the smile but quite missing the subversion, Harold nodded pompously back.

'Well . . .' Colin Smy got to his feet and struck a no-nonsense pose as if to emphasize both his importance to and difference from the surrounding actors. 'Some of us have got work to do.' Having placed his banderilla he gave it a moment to sink in. Standing chunkily on slightly bowed legs, he wore jeans and a tartan shirt and had rough, wiry hair cut very short. Tufts of it stuck up here and there and this, combined with a great deal of snapping energy made it, someone had once said, like having a rather ferocious fox terrier charging around the place. Now he disappeared into the wings, calling pointedly over his shoulder, 'If I'm wanted you'll find me in the scene dock. There's plenty going on down there if anyone's interested.'

No one seemed to be and the hammering which shortly reached their ears remained aggrievedly solitary. Over their heads Dierdre turned on hot water and scrubbed at the mugs, clattering them crossly and adding yet more chips. Not a single person ever came up to give her a hand with the exception of David Smy who was often waiting around to drive his father home. She knew this was her own fault for not putting her foot down long ago, and this made her crosser than ever.

'Well, I think we should give Tim five more minutes,' the Emperor Joseph was saying back in the stalls, 'and then get on.'

17

'No doubt you do,' replied Esslyn. 'But I have no intention of "getting on" until we have this practical problem solved. It's all very well to say these things can be left till the last second . . .'

'Hardly the last second,' murmured Rosa.

'. . . but I'm the one who's going to be out there facing the serried ranks.' (Anyone'd think, observed Nicholas to himself, that we were going on at the Barbican.) 'It's horrendous enough, God knows, a part that size.' (What did you take it on for then?) 'But after all, Salieri's attempted suicide is the high point of the play. We've got to get it not only right but brilliantly right.'

Nicholas, who had always regarded Mozart's death as the high point of the play, said: 'Why don't you use an electric razor?'

'For Christ's sake! If this is the sort of —'

'All right, Esslyn. Simmer down,' Harold soothed his fractious star. 'Honestly, Nicholas —'

'Sorry.' Nicholas grinned. 'Sorry, Esslyn. Just a joke.'

'Stillborn, Nico,' said Esslyn loftily, 'like all your jokes. Not to mention your . . .' He buried his lips in the golden fronds tenderly curling on Kitty's neck and the rest of the sentence was lost. But everyone knew what it might have been . . .

Nicholas went very white. He said nothing for a few moments then spoke over-calmly, picking his words with care. 'It might not seem like it but I am concerned about this problem. After all — if Esslyn doesn't have enough time to get used to handling what's going to be a very vital prop, the whole business is going to look completely amateurish.' There was a crescendoed hum and breaths were held. Harold got to his feet and fixed his Mozart with a rabid eye.

'Don't you ever so much as breathe that word in my presence, Nicholas — OK? There is *never* anything amateurish about my productions.'

In so boldly refuting the adjective Harold was being a mite economical with the truth. The whole company was proud of what it fondly regarded as its professional standards, but let a breath of adverse criticism be heard and suddenly they were only amateurs mostly with full-time jobs and really it was a miracle any of them found time to learn their lines at all let alone get a show on the road. Now Nicholas, having drawn blood all round, appeared mortified at his clumsiness. But before he could open his mouth to make amends the auditorium doors swung open and Tim Young appeared. He walked quickly towards them, a tall man in a dark Crombie overcoat and Borsalino hat, carrying a small parcel.

'Sorry I'm late.'

'Where have you been?'

'The paperwork seemed to take for ever . . . then the phone started. You know how it is.' Tim spread his answer around the group rather than replying directly to Avery, who then said:

'Who? Who phoned?'

Tim slipped off his overcoat and started to undo his parcel. Everyone gathered round. It was very carefully wrapped. Two layers of shiny brown paper then two of soft cloth. Finally the razor was revealed. Tim opened it and laid it across his palm.

It was a beautiful thing. The handle, an elegant curve of ebony, was engraved in gold: E.V. Bayars. Master Cutler. (C.A.P.S.) Around this imprint was a wreath of acanthus leaves and tiny flowers inlaid in mother of pearl. The reverse side was plain except for three tiny rivets. The blade, its edge honed to a lethal certainty, winked and gleamed.

Esslyn, mindful of its reason for being there, said: 'Looks bloody sharp.'

'As it must,' cried Harold. 'Theatrical verisimilitude is vital.'

'Absolutely,' seconded Rosa, rather quickly some thought.

'I don't give a fairy's fart for theatrical verisimilitude,' enjoined Esslyn, holding out his hand and gingerly taking the razor. 'If you think I'm putting this thing within six inches of my throat you can think again.'

19

'Haven't you ever heard of mime?' inquired Harold.

'Yes I've heard of mime,' replied Esslyn. 'I've also heard of Jack the Ripper, Sweeney Todd and death by misadventure.'

'I'll work something out by the next rehearsal,' said Harold reassuringly. 'Don't worry. Wrap it up again for now, Tim. I want to get on with act two. Dierdre?' Pause. 'Where is she *now*?'

'Still washing up, I think,' said Rosa.

'Good grief. I could wash up the crockery from a four-course banquet for twenty in the time she takes to do half a dozen cups. Well . . . to our muttons. Phoebe – you'd better go on the book.' Everyone dispersed to the wings and dressing rooms with the exception of Esslyn who remained still studying the razor thoughtfully. Harold crossed to his side. '*Pas de problème!*' he said. 'You have to get used to handling it, that's all. Look – let me show you.'

He took the beautiful object and carefully eased the blade back towards the handle. Suddenly it sprang to forcefully, with a sharp click. Harold let out a little hiss of alarm and Esslyn a longer one of satisfaction.

'You don't seem to have trained this very well, Tim,' called Harold, giving Esslyn a smile of rather strained jocularity. Then he put the razor down and took the other man's arm matily. 'Now, when have you ever known me with a production headache I couldn't put right? Mm? In all our years together?' Esslyn responded with a wary look, rife with disenchantment. 'Believe me,' said Harold, spacing out his words and weighting them equally to emphasize the power of his conviction, 'you are in safe hands. There is nothing whatsoever to worry about.'

He spoke with absolute sincerity, but his confidence was sadly misplaced. For wheels were already within wheels. And there were plans afoot of which he was, as yet, completely ignorant.

DRAMATIS PERSONAE

In his room over the Blackbird bookshop Nicholas lay on the floor doing his Cicely Berry voice exercises. He did them night and morning without fail, however late he was getting up or getting in. He had reached the lip and tongue movements, and rat-a-tat sounds filled the room. Fortunately the neighbours on both sides (Brown's the funeral parlour and a butcher's) were past caring about noise.

Nicholas had been born nineteen years ago and brought up in a village midway between Causton and Slough. At school he had been regarded as just above average. Moderately good at games, moderately good at lessons and, as he was also blessed with an amiable disposition, moderately good at making friends. He had been in the upper sixth and thinking vaguely of some sort of future in a bank or on the management side of industry when something happened which for ever changed his life.

One of the texts for his English A level was *A Midsummer Night's Dream*. A performance of the play by the Royal Shakespeare Company was booked to take place in the vast gymnasium of Nicholas' comprehensive. Within two days of the announcement the performance was sold out. Several of the sixth form went, Nicholas more for the novelty of the thing than anything else. He had never been to the theatre and knew as much about acting as he did about farming, coal mining or deep-sea fishing. That it existed as a craft to be cultivated and practised had never occurred to him.

When he arrived there seemed to be hundreds of people milling about and the gym was transformed. There were rostrums and flights of steps, trestle tables, artificial green grass and a metal tree with golden apples on it. Scattered about the floor were huge cushions made of carpet

21

material. Five musicians were sitting on the vaulting horse. Overhead was an elaborate grid of metal with dozens of lights attached. Then Nicholas noticed, on a dais at the other end of the hall, a stocky man in evening clothes with a broad red ribbon across his breast pinned with a jewelled star and medals. He was chatting to a woman in a dark green bustled dress wearing diamonds in her ears and a tiny crown. Suddenly he held out his arm, she rested her gloved hand on his wrist and they stepped down from the platform. The lights blazed white and hard and the play began.

Immediately Nicholas was enthralled. The vigour and attack and intense proximity of the actors took his breath away. The brilliant costumes, their colours blurred by the quickness of the players' movement and dance, dazzled him. He was caught up in the sweep and power of emotions that defied analysis. And they changed so quickly. He no sooner felt the most intense sympathy for Helena than he was compelled to laugh at her incoherent rage and the scenes between Titania and Bottom were so sensual he felt his face burn.

He had to move lots of times. Red ropes were set up at one point and, standing just behind them, he was a part of Theseus' court. Then he got bundled on to the dais to watch Bottom carried shoulder high by a shouting cheering mob to his nuptials. The ass's head turned and the yellow eyes glared at him as the man went by braying and raising one brawny arm in unmistakable sexual salute. And in the midst of this seemingly unstoppable splendid flux of dance and movement and energy and rhythm were remarkable points of stillness. Oberon and Titania, each spinning casually on a climbing rope, silk robes fluttering, swinging nearer and nearer to each other, exchanging glances of passionate hatred, unexpectedly stopped and shared a chaste ironic kiss. Pyramus' grief at Thisbe's death expressed simply but with such pain that all the court and audience too became universally silent.

And then the wedding feast. After a great fanfare the court and servants threw plastic glasses into the audience, then ran around with flagons to fill them. Everyone toasted Theseus and Hippolyta. Balloons and streamers descended from the grid. Faerie and human danced together and the hall became a great swirling mass of colour and light and melodious sounds. Nicholas climbed a flight of steps and stood watching, his throat closed and dry with excitement and then, as if on the stroke of midnight, all movement ceased and Nicholas realized that Puck was standing next to him. So close their arms were touching. The actor spoke: 'If we shadows have offended . . .'

Then Nicholas realized that it was coming to an end. That the whole glorious golden vision was going to fade away and die . . . 'no more yielding but a dream'. And he thought his heart would break. Puck spoke on. Nicholas studied his profile. He could feel the dynamic tension in the man. See it in the pugnacious tightness of his jaw and the rippling muscles of his throat. He spoke with tremendous force, emitting a small silver spray of saliva as he declaimed the closing lines. And then on 'give me your hand if we be friends' he stretched out his arm to the audience in a gesture that was all benevolence and, with his right, reached out to Nicholas and seized his hand. For the space of one more line they stood, the actor and the boy whose life would never be the same again. Then it was over.

Nicholas sat down as the applause went on and on. When the company finally dispersed and the audience drifted away he remained, clutching his glass, in a daze of passionate emotion. Then one of the stage hands took the steps away. Nicholas emptied his glass of the last spot of blackcurrant, then spotted a red streamer and a pink paper rose on the floor. He picked them up and put them carefully in his pocket. The lighting grid was being lowered and he felt in the way so he took himself off with the deepest reluctance.

Outside in the road were two vast pantechnicons. Someone was loading the metal tree with golden apples. Several of the actors emerged. They set off down the road and Nicholas followed, knowing that tamely going home was out of the question. The group went into the pub. He hesitated for a while by the door then slipped in and stood, a rapt observer, just behind the cigarette machine.

The actors stood in a circle a few feet away. They were not dressed stylishly at all. They wore jeans, shabby Afghans, sweaters. They were drinking beer; not talking or laughing loudly or showing off, and yet there was something about them . . . They were simply different from anyone else there. Marked in some subtle way that Nicholas could not define. He saw Puck, a middle-aged man in an old black leather jacket and a peaked denim cap, smoking, waving the smoke away, smiling.

Nicholas watched them with a degree of longing so violent it made his head ache. He wanted desperately to overhear their conversation and was on the point of edging nearer when the door behind him opened and two teachers came in. Immediately he dodged behind their backs and into the street. Apart from feeling that he could not bear to be exposed so soon to the banalities of everyday conversation Nicholas felt sure that the enthralling experience through which he had just passed must have marked him physically in some way. And he dreaded what he felt would be clumsy and insensitive questioning.

Fortunately when he got home everyone had gone to bed. He looked at himself in the kitchen mirror, surprised and a little disappointed at the modesty of his transformation. His face was pale and his eyes shone but apart from that he looked pretty much the same.

But he was not the same. He sat down at the table and produced the glass, the flower, the streamer and his free cast list. He smoothed the paper out and ran down the column of actors. Puck had been played by Roy Smith. Nicholas drew a careful ring around the name then washed and dried his glass carefully, put the rose and the paper and the streamer inside, then went to his room. He lay on his bed reliving every moment of the evening till daylight broke. Next day he went to the library, asked if there was a local drama group and was given details of the Latimer. He went to the theatre that same evening, told them he wanted to be an actor and was immediately co-opted to help with the props for *French without Tears*.

Nicholas quickly discovered that there was theatre and theatre, and adapted philosophically. He had a lot (everything) to learn and had to start somewhere. He was sorry that none of the CADS, with the exception of Dierdre, had been to see *The Dream* but sensed very quickly that to attempt to describe it let alone mention its effect on him would be a mistake. So he made and borrowed props and ran about and made himself so useful that he was co-opted permanently. For the next play, *Once in a Lifetime*, he went on the book. He made a hash of prompting at first, bringing down upon himself Esslyn's scorn and Harold's weary disdain, but he took the play home and read it over and over, absorbing the quick-fire rhythms, getting to sense the pauses, making himself familiar with exits and entrances, and became much better. He helped to build the set for *Teahouse of the August Moon* and Tim taught him basic lighting, letting him share the box and patting his bottom absentmindedly from time to time. He did the sound effects and music for *The Snow Queen* and, in *The Crucible*, he got a speaking part.

Nicholas learnt his few lines quickly and was always the first actor at rehearsals and the last to leave. He bought a cheap tape recorder and worked on an American accent, ignoring the amused glances between certain members of the cast. He made up an entire history for his character and listened and reacted with intense concentration to everything that went on around him on stage. Long before the first night he could think of nothing else. When it arrived and he was cackhandedly putting on too much make-up in the packed dressing room he realized he had forgotten his lines. Frantically he sought a script, wrote them down on a piece of paper and tucked it into the waistband of his homespun trousers. Waiting in the wings he was overcome with a wave of nausea and was sick in the firebucket.

As he stepped on to the stage terror struck him with hurricane force. Rows of faces swam into his line of vision.

He looked once and looked away. He spoke his first line. The lights burned down but he felt cold with exhilaration and excitement as one after the other the rest of his lines sprang to the forefront of his mind when needed and he experienced for the first time that strange dual grip that an actor must always keep on reality. Part of him believed in Proctor's kitchen in Salem with its iron pots and pans and crude furnishings and frightened people, and part of him was aware that a stool was in the wrong place and that John Proctor was still masking his wife and Mary Warren had forgotten her cap. Afterwards in the club-room he experienced a warm close camaraderie ('give me your hands if we be friends') which seemed fleetingly to surmount any actual likes and dislikes within the group.

In the pantomime he played the back legs of a horse and then was offered the part of Danny in *Night Must Fall*. Rehearsals started six weeks before his A levels and he knew he had failed the exams. The endless grumblings that had been going on at home for months about all the time he was spending at the Latimer erupted into a blazing row and he walked out. Almost immediately Avery offered him the tiny room over the Blackbird book-shop. It was rent free in exchange for dusting the shop every morning and cleaning Avery's house once a week.

He had lived there now for nearly a year and subsisted (sometimes, superbly, on Avery's leftovers) mainly on baked beans purloined from the supermarket where he worked. Nearly all his wages went on voice and movement classes – he had discovered an excellent teacher in Slough – and on theatre tickets. Once a month he hitched up to London to see a show, determined to keep his batteries re-charged by frequent injections of what he thought of as the real thing. (It was after an exhilarating performance of *The Merry Wives of Windsor* at the Barbican that he had chosen Ford's Epicurean speech for his Central audition.)

He still didn't know if he was any good. Brenda Leggat, first cousin to the Smys, reviewed the CADS productions in the local rag, and her perceptions were about as original as her prose. Every comedy was sparkling, every tragedy wrenched the heart. Performances if not to the manner born were all we have come to expect from this actor/actress/soubrette/ingenue/cocktail cabinet. And Nicholas soon understood the group well enough to know that any direct questions regarding his performance would receive anodyne if not gushing reassurances. Plenty was said in the clubroom about absent friends but it was almost impossible for an actor to get an honest opinion to his face. Everyone except Esslyn and the Everards (and Harold of course) told Nicholas that he was marvellous. Harold rarely praised (he liked to keep them on their toes) except at first nights when he behaved like a Broadway impresario surging about hysterically, kissing everyone, distributing flowers and even squeezing out an histrionic tear.

Nicholas finished his exercises, did a series of stretches and some more deep breathing, undressed, cleaned his teeth, climbed into bed and promptly fell into a deep sleep.

He dreamed it was the first night of *Amadeus* and he stood in the wings dressed all in black with wrinkled tights and a skull under his arm, having learnt the part of *Hamlet*.

Rosa Crawley's husband was waiting up, having spent the evening in the Cap and Bells with some fellow Rotarians and their Crimplened spouses. He always tried to get home before his wife not only because she hated finding the house empty but because he looked forward to hearing the continuing saga of theatrical folk that started almost the minute she came through the door. She never accompanied him to the pub of course and Ernest basked a little in her absence knowing that his companions were aware that his wife had much more interesting fish to fry. Tonight he was home only minutes before her and had just made his cocoa when she arrived. Ernest plumped up the sofa cushions, poured a double scotch on the rocks so that his wife could unwind and sat back with his own drink, his face bright with anticipation.

Rosa sipped her whisky and watched Ernest pushing aside the wrinkled skin on his steaming cocoa a little enviously. Sometimes, especially on a night like this, she quite fancied a cup of cocoa but felt that it was surely, (Slippery Elm Food apart) the least sophisticated drink in the entire world. Starting to take it of an evening could well be the first step on the sliding slope to cosiness and a public admittance of middle age. Next thing she'd be padding round in a warm dressing gown and wearing vests. She slipped off her high-heeled shoes and massaged her feet. The shoes lay, vamp down, spiky four-inch heels stabbing the air.

She was a short woman, just over five feet tall with a gypsyish appearance which she nurtured to an extreme degree. The black of her dark hair was regularly intensified, her fine dark eyes ringed with khol and decorated with a double fringe of false lashes whilst her coppery complexion spoke of the wind on the heath and a star to steer by. Her nose was larger than she would have liked but she capitalized on this by hinting at a rather tragic immigrant Jewish background. A suggestion that would have horrified her grandparents, sturdy Anglo-Saxon farm workers from Lincolnshire. She nourished this vaguely semitic Tziganery by wearing dark clothes with accessories that were so dazzling they seemed to be going off like fireworks rather than making a fashion point.

Looking over at Ernest placidly sipping his nightcap she wondered anew at the strange fact of their marriage. It had been out of the question of course that she remain single after her divorce from Esslyn. Apart from the matter of pride she couldn't bear to be alone for more than five minutes. She had assumed that, with her looks and personality, men would come flocking out of the woodwork once the word got round that she was available, but this had not been the case. Ernest Crawley, local builder, widower and comfortable had been the only serious suitor.

He was a sweet man who knew his place and she accepted him the first time of asking. He was shy of and a little alarmed by the CADS and, apart from going to

Rosa's first nights and the last-night party, kept well away, perhaps sensing that this would please her best. Occasionally Rosa gave the leading lights in the company lunch and then Ernest played mine host barricaded behind a trestle table and pouring out the Frascati. They all drank like whales it seemed to him and he was glad when it was all over and the hot-house atmosphere damped down to normal again. He asked how it had all gone.

'Ach,' said Rosa exhaustedly, resting the back of her hand against her forehead, 'quite horrendous. Joyce still hasn't done a thing about my costume, David Smy is like an elephant loose on the stage and the Venticelli are hopeless.'

Ernest finished his cocoa, picked up his pipe and tamped it in contented anticipation. He had his own dramas at work, of course. Complaints from the foreman, rows in the hut, occasionally a serious accident. But there was something about the activities at the theatre. Rosa relayed them with such panache that they rose far above the ordinary pettinesses of his working day.

'Harold says he's going to strangle them.' (Rosa always opened her monologues with a flourishing bit of hyperbole.) 'One at a time and very slowly if they don't pick up their cues.'

'Does he now?' Ernest made his response deliberately noncommittal. Rosa's attitude to her director was variable. Sometimes her loathing and jeers at his affectations knew no bounds; at others – usually when Harold had had a clash with some supporting actress – he had all her sympathy. Then they were coevals, talent burnished bright, swimming in harness in a sea of mediocrity. This was clearly going to be one of those nights.

'The Venticelli open the show, right? Just the two of them . . . quick fire . . . non stop. Like Ros and Gil . . . you know?' Ernest nodded sagely. 'I mean they will kill this production . . . absolutely kill it before it even gets off the ground.'

Ernest nodded again and did a bit more tamping. He

didn't know who or what the Venticelli might be but the poor buggers had obviously better get their skates on if they wanted to survive the course. Rosa had now moved on to Boris who, she said, had painted his face up to the hilt and was playing the Emperor Joseph like a mad Bavarian hausfrau.

If it occurred to Ernest to think it odd that, never in the past two years, during which twelve plays had been produced, had Rosa's tongue, so sharply dismembering performance after performance, ever alighted on the name of her first husband, he wisely kept this observation to himself.

'Ruined, ruined!' Avery ran through the carpeted hall pulling off his cashmere scarf and dropping it as he went. Gloves fell on the Aubusson, his coat on the raspberry satin sofa. Tim strolled along in the wake of all this turbulence picking up Avery's things and murmuring 'Bad luck for some' when he came to the gloves. He stuffed one into each pocket of the coat and hung it up in the tiny hall next to his own, amused by the contrast between the tattersall check, with its garland of turquoise cashmere and little chestnut fingers sticking beseechingly up in the air, and his own sombre dark grey herringbone and navy muffler.

Avery, already wrapped in his *tablier* and wearing his frog mittens, was pulling the le Creuset out of the oven. He put it down on a wooden trivet and eased the lid off a millimetre at a time. Whilst hurrying home he had made a bargain with the Fates. He would not question Tim about the source and content of the previously mentioned phone calls if they would keep an eye on the *daube*. Avery, knowing the superhuman restraint that would be necessary to stick to his side of the agreement, had felt an almost magical certainty that the least the other party could do was to honour theirs. But, running up the garden path, sure that he smelt a whiff of carbon on the cold night air, his certainties evaporated. And, as he ran with quailing anticipation through the sitting room, he became

30

firmly convinced that the bastards had let him down again. And so it proved to be.

'It's got a crust on!'

'That's all right.' Tim sauntered into the kitchen and picked up a bottle opener. 'Aren't you supposed to break that and mix it in?'

'That's a cassoulet. Oh God . . .'

'For heaven's sake stop wringing your hands. It's only a stew.'

'A stew! *A stew*.'

'At least we won't be able to say there's not a crust in the house.'

'That's all it means to you, isn't it? A joke.'

'Far from it. I'm extremely hungry. And if you were that worried you could have come home earlier.'

'And you could have come to the theatre earlier.'

'I was doing the Faber order.' Tim smiled and smoothed the irritation from his voice. With Avery in this state it could be midnight before a morsel crossed his lips. 'And the phone calls were from Camelot Antiques about your footstool and Derek Barfoot rang asking us for Sunday lunch.'

'Oh.' Avery looked sheepish, relieved, grateful and encouraged. 'Thank you.'

'Look. Why don't we use this spoon with the holes in –'

'No! You'll never get it all!' Avery stood in front of his casserole like a mother protecting her child from a ravening beast. 'I've got a better idea.' He produced a box of tissues and lowered half a dozen with slow and exquisite care on to the crumbling top layer. 'These will absorb all the bits then I can lift the whole thing off with a fish slice.'

'I thought it was in the topsoil where all the goodness lay,' murmured Tim, going to the larder to get the wine.

The larder was really Avery's domain but it had a deep quarry-tiled recess with a grilled window on to the outside wall which made it beautifully cool and the perfect place for a wine rack. The tiny room was brilliantly lit and crammed with provisions. Walnut and hazelnut and sesame oils. Olives, herbs and pralines from Provence. Anchovies and provalone; truffles in little jars. Tins of clams and Szechwan peppercorns. Potato flour and many mustards. Prosciutto, water chestnuts and a ham with a wrinkled leathery skin the colour of liquorice hanging from the ceiling next to an odoriferous salami. Tiny amaretti and snails. Tomato paste and marron paste, cured fish and lumpfish, gull's eggs and plover's eggs and a chilli sauce so hot it could blast the stones from a horse's hoof. Tim moved a crock of peaches in brandy, took a bottle from the rack and returned to the kitchen.

'What are you opening?'

'The Chateau d'Issan.'

Chewing his full marshmallow lip (the tiny drop of reassurance re the phone calls having already vanished into a vast lake of more generalized anxiety) Avery watched Tim twist the corkscrew, press down the chrome wings and, with a soft pop, pull the cork. Avery thought it the second most beautiful sound in the world (following hard on the easing of a zip) whilst having a terrible suspicion that for Tim it might be the first. Now, looking at the flat dark silky hairs on the back of his lover's wrist glinting in the light from the spotlamps, noticing his elegant hands as they tilted the bottle and poured the fragrant wine, Avery's stomach lurched with a familiar mixture of terror and delight. Tim took off his suit jacket revealing an olive-green doeskin waistcoat and snowy shirt, the sleeves hitched up by old-fashioned elasticated armbands. Then he lowered his narrow, ascetic nose into the glass and sniffed.

Avery could never understand how anyone who cared so passionately about what he drank was not equally fastidious when it came to what he ate. Tim would consume anything that was what he called 'tasty', and his range was catholic to say the least. Once, stranded for an hour on Rugby station, he had demolished cheeseburger and chips, several squares of white, sponge-like bread, a lurid pastry with three circles of traffic-light-coloured jam, two Kit-Kats and a cup of pungent, rust-coloured tea with every appearance of satisfaction. And he did not even, Avery had reflected whilst toying miserably with an orange and a glass of lukewarm Liebfraumilch, have the excuse of a working-class background. (Tim had declined the Liebfraumilch on the grounds that it was not only likely to be the produce of more than one country but liberally laced with antifreeze to boot.)

So why, Avery sometimes asked himself as he leafed through his vast collection of cook books, did he labour so long and ardently in the kitchen? The answer was immediate and never changing. Avery prepared his wood pigeon *à la paysanne, truites à la crème* and *fraises Romanof* out of simple gratitude. He would place them before Tim in a spirit of excitable humility because they were his supreme attainment; the very best his loving heart could offer. In the same manner he ironed Tim's shirts, chose fresh flowers for his room, planned little treats. Almost unconsciously when shopping his eye was alert for something, anything that would make a surprise gift.

He never ceased to marvel at the fact that he and Tim had been together for seven years, especially when he discovered the truth about his friend's background. Avery had always been homosexual and had innocently supposed that Tim's experience had been the same. Then he discovered that Tim's understanding of his true nature had come painfully and gradually. That he had regarded himself as heterosexual as a teenager and bisexual for several years after that. (He had even been engaged for eighteen months whilst in his early twenties.)

The acquisitiion of this knowledge had thrown Avery into a turmoil of fear. Tim's assurances and his reminder that this had all happened twelve years ago had done little to calm a temperament that was volatile by nature. Even now Avery would watch Tim without seeming to, looking furtively for signs that these earlier inclinations were reasserting themselves just as a showily coloured plant occasionally reverts to its more pallid origins.

Avery reasoned thus because he could never, ever, in a trillion zillion years understand what Tim saw in him.

For a start there was the physical contrast. Tim was tall and lean with hollow cheeks and a mouth so stern in repose that his sudden smile seemed almost shocking in its sweetness. Avery thought he was like a figure in a Caravaggio painting. Or perhaps (his profile at the moment looked alarmingly austere) a medieval monk. Nicholas had said he thought that Tim, although emotionally lean, was spiritually opulent. This was not what Avery wanted to hear. He didn't give a fig for spiritual opulence. Give him, he had replied, a nice *filet mignon* and a fond caress any old day of the week.

Avery knew he cut a ridiculous figure when compared to Tim. For a start he was tubby and his features, like his personality, were sloppy and spread all over the place. His lips were squashy and overfull, his eyes a washed-out blue and slightly protruberant with almost colourless lashes, and his nose, just to be different, was neat and small and seemed quite lost in the pale pink expanse of his face. His head was very round with a fringe of curls, butter yellow and softly fluffy like duckling down. He had always been agonizingly conscious of his baldness and, until he met Tim, had worn a wig. The morning after their first night together he had found it in the dustbin. It had never been mentioned between them again and Avery bravely continued to live without it, treating himself and his scalp to a weekly going over with a sun lamp instead.

Then there was the difference in their dispositions. Tim was nearly always calm whilst Avery veered excitedly between elation and despair, touching all the psychological stations of the cross on the way. And he reacted so dramatically to things. This had always seemed to amuse Tim but, once or twice lately, Avery had noticed a twitch or two of impatience, a spot of lip tightening. Now, draining his glass of Bordeaux he framed in his mind the latest of many small vows. He would learn to take things more calmly. He would think before speaking. Take several deep breaths. Perhaps even count to ten. He turned his attention back to the le Creuset. All the tissues had sunk without trace. Avery let out a scream that could have been heard halfway down the street.

'Bloody hell.' Tim banged his glass down on the work top. 'What's the matter now?'

'The Kleenex have sunk to the bottom.'

'Is that all? I thought at the very least you were being castrated.'

'I meant them to soak up all the bits,' sobbed Avery.

'Well now you've discovered that they won't. Knowledge is never wasted. We'll just give it to Nicholas.'

'You can't do that – it's full of tissue paper.'

'Riley then.'

'Riley! There's half a bottle of Beaune in there.'

'So he'll think it's Christmas.'

'Anyway Riley's a fish man, not a meat man. What are you doing?'

'Toast.' Tim was slicing bread on the marble pastry slab. Now he reached across Avery and switched on the grill. Then he refilled both their glasses. 'Drink up, sweetheart. And stop flowing all over the furniture.'

'Sorry . . .' Avery sniffled and snuffled and drank up. 'You're . . . you're not angry with me are you, Tim?'

'No, Avery, I'm not angry with you. I'm just bloody starving to death.'

'Yes. So –'

'Don't keep saying you're sorry. Get off your backside and give me a hand. There's some duck pâté left over. And we could finish the mango ice cream.'

'All right.' Still mopping and mowing, Avery crossed to the fridge. 'I don't know why you put up with me.'

'Stop being ingratiating, it doesn't suit you.'

'Sor –'

'And if I didn't who else would?'

This question so casually posed seemed to Avery no more than the simple truth. Awash with sorrow, he hung his head and pondered, looking down at his round tummy and chubby little feet. Then he looked up and met Tim's sudden brilliant smile. Oh frabjous day! thought Avery, beaming widely in his turn. And then, to make things absolutely perfect and he and Tim equal in carelessness, the toast caught fire.

'We can pretend they're charcoal biscuits,' said Avery, draining the rest of his wine. Then, quite forgetting the earlier strictures about him being ingratiating, 'I wish I were more like you. More calm.'

'Good grief, I don't. I'd hate to live with someone like me. I'd be bored to death in a week.'

'Would you, Tim?' Magically the dolorous beat of Avery's heart quickened. 'Would you really?'

'A drama a day keeps the doldrums away.'

'Mmm.' Avery helped himself to some more wine. 'That's true, I suppose.'

'But we've had our ration for tonight. Now we must get on.'

'Yes, Tim.' Avery bustled happily about finding unsalted butter, celery, the pâté and a white china bowl of tomatoes. Tim was quite right, of course. Everyone knew about the attraction of opposites. That's why it all worked so well on the whole. Why they were so happy together. It was just foolishness for him to struggle to destroy the very characteristics that his partner found attractive.

Avery took the hand-operated coffee grinder and put some beans in the little wooden drawer. He refused to use an electric contrivance, believing that the uncontrollably high speed overheated the beans, sent by post by the Algerian Coffee Company, and impaired their flavour. The fragrance of the beans met and mingled with the succulent scent of the wine and the very ordinary but always to Avery deeply satisfying smell of fresh toast. He sat down at the scrubbed deal table full of anticipation. This was the time he loved best of all. (Well, nearly.) When there was food and wine and gossip and jokes.

Even if all they had done during the day was sell books and get on with the paperwork there was always at least one customer who was ripe for exaggerated mimicry or grotesquely imaginative suggestions as to how they got their jollies. But of course the nights that sparkled, the nights that offered the most superlative entertainment, were the nights when they had been to the Latimer. Then performances could be put through the mincer, relationships scrutinized and surmises made and opinions mooted as to Harold's precise degree of sanity (always open to question and anybody's guess).

But occasionally, if there had been 'a drama' in the home Tim might withdraw a little and affect a lack of interest in the theatrical proceedings. These were anguished times for Avery who gossiped as easily as he drew breath and with almost the same urgent necessity. Now, as he slathered butter over his toast he looked across at Tim, spreading neatly, with a small degree of perturbation. But it was all right. Tim looked back at Avery and his slaty eyes which could look so cold were warm with a sudden flare of malice.

'But apart from that, Mrs Lincoln,' he said, reaching for the celery, 'how did you enjoy the play?'

When Joyce Barnaby entered the sitting room her husband was dozing in front of the fire. He had been drawing a sprig of Elisha's tears and his pencil was cradled in his hand although the sketch pad had fallen to the floor. He woke when his wife standing behind his chair folded her arms across his chest and gave him a hug. Then she picked up the pad.

'You haven't finished?'

'I dropped off.'

'Did you eat your lasagne?'

Tom Barnaby gave a noncommittal grunt. When Joyce had come home from the casting evening of *Amadeus* and told him she was playing Keeper of the Cakes only the fact that a raging heartburn was running amok in his breast at the time had stopped him laughing aloud. He could never get over the fact that she ate her own cooking if not with relish at least with no evidence of distaste. He wondered sometimes if his genuine expressions of dismay at mealtimes had, over the years, assumed a ritualistic or even a fossilized stamp and that Joyce had decided they were some sort of running gag. He watched her bend over the sprig of whitish-mauve flowers and inhale appreciatively.

'How did it go, my lovely?'

'Like an evening with the Marx Brothers. I've never know so many things go wrong. Fortunately Tim arrived in the break with his razor, which cheered Harold up. Until then he'd been grousing all night. *Molto disastro*, my darlings!'

'What's the razor for anyway?'

'You wait and see. If I tell you now it'll spoil the first night.'

'Nothing could be spoiled for me that has you in it.' He took her hand. 'What's that big bag for?'

'Wardrobe. Trousers to be let out. Broken zips. Some braid to replace.'

'You do too much.'

'Oh Tom.' She nudged his feet off a low stool and sat on it herself, holding her other cold hand out to the fire. 'Don't say that. You know how I love it.'

He did know. Earlier on he had been listening to a tape she had made of the arias sung by Katherina Cavalieri. Joyce had a beautiful voice; a rich soaring soprano. A little blurred now in the higher register but still thickly laced with plangent sweetness. 'Marten Aller Arten' had moved him to tears.

His wife had been a student at the Guildhall School of Music when they had met and fallen in love. When he had first heard her sing at a public performance in her final year he sat there listening to the marvellous sounds, stunned and afraid. For a long while after that he had been unable to belive that she could really love the ordinary man that he knew himself to be. Or that she would ever be safely his.

But they had married and for four years she had continued to sing, at first giving small, ill-attended recitals then joining the chorus at the Royal National Opera House. After Cully was born it all came to an end. Only for a while, she and Barnaby agreed. Temporarily. But progress in the Force had been slow and money tight, and when Cully was two Joyce got a job understudying in *Godspell*. But Tom was frequently on night duty and one or two very unsettling experiences with babysitters left her so full of guilt and anxiety that when she did get to the theatre she was quite unable to concentrate. So, pro tem, she joined the Causton Light Operatic Society to keep her voice supple then, when that folded, the CADS. Not what she'd been used to, of course, but better than nothing. And she and Tom both agreed it was only until Cully was old enough to be left by herself.

But, when that time came, Joyce found that the musical world had moved on and was full of bright gifted tough pushy young singers. And the years of more or less contented domesticity had blunted the knife edge of her ambition. She found she didn't want to drag herself up to London and stand in a vast dim theatre and sing to a faceless trio somewhere out there in the dark. Especially with a crowd of twenty-year-olds watching from the wings sharp as ninepence with determination and buoyant with energy and hope. And so, gradually and without any fuss or visible signs of dismay, Joyce relinquished her plans for a musical career.

But her husband never saw her playing with such perceptive truthfulness the modest parts that were her lot, or heard her lovely voice in the Christmas pantomime gloriously leading all the rest, without a terrible pang of sorrow and remorse. The pang had become muted over the years given their continuing happiness but now, 'Marten Aller Arten' fresh in his ears and the great sack of alterations seen out of the corner of his eye, a sudden shaft of sadness, of pity at the waste, went through him like a knife.

'Tom . . .' Joyce seized his other hand and stared intently into his face. 'Don't. It doesn't matter. All that. *It doesn't matter*. It's you and me. And now there's Cully. Darling . . . ?' She held his gaze forcefully, lovingly. 'All right?'

Barnaby nodded and allowed his face to lighten. What

else could he do? Things were as they were. And it was true that now there was Cully.

Their daughter had been obsessed with the theatre since the age of four when she had been taken to her first pantomime. She had been quickly on stage when the dame had asked for children to watch for the naughty wolf and had had to be forcibly removed, kicking and screaming, when the scene was over. She had performed at her primary school with great aplomb, (oak leaf/young rabbit) and had never looked back. Now in her final year reading English at New Hall, her performances in the ADC were formidable to behold.

'I thought you knew all that,' continued Joyce. 'Silly old bear.'

Barnaby smiled. 'Been a long while since anyone called me that.'

'Do you remember when Cully used to? There was that programme she loved on television . . .' Joyce sang, 'Barnaby the bear's my name . . . I forget the rest.'

'Ahhh yes. She was a little cracker when she was seven.' The conversation rested for a moment then Joyce continued, 'A message from Colin.' Barnaby groaned. 'Could you paint the fireplace. Please?'

'Joycey – I'm on holiday.' He always demurred when asked to help out with the set and he always, work permitting, gave a bit of a hand.

'I wouldn't ask if you weren't on holiday,' lied Joyce brazenly. 'We can all chuck a bit of paint on flats but this fireplace Colin's made . . . it's so beautiful, Tom – a work of art. We can't let any old slaphappy Charlie loose on it. And you're marvellous at that sort of thing.'

'Soft soap and flannel.'

'It's true. You're an artist. Do you remember that statue you did? For *Round and Round the Garden*?'

'Only too well. And the letters to the local press.'

'You could do it Saturday afternoon. Take a flask and some sandwiches.' She paused. 'I wouldn't ask if it were gardening weather.'

'I wouldn't do it if it were gardening weather.'

'Oh thank you, Tom.' She rubbed his hand against her cheek. 'You are sweet.'

Detective Chief Inspector Barnaby sighed, seeing the last few precious days of his annual leave filling up with bustling activity. 'Try telling them that at the station,' he said.

Harold aimed his Morgan at the space between the gate-posts topped with polystyrene lions at 17 Wellington Close and bombed up to the car-port. He encouraged the engine to give a final great full-throated roar then switched off and braced himself for the awkward business to follow. Getting in and out of the Morgan was not easy. On the other hand driving along in it, handling it, being seen in it was tremendous. Heads were turned as the scarlet bonnet flashed past, slaking temporarily Harold's ultimately unquenchable thirst for admiration. The fact that his wife disliked the car added to his pleasure. He withdrew his keys and patted the dashboard appreciatively. One instinctively knew when something was right, mused Harold, having long ago taken this cunning adman's lie to his heart.

On the leather bucket seat next to him lay a sheaf of posters which Mrs Winstanley would dish out to fellow members of the Townswomen's Guild, her flower arranging class and the local shops. Apart from scouring his thinking promotion wise and being interviewed when-ever he could create the opportunity Harold had no truck with publicity. After all, he would tell any jibbers, you didn't see Trevor Nunn popping in and out of his local newsagents with footage on the latest extravaganza. Briefly reflecting on that famous name, Harold swallowed hard on the bile of dissatisfaction. He had long been aware that if it had not been for his careless early marriage and the birth of three numbingly dull children – now, thankfully, boring themselves and their consorts to death miles away – he would currently be one of the top direc-tors in the country. If not (Harold had never been one to shirk home truths) in the world.

All you needed was luck, talent and the right wife. Harold believed you made your own luck, talent was no problem. He had that, God knew, burgeoning from every pore. But the right wife . . . ah, there was the rub. Doris was a simple bourgeois. A Philistine. When they were first married, (she had been a slim shy pretty girl) the children had kept her occupied and she had had no spare time to take an interest in the Latimer. Later, when they were growing up and following their own pursuits, her attempts to comment on the productions had been so inept that Harold had forbidden her to come to the theatre at all except on first nights.

He had briefly considered trading her in when Rosa had come on the market, seeing the latter as a far more suitable mate for a producer. (Sometimes he wondered if Doris was really grateful for, or even aware of, the status that his position as the town's only theatrical impresario conferred.) However, after exposing this fleeting fancy to the cold light of reason Harold had to admit that it was gravely flawed. Rosa was used to, nay, revelled in, her role as leading lady and he could not see her deliberately lowering her wattage to show him to best advantage. Whereas Doris, in spite of her peculiar absorptions – pickling eggs, drying flowers and stuffing innocent knitted creatures with chunks of variegated foam – did have the supreme virtue of dimness. Indeed Harold was pleasurably aware that when he entered a room she practically vanished into the woodwork like the *melanchra persicariae*. And, perhaps most important of all, she was not grasping. He had provided modestly for his wife and children, far more modestly in fact than he might have done. Over half the profits he made from his business (Joyce had been quite right in thinking) went into his productions so that whatever snipers might find to criticize in any other direction, they could never say the play was not well dressed.

An amber rectangle of light fell across the windscreen. 'Harold?'

Harold sighed, gave the mileage dial a final quick polish with his hanky and called: 'Give me a chance.'

He struggled out of the cockpit. This was the cut-off point for him. The moment when he turned away from the full-blooded rumbustious razzle-dazzle rainbow ring of circus and stepped into the shady grey half-formed and quite unreal world of bread.

'Your supper's getting cold.'

'Dinner, Doris.' Already consumed with irritation, he pushed past her into the kichen. 'How many times do I have to tell you?'

'How has he been, Mrs Higgins?' Dierdre entered the kitchen quietly through the back door and the elderly woman dozing by the fire jumped. 'I'm sorry. I didn't mean to startle you.'

'He's been ever so good,' replied Mrs Higgins. 'Considering.'

Dierdre thought the considering uncalled for. They both knew that Mr Tibbs wasn't always ever so good, and why. Dierdre glanced at the mantelpiece. Mrs Higgins' envelope had gone and Dierdre spied it, sticking out of her grubby apron pocket as she heaved herself to her feet. 'Upsadaisy.'

'Is he still asleep?'

'No. Just chatting away to hisself. I made him a lovely plate of soup.'

Dierdre spotted the tin in the sink, said, 'You're so kind,' and helped Mrs Higgins on with her coat. The thankfulness and gratitude in her voice were not feigned. If it were not for Mrs Higgins, Dierdre would have no life at all. No life that is apart from home and the Gas Board. Because where else would she find someone to sit with a befuddled old man for a couple of pounds? Not that the money was ever mentioned. The first time Mrs Higgins came Dierdre had offered, only to be told: 'Don't you worry, dear, I'd only be sitting next door on me tod watching the goggle box.' But the coins Dierdre had left under the teapot disappeared and so, always since then, had the manila envelope.

When Mrs Higgins had gone Dierdre locked and bolted

the door, put some milk for her Horlicks on a very low heat and climbed the stairs. Her father was sitting up, ramrod straight in crisp pyjamas under a large dimmish print of *The Light of the World*. His grey still faintly gingery moustache was soaked with tears of joy and his eyes shone. 'He is coming,' he cried as Dierdre entered the room. 'The Lord is coming.'

'Yes, Daddy.' She sat on the bed and took his hand. It was like holding a few slippy bones in a bag of skin. 'Would you like another drink?'

'He will take us away. Into the light.'

She knew it was no good trying to settle him. He always slept upright, his back bolted into a perpendicular line against a cumulus of pillows. She patted his arm and kissed his damp cheek. He had been a little bit disturbed for several months now. The first indication that all was not well had occurred when she arrived home from the theatre one night after set-building to find him in the street going from house to house, rapping on doors and offering the startled occupants a shovelful of live coals.

Horrified and amazed she had led him back home, replaced the coals on the kitchen fire and questioned him gently, trying to find a rational explanation. Of course there had been none. Since then he had frequently been befuddled or confused. (Dierdre always used these unemphatic terms, avoiding the terrible official definition. When one of the workers at the Centre where Mr Tibbs spent his days had used the word Dierdre had screamed at her in fear and anger.)

He still had lengthy periods of marvellous clarity. There was just no way of knowing when they would arise or for how long they would last. The previous Sunday had been a lovely day. They had gone for a walk in the afternoon and she had been able to tell him all about *Amadeus*, exaggerating her role in the production as she always did to make him proud of her. In the evening they had had a glass of port and some lumpy home-made cake and he had sung songs that he remembered from his childhood. He had been over forty when Dierdre was born so the songs were very old ones. 'Red Sails in the Sunset', 'Valencia' and 'Oh, Oh Antonio'. He had put on his bowler hat and tapped and twirled his stick, shuffling in a sad transmogrified echo of the routines he had leapt through when, years before, he had so delighted Dierdre and her mother. His hair had been reddish gold then and his moustache had gleamed like a new conker. They had both wept before going to sleep last Sunday.

Dierdre crossed to the window to draw the curtains and stood for a moment looking up at the sky. There was a brilliant moon and a cavalcade of scudding clouds. Gabriel, her guardian angel, lived up there. As well as on the earth walking, bright and shining, just an immortal breath away, keeping a loving eye on the Tibbs' worldly concerns. When she was a little girl Dierdre would whip round quickly sometimes, as she did in a game of Statues, hoping to catch sight of his twelve-foot wings before he put on his invisible cloak. Once she was convinced she had found the outline of a golden footprint before hearing, over her head, a rushing beating swoosh of sound like the passing of a thousand swans.

As well as the archangel everyone had a star to watch over them. When she had asked her father which was hers he had said: 'It's always the star that shines the brightest.' They all looked the same tonight, thought Dierdre, letting the curtain fall, and rather cold. She remembered the milk and hurried down to the kitchen just too late to stop it boiling over.

She refilled and replaced the pan then took her script for the next production (*Uncle Vanya*) from the dresser. It had been dissected and reassembled, interleaved with blank pages, as had all the copies of plays on which she had been Assistant Stage Manager. Dierdre worked long and ardently on every one before the first rehearsal. She would read and re-read the play getting to know the characters as well as if she had lived with them. She struggled to realize the sub-text and sense the tempo. Her head buzzed with ideas on staging and she used long rolls of thin card to design her sets. She was as enthralled by

Uncle Vanya as she had been by *The Cherry Orchard*, intoxi-
cated by Chekov's particular ability to produce a seemingly natural world full of real human beings then
reconcile this world with the dramatic limitations of the
theatre.

Now, becoming aware that she was hungry, she closed
Uncle Vanya and put the book aside. She hardly ever
managed to eat on theatre evenings, not if she wanted to
be on time. She found a bit of salad cream in the fridge
together with a small hard piece of leftover beef and two
slices of beetroot, and, whilst spreading margarine on the
stretchy white bread that was all her father's gums could
tackle, she slipped into a frequent and favourite reverie
in which she reviewed edited lowlights from the latest
rehearsal, rewriting the scenario as she went along.

DIERDRE: I think the Venticelli are far too close to
Salieri in the opening scene. They
wouldn't huddle in that intimate way. And
they certainly wouldn't be touching him.

ESSLYN: She's quite right, Harold. They've been
getting more and more familiar. I thought
if someone doesn't say something soon I'd
have to myself.

HAROLD: Right. Stop nudging the star, you two. And
thanks, Dierdre. Wish I'd taken you
aboard years ago.

OR

HAROLD: Coffee all round I think, Dierdre.

DIERDRE: Do you mind? Assistant directors don't
make coffee.
(GENIAL LAUGHTER)

HAROLD: Sorry. We're so used to you looking after
us.

ROSA: We've been taking you too much for
granted, darling.

ESSLYN: And all the time you've been hiding all

	these dazzling ideas under your little bushel.
HAROLD:	Careful – I'm turning green.

> (MORE GENIAL LAUGHTER.
> KITTY GETS UP TO MAKE THE
> COFFEE)

OR

HAROLD:	(SLUMPED IN A CHAIR IN THE CLUBROOM) Now the others have gone I don't mind telling you, Dierdre, I just don't know what I'd have done without you on this production. Everything you say is so fresh and original. (HEAVY SIGH) I'm getting stale.
DIERDRE:	Oh no, Harold. You mustn't think –
HAROLD:	Hear me out, please. What I'm working round to is our summer production. There's such a lot of work involved in *Uncle Vanya* . . .
DIERDRE:	I'll be happy to help.
HAROLD:	No, Dierdre, *I'll* help. What I'd like – what we'd all like – is for you to direct the play.

Even Dierdre's feverishly yearning soul found this final duologue a bit hard to credit. As she scraped out the last bit of solid shiny yellow salad cream and distributed it patchily on the spongy bread she reverted to simpler fantasies. Harold crashing his car. Or Harold having a heart attack. The latter was the most likely, she thought, recalling his stout tummy under its popping brocade waistcoat. She surveyed her completed sandwich. The beetroot was falling out. She caught it, stuffed it back in and took a bite. It wasn't very nice. The milk boiled over again.

'How do you think it went then, Constanza?'
Kitty was sitting by the dressing table. She had peeled

off her tights and propped up her milk-white legs on an embroidered footstool. Although she had announced her pregnancy barely three months ago she was already inclined to hold the small of her back and smile, brave aching smiles. She winced sometimes too in the manner of one reacting to tiny blows. Now she carefully dotted cleansing cream over her face before giving the expected response.

'Well, darling, I thought you were wonderful. It's coming along brilliantly.'

'Almost there, wouldn't you say?'

'Oh I would. And with so much against you.'

'Absolutely. Christ knows what Nicholas thinks he's doing. I'm amazed Harold lets him get away with it.'

'I know. Donald and Clive are the only ones who say anything. And then only because they know how you feel.'

'Mm. They're useful creatures in many respects.'

Esslyn had cleaned his teeth, put on his mid-calf-length pyjamas with the Judo-style top and was sitting up in bed tautening his facial muscles. Mouth dropped open, head tilted back, mouth closed aiming bottom lip at the tip of his nose. He had the jawline of a man of twenty-five which, on a man of forty-five, couldn't be bad. He blew out his cheeks and let them collapse slowly. (Nose to mouth lines.) Then studied his pretty wife as she finished taking off her make-up.

He always fell slightly in love with the most attractive female member of the cast (they expected it) and in *Rookery Nook* had got really carried away in the props room with the frisky young ingenue who was now Mrs Carmichael. She had been playing Poppy Dickie at the time. Unfortunately when the pregnancy was discovered he was unmarried so he felt it incumbent upon him to propose to Kitty. He did this rather ruefully. He had been looking forward to several years of louche living before finding someone to care for him in his old age. But she was a biddable little piece and he couldn't deny that this latish fatherhood had upped his status potentwise in the office. And of course it had been the most tremendous sock in the eye for Rosa.

He felt he owed her one for the way she had behaved when he had asked for a divorce. She had screamed and wailed and wept. And bellowed that he had had the best years of her life. Esslyn, he felt reasonably enough, pointed out that if he hadn't had them someone else would have. She could hardly have kept them, pristinely unlived, in a safe-deposit box. Then she had sobbed that she had always wanted children and now it was too late and it was all his fault. This seemed to Esslyn just plain ridiculous.

They had sometimes discussed starting a family, usually when cast as parents in the current production, but Esslyn always felt it only right to point out that, whilst their stage children would disappear after the final performance, real ones would be around for a whole lot longer. And that, although his own life might not be much affected, Rosa's, since he would definitely not be shelling out for a nanny, would never be quite the same again. He'd thought she'd appreciated the logic of this but she brought it all up when the question of moving out of White Wings was broached, refusing to budge until she had had some compensation for her 'lost babies'. Quite a hefty sum they had cost him too. He had got his own back, though. When Kitty had become pregnant he had announced it and their forthcoming nuptials at the end of a rehearsal of *Shop at Sly Corner*. Tenderly holding Kitty's hand, his eyes on Rosa's face, Esslyn had more than got his money back.

Of course by then she had married that boring little builder. To be fair though, Esslyn admitted to himself, finishing his cheek exercises and starting on some head rolling to reduce the tension in his neck, there were people who thought accountancy just as dreary a job as putting up houses. Perhaps even drearier. Esslyn could not agree. To him the sorting and winnowing of claim and counter claim, the reduction of stacks of wild expense-account imaginings to a column of sober, acceptable figures and the hunting down of obscure wrinkles and loopholes in the law enabling him to reduce his client's tax bill was a daily challenge which he would not have felt it too imprecise to call creative.

Esslyn preferred to handle the accounts of individuals. His partner, a specialist in company law, dealt with larger concerns with the single exception of the charitable trust that supported the Latimer. As an insider with an intimate knowledge of the company's affairs Esslyn had automatically taken this on together with the accounts for Harold's import/export business, which was a modest one but not without interest. He never charged Harold quite as much as he would a non-acquaintance and often wondered if his producer really appreciated this.

Having come to the end of his reminiscences and rolling his head about, Esslyn returned his attention to Kitty. Becoming aware of his regard she tossed her high-lit curls in a coquettish gesture which a less complacent husband might have thought a touch calculated. Then she admired her neck in the mirror. Esslyn admired her neck as well. Not a ring or a blur or a fold in sight. She had a charming little face. Not quite pointed enough to be called heart shaped it obtained more to a neat foxiness which, combined with the narrow tilt of her sparkling eyes, was very appealing. Now she stood up, smoothing the rosy fabric of her nightdress close against her belly, as yet no rounder than when they had wrestled in the props room, and smiled into the glass.

Esslyn did not smile back but contented himself with a simple nod. He was very sparing with his smiles, bringing them out only on special occasions. He had long been aware that, whilst they lit up and transformed his face, they also deepened and reinforced the nose to mouth lines somewhat. Now he called 'Darling' in a manner that spoke more of instruction than endearment.

Obediently Kitty crossed to the fourposter and stood by his side. Esslyn made a 'going up' gesture with his hand, palm held flat, and his wife lifted her nightdress over her head and let it fall, a cool raspberry ripple of satin, into a pool around her feet. Esslyn let his gaze slide over her lean almost boyish flanks and hips and small apple breasts, and his lips tightened with satisfaction. (Rosa had allowed herself to become quite grotesquely fat during the last years of their marriage.) Esslyn tugged at the cord of his pyjamas with one hand whilst patting his wife's pillow with the other.

'Come along, kitten.'

She felt really nice. Firm and young and strong. She smelt of honeysuckle and the iffy white wine they sold in the clubroom. She was sweetly compliant rather than saucily active which, it seemed to Esslyn, was just how things should be. And, to round off her character to perfection, she couldn't act for toffee.

This last reflection recalled the rehearsals for *Amadeus* and, as Esslyn started to move briskly inside his wife, he mulled over his latest role at the Latimer. Quite a challenge (Salieri was never off stage) but he was starting to feel that acting was no longer quite enough. It had been suggested that he might try a spot of directing and the truth was that Esslyn was rather drawn to this idea. He had once read a biography of Henry Irving and quite fancied himself in a long dark coat with an astrakhan collar and a tallish hat. He might even grow sideboards –

'How was that for you, darling?'

'How was what? Oh –' He gazed down at Kitty's face. Her lips shinily parted, her eyes closed in soft eclipse. 'Sorry. Miles away as per usual. Fine . . . fine.' He gave her a post-coital peck on the cheek in the manner of one putting the finishing touch to an iced cake, and rolled over to his own side of the bed. 'Do try and get your lines down for Tuesday, Kitty. At least for the scenes when we're together. I can't stand being held up.' Unconsciously he echoed Harold. 'I don't know what you find to do all day.'

'Why' – Kitty got up on one elbow and beamed a shining, sky-blue glance in his direction – 'I think of my pettipoos, of course.'

'And I think of you too, puss-wuss,' rejoined Esslyn, really believing at that moment that he did. Then he said,

'Don't forget – by Tuesday,' plumped up his pillows and, two minutes later, was fast asleep.

The Everards, toadies to the company's leading man, lived in unspeakable disarray in a crumbling terraced house down by the railway lines.

They were objects of curiosity to the rest of the street who could not make them out. They did not seem to have jobs (the curtains were sometimes still drawn at midday) and would often not come flitting out with their little expandable string shopping bags until well past tea-time.

That they had little money seemed obvious. They never gave at the door and could occasionally be seen at five o'clock on market day scavenging behind the stalls with dainty precision picking over the left-over fruits and vegetables. Various subtle and not so subtle attempts by the neighbours to get into the house had failed. They had not even managed to set foot on the tacky linoleum in the hall. And the windows were thickly coated with grime so that, even when the tattered curtains were pulled aside, the interior of the house remained a mystery.

The sour patch of ground standing in for a back garden was overgrown with nettles, thistles and tall grass which occasionally swayed and rustled, disturbed by the passing of rodents. On the asphalt beneath the front bay window their car slumped. This was a fifteen-year-old Volkswagon held together by spot welding and willpower with a Guinness label where the tax disc should have been. Mrs Griggs at the corner newsagents had reported them to the police over this and the label disappeared for a while but was now back again. The Everards, Mrs Griggs was fond of saying, gave her the creeps. She couldn't stand Clive's front teeth which looked very sharp and protruded slightly, or Donald's habit of blinking and squinting. She called them Ratty and Moley although never in their presence.

They were rarely seen apart and if they were, a certain dimness about the single Everard was noticeable. It was as if only by close physical proximity could the spark be struck that enabled them to shine with their full malevolent wattage. They seemed to feed off each other; to wax fat on spiteful prediction and exchange. Nothing gave the brothers more happiness than the intense discomfiture of their fellow man although they would never have been honest enough to say so. Indeed hypocrisy was their stock-in trade. Nobody could have been more surprised than they when someone took a remark amiss. Or when a plot or a plan resulted in the collapse of frail parties and distress all round. Who would have thought it? they would cry and retire to their appalling kitchen to plot and plan some more.

Passers by number thirteen Axon Street would stare at the grey windows and mutter and raise their eyebrows. Or tap their foreheads. The question 'what are they up to?' was not infrequently posed. Answers ranged pleasureably over a wide spectrum of subversive activities from the stealthy printing of underground literature to the making of bombs for the IRA. They were all quite wide of the mark. The beam of the Everards' malice, though powerful, was a narrow one and if they could make just a little mayhem within the immediate circle of their acquaintances, then they were quite content.

REHEARSALS

The theatre was perfectly situated in the very centre of Causton at the corner of the main thoroughfare. Actually it turned the corner, having originally been the last shop (a baker's) on the High Street and the first, (haberdashery and sewing machine repairs) on Carradine Road. Both shops went back a long way (the bread had been baked on the premises) and they each had several poky rooms above. Having the strong support of the then Mayor Councillor Latimer, the Causton Amateur Dramatic Society leased the two buildings and, with the aid of a grant from the council, the proceeds from various fundraising activities and a modest amount of professional help, had gutted them both and transformed the shell.

They had built a stage with a plain proscenium arch, fitted a hundred dark grey plastic seats to a raked floor and installed a simple lighting grid, There was a stage door and two large plate-glass doors which fronted the tiny foyer. This doubled as an office and had in it a desk, a chair, a telephone, an old filing cabinet and a pay phone. There was also a board showing colourful photographs of the current production. A huge cellar running between both shops became the scene dock and dressing rooms. These were more than adequate except at panto time or during the run of a play with an exceptionally large cast such as *Amadeus*. Toilets for the actors were halfway along a corridor connecting the wings to the foyer.

Three quarters of the top floor was taken up by the clubroom which was open to the public at performance times when coffee and glasses of wine were available. Plastic tables and chairs were scattered about and there were a couple of settees which, imperfectly disguised, performed on stage as often as some of the actors and, it must be said, frequently with more conviction. The rest of the upstairs space was taken up by two loos for the audience and Tim's lighting box which had a notice on the door: PRIVATE. KEEP OUT. The Latimer was carpeted throughout in charcoal haircord and the walls were rough-cast white.

Many of the CADS now looked back wistfully to those early days fifteen years past when, surrounded by rubble and timber and cables and choking on brick dust, they had wrought out of chaos their very own theatre. Things had been different then. Harold for example. Beardless and slim in old corduroys, he had mucked in, getting filthy in the process, cheering them on when they were tired, holding the dream before their flagging spirits and their gritty, dust-filled eyes.

They had all seemed equal then, in those glorious early days. Each with his part to play and no part more valuable than any other. But after the theatre was officially opened and Mayor Latimer had made his long-winded speech, imbibed hugely and vanished under the drinks table, things started to change and it soon became plain that some were very much more equal than others. For gradually, sinuously, Harold had eased his way to the top, stepping firmly on the necks of those too timid, too dim or just too lazy to complain until (no one could quite put their finger on the point of no return) a czar was born. And now occasionally people joined the company who knew nothing of those grand pioneering times when each member could have his say and be treated with respect. Renegade newcomers who couldn't care less about the past.

Like Nicholas for instance, now approaching the Latimer stage door. As far as Nicholas was concerned the Causton Amateur Dramatic Society came into existence during the rehearsals of *French without Tears* and would die the death if his audition at Central was successful (as it must be, *it must*) with *Amadeus*. He fumbled in his pocket for the key. He had been given his own as soon as Colin became aware of his willingness to appear early, stay late, run about, fetch and carry and generally make himself useful. Even now, in his illustrious position as what Esslyn grudgingly admitted to be second lead, Nicholas had arrived a good half hour before the stage management.

In fact it was barely six o'clock when he entered the building so he was not surprised to find himself immediately swallowed up by silence. He stood for a moment inhaling voluptuously and although the air smelt of nothing more exotic than the peel of an orange left in a tin waste-paper basket it became transmuted in his apprentice's nostrils to something rare and ambrosial. Nicholas padded silently, happily down the stone stairs to the dressing rooms.

He flung his anorak down, slipped on Mozart's brocade coat and picked up his sword. Nicholas was a short man, barely five feet six, a fact which caused him considerable anguish – Ian Holm, Anthony Sher and Bob Hoskins notwithstanding. Even on a good day when the wind was southerly the sword caused him problems, especially when getting up and sitting down at the pianoforte. He had planned to take it home with him to practise wearing it about the place but had foolishly asked Harold's permission, which had promptly been refused. 'You'll only lose it and then where shall we be?'

Now Nicholas buckled it on and made his way towards the stage, muttering the lines leading up to his move, anticipating the first night when he tripped over the thing and fell flat on his face, firmly putting this anticipation aside. A moment later, trainers muffling his footsteps, he was on the set. He stood for a moment excitedly aware of that frisson – half terror, half delight – that seized him whenever he walked on to a stage even when the theatre was empty.

But in fact it wasn't. There was a sound. Startled, he looked around. All the seats were unoccupied. He turned facing the way he had come but there was no one in the wings. Then he crouched and looked along the raked floor of the auditorium expecting to see Riley mauling some disgusting titbit. But no cat. Then it came again. Squeaky. Almost rubbery sounding in its effect. Such as might be made if you dragged your finger over a window pane. What could it be? And where was it coming from? Having checked the stage, the wings and the auditorium Nicholas was quite baffled. Until he lifted his head.

The sight that met his eyes was so surprising that it took him a couple of seconds to realize precisely what he was staring at. Someone was in Tim's lighting box. A girl. Nicholas swallowed hard. A naked girl. At least naked as far as he could see which was to just below her waist. Below this the glass panel changed to solid wood. The girl had tumbling fair hair and narrow shoulders and her back was pressed against the glass. When she arched it as she now did her skin imprinted uneven misty circles like pearly flowers. Her arms were outstretched and it was her fingers, clenching and unclenching against the glass, that had made the strange sound. He knew who it was. Even before she wrenched her body suddenly sideways revealing one small pointed breast and a swooning profile. Her eyes (thank God) were closed. Cemented to the floor he stared and stared, unable to drag his eyes away and Kitty smiled, an intense private smile gluttonous with satisfaction.

Whoever else was in the box must either be kneeling or crouching in front of her. Vivid pictures of what the lucky devil might be doing crowded Nicholas' brain and he was swept by a wave of lust so powerful that it left him with a bone-dry throat and gasping for air. When the wave had receded somewhat he took several deep breaths and ruminated on the extreme awkwardness of his position. Then the sound started again and he watched Kitty slowly slide down the glass, her shoulder blades leaving two damp, equidistant tracks. She turned her head away again as she disappeared and laughed, a raucous throaty chuckle quite unlike her usual tinkling carillon.

Released, Nicholas exhaled very carefully even though common sense told him the sound must be barely audible (he was amazed they had not heard the beating of his heart) then he tiptoed off stage and bore his bulging groin off to the loo. Once there he stayed longer than was absolutely necessary, mulling over the best course of action and praying that Kitty's playmate didn't decide to come in for a pee. He had just decided to creep out to the street and make a great noise coming back in again when he heard beneath him the slam of a door. He waited for another five minutes then made his way back to the basement.

As he passed the ladies' dressing room he heard a clatter as if someone was moving a bottle or jar. Nicholas opened the door. Kitty, demurely buttoned up in an apricot blouse and securely, nay chastely swathed in a long matching skirt, chirruped with alarm then said, 'You made me jump.'

'Sorry . . . hello.'

'Hello yourself.' Kitty frowned at him. 'What's the matter?'

'Mm?'

'You're not getting a sore throat, are you?'

'Don't think so.'

'You're croaking.'

'Ah. Just the proverbial frog.' He cleared his throat once or twice. Then did a mock gargle. But the dryness at the sight of her remained. 'That's better.'

'It doesn't sound better. You look a bit peaky actually, Nico . . . quite drained.' She narrowed her eyes at her reflection. '*Now* what's the matter?'

'Nothing.' Nicholas turned his sudden laugh into a cough. 'You first here then? You and Esslyn?'

He linked the names automatically then, finding ignorance established and Kitty misled, congratulated himself on his cleverness. But no sooner had he done this than a further thought developed. What if Kitty had actually been with Esslyn in the box? Stranger things had happened. Married couples were supposed to sometimes need peculiar settings or bizarre games to turn them on. Look at that Pinter play. Him coming home 'unexpectedly' in the afternoons; her in five-inch heels. But surely that was only after decades of marital boredom? The

Carmichaels hadn't been together five minutes. Kitty was speaking again.

'Oh, Esslyn's working till half six. So I came on early in my little Suzuki. I need lots of time to get ready. In fact' – she smiled, her lovely lips parting like the petals of a rose – 'I thought I'd find you here when I arrived.'

'. . . Er . . . no . . .' stammered Nicholas. 'Tried to get away but it was one of the manager's keen-eyed days.'

'Oh what a shame.' Another smile, warmly sympathetic. 'We could have gone over our lines together.'

Nicholas absorbed the impact of the smile (a soft, feather-light punch to the solar plexus) and his knees buckled. He hung grimly on to the door handle. For the first time in his life he cursed the enthusiasm that had brought him to the Latimer long before anyone else could reasonably have been expected to be present. Then he wondered how the hell, feeling like this, he was going to be able to concentrate on stage. Forcefully he reminded himself that this was only Kitty. Pretty, silly, ordinary Kitty. Her very silliness and the fact that she was an indifferent actress would normally have been enough to ensure his complete lack of interest. And if his mind could reason thus, reasoned Nicholas, why then should his viscera, still churning rhapsodically, not be brought under equally firm control? As he continued to argue against this onrush of carnality Kitty picked up a wire brush and started to rearrange her hair. She brushed it up and away from her face, which looked even more piquantly heart shaped without the surrounding aureole of golden curls.

Nicholas told himself it was more pointed than heart shaped. Sharp. A bit ferrety really. Then she opened her mouth, filled the damp rosy cavity with grips and started to pile the hair on top of her head. This movement pushed her bosom out. It strained against her blouse. Then, as Nicholas watched, every button burst its moorings. The fabric fell apart and her small exquisite breasts were revealed, doubly dazzling by being reflected in the mirror. She stood up and, with a light, thrillingly lascivious shrug, magically shed the rest of her garments except for silky, lace-topped stockings and thigh-high boots. Then she turned, placed one foot firmly on the seat of her chair and beckoned to him.

'Nico . . . ? What on *earth's* the matter with you tonight?'

'Ohhh . . . nerves, I guess.'

'Right. You and me both. Oh drat –' Kitty's hair collapsed. 'It's going to be one of those days when it just won't stay up.'

Nicholas, whose problem could hardly have been further removed from his companion's, was temporarily distracted by something being shifted around in the adjacent scene dock. 'Ah,' he murmured, 'seems we're not the only ones here early.'

'I'd like to have it cut,' – Kitty re-skewered the grips forcefully – 'but Esslyn'd go mad. He doesn't think a woman's truly feminine unless she's got long hair.'

'I wonder who it is.'

'Who what is?'

'In the workshop.'

'Colin, I suppose. He was moaning the other night about how much he had to do.'

'Par for the course.'

'Mmm. Nico . . .' Kitty put down her brush and turned to face him. 'You won't . . . well . . . go to pieces on the first night will you,. darling? I should be absolutely frantic.'

'Of course I won't!' cried Nicholas indignantly. This insult managed to damp his ardour in a way that all the earlier rationalizations had failed to do. Silly cow. 'You should know me better than that.'

'Only you've so many lines . . .'

'No more than in *Night Must Fall*.'

' – and Esslyn said . . . with your inexperience . . . you'd probably just dry up and leave me stranded . . .'

'Esslyn can get stuffed.'

'Oohh!' Neat foxiness beamed. Then she cocked her head on one side conspiratorially. 'Don't worry. I shan't pass it on.'

'You can pass it on as much as you like as far as I'm concerned.'

Nicholas went out, slamming the door. Patronizing bastard. 'It won't be me who goes to pieces on the first night, mate,' he muttered. In the men's dressing room he slung his coat and sword, glanced at his watch and discovered that, incredibly, barely twenty minutes had passed since he had entered the theatre. He decided to pop along and have a look at the scene dock.

A man was there putting the finishing touches to a small gilt chair. He stood back as Nicholas entered, studying the tight hoop of the chair back, his brush dripping glittering gold tears on to an already multicoloured floor. It was not the man Nicholas expected to see but he experienced an immediate warmth, almost a feeling of kinship towards the figure who was regarding his handiwork so seriously. Anyone who could make a cuckold out of Carmichael, thought Nicholas, was a man after his own heart.

'Hullo,' he said. 'The boss not in yet?'

David Smy turned, his handsome bovine face breaking into a slow smile. 'No, just me. And you of course. Oh' – his brush described a wide arc and Nicholas, not wishing to be gilded, jumped briskly aside – 'and the furniture.'

'R.i.g.h.t.' Nicholas nodded. 'Got it.' Then he performed the classic roguish gesture seen frequently in bad costume dramas but rarely in real life. He laid his finger to the side of his nose, tapped it and winked. 'Just you and me and the furniture it is then, Dave,' he replied and went back to the stage for some more practice.

After fifteen minutes or so at sitting down at and standing up from the piano and striding about getting used to his sword Nicholas went up to the clubroom to see who else had arrived. Tim and Avery sat at a table, their heads close.

They stopped talking the moment Nicholas entered and Tim smiled. 'Don't worry,' he said. 'We weren't talking about you.'

'I didn't expect you were.'

'Didn't you really?' asked Avery, who always thought that everyone was talking about him the second his back was turned and never very kindly. 'I would have.'

'Oh not your childhood insecurities, Avery,' said Tim. 'Not on an empty stomach.'

'And whose fault's that? If you hadn't been so long at the post office –'

'Nico . . .' Tim indicated a slender bottle on the table. 'Some De Bortoli?'

'Afterwards, thanks.'

'There won't be any afterwards, dear boy.'

'What were you whispering about anyway?'

'We were having a row,' said Avery.

'In *whispers?*'

'One has one's pride.'

'More of a discussion,' said Tim. 'I'm sorry I can't tell you what it's about.'

'We're burning our boats.'

'Avery!'

'Well, if we can't tell Nico who can we tell?'

'No one.'

'After all, he's our closest friend.'

Nicholas tactfully concealed his surprise at this revelation and the silence lengthened. Avery was biting his bottom lip as he always did when excited. He kept darting beseeching little glances at Tim and his fists opened and closed in purgatorial anguish. He looked like a child on Christmas morning denied permission to open its presents. Even his circle of curls danced with the thrill of it all.

Nicholas bent close to Avery's ear. 'I've got a secret as well. We could do a swop.'

'Ohhh . . . *could* we, Tim?'

'Honestly. You're like a two-year-old.' Tim looked coolly at Nicholas. 'What sort of secret?'

'An *amazing* secret.'

'Hm. And no one else knows?'

'Only two other people.'

'Well it's not a secret then, is it?'

'It's the two other people that the secret's about.'

'Ah.'

'Oh go on, Tim,' urged Nicholas. 'Fair exchange is no robbery.'

'Where do you find these ghastly little homilies?'

'*Please* . . .'

Tim hesitated. 'You must promise not to breathe a word before the first night.'

'Promise.'

'He said that rather quickly. If you break it,' continued Avery, 'you won't get into Central.'

'Oh God.'

'He's gone quite pale.'

'That was a stupid thing to say. Since when have you had crystal balls?'

'Why the first night?' asked Nicholas, recovering his equilibrium.

'Because after then everyone will know. Do you promise?'

'Cut my throat and hope to die.'

'You've got to go first.'

Nicholas told them his secret, looking from face to face as he spoke. Avery's mouth opened like a starfish in an ooo of astonishment and pleasure. Tim went scarlet, then white, then red again. He was the first to speak.

'*In my box*.'

Nicholas nodded affirmation.

'Of all the fucking cheek.'

'Ever the *mot juste*,' chuckled Avery, practically rocking on his chair with satisfaction. Nicholas thought he was like one of those weighted Daruma dolls that, no matter how hard you pushed them down, sprang straight back up again. 'But . . . if you couldn't see the man how do you know it was David?'

'There was no one else in the place. Just me, Kitty who surfaced in the dressing room about ten minutes later, and David in the scene dock. And I know he and his dad are often early. But they're never *that* early.'

'I thought you always kept your box locked,' said Avery.

'I do. But there's a spare key on the board in the prompt corner,' said Tim, adding, 'I shall take it home with me in future. I must say,' he continued, 'he's a bit . . . lumpen . . . David. For Kitty I mean.'

'Constanze's bit of rough,' Avery giggled. 'Must have given you quite a thrill, Nico. If you like that sort of thing.'

'Oh,' said Nicholas pinkly, '. . . not really'.

'Still, he's a nice lad,' continued Tim, 'and I should think almost anyone'd be a relief after Esslyn. It must be like going to bed with the Albert Memorial.' He pulled back his cuff. 'Nearly the quarter. Better go and check the board.'

He picked up his bottle and moved quickly to the door, Avery scuttering after. Nicholas, in hot pursuit cried: 'But what about your secret?'

'Have to wait.'

'I've got time. I'm not on for twenty minutes.'

'And I'm not on,' echoed Avery, 'at all. I can tell him.'

'We tell him together.' Tim tried the door of his box then got out his key. 'At least David locked up after him.'

He opened the door, and just for a moment the three of them stood on the threshold, Avery quivering like the questing beast. His button nose pointed (as well as it was able) and he sniffed as if hoping to detect some faint residual flavour of wickedness on the stuffy air.

'For heaven's sake, Avery.'

'Sorry.'

The image of Kitty rushed back to Nicholas so vividly that it seemed impossible that the tiny place could have remained unmarked by her presence. Then he saw faintly on the glass the now barely visible tracks made by her dragging shoulder blades.

Avery said: 'I wonder what made them choose here?'

'Sheer perversity, I should think. Well . . . see you later, Nicholas.'

Dismissed, Nicholas was just turning away when a

thought struck him. 'Oh Avery . . . you won't repeat what I've told you to anyone?'

'*Me?*' Avery was outraged. 'I like the way you ask me. What about him?'

Nicholas grinned. 'Thanks.'

Downstairs he collided with Harold, who arrived as he did everything else, Napoleonically. He started shouting as he entered the foyer and didn't stop until he had seen some flurry of movement, however unnecessary, in every corner of the auditorium. He called it keeping them on their toes. 'So who's ahead of the game?' he cried, subsiding into Row C, lighting a Davidoff and removing his hat. Harold had quite a collection of fur hats. This one was black and cream and yellowish-grey and definitely the product of more than one animal. It had a short tail, squatted on his head like a ringtailed lemur and was known throughout the company as Harold's succubus.

'Come on, Dierdre,' he roared. 'Chop, chop!'

The play began. The Venticelli loped down to the footlights and stood, secretively entwined, like a pair of gossipy stick insects. They were an unattractive pair, with pasty open-pored complexions and most peculiar hair. Flossy and fly-away, it was that strange colour – dirty blonde with a pinkish tinge – that hairdressers call champagne. Their eyelids drooped in the lizard-like manner of the old although they were barely thirty. They always seemed to be on the verge of imparting some distasteful revelation and spoke in a sort of snittering whisper. Harold was always having to tell them to project. Seemingly secure under Esslyn's patronage, they discussed anyone and everyone poisonously and their breath smelt dank and malodorous like a newly opened grave. Now, having finished their opening dialogue and wrapped their cloaks tightly about them, they pranced off.

Esslyn took the floor and Nicholas in the wings watched the tall figure with a certain degree of envy. For there was no denying that his rival cut a splendid figure on stage. Take his face for a start. High cheekbones, rather thick but beautifully shaped lips and, that rare feature, truly black eyes. Hard and bright the pupils glittered like tar chippings. His jowls were always a faint steely blue like those of the villains in gangster cartoons.

Nicholas' own face could not be more ordinary. It was an 'ish' face. Brownish hair, greyish eyes, straightish nose. Only the fact that his even features were unevenly distributed gave it any distinction at all. Rather a lot of space between the tip of the nose and the top lip which he thought made him look a trifle monkeyish, although Hazel at the check-out had pronounced it 'very sexy'. A wide space also between his eyes and a very wide one indeed after the eyebrows and before the hairline. So apart from being dwarfish and clumsy with nondescript features, Nicholas reflected sourly, he would probably be completely bald before the age of twenty-one. He stared aggrieved at Esslyn's crisp sloe-black hair. Not even a flake of dandruff.

'Cheer up,' whispered David Smy, arriving ready for his first entrance. 'It might never happen.'

Nicholas barely had time to smile back before his companion went on. Poor old David, thought Nicholas, watching Salieri's valet sidling across the boards with that constipated cringe that afflicts people who loathe acting and are coaxed on to a stage. Fortunately the valet was a non-speaking part. The only time David had been given a line to say containing seven words he had managed to deliver them in a different order every night of the run without repeating himself once.

'*David* . . .' Nicholas heard from the stalls. 'Try not to walk as if you've got a duck up your knickers. Get off and come on again.'

Blushing, the boy complied. On re-entering he strode manfully to his position only to hear the Venticelli sniggering behind his back.

'My God – it's the frog footman.'

'No it's not. It's Dandini.'

'You're both wrong,' mouthed Esslyn in a Restoration aside. 'It's the Fairy Quasimodo.'

'For heaven's sake get on with it!' cried Harold. 'I'm

putting on a play here, not running a bear garden.' He sat back in his seat and the rehearsals rolled on. *Amadeus* was not an easy play but Harold had never been one to shirk a challenge to his directorial skills, and the fact that it had a large cast and thirty-one scenes did not deter him. Six keen fifth formers from the local comprehensive had been recruited to help on stage management and Harold watched them now drifting vaguely on and off the set, an exasperated expression on his face. It was all very well for the author to suggest that their constant coming and going should by a pleasant paradox of theatre be rendered invisible. He wasn't lumbered with a crew of sleepwalking zombies who didn't know their stage right from a ninety-seven bus. And Esslyn, who was on stage throughout and could have been a great help, was worse than useless. Years ago Harold had made the mistake of saying that when he was in the business no actor of any standing would demean himself by touching either stick or stone during a performance. All that was strictly stage management. Since then their leading man had steadfastly refused to handle anything but personal props.

'Dierdre,' shouted Harold. 'Speed this lot up. The set changes are taking twice as long as the bloody play.'

'If he'd read Shaffer's notes,' murmured Nicholas to Dierdre who had been testing a pile of newly stacked furniture in the wings for rockability and was now back in the prompt corner, 'he'd know you're supposed to carry on acting through the changes.'

'Oh you won't find Harold bothering with boring old things like author's notes,' said Dierdre, as near to malice as Nicholas had ever heard her, 'he has his own ideas. I hate this scene, don't you?'

Nicholas, poised for his entrance, nodded briefly. The reason they both disliked 'The Abduction from the Seraglio' was the lighting. Futilely when Harold had asked for crimson gels Tim had attempted one of his rare arguments. In reply, speaking very slowly as if to an idiot child, Harold explained his motivation.

'It's all about a seraglio. Right?'

'So far.'

'Which is another word for a brothel – right?'

Tim murmured 'Wrong' but could have saved his breath.

'Which is another word for a red-light house. Ergo . . . surely I don't have to further spell it out? I know it's theatrical, Tim, but that's the kind of producer I am. Bold effects are my forte. If what you want is wishy-washy naturalism you should stay at home and watch the telly.'

Nicholas was always glad when the scene was finished. He felt as if he was swimming in blood. He came off stage dissatisfied with his performance and irritated with himself. Avery's secret was snagging at his mind. He wondered what on earth it could be. Probably some piddling little thing. Nowhere near as scandalously interesting as Nicholas' own secret. He wished they'd either told him at once or not mentioned it at all. Perhaps he could persuade them to cough it up in the interval.

Pausing only to give David Smy a very insinuating moue and a nudge in the ribs, Nicholas returned to the dressing room. Next time Colin came up from the paint shop David approached his father and asked him if he thought Nicholas could possibly be gay.

Three rehearsals later the difficulties with the razor had still not been sorted out. When the moment arrived to wield it and David stood deferentially by holding his tray with the water, wooden bowl of shaving soap and towel, the action ground to a halt. Esslyn moved downstage and stared challengingly at Row C. The Everards, lizard lids aflicker, capered behind. Tim and Avery, sensing a possible fracas, left the lighting box and the stage staff gathered round. Harold rose and, with an air of quite awesome capability, took the stage.

'Well, my darlings,' he cried as he mounted the steps, 'we have a wide-open situation here and I'm offering it to the floor before I sound off with any of my own suggestions, which I need hardly say are myriad.' Silence. 'Never let it be said that I'm not open to new ideas from whatever direction they may arise.' The silence took on an incredulous slightly stunned quality as if someone had thwacked it with a baseball bat. 'Nicholas? You seem to be on the verge of suggestive thought.'

'He always is,' said Avery.

'Well . . .' said Nicholas, 'I was wondering if it might not look very exciting done with Salieri's back to the audience. An expansive movement.' He leapt to his feet to demonstrate. 'Like so –'

'I don't believe this,' retorted Esslyn. 'Is there nothing you wouldn't do to sabotage my performance? Do you really think you could persuade me to play the most exciting moment of my entire career facing up stage?'

'What career?'

'Of course everyone knows you're jealous –'

'*Me? Jealous? Of you?*' The smidgeon of truth in this assertion caused Nicholas to splutter like fat in a pan. 'Hah!'

'I should climb back into your swamp, Nicholas,' snickered a Venticelli. 'Before you have yet another brilliant wheeze.'

'Yes,' agreed his twin. 'Back to the Grimpen Mire with you.'

'It'll be a funny old day,' snapped Nicholas, 'when I take any notice of a pair of bloody book ends.'

'Now, now,' beamed Harold. He adored displays of temperament by his actors, fatuously believing them to be a sign of genuine talent. 'Actually, Esslyn, you know it might look quite effective –'

'Forget it, Harold.'

Everyone sat up. Confrontation between the CADS director and his leading man was unheard of. Harold directed Esslyn. Esslyn went his own way. Harold ignored this intransigence. It had been ever thus. Now every eye was on Harold to see what he would do. And he was worth watching. Various emotions chased over his rubicund features. Amazement, disgust, rage, then finally (after a great struggle) compliance.

'Obviously,' he said, presaging the frankly incredible,

'I would never force an actor to do something that was totally alien to his way of working. It would simply look wooden and unconvincing.' Then, quickly, 'Does anyone else have any ideas?'

'What happened about those bag things?' asked Rosa. 'That we talked about earlier on?'

'They didn't work. Or rather,' continued Harold, evening the score, 'Esslyn couldn't make them work.'

'You don't pull off a trick like that the first time,' retorted Esslyn. 'You have to practise, which I could hardly do with you yelling *molto costoso* in my face every time I asked for another.'

'Then you'll have to mime streaming with blood,' said Rosa, smiling sweetly. 'I'm sure if anyone can do it you can.'

'Ouch!' said Kitty, exchanging a rueful, collusive glance with her husband. It was a complicated glance and managed to suggest not only that Rosa was jealous of her husband's present happiness but also that she was not quite right in the head. The assistant director cleared her throat.

'Whoops,' whispered Clive Everard. 'Page the oracle.'

'The problem's as good as solved.'

'Perhaps,' Dierdre began hesitantly, 'we could cover the blade with Sellotape. I'm sure it wouldn't show from the front.'

There was a pause then a deep sigh from Harold. 'At last.' He nodded, a wry, reproachful nod. 'I was wondering who would be the first to think of that. Got some here, I trust, Dierdre?'

'Oh yes . . .' She took the razor from David's tray, holding it carefully by the handle, and bore it off to her table. There she tipped her carrier bag on to its side. The Sellotape rolled out, closely followed by a bottle of grudgingly-carried milk. She saved the milk just in time, sat down beneath the anglepoise, picked up the tape and started scratching at it to find the ends. Then she cut off a strip and laid it lengthwise against the cutting edge. It was too short (she should have measured before she started) as well as being too narrow to wrap over the steel completely. She hesitated wondering if it was necessary to take the first piece off before trying again and decided she wouldn't dare come so close to that gleaming steel. Even at the thought her hands started to sweat. She felt all hot and bothered as if everyone was watching her, glanced up and discovered she was right.

'Shan't be a sec,' she called jollily. The tail of the tape had vanished and she started scratching again. 'More haste less speed.'

'I always find,' Rosa returned the call, 'that folding the end bit over every time is a great help.'

'Oh, what a good idea,' gritted Dierdre, 'I must remember that.' Holding the razor firmly she attached the tape to the handle end and wound the reel round and round, up and down the blade until it was well and truly covered. Then she cut off the tape. The result was dreadful. Very uneven and bumpy, with half a dozen thicknesses in one place and two or three in others, all of which would be clearly visible from the stalls in that intimate theatre. Oh God, thought Dierdre, what on earth am I going to do? The thought of trying to remove the tape again terrified her. Even supposing she could find the tag end.

'What's the problem, Dierdre?' David Smy put his valet's tray down and pulled up one of the little gold chairs.

'It's all gone wrong.' Dierdre blinked hard behind her pebbled lenses. 'I had a terrible job getting it on. Now I'm frightened to try and take it off in case I cut myself.'

'Let's have a look.'

'Be careful.' Dierdre handed the razor over.

'Got some scissors? No . . . smaller than those.' When Dierdre shook her head David produced a Victorinox Swiss army knife and eased out a tiny pair of clippers. Dierdre watched his brown fingers tipped with clean short nails which had dazzlingly white half moons. He handled things so precisely, almost gracefully, and without any floundering or wasted movements. Snip, snip and the tape

71

was off. Dierdre unrolled more. David measured the blade against it, cut off two lengths, and with Dierdre holding the handle folded them carefully over the length of the blade, first one side then the other. Then he ran the razor hard down the prompt copy. It fell apart. 'That should do it.'

'*David*. You mustn't say that. Not even in fun. We'll have to put some more on.'

'If you insist.' His slow smile was reassuring. 'I was only pulling your leg.'

'I should hope so.' After a few moments she smiled rather nervously in return. David re-covered the blade and this time produced no more than a faint indentation when he pressed the page.

'Come *on*, Dierdre – chop, chop. We could all have cut our throats ten times over by now.'

'Sorry, Harold.'

'You go when you're ready,' said David. 'You don't want to let that lot run you about. Load of wankers.' Then he added hastily: 'Pardon my French.'

'Oh if it's French,' Dierdre murmured apologetically, 'it's right over my head, I'm afraid. Well . . . let's see how this goes down.' She handed the razor to Esslyn who received it warily. 'You could try it out on your thumb first.'

'I shall certainly try it out on someone's thumb,' replied Esslyn crisply, handing it straight back. Obligingly Dierdre illustrated its newly rendered bitelessness. Esslyn said: 'Hmm,' and sawed tentatively then more firmly back and forth across his knuckles. 'Seems OK. Right . . . Harold?'

Esslyn waited until everyone's attention was upon him then stood, centre stage, in a martyr's pose: hands across his breast, eyes on a glorious horizon, looking for all the world, as Tim said later, like Edith Cavell in drag. He spoke loudly, in a doom-laden voice: '. . . And in the depth of your downcastness you can pray to me . . . And I will forgive you. *Vi Saluto!*' Then, throwing his head back and holding the razor in his right hand he drew it quickly

72

across his throat. One sweeping dramatic movement from ear to ear. There was a terrible silence then someone murmured, 'My God.'

'Works, does it?'

'You could practically see the blood,' squawked Don Everard.

'They'll be carrying people out.'

Esslyn smirked. He liked the idea of people being carried out. Harold swung round, letting his satisfied smile embrace them all. 'I knew that would work,' he said, 'as soon as I thought of it.'

'I really believe that's the secret of our success,' chipped in Nicholas, 'an ideas man at the helm.'

'Well of course that's not for me to say,' demurred Harold, who never stopped saying it.

'Wasn't it Dierdre,' said David Smy loudly, 'who thought of it?'

'David,' whispered Dierdre across the table, 'don't. It doesn't matter.'

'It was Dierdre,' said Harold, 'who *vocalized* it. I thought of it weeks ago when the production was in the planning stage. She simply caught my idea on the ether, as it were, and vocalized it. Now, if the stage management have stopped showing off, we really must get on . . .'

But the rehearsal was further delayed by Kitty who, white faced, was now clinging to her husband, her arms around his waist, her head buried in his chest. '. . . It looked so real . . .' she mewed, 'I was frightened . . .'

'There, there, kitten.' Esslyn patted her as if soothing a fretful animal. 'There's absolutely nothing to be frightened about. I'm quite safe. As you can see.' He let loose a smug apologetic look over her head.

Now if she could act like that, thought Nicholas, when she's on stage with me, I'd be a happy man. He glanced across at Kitty's lover to see how he was reacting to this little display, but David was continuing his conversation with Dierdre and affecting not to notice. Nicholas observed the rest of the company. Most were looking indifferent, one or two embarrassed, Boris ironical, Harold

73

impatient. The Venticelli, to Nicholas' surprise, appeared jealous. He was sure this was not romantic resentment. In spite of their affectations and flouncings and toadily awful obsequiousness Nicholas did not believe they were sexually interested in Esslyn. In fact they both struck him as almost asexual. Dry and detached and probably more interested in making mischief than in making love. No, Nicholas guessed they were simply peeved that the object of their sycophancy was being so crass and ungrateful as to show public affection for another.

Then, eyes travelling on, Nicholas received a shock. Sitting a little behind the others and surely believing herself to be unobserved, Rosa was staring at Esslyn and his wife. Her face showed pure hatred. Not a muscle moved and the emotion was so concentrated, so extreme that she might have been wearing a mask. Then she noticed Nicholas' gaze, dropped her rancorous eyes and immediately became herself again. So much so that by the time, half an hour later, she made her usual flurried departure (trailing her scarf, dropping her script, whirling her Madame Ranyevskaia coat about and crying 'night-night my angels') he was almost convinced that he had imagined it.

The book arrived about a week before the dress rehearsal. Dierdre found a small parcel neatly wrapped in brown paper on the floor in the foyer. It was directly beneath the letter-box flap set in the wooden surround of the plate-glass doors. She turned the parcel over, frowning. On the front, hand printed in small capital letters, were the words HAROLD WINSTANLEY. She laid it on top of her basket and made her way up to the clubroom to unload her two bottles of milk and tea and sugar replenishments. As she entered Riley hurried forward to greet her. She put the milk bottles in a pan of cold water then bent down and rubbed his ears. He permitted this for as long as it took him to realize that she was not bearing gifts, then stuck his tail in the air and wandered off. Dierdre watched him go sadly, wishing he was not so mingy with his affections.

Only Avery got the full treatment – purring, rubbing round the legs, little 'mrrs' of satisfaction – but then only Avery dished up the dinner. He bought fish trimmings or 'cheeks' for the cat, which Riley would remove from his dish to consume at his leisure. Dierdre was always coming across the bluish white pearly wings of bone that remained.

He was a handsome animal. White bib and socks, mixed whiskers and a white tip to his tail. The rest of his coat, once black and gleaming like newly mined coal, now had a rusty tinge which made him look a bit seedy. He was a full-blooded tom and had a hairless patch above one eye which was no sooner grown over than some bold adversary clawed it back to its original glabrous state. He had brilliant emerald green eyes and, when the theatre was dark, you could see them walking about on their own between the lines of seats.

No one knew how old he was. He had appeared two years ago, suddenly strolling across the set during a run-through of *French without Tears.* The immense almost magical theatricality of this appearance had at once appealed to everyone. He had got a round of applause, a piece of haddock, (Dierdre having been sent to Adelaide's) and been adopted on the spot. This, although he had not been able to say so in so many words, had not been his intention. For Riley was looking for a more orthodox establishment. He had been vastly deceived in the sitting room of *French without Tears* which had disappeared shortly after he had made its acquaintance, only to re-appear in a totally different guise several weeks later. This was really not his scene. He wanted an ordinary, even humdrum, home where the furniture was fairly stable, with at least one human being more or less constantly in worshipful attendance. He often tried to follow Avery when he left the theatre but had always been firmly brought back. Dierdre, who had always longed for a pet, would have loved to have taken him home but her father was allergic to both fur and feather.

Now, having unpacked the tea and sugar and set out

the cups, Dierdre made her way to the auditorium to chalk up the stage for act one. As Nicholas was already there going over his 'opera' speech she slipped silently into the back row to listen. It was a complicated piece and Nicholas was making a hash of it. It started on a high point of anger, broke in the middle into giggling of almost frenzied effusiveness, and ended on a note so elated as to be almost manic.

He had been going over it at home every night the previous week and was agonizingly conscious that it wasn't working. Now he pumped amazement into his voice: 'Astonishing device. A Vocal Quartet!' Following up with forced excitement: 'On and on, wider and wider – all sounds multiplying and rising together . . .' He ploughed on, ending with an empty rhetorical shout: 'And turn the audience into God!'

Despair filled him. Nothing but ranting. But what was he to do? If emotion wasn't there it couldn't be turned on like a tap. A dreadful thought lurking always in the back of his mind leapt to the fore. What if he felt dry and stale like this on the first night? Without technique he would be left clinging desperately to the text like an ill-equipped mountaineer on a rock face. He almost envied Esslyn his years of experience; his grasp of acting mechanics. It was all very well for Avery to describe their leading man's performance as 'just like an Easter egg, darling. All ribbons and bows and little candied bits and pieces with a bloody great hollow at the centre.' Nicholas was not comforted, being only too aware that, when his emotions let him down, he could offer neither ribbon nor bow, never mind anything as fancy as a candied trimming. Dierdre came down the aisle.

'Hi,' said Nicholas morosely. 'Did you hear all that?'

'Mmn,' said Dierdre, putting her basket on the edge of the stage and climbing up.

'I just can't seem to get it right.'

'No. Well – you haven't got the feeling, have you? And you're just not experienced enough to put it over without.'

Nicholas, who had expected some anodyne reassurance,

stared at Dierdre who crossed to the prompt corner and
started to unpack her things saying,

'If I could make a suggestion . . . ?'

'Of course.' He followed her round the stage as she
crouched to re-mark the entrances and exits smudged or
quite erased at the previous rehearsal.

'Well . . . first you mustn't take the others into account
so much when you're speaking. Salieri . . . Van
Swieten . . . they matter in Mozart's life only so far as
they affect his income. They mean nothing to him as
people. Mozart's a genius – a law unto himself. You seem
to be trying to relate to them in this speech, which is fatal.
They are there to listen . . . to absorb . . . Perhaps to be
a little . . . afraid . . .'

'Yes . . . yes I see . . . I think you're right. And God –
how do you think he sees God?'

'Mozart? He doesn't "see" God as something separate
like Salieri does. Music and God are all the same to him.
As for the delivery, you're working the wrong way round.
That's why it sounds stale before you've even half got it
right –'

'I know!' Nicholas smote his forehead. '*I know.*'

'If you stop thinking about the words and start listening
to the music –'

'There isn't any music.'

'– in your head, silly. If you're making a passionate
speech about music you have to *hear* music. Most of the
other set pieces either have music underneath them or
just before. This is very . . . dry. So you must listen to all
the tapes and see what evokes the emotion you need, then
marry it in your mind to the lines. I don't mean "must"
of course' – Dierdre blushed suddenly – 'only if you like.'

'Oh but I do! I'm sure that would . . . it's a terrific
idea!'

'You're in the way.'

'Sorry.'

Nicholas looked down at Dierdre's bent head and
chalky jeans. He had not, unlike most of the rest of the
company, underestimated her proficiency behind the

scenes. But he had never talked to her about play production and, although he was aware of her ambitions in that direction, had thought (also like the rest of the company) that she would be no better at it than Harold was. Now he gazed at her rather as men gazed at girls in Hollywood films after they had taken off their glasses and let their hair down. He said: 'It's a wonderful play, don't you think?'

'Very exciting. I saw it in London. I'll be glad when it's over, though. I don't like the way things are going.'

'What do you mean?'

'Oh, nothing specific. But there's not a nice feeling. And I'm dying to get on to *Vanya*. I do love Chekov, don't you, Nicholas?' She regarded him with shining eyes. 'Even *The Cherry Orchard*, after all Harold managed to do to it . . . there was still so much left.'

'Dierdre . . .' Nicholas followed her around in the wings where, clipboard in hand, she started to check the props for act one. 'Why on earth . . . I mean . . . you should be with another company. Where you can really do things.'

'There isn't one. The nearest is Slough.'

'That's not far.'

'You need your own transport. At night anyway. And I can't afford to run a car. My father's – He can't be left alone. I have to pay someone to sit with him on theatre evenings . . .'

'Oh, I see.' What he did see – a sudden yawning abyss of loneliness, creative imagination starved of expression and stifled, unrealized dreams – made him deeply, shamedly embarrassed. He felt as if he were with one of those awful people who, uninvited, hitch up their clothes and show you their operation scar. Aware of the unfairness of this comparison and the banality of his next remark, Nicholas mumbled, 'Bad luck, Dierdre,' and retreated to the stage. Here, more for the sake of bridging an awkward moment than anything else, he picked up the parcel. 'Someone sending Harold a bomb?'

'Heavily disguised as a book.'

Nicholas eased the brown paper lightly Sellotaped folds and attempted to peer inside.

'Don't do that,' called Dierdre, 'he'll say someone's been trying to open it. And he's bound to blame me.'

But Harold seemed to notice nothing untoward about his parcel. He arrived rather later than usual and was changing into his monogrammed directing slippers when Dierdre gave him the book. There had been a time when Harold had always removed his footwear during rehearsals, explaining that only by doing so could he arrive at the true spirit of the play. Then he had seen a television interview with a famous American director during which the great man had stated that people who took off their shoes to direct were pretentious pseuds. Harold, naturally, did not agree but just in case other members of the company had also been viewing he covered up his feet forthwith.

As he took the parcel Rosa, noticing, called out: 'Oohh look . . . Harold's got a prezzie.' And everyone gathered round.

The prezzie proved to be a bit of a letdown. Nothing unusual or exciting. Nothing to do with Harold's only real passion in life. It was a cookery book. *Floyd on Fish*. Harold gazed at it blankly. Someone asked who it was from. He spun the pages, turned the book upside down and shook it. No card.

'Isn't there something written inside?' nudged an Everard. Harold turned the first few pages and shook his head. 'How extraordinary.'

'Why on earth should anyone send you a recipe book?' asked Rosa. 'You're not interested in cooking, are you?' Harold shook his head.

'Well if you're going to start,' said Avery, 'I shouldn't start with that. The man's basically unsound.'

'Gosh, you are a snob,' said Nicholas.

'Right, young Bradley. That's the last time you sit down at my table.'

'Oh! I didn't mean it, Avery – honestly.' Half frantic, half laughing, Nicholas continued. '*Please*. I'm sorry . . .'

'I shall think of it,' said Harold, 'as a gift from an unknown admirer. And now we must get on. Chop, chop everyone . . .'

He put the parcel inside his hat. The momentary warmth that its appearance had engendered (it had been years since anyone had given him a present) had vanished. In its place was a faint unease. What a peculiar thing for anyone to do. Spend all that money on a book then send it anonymously to someone for whom it could be of no interest whatever. Ah well, thought Harold, he certainly didn't have time to ponder on the mystery at the moment. The mystery of the theatre – that was his business. That was what he had to kindle up. And plays did not produce themselves.

'Right, my darlings,' he cried, 'from the top. And please . . . lots and lots of verismo. Nicholas, you remember – Where *is* Nicholas?'

Mozart stepped out from the wings. 'Here I am, Harold.'

'Don't forget the note I gave you on Monday. *Resonances*. OK? That's what I want – plenty of resonances. You're looking blank.'

'. . . Sorry, Harold?'

'You know the meaning of the word resonances, I assume?'

'. . . Um . . . Don Quixote's horse, wasn't it?'

'Oh God!' cried Harold. 'I'm surrounded by idiots.'

Several days passed. None of the rehearsals went well and the first couple of run-throughs were absolutely dreadful. But it was at the dress rehearsal (so everyone later told Barnaby) that things really came to a head.

As Esslyn strode around the stage with his springheeled tango dancer's walk in his blue and silver coat so his performance grew in glossy fraudulence. He had stopped acting with – indeed he hardly even looked at – his fellow players and strutted and posed in splendid isolation. Backed up by his snickersnees, he continued to snipe at David and Nicholas.

Nicholas was coping with all this very well. His earlier talk with Dierdre had been the first of three and he was now groping his way towards what he believed would be a truthful, intelligent and lively rendering of the part of Mozart. He was halfway through the opening scene and playing to the back of Salieri's neck when Esslyn suddenly stopped what he was saying and strolled down to the footlights.

'Harold?' Harold, his face marked with surprise, climbed out of his seat and walked forward. 'Any particular stress on *che gioia?*'

'What?'

'Sorry. To be frank, my problem is . . . I'm not quite sure what it means.' Silence. 'Perhaps you could enlighten me?' Long pause. 'I'd be most grateful.'

'Now who's being *cattivo?*' murmured Clive.

'Don't you know?' said Harold.

'I'm afraid not.'

'Do you mean to tell me that you've been saying those lines over and over again for the last six weeks and you don't know what they mean?'

'So it appears.'

'And you call yourself an actor?'

'I certainly call myself as much of an actor as you are a director.'

An even longer pause. Then, softly on the air it seemed to everyone present came a faint reverberation like the roll of distant drums. Harold said, very quietly: 'Are you trying to wind me up?'

'Didn't think it was necesary,' muttered Donald.

'Thought he ran on hot air.'

'Of course not, Harold. But I do think –'

'I'm not going to translate it for you. Do your own homework.'

'Well, that seems a bit –'

'All right, everyone. Carry on. And no interval. We've wasted enough time as it is.'

Esslyn shrugged and sauntered back to his previous position and the reverberations rippled away into a silence shot with disappointment. The first real confrontation, you could almost see everyone thinking, and it's over before it really gets going. But their frustration was short lived, for a few minutes later Esslyn stopped again, saying: 'Do you think it's true he's never really laid a finger on Katherina?'

'Of course it's true,' shouted back Harold. 'Why on earth should he tell himself lies?'

Then there was a query on court etiquette, on the timing of the Adagio in the library scene and on the position of the pianoforte. Harold once more made his way to the footlights, this time with a savage tic in one eyelid.

'If you've noticed all these hiccups before,' he said icily, 'may I ask why you have left it till this late stage to say so?'

'Because I'm not in charge. I was waiting for you to pick them up. As you're obviously not going to I feel, for the good of the play and the benefit of the company, I have to say something.'

'The day you have any concern for the rest of the company, Esslyn, will be the day pigs take to the skies.'

After this, as if the earlier interruptions had been just appetizers, the merest titillations, things started to go more splendidly wrong. Kitty's padding would not stay up. The more it slid about the more she grabbed at it. The more she grabbed at it the more she giggled until Harold stood up and yelled at her, when she promptly burst into tears.

'It's not so easy,' she wept, 'when you're already pregnant in the first place.'

'How many places are there, for God's sake?' retorted Harold. 'Wardrobe!' He stood tapping his foot and sucking his teeth until Joyce had secured Baby Mozart. Then the manuscript paper was not in its place on the props table. Or the quill pen. Or Kitty's shawl. Dierdre apologized and swore they had been there at the start of rehearsal. Salieri's wheelchair jammed, and gold railings, not quite dry, imprinted themselves on to the Emperor Joseph's white satin suit.

But the most dramatic, alarming and ultimately hilarious *contretemps* was that the trestle table holding the bulk of the audience for the first night of *The Magic Flute* collapsed. It was piled high with sausage-chewing, pipe-smoking Viennese rabble. Belching, joshing, pushing each other about and generally overacting, all this to the loud accompaniment of rustic accents. These were mainly Zummerset but one conscientious burgher who had really done his homework kept shouting: 'Gott in Himmel.'

Then, as the glorious *'Heil sei euch Geweihten'* soared above their heads the trestle creaked, groaned and gave way, tumbling the by now hysterical peasantry into a large heap in the centre of the stage. Everyone except Harold thought this wondrously droll. Even Esslyn jeered with cold delicacy into his lace cuff. Harold rose from his seat and smouldered at them all.

'I suppose you think that's funny?'

'Funniest thing since the black death,' replied Boris.

'Right,' said his director. '*Colin.*' A helpful soul repeated the cry as did someone in the wings followed by someone in the dressing rooms then, finally, a faint echo was heard under the boards of the stage.

'Good grief,' grumbled Harold as he stomped down yet again, 'it's like waiting for the star witness at the Old Bailey.'

Colin arrived with a wooden shaving curl on his shoulder as if to designate rank, a hammer in his hand and his usual air of a man dragged away from serious work to attend to the whims of playful children.

'You knew how many people this table had to hold. I thought you said you were going to reinforce it.'

'I did reinforce it. I nailed a wooden block in each corner where the struts go in. I'll show you.' Colin picked his way over the still supine actors, lifted the table then said, 'Stone me. Some silly sod's taken them out again.'

'Ohhh God!' Harold glared at his cast, one or two of whom were still weeping quietly. 'You have no right to be in a theatre, any of you. You're not fit to sweep the stage. Better make some more, Colin. Now, *please*, let us get on.'

He was walking back to his seat when Clive Everard, hardly bothering to lower his voice, said: 'That man couldn't direct his piss down an open manhole.'

Harold stopped, turned and replied forcefully into the shocked silence. 'I hope you don't see yourself appearing in my next production, Clive.'

'Well . . . I did rather fancy Telyeghin . . .'

'Well,' repeated Harold, 'I suggest you start fancying yourself in an entirely different company. Preferably on an entirely different planet. Now, I want to get to the end of the play with No. More. Interruptions.'

And they just about did. But by this time nerves were in shreds. Umbrage had been given and taken and returned again with interest. More props had erred and strayed in their ways like lost sheep. The scenery had learned the wisdom of insecurity and at least one door left the set almost as smartly as the actor who had just pulled it to behind him. As the final great funeral chords of music died away actors gathered on stage, drifting into despondent clumps. Harold, after making one grand gesture of despair, flinging his arms above his head like an imperial bookmaker, joined them.

'There's no point in giving notes,' he said. 'I wouldn't know where to start.' This admission, the first such that had ever passed his lips, seemed to shake Harold as much as his companions. 'You're all as bad as one another and a disgrace to the business.' Then he left, striding out into the winter night in his embroidered directing slippers, not even waiting to put on his coat.

No sooner had he left than the atmosphere lightened. And, as tension was released, laughter broke out and some healthy moaning on the lines of who did Harold think he was and it was only a bit of fun for heaven's sake, it's not as if we're getting paid.

'Personally,' said Boris, 'I'm sick of saying Heil Harold.'

'No one can do a thing right, it seems to me,' said Rosa. 'One might as well be in the Kremlin.'

'I wouldn't mind if he were competent,' whispered a Venticelli.

'Quite,' agreed the other. Then, aside to Esslyn: 'The peasants are revolting.'

There was a bit more Bolshevik rumbling, then Riley strolled down the aisle and jumped on to the stage. Several of the fifth formers who didn't know his nasty little ways, and Avery who did, said, 'Aahhh . . .'

The cat took a crouching position. His haunches quivered, his shoulders contracted then started to jerk. He made several loud gulping noises and a strangulated cough then deposited a small glistening heap of skin and bones and fur and blood on the boards and walked off. There was a long pause broken by Tim.

'A critic,' he said. 'That's all we need.'

'Ah well,' said Van Swieten, 'let's look on the bright side. Everyone knows a bad dress rehearsal means a good first night.'

Above his head, above the lighting grid and the theatre roof and the night sky and the limitless deep black arc of the heavens Thalia, the comic muse, was playing Chinese checkers with the Eumenides. Catching these words on a misdirected breeze, she was overcome by hysterical laughter and had to be helped from her cloud to the nearest comfort station.

ENTRACTE
(SATURDAY MORNING,
CAUSTON HIGH STREET)

Causton was a nice little town, but small. People who could not adequately function without their Sainsbury's or Marks and Spencer's had to travel to Slough or Uxbridge. But those who stayed at home were capably if unadventurously served. In the main street was a supermarket and a fishmonger's, a dairy, a bakery and a very basic greengrocer. Two butchers (one first class who hung his meat properly and could prepare it in the French way), McAndrew's Pharmacy which also sold perfumes and cosmetics, two banks and a hairdresser's, Charming Creations by Doreece. There were two funeral parlours, a bookshop, the wine merchants and post office and a small branch library.

Causton also had three eating places. Adelaide's which produced every combination of fry-up known to man from behind a phalanx of hissing tea-urns and the Soft Shoe Café which served home-made cakes, cream teas, dainty triangular sandwiches with the crusts cut off and morning coffee. There was also a pub the Jolly Cavalier (née the Gay Cavalier) which sold shepherd's pie and goujons in a basket. And, of course, there was the theatre.

Saturday 17 November was a brilliant day. The pavement sparkled crystalline with frost and people strode briskly about, visibly preceded by the white exhalations of their breath. Carol singers held forth. Dierdre and her father stood, arm in arm, outside the fishmonger's. She was worried about the cold air on his chest but he had so wanted to come out and had seemed very calm and collected so she wrapped him up in two scarves and a balaclava and here they were. Mr Tibbs held tightly on to the empty shopping basket and gazed at his daughter with the same mixture of pride in achievement, anxiety in case he might be found wanting and simple love that might have been found on the face of a labrador in a similar position. Together they studied the display.

Red mullet and a huge turbot flanked by two crabs rested on a swell of pale grey ice. Humbler creatures lay, nose to tail, on white trays, plastic parsley flowering in their mouths. Mr Tibbs regarded this piscatorial cornucopia with deep interest. He was very fond of fish. Dierdre opened her purse, guiltily aware that, if it wasn't for her involvement with the Latimer, her father could dine on fish every day of his life.

'D'you think . . . the herrings look nice, Daddy.'

'I like herrings.'

'I could do them in oatmeal.' Dierdre smiled gratefully and squeezed his arm. 'Would that be all right? With brown bread and butter?'

'I like brown bread and butter.'

They joined the queue. Dierdre was so used to people ignoring her father, even when she knew those same people to be his former pupils, that she was quite overwhelmed when a woman next to them turned and said how nice it was to see him up and about and how well he was looking.

And he did look well, agreed Dierdre, taking a sidelong glance. His eyes were clear and shining and he was nodding in reply to the greeting and offering his hand. He evinced some concern when the plump glittering herrings disappeared inside sheets of *The Daily Telegraph* but relaxed again once they were safely in his basket. Then he shook hands with the rest of the queue and he and his daughter left and made their way to the greengrocer.

Here Dierdre bought potatoes, a cabbage, carrots and a pound of tangerines which the assistant tipped loose into her basket where they lay, like glowing coals, on top of the other vegetables. She tried to take over the basket then, fearing it would be too heavy for her father, but he insisted on carrying on and they made their way, still arm in arm, to the library. On the way they passed the Blackbird and Dierdre waved to Avery, pleased when he waved back.

At the library Mr Tibbs let his daughter choose the books. This she did every Saturday, taking out one for herself and two for her father. He asked every week, sometimes quite urgently, for his new books and Dierdre, feeling that the wish to persevere with any previous activity must be a healthy sign, always complied. However bulky the volumes her father always handed them back the following Saturday, thanking her politely and saying how much he had enjoyed them. But she had seen him once with a volume of G.K. Chesterton. He perused the page on both sides, reading along to the end of the first line then turning over to continue then back again for the second line and so on to the end. Then he had lifted the book and held the page against the light as if to wring out the last possible drop of information before going on to the next one. Now Dierdre chose a travel book with photographs of beautiful serene landscapes, something by Monica Dickens and David Mamet's *Writing in Restaurants* which she had reserved six weeks before.

After listening to the carols for a few minutes and putting something in the vicar's box they went to the bakers where Dierdre bought a large sliced white loaf and a cheap sponge cake oozing scarlet confectioner's jelly and mock cream, then they went home. Mr Tibbs took to his bed saying he was tired after his walk and Dierdre made some tea.

She made her own bed whilst waiting for the kettle to boil and, whilst smoothing the coverlet, caught sight of herself in the wardrobe mirror. She avoided mirrors usually except for the briefest of toilets in the morning. What was the use? There was no one special to make an effort for. This had not always been the case. Ten years ago, when she was eighteen, and a boy at the office seemed to be interested, she had studied the magazines for a while and tried to do things with her dark curly hair that stuck out in all directions and her over-rosy complexion, but then her mother had died and she had got so involved with domestic affairs that the boy had, understandably, drifted off and was now happily married with three children.

It wasn't that she was a bad shape, thought Dierdre, removing her glasses so that her image became a reassuring blur. She was quite tall and quite slim although her bottom was a bit droopy. And she had nice eyes if only she didn't have to wear the hideous glasses. Joyce had suggested contact lenses at one point but the expense made them out of the question, and in any case Dierdre feared her prescription was too strong. She had worn the glasses since she was three. At school a Catholic friend, knowing her loathing for the wretched things, had offered to petition Lucia, patron saint of the shortsighted on her behalf. But although she assured Dierdre a few days later that this had been done the results were negligible. Either the deity had not been in the giving vein that day or, more likely, had sniffed out an heretical supplicant and resolutely withheld the 'fluence. Dierdre gave a brief sigh, put them back on and, hearing the kettle whistle, hurried downstairs.

She took some tea and a piece of cake upstairs, waiting to make sure her father drank it. Suddenly he said: 'How's it all coming along, dear? *Amadeus?*'

'Ohh . . .' Dierdre looked at him, surprised and pleased. It had been so long since he had shown any interest in the drama group. She always talked to him about the current production, playing down her subservient role, telling him only about her ideas for the play, but not for months had he been responsive. 'Well . . . we had the most appalling dress rehearsal yesterday. In fact it was so bad it was funny . . .' She retailed some of the highlights and when she came to the collapsing table her father laughed so much he almost spilt his tea. Then he said, 'D'you know I think I might come to your first night. That is,' he added, 'if I don't have one of my off days.'

Dierdre picked up his cup and turned away. She felt the quick sting of tears yet at the same time a flood of hope. This was the first time he had referred directly to his illness. And what a brave, light-hearted way to speak of it. 'One of my off days.' What a calm, rational, intelligent, *sane* way to describe things. Surely if he could talk about his other self in this detached manner he must be getting better. Going to the theatre, mingling with other people, above all listening to the glorious music could surely do him nothing but good. She turned back, smiling happily.

'Yes, Daddy,' she said. 'I think that's a lovely idea.'

The Blackbird bookshop was, briefly, empty of customers. Avery sat at his beautiful *escritoire* near the door. The shop was on two levels connected by an ankle-snapping stone step glossy with use. There was a convex mirror over the step revealing the only hidden corner so that Avery had a comprehensive view. People still managed to pinch things of course, especially during the run-up to Christmas. Avery got up, deciding to put away some of the volumes that browsers had left out anyoldhow on the two round tables. The Blackbird's stock was displayed under general headings and customers occasionally replaced books themselves, often with felicitous results. Tutting loudly Avery pulled *The Loved One* from the Romance shelf and *A Room with a View* from Interior Design.

'Look at this,' he called a moment later to Tim who was stirring something on the gas ring in the cubbyhole at the rear of the shop. '*A Severed Head*' under Martial Arts.

'I'm not sure that Martial Arts is an entirely innapropriate designation for Murdoch,' said Tim, lifting the spoon to his lips.

'I don't know why you're stirring and tasting in that affected manner,' cried Avery, moving to the cubbyhole, 'we all know what a cunning way Mr Heinz has with a tomato.'

'You said I could have what I liked for lunch.'

'I must have been mad. Even a bayleaf would add a smidgeon of veracity.'

'All right, all right.'

'Or a little yogurt.'

'Don't make a meal of it.'

'No danger of that, duckie.' They both laughed. 'What's in the rolls?'

'Watercress and Bresse Bleu. And there are some walnuts. You can open the Chablis if you like.'

'Which one?' Avery started pulling bottles out of the wine rack under the sink.

'The Grossot. And give Nico a shout.'

'Isn't he at work, then?' Avery opened the bottle then pulled aside the thick chenille curtain and bawled upstairs.

'Says he couldn't concentrate with the first night so close.'

'All those empty shelves. The housewives of Britain will be in a tizz. *Nico . . .*'

'Who were you waving to just now?'

'When?' Avery frowned. 'Oh, then.. Poor old Dierdre and her papa.'

'God – what a life. Will you promise to shoot me if I ever get like that?'

Dazed with joy at this casual assumption that they would be together when Tim was old and grey, Avery took a deep breath then replied crisply: 'I shall shoot you long before you get like that if you bring any more muck into my kitchen.'

There was a clattering of footsteps on the uncarpeted stairs and Nicholas appeared. 'What's for lunch?'

'Cheese and whine,' said Tim. 'You'd be better off upstairs, believe me.'

'I thought I smelt something nice.'

'There you are,' said Tim. 'Someone else with a nose for a bargain.'

'Like Dostoevsky's for a dead cert.'

'Clever dick.'

'Famous for it.'

'Be quiet,' said Tim. 'We're embarrassing Nicholas.'

'No you're not,' replied Nicholas truthfully, 'but I am jolly hungry.'

'Oh lord . . .' A woman wearing a squashed felt hat was staring urgently in at the window. 'Nico – run and put the catch down, there's a love. And turn the sign. I know her of old. Once she's in you'll never get her out.' When Nicholas returned Avery added: 'She's very religious.'

'Obviously. What other reason would anyone have for wearing a hat like that.'

'D'you know,' said Avery approvingly, 'I think we shall make something of this boy yet. Would you like a little wine, Nico?'

'If it's not too much trouble.'

'Oh don't be so *silly*,' retorted Avery, sploshing the Chablis into three large tumblers. 'I hate people who say things like that. They're always the sort who never mind how much trouble they give you. She came in the other day, prosing on –'

'Who did?'

'Her out there. Came rushing up and asked me what I knew of the Wars of the Spanish Succession. I said absolutely nothing. I hadn't stirred from the shop all day.' Avery looked at his companions. 'Laugh. I thought they'd never stop.'

'Start.'

'Start what?'

'The joke is,' explained Nicholas patiently, 'laugh, I thought they'd never start.'

'You're making it up.' Nicholas reached out for a second roll and got his fingers slapped. 'And don't be such a pig.'

'Don't mention pigs to me. Or meat of any kind.'

'Oh God – he's turned vegetarian.' Avery blanched. 'I knew all those beans would go to his head.'

'That would make a change,' said Tim. 'What's up, Nicholas?'

'The first-night frantics, I'll be bound,' said Avery. 'If you're worried about your lines I'll hear them after we close.'

92

Nicholas shook his head. He knew his lines and no longer feared (as he had in *The Crucible*) that they would vanish for good and all the moment he stepped on stage. What was disturbing him were his pre-first-night dreams. Or rather dream. He was now quite used to having some sort of nightmare before the opening of a play and had discovered most of his fellow actors had similar experiences. They dreamed they had learned the wrong part or their costume had vanished or they stepped on stage into a completely strange drama or (very common) they were in a bus or car which went past the theatre again and again and refused to stop. Nicholas' dream fell into this last category except that he was travelling under his own steam to the Latimer. On roller skates. He was late and flying along, down Causton High Street, knowing he would only just make it when his feet turned into the butcher's shop. No matter how hard he fought to carry straight on that is where they would go.

Inside the shop everything had changed. It was no longer small and tiled with colourful posters but vast and cavernous; a great warehouse with row after row of hanging carcasses. As Nicholas skated frantically up and down the aisles trying to find a way out he passed hundreds of slung up hares with their heads in stained paper bags, lambs with frills around newly beheaded necks and huge sides of bright red marbled meat rammed with steel hooks. Sweating with fear he would wake, the reek of blood and sawdust seemingly in his nostrils. He had had this dream now every night for a week. He just hoped to God once the first night was over he never had it again.

He described it light-heartedly to his companions but Tim picked up the underlying unease. 'Well,' he said, 'there's only two more to go. And don't worry about Monday, Nico. You're going to be excellent,' Nicholas looked slightly less wan. 'Avery was in my box last night and he cried at your death scene.'

'Ohhh.' Nicholas' face was ecstatic. 'Did you really, Avery?'

'That was mostly the music,' said Avery, 'so there's no need to get above yourself. Although I do think, one day, if you work very hard, you are going to be quite good. Of course, appearing opposite Esslyn anyone would look like the new Laurence Olivier. Or even the old one, come to that.'

'He's so prodigiously over the top,' said Tim. 'Especially in the Don Giovanni scene.'

'Absolutely,' cried Nicholas, and Tim watched with approval as some colour returned to his cheeks. 'That's my favourite. "Makea this one agood in my ears. Justa theesa one . . ." ' His voice throbbed with macaronic fervour. ' "Granta thees to me . . ." '

'Oh! Can I play God?' begged Avery. '*Please*.'

'Why not?' said Tim. 'What's different about today?'

Avery climbed on to a stool and pointed a chubby Blakean finger at Nicholas. 'No . . . I do not need you, Salieri. I have . . . *Mozart!*' Demon king laughter rang out and he climbed down holding his sides. 'I've missed my vocation – no doubt about it.'

'Didn't you think,' said Nicholas, 'that there was something funny about the whole dress rehearsal?'

'Give that man the Barbara Cartland prize for understatement.'

'I mean funny peculiar. I can't believe all those upsets were accidental, for a start.'

'Oh, I don't know. One sometimes has glorious evenings like that,' said Tim. 'Remember the first night of *Gaslight*?'

'And the Everards. They're getting more and more contemptuous,' continued Nicholas. 'That remark about the manhole. I don't know how they dare.'

'They dare because they're under Esslyn's protection. Though what he sees in them is an absolute mystery.'

'Don't talk to me,' said Nicholas, sulkily sidetracked, 'about mysteries.'

'You're not going to start on that again,' said Avery.

'I'm sorry, but I don't see why I should let it drop. You promised if I told you my secret you'd tell me yours.'

'And I will,' said Tim. 'Before the first night.'

'It's before the first night *now*.'

'We'll tell you on the half honeybun,' said Avery. 'And that's a promise. Just in case you tell someone else.'

'That's ridiculous. I trusted you and you haven't told anyone else . . . have you?'

'Naturally not.' Tim was immediately reassuring but Avery said nothing. Nicholas looked at him, eyebrows raised interrogatively. Avery's watery pale blue eyes wavered and slid around, alighting on the remaining crumbs of cheese, the walnuts, anything it seemed but Nicholas' direct gaze.

'Avery?'

'Well . . .' Avery gave a shamefaced little smile. 'I haven't really *told* anyone. As such.'

'Oh Christ – what do you mean "as such"?'

'I did sort of hint a bit . . . only to Boris. He's the soul of discretion, as you know.'

'*Boris?* You might as well have had leaflets printed and handed them out in the High Street!'

'There's no need to take that tone,' shouted Avery, equally loudly. 'If people don't want to be found out they shouldn't be unfaithful. And anyway you're a fine one to talk. If you hadn't passed it on in the first place no one else would know at all.'

This was so obviously true that Nicholas could think of nothing to say in reply. Furiously he pushed back his chair and, without even thanking them for lunch, clattered back upstairs.

'Some people,' said Avery and looked nervously across the table. But Tim was already stacking the glasses and plates and taking them over to the sink. And there was something about the scornful set of his shoulders and his stiff repudiating spine that warned against further overtures.

Poor Avery, cursing his careless tongue, tidied and bustled and kept his distance for the rest of the afternoon.

Colin Smy was replacing the blocks of wood in the trestle

table and Tom Barnaby was painting the fireplace. It was a splendid edifice which Colin had made from a fragile frame of wooden struts covered with thick paper. It had then been decorated with whorls and loops and arabesques and swags made from heavily sized cloth. It now looked, even without the benefit of lighting, superb. Tom had mixed long and patiently to find exactly the right faded brickish-red which, together with swirls of cream and pale grey, gave a beautiful marbled effect. (In the Penguin *Amadeus* the fireplace had been described as golden but Harold hoped he had a bit more about him than to slavishly copy other people's ideas, thank you very much.)

Although Barnaby ritually grumbled, there had been very few productions over the past fifteen years that he hadn't spent at least an hour or two on, sometimes even tearing himself away from his beloved garden. Now, looking around the scene dock, he remembered with special pleasure a cut-out garden hedge, all silver and green, which had represented the forest in *A Midsummer Night's Dream* and how it had shimmered in the false moonshine.

Barnaby derived great nourishment from his twin leisure activities. He was not greatly given to self-analysis, believing the end result, given man's built-in capacity for self-deception, to be messy and imprecise. But he could not but observe, and draw conclusions from, the contrast between the fruitfulness of his off-duty time and the aridity of much of his working life. Not that there was no call for imagination in his job: the best policemen always had some (not too much) and knew how to use it. But the results when it was applied were hardly comparable with those of his present occupation.

If he failed, the case would be left as a mass of data awaiting a lucky cross-reference from some future keen-eyed constable eager for promotion. If he succeeded the felon would end up incarcerated in some institution or other whilst Barnaby would experience a fleeting satisfaction before facing once more, for the umpteenth thousandth time, the worst humanity had to offer which, if you caught it on a bad day, could be terrible indeed.

So was it any wonder, he now reflected, that in what little spare time he had, he painted pictures or stage scenery or worked in his garden? There at least things grew in beauty, flowered, withered and died all in their proper season. And if freakish Nature cut them down before their alloted span at least it was without malice aforethought.

'You've done a grand job there, Tom.'

'Think so?'

'Our Fuehrer will be pleased.'

Barnaby laughed. 'I don't do it for him.'

'Which of us does?'

They worked on in a companionable silence surrounded by fragments from alien worlds. There was the bosky world (spotted toadstools from *The Babes in the Wood*), the chintzy (fumed oak from *Murder at the Vicarage*) and the world of pallid chinoiserie (*Teahouse of the August Moon* – paper screens). Barnaby glanced up and caught the shy eye of a manky goose peering through the frame of a French window (*Hay Fever*).

Colin finished hammering four new blocks into the trestle then upended it, saying: 'That'll do it. They can dance on that with hobnail boots and it should hold.'

'Who do you think took the others out?' said Tom, Joyce having described the scene to him.

'Ohh . . . some silly bugger. I shall be glad when this play's over and done with. Every rehearsal something goes wrong. Then it's Colin do this . . . Colin fix that . . .'

Barnaby selected an especially fine brush for one of the curlicues and stroked the paint on carefully. Colin's automatic grumbling flowed peacefully around his ears. The two men had worked together, on and off, for so long that they had now reached the stage of feeling that really they'd said all they had to say and, apart from certain ritualistic remarks, kept a silence as comfortable as a pair of old slippers.

Barnaby knew all about his companion. He knew that

Colin had brought up his son, motherless since the age of eight. And that he was a gifted craftsman who carved delicate high-stepping animals full of lively charm. (Barnaby had bought a delightful gazelle for his daughter's sixteenth birthday.) And that Colin loved David with a protective devotion that had not grown less as the boy developed into a young man more than capable of taking care of himself. The only time Barnaby had seen Colin lose his temper was on David's behalf. He thought how fortunate it was that Colin was rarely in the wings at rehearsal and so missed most of the sniping that David was having to put up with. Now, knowing of the younger Smy's reluctance to perform, Barnaby said: 'I expect David'll be glad when next Saturday comes.'

Colin did not reply. Thinking he had not heard, Barnaby repeated his remark, adding, 'At least he hasn't got any lines this time.' Silence. Barnaby took a sideways look at his companion. At Colin's stocky frame and tufty hair, black when they had first met, now brindled silver like his own. Colin's usual expression of sturdy self-containment was slightly awry and a second, much less familiar, lurked beneath. Barnaby said, 'What's up?'

'I'm worried about him.' Colin looked sharply at Barnaby. 'This is just between us, Tom.'

'Naturally.'

'He's got involved with some girl. And she's married. He hasn't been himself for some time. A bit . . . quiet . . . you know?' Barnaby nodded, thinking that David was so quiet anyway it would take a father to spot the silence deepening. 'I thought it might be that,' continued Colin. 'I'd be really chuffed to see him settled – after all he's nearly twenty-seven. So I said bring her home then and let's have a look at her, and he said she wasn't free. He obviously didn't want to talk about it.'

'Well . . . I suppose there isn't a lot of point.'

'Not what you hope for them though, is it, Tom?'

'Ohhh,' said Barnaby, 'I shouldn't worry too much. Things might still work out.' He smiled. 'They don't mate for life these days, you know.'

'I pictured him going out with some nice local girl. A bit younger than himself . . . perhaps courting in the front room on the settee like me and Glenda used to . . . and grandchildren. What man our age hasn't pictured his grandchildren?' Colin sighed. 'They never turn out like you think, do they, Tom?'

Barnaby pictured his little girl, now nineteen. Tall, clever, malicious, stunningly attractive with a heart of purest platinum. He could not help being proud of her achievements but he knew what Colin meant.

'That they don't,' he said. 'Nothing at all like you think.'

Ernest Crawley was carving the joint. He worked like a surgeon, unemotionally but with great precision and a certain amount of éclat, wielding the long shining knife like a scimitar and laying the slices of meat tenderly on the hot plates.

Rosa browned the potatoes on top of the stove. She wore a loose flowing garment, the cuffs of which sailed dangerously close to the fragrant, spitting fat.

'How are them fellas getting on with their part then, love?'

'What fellows?'

'The ones that sound like an Italian dinner.'

'Oh – the Venticelli. Awful – in more ways than one.'

As Rosa retailed one or two of the more amusing incidents from the dress rehearsal she could not help comparing Ernest's innocent and rather touching curiosity with Esslyn's grandiose self-absorption, always present but intensified to an incredibly high degree on the eve of a new production. The whole house had fizzed then with prima-donna emotion. In fact all their married lives had been conducted with as much noise and flourish as a carnival procession. A fanfaronade of first nights, last nights, rehearsals, parties and non-stop dramas both on and off the set.

Caught off guard and drawn carelessly into bitter recollection, Rosa corrected herself. All *her* married life. Esslyn, fortunate man, had inhabited another world for a large part of the working week. He went to the office, dined with clients, had drinks with acquaintances (never friends) who were not of the theatre. Rosa had lost, through neglect and narrowing interests, the few women friends she had ever had. And so intertwined had her role as Mrs Carmichael become with her many performances at the Latimer that it had grown to seem equally chimerical until the crunch came.

She had become aware quite early in the marriage that Esslyn was playing around. He'd said that sort of behaviour was expected of a leading man in a theatrical company and he would always come safely home. Rosa, furious, had yelled back that if all she'd wanted was something that would come safely home she would have linked her future to a racing pigeon. However, as the years flew by and he always did come safely home, she became not just resigned to his philandering but also in a strange way rather proud of what she saw as his continuing popularity, like a mother whose child consistently brings home all the prizes. There was also a positive side to all this unfaithfulness, namely that he had less sexual energy to spare for his wife. Like many people who live in a cloud of high-flown romanticism Rosa didn't care for a lot of heavy activity in the bedroom. (Here again as in so many other ways dear Ernest was ideal, seeming quite happy to bounce about, gently and rather apologetically, in the missionary position, usually after Sunday lunch.) So, as far as Rosa was concerned, Esslyn's announcement that he wanted a divorce had come out of the blue. He said he had fallen in love with the seventeen-year-old playing Princess Carissima in *Mother Goose*, and although, within a few weeks, the girl had found a boyfriend of her own age, passed her A levels and sensibly taken herself off to university, Esslyn, having tasted the heady wine of freedom, had still pressed ahead.

Rosa's reaction to his defection had frightened and amazed her. At first so accustomed was she to living in a state of almost perpetual mimesis, she hardly recognized that a great core of real pain lay behind her shoutings and ravings and great sweeps of dramatic movement. Then, after she had been bought off and left White Wings, she had spent long terrible weeks in her new flat picking over her emotions, struggling to separate the false regrets from the true, attempting to follow the wretched thread of her anguish to its source. During this time she would prowl about, her arms locked across her chest as if she were literally holding herself together; as if her whole body was an open wound. Gradually she started to understand her true feelings. To be able to examine them, test them, give them a name. The bleak regretful sorrow which persistently invaded her mind she now recognized as a state of mourning for the child she'd never had. (Had not even realized she'd really wanted.) She carried this bereavement continually, like a small stone, in her breast.

During this period she had forced herself, buttressed by natural pride and tremendous efforts of self-control, to continue her activities at the Latimer, and the second emotion was named for her the moment Esslyn announced Kitty's pregnancy. Although Rosa was looking fixedly elsewhere she could tell by the sideways stretch to his voice that he was smiling broadly. Hatred had rampaged then so furiously and with such power through her body that she felt had she opened her mouth she must have roared. She had been terrified, fearing this hot malevolence would control her. That she might simply go out one dark night and savage them both. Now she no longer thought that. But the bruising embers still slumbered and sometimes she would open the furnace door to peep and poke at them a little and the burning would scorch her cheeks.

'Are you all right, dear?'

'Oh.' Rosa turned her attention to the potatoes. 'Yes love . . . I'm fine . . .'

'Don't let them catch.'

'I won't.'

The potatoes looked and smelt wonderful; buttery deep brown with little crisp bits around the edges. Rosa gave them another minute, more to regain her equilibrium than because they needed it, then decanted them into a Pyrex dish and flung over some chopped parsley. They sat down. Ernest helped himself to the vegetables then passed them to Rosa, who did the same.

'Only three potatoes?'

'Well . . . you know . . .' She patted the folds of her tummy concealed beneath the billowy robe.

'What nonsense,' cried Ernest. 'If Allah had meant women to be thin he'd never have invented the djellabah.'

Rosa laughed. He had surprised her more than once had Ernest with his witticisms. She helped herself to several more potatoes whilst Ernest congratulated himself, not for the first time, on his foresight in placing a regular order for the *Reader's Digest*.

Esslyn sat at the breakfast table with *The Times* and squares of Oxford marmalade-coated toast, patronizing his wife. 'You'll be perfectly all right. After all you're not actually overloaded with lines. Hardly any more than with Poppy Dickie.'

'I feel sick.'

'Of course you feel sick, my angel. You're pregnant.' Esslyn folded back the business section before reverting to the matter in hand. 'How on earth would you cope if you were tackling Salieri? I'm never off.'

'But you love it.'

'That's hardly the point.' Esslyn abandoned his attempt to follow the fortunes of Rio Tinto Zinc and looked at his wife severely. 'Apart from the satisfaction of knowing that one has given a great deal of pleasure to a great many people, if one has a talent it is one's duty to exercise it to the full. I hate waste.'

Kitty followed his glance, picked up her remaining square of toast, now a bit clammy and congealed, and chewed on it morosely. 'I'd hardly call our audiences a great many people.'

'I was speaking figuratively.'

'Huh?'

'Try not to look so vacant, kitten.' Esslyn scraped back his chair. 'What have you done with my briefcase?'

'I had it with some mushrooms and bacon before you came down.'

'Ah –' Esslyn crossed to the old deal dresser holding pretty blue and white jugs and plates, picked up his case and put *The Times* into it. Then he returned to the table and brushed her cheek with his cool lips. 'Back soon.'

'Where are you going?'

'Work. I have to call in –' He moistened his finger and pressed a crumb to it which had strayed from his plate. '– something at the office.'

'But you never go in on Saturday!' exclaimed Kitty, turning down her pretty lips.

'Don't whinge, my precious. It doesn't become you.' Esslyn deposited the crumb in the bread basket. 'I shan't be long. Come and help me on with my coat.'

After she had wound Esslyn's silk Paisley muffler perhaps a trifle too snugly around his neck and buttoned his coat on the wrong side Kitty insisted on feathering her husband's lips with many little kisses. Then she clip-clopped back to the kitchen window and watched him back the BMW out of the double garage and down the drive. She opened the window, flinching a little in the sharp air, and waved. She listened, loving the machine-gun spatter of tyres on gravel. There was something about that sound. Why it should give her such intense satisfaction she could never understand. Perhaps it was simply a matter of luxurious association – all those wealthy cardboard cut-outs in American soaps crunching grandly around pillared porticoes in their stretch limos. Or maybe it was because the sound reminded her of happy childhood holidays in Dorset with the cold waves dragging the pebbles to and fro. Or perhaps it was simply that the rattling gravel meant her husband had finally left the house.

Kitty gave a last wave for luck and went upstairs to their bedchamber, scene of mutual delights, where Salieri's blue and silver coat, lace-ruffled shirt and cream trousers were laid over a chair back. Whilst everyone else had been happy to leave their costumes in the dressing room (which was, after all, securely locked) Esslyn had ostentatiously brought his back to White Wings, insisting that, after such a dress rehearsal, he wouldn't trust the stage management to look after a pair of worn out Y-fronts.

He had tried the costume on before getting properly dressed this morning, strutting his stuff in front of the cheval glass, anticipating aloud the moment when he would stand up from his wheelchair, fling off his tattered old dressing gown and take the audience's collective breath away. Kitty only half listened. He had paraded a bit more then said something in garbled French before changing into his business suit and properly subduing the day. Now Kitty scrunched the coat into a tight ball, threw it in the air and kicked it as far as she could before tripping into the en suite bathroom.

She turned the necks of two golden swans and tipped some Floris Stephanotis bath oil into the steaming water. Then she poured a generous amount of the sweet-scented stuff into her cupped hand. She massaged her calves and thighs, then her stomach and, last of all, her breasts. She closed her eyes, swaying with pleasure. Reflected in the dark glass wall tiles, four glittering bronzy Kittys swayed too. Then, fully anointed, she turned off the taps and slid into the sunken circular bath.

Around the rim, carpeted in ivory velour, were creams and unguents, several bottles of nail varnish, her copy of *Amadeus* and a telephone covered with mock ermine. She picked up the receiver, dialled, and a male voice said 'Hullo'.

'Hullo yourself, scrumptious. Guess what? He's gone to work.' The voice rumbled and Kitty said, 'I couldn't let you know. I didn't know myself till he was halfway through his boiled egg and soldiers. I thought you'd be pleased ... Ohh ... can't you?' She pouted prettily. 'Well, I haven't. In fact I've got nothing on at all at the moment. Listen ...' She splashed the water with her hand. A chuckle came down the line and Kitty laughed too. The same raunchy harsh sound that Nicholas had heard in the lighting box. 'I shall just have to settle for the Jacuzzi then, darling. Or a go on the exercise bike.' Another snort. 'But it won't be the same. See you Monday, then.'

Kitty hung up and as she did so the flex caught on her script and it fell into the bath. Kitty sighed and her lovely coral lower lip pushed forward delightfully, half covering the twin lascivious peaks of the upper. Sometimes, she thought, life was just too too much. Paul Scofield, clutching his shabby shawl, glared up at her from beneath the blue water like some astonishing new specimen of marine life. She poked him crossly with her toe, leaned back, closed her eyes, rested her head on the herb-filled pillow, and thought of love.

Harold was meeting the press. The real press, not just the regular, pot-bellied, beer-swilling hack from the *Causton Echo* who had interviewed Harold during the run of *The Cherry Orchard* then described the play as an epic agricultural drama by Checkoff. Although, to be fair to the man, this might have been due to Harold referring to the play simply as *The Orchard*. He always tried to shorten titles, believing this made him appear more *au fait* with theatrical parlance. He had spoken of *Rookers (Rookery Nook)*, *Once (in a Lifetime)*, *Night (Must Fall)*, and *Mother (Goose)*. 'This *Mother's* going to be quite a show,' he had confided to the local inkslinger who had, perhaps fortunately, replaced the missing noun before submitting his copy.

But today ... aahh ... today Harold was meeting Ramona Plume from the features page of the *South-East Bucks Observer*. Naturally he had always let them know about his work but the response until now had been, to say the least, tepid. However two letters, followed by a diligence of phone calls extolling the dazzlingly inventive nature of the current production, had finally produced a response. Anticipating a photographer, Harold had dressed accordingly in a longish grey overcoat with an astrakhan collar, shining black knee boots and a persian-lamb hat. The weather was bitterly cold and hailstones like transparent marbles were bouncing about on the pavement. A pigeon, its wing feathers stiff with ice, regarded him glumly from the Latimer doorway.

They were late. Harold had rather ostentatiously looked at his watch, shaken it, lifted one of his ear flaps and listened then started to pace tubbily up and down looking like a cross between Diaghilev and Winnie the Pooh. The pigeon, perhaps thinking a spot of exercise might warm up the feathers, left the doorway and joined him. Harold was very much aware that people were noticing him and favoured the occasional passer-by with a gracious nod. Most of them would know who he was – he had, after all, been the town's theatre director for many years – the others, as became plain from their glances and whispered comments, recognized his quality. For Harold walked in an aura of barnstorming splendour. In him the strenuous creative struggle of rehearsal, the glamour of first nights and the glittering aftermath of post-performance soirées were made manifest.

Sometimes, to underline the humdinging superiority of his position, Harold would torture himself, just a little, with one of his most magnetic and alarming daydreams and, to pass the time, he slipped into it now. In this dream he would fantasize, rather like Marie Antoinette milkmaiding about at the Trianon, that he was living in Causton as a nonentity. Just another middle-aged dullard. He saw himself at the Rotarians with other drearies pomp-ously discussing local fundraising or, worse, serving on the Parish Council where an entire evening could be maundered away delving into the state of the drains. Activities generating a self-righteous glow whilst filling in an abyss of boredom. On Sunday he would clean the car (a Fiesta) and in the evening there would be television with programmes of interest ringed well in advance. After this would come the writing of a why-oh-why letter to the *Radio Times* pointing out some faulty pronunciation or error in period costume or setting and a temporary leg-up, statuswise, in the community if it was actually printed.

It was usually at this point that Harold, his face sheened with the cold sweat of terror, stopped the panorama, leapt down from the tumbril and legged it back to reality. Now he was helped on his way by the sight of a shabby Citroën 2CV parking at the corner of Carradine Street on a double yellow line. He collected himself and hurried forward.

'You can't stop there.'

'Mr Winstanley?'

'Oh.' Harold adjusted his hat and facial expression. He said, disbelievingly, 'Are you from the *Observer?*' She hardly looked old enough to be in charge of a paper round let alone a feature column.

'That's right.' Ramona Plume pointed at the wind-screen as she scrambled out. A large disc was stamped PRESS. 'I'm OK for a few minutes, surely?'

'*A few* . . .' Harold led the way to the Latimer's glass doors. 'The story I have to tell, my dear, will take a lot longer than a few minutes.'

As the girl followed him into the foyer she laughed and said: 'Is he with you?' jerking her head at the pigeon. Harold tightened his lips. Ms Plume opened a small leather case slung on a thin strap across her chest. Harold, who had assumed this to be a handbag, watched discon-certedly as she undid a flap, pressed a button and started a tape. He leapt into speech. 'I first thought of producing *Ama* –'

'Hang on. Just rewinding.'

'Oh.' Miffed, Harold strolled over to the photograph board and stood in a proprietorial stance, one arm draped across the top. 'I thought – when your colleague turns up – the first set of photographs might be here?'

'No piccies.'

'What!'

'It's Saturday. Nobody free.' She tossed back a long fall of blonde hair. 'Weddings. Dog Shows. Pudding and Pie. Scouts' Xmas Fayre.'

'I see.' Harold bit back a sharp rejoinder. It never did

to antagonize the press. And he had plenty of stills including a recent one of himself wreathed in a Davidoffian haze directing Nicholas in *Night Must Fall*.

Ms Plume poked a microphone not much bigger than a toothbrush at him, saying: 'I understand from your letter that this is the Latimer's ninetieth production?'

Harold smiled and shook his head. There was an awful lot of ground to be covered before they discussed the precise place of *Amadeus* in the Winstanley pantheon. He took a deep breath. 'I always knew,' he began, 'that I was destined for –'

'Just a sec.' She dashed into the street, looked up and down and dashed back. 'They're getting very sniffy at the office about paying fines.'

'As I was saying –'

'Are the programmes done yet?'

'What for?'

'*Amadeus* of course.'

'I should hope so. It's the first night on Monday.'

'Could I have one?'

'What . . . now?'

'In case I have to zip off. Get the names right – that's the main bit, isn't it? With Amdram.'

Amdram! Harold went to the filing cabinet feeling sourly that the way things were going it might be a good idea to skip his formative years. He took two first-night tickets from the cash box and slipped them into a programme, saying: 'I don't know if you're familiar with the play at all?'

'I'll say. Saw it at the National. That Simon Callow. Am*aay*zing.'

'Well of course Peter Hall and I do approach the text from an entirely different –'

'Did you see *Chance in a Million?*'

'What?'

'On the telly. Simon Callow. *And* Faust. Totally in the nuddies at one point.'

'I'm afraid I –'

'Am*aay*zing.'

'You seem very young,' said Harold acerbically, 'to be a reporter.'

'I'm their cub.' The fubsiness of the noun did not mollify, especially when she added, 'I always get the short straw.'

'Look. If we could go on to my next –'

A black and yellow shape peered through the doors. The girl gave a piercing squeal and flew across the carpet. '*I'm coming* . . . Don't book me . . . *please* . . . Press. Press!' She waved her microphone at the phlegmatic profile and disappeared into the street. Harold hurried after and caught up with her as she climbed back into the car. She wound the window down. 'Sorry it was a bit rushed.'

'There's some tickets inside the programme.' He dropped it into her lap as she took first gear. 'Front row. Do try to come . . .'

On the way back to Slough the *Observer*'s cub drew into a layby, changed her tape of Bros for The Wedding Present and checked her appointments list. In half an hour Honey Rampant, the TV personality, was opening a garden centre. There'd probably be snackies and nibblies so Ms Plume decided to drive straight there instead of stopping for a sarnie. Before driving off again she tore up the front-row tickets for *Amadeus* and threw the fragments out of the car window, thus missing the scoop of a lifetime.

FIRST NIGHT

Everything was ready. Checked and counter-checked. Dierdre sent her young assistants up to the clubroom for some orange squash or a cup of coffee, leaving Colin to set the pianoforte. It was already past the half, and a buzz of excited conversation came up from the dressing rooms.

'I shall come in on a wing and a prayer,' Boris was informing everyone.

'I thought you were an atheist.'

'No one's an atheist on first nights, darling.'

'Where's Nicholas?'

'He's always here *hours* before anyone else.'

'Someone's pinched my eyebrow pencil.'

'I've forgotten every line. You'll all have to cover for me.'

'Has anyone seen my stockings?'

'I hear Joyce's daughter's coming.'

'Oh God. Well, I hope she keeps her opinions to herself. I can still remember what she said about *Shop at Sly Corner*.'

'I thought Harold was going to go into orbit.'

'I mean – no one minds *constructive* criticism.'

'*You've* got my stockings.'

'No I haven't. They're mine!'

'If any of the furniture collapses tonight I shall corpse rigid.'

'They are *not* yours. Look – here's the stain where I upset my wet-white.'

'We've got an almost full house.'

'Oh the master will be pleased. "A bum on every seat, my loveys." '

' "And mass genuflexion." '

'It's nearly the quarter. Where on earth can Nicholas *be?*'

Nicholas was late for the most thrilling of reasons. Tim and Avery had just told him their secret and he had been so excited and alarmed that he had stayed in the electrician's box questioning them until the very last minute. The facts were these: Tim always designed his own lighting for each production, working at home with a model of the set. He was especially pleased with his plan for *Amadeus*, amber and rose for Schönbrunn, greys behind the whispering Venticelli, crepuscular violet when Amadeus died. Harold, as always, would have none of it. ('Just who is directing this epic? No – I'm serious. I really want to know.') That same night Tim carried out Harold's lighting plot for the first time and when he and Avery got home Avery burst into tears, saying his beautiful set looked as if it were part of a sewer after their star product hit the fan.

It was then that Tim decided that he had had enough and put forward his proposition. It was simply that, on the first night, he would light the play from his own original plan. Once the curtain was up there would be nothing Harold or anyone else could do about it and he would hardly wish to make a scene at the interval. Of course it would mean the end of their time at the Latimer but both were prepared to face that and had already put out feelers towards a group in Uxbridge. They had sneaked into the theatre on Sunday afternoon to reset everything and run through the new plot.

Now Nicholas entered the dressing room bursting with suppressed information and squeezed into the only remaining space. Around him actors were nearly all in costume. Van Strack was pulling on white stockings, David Smy struggled with his cravat, the Venticelli – caped and masked and looking more like bats than stick insects – whirled about with seedily sinister affection. The air smelled of powder, aftershave and hair lacquer. Nicholas got into his lace-trimmed shirt, picked up a tube of Kamera Klear and rubbed some in, watching his pallid complexion turn a warm apricot. He wore very little make-up now and looked back to his debut in *The Crucible*

111

where he sported heavy lake wrinkles and wisps of crinkly snow-white hair with not a little condescension.

On the other side of the room Esslyn was shaking powder on to his wig and Nicholas, seeing in his mirror the other man's reflection, was uncomfortably reminded of his own loose-lippedness. Behind Nicholas the Emperor Joseph, heavy in white satin and jewelled decorations, paced slowly up and down like a great glittering slug. Nicholas imagined the small rouged lips pushed forward and whispering what had once been his own secret into the collective company ear.

Esslyn, apparently unaware of his invisible horns, was looking especially pleased with himself like a cat that has swallowed a particularly succulent canary. He lifted his hands and adjusted his wig and Nicholas saw his rings sparkle. He wore six. Most were encrusted with stones and one had short savage spines and perched on his finger like an embattled baby porcupine. Now he pushed a tin of Cremine which had had the temerity to stray on to his patch smartly aside and began to speak.

Even as he tuned in Nicholas knew he would not like what the other man was going to say. There was relish in his voice; it curled with spite. He was talking about Dierdre. Relaying something that she had told him in confidence but which he felt was too delightful not to pass on. Apparently she had received a telephone call at work last week from the police. It seemed her father had wandered off from the day centre in the rain without a coat or even a jacket and had been found half an hour later attempting to direct the traffic at the junction of Casey Street and Hillside.

'So I said,' continued Esslyn, 'trying to keep a straight face at the thought of that senile old fool out in the pouring rain, "How dreadful". And she said, "I know." ' He paused then, giving them the benefit of his immaculate timing, ' "He doesn't know that area at all." '

Spontaneously they nearly all roared, Nicholas included. True he laughed less long and heartily than the others but still, he did laugh. A moment later Dierdre appeared in the doorway.

'A quarter of an hour, everyone.'

There was an immediate chorus of overloud and falsely grateful thankyous. Only Esslyn, carefully applying lip liner, said nothing. It was hard to tell, thought Nicholas, whether she had overheard or not. Her high colour would conceal a blush and, as her expression was always riddled with anxiety, this gave no clue either. She stood poised in the doorway for all the world, as the Everards said the second she'd disappeared, as if she were about to break into a gallop. To do the dressing room credit there was no laughter this time.

Someone got up and followed her out and Nicholas nearly got up and followed him, he was so sick of them all. He felt he should try to make amends and pictured himself approaching Dierdre in the wings. But what could he say? I wasn't one of those who laughed? Deeply embarrassing as well as untrue. I'm sorry, Dierdre – I didn't mean to be hurtful and I'm really sad about your father? Even stickier, and what if she hadn't overheard at all? In that case putting her so firmly in the picture would simply cause unnecessary pain. Then, to make himself feel better, he started to feel irritated with her. Honestly, he thought, for someone always dependent on the kindness of strangers she could certainly pick her confidantes. A callous sod like Esslyn was the last person she should be opening her heart to. What else did she expect? But shifting a fair proportion of his guilt on to Dierdre's already bowed shoulders made him feel even worse. He became aware that he was furious with Esslyn for catapulting him into this emotional distraction when all his thoughts should be channelled towards act one, scene one. Almost before he knew he meant to, he spoke.

'You know your trouble, Esslyn?' Esslyn's hands were still. He looked inquiringly into his glass. 'You're too full of the milk of human kindness.'

There was an immediate hush. Blanched faces turned exaggeratedly to each other. Boris stopped pacing and stared aghast at the back of Nicholas' head. Van Swieten said: 'You fool.' Nicholas stared back at them all defiantly. This respect for Esslyn could be taken too far. He may have been the company's leading man for fifteen years but that didn't make him God Almighty.

'Do you know what you've done?' said Boris.

'I've spoken my mind,' said Nicholas. 'Anyone'd think it was a hanging matter.'

'*You've quoted from* Macbeth.'

'What?'

'Yet I do fear thy nature,' quavered Boris. 'It is too full of the milk of human kindness –'

'Shut up!' yelled Orsini-Rosenberg. 'You'll make it worse.'

'That's right,' said Clive Everard. 'Nicholas did it unknowingly.'

'It's Boris who'll bring trouble on our heads.'

'You must both go out and turn round three times and come back in,' said Van Strack.

'I'll do nothing of the sort,' said Nicholas, but hesitantly. After all if he was going to enter the profession, he should (longed to) embrace all its myths and mysteries. 'It's not as if I did it on purpose.'

'Come *on*.' Boris was already in the doorway. Nicholas hovered half out of his seat. 'It's the only way to avert disaster.'

'That's true, Nicholas. There are terrible stories about what happens if you quote *Macbeth* and don't put it right.'

'Ohh . . . if you say so.' Nicholas joined Boris at the door. 'Which way do we turn? Clockwise or anticlockwise?'

'How should I know?'

'I don't suppose it matters.'

'It matters terribly,' called Van Swieten.

'In that case we'll turn three times each way.'

'But' – Boris had almost chewed off all his carmine lip rouge in his anxiety – 'won't they cancel each other out?'

So Nicholas turned clockwise and Boris anti, although

as things turned out they could both have saved themselves the trouble.

Colin had finished setting the pianoforte and now disappeared behind his superb fireplace to check that the struts and weights which held it secure were firmly in position. Crouching down he heard footsteps and, looking through the huge space beneath the mantel, saw Dierdre almost run through the wings opposite. A second person followed and disappeared into the toilet, coming out again almost immediately. Colin was about to stand up and call across the stage when he was struck by something intensely furtive about the figure. It stood very still looking round the deserted wings, then it moved to the dark area at the back of the props table and bent down. A minute later it straightened up, glanced around once more and hurried back into the loo. Colin crossed the stage and approached the table but he had no time for more than a quick check (it all looked perfectly in order) when Dierdre returned from the clubroom shepherding her giggling gaggle of assistants. She crossed to him and said, 'Oh Colin, would you call the five, please? My father's taxi's due in a minute and I have to get him to his seat.'

The foyer was packed. Tom Barnaby, carrying a glass in one hand and a programme in the other, accompanied by a tall girl, darkly beautiful, pushed his way towards the Winstanleys. Strings played over the Tannoy.

'What awful music. It simpers.'

'Salieri.'

'Ahhh . . .' said Cully, adding, 'Can you see the divine afflatus?'

'You behave yourself, my girl. Or I'll take you home.'

'Dad,' Cully laughed delightedly. 'You are a hoot. Look – there he is.'

Harold was in evening dress. A large yellow silk hanky peeped out of one jacket pocket. He also wore a maroon cummerbund and a dress shirt so stiffly starched you could have sliced tomatoes with the ruffles. He was welcoming the audience graciously. Harold adored first

115

nights. They came closer to satisfying his longing for recognition than any other occasion. Mrs Harold, in a black button-up cardie unevenly spattered with pearls teamed with a tartan skirt of uncertain length, drifted dimly in his glorious wake echoing the greetings, getting the names wrong and wishing she was at her flower arranging class.

'Hello, Doris.'

'Oh, Tom . . .' Relieved at the sight of a friendly face, Mrs Winstanley thrust out her hand and blushed when her companion was unable to take it. 'Harold tells me you've done a wonderful job on the set.' Knowing it would never occur to Harold to do anything of the kind, Barnaby just smiled and nodded. 'And I understand,' continued Doris, 'that Joyce is singing better than ever.' She didn't add, as she had been wont to do when they first met, you must come and have a meal with us soon. Harold had really torn her off a strip as soon as they were alone, saying that when he wanted a great clod-hopping Philistine of a policeman cluttering up his lounge she would be the first to know.

Barnaby was aware of this attitude, which caused him not a little quiet amusement. Now he talked to Doris about horticulture, having long ago recognized a passion as great as his own. In fact all the shrubs in the Winstan- leys' garden were grown from cuttings from Arbury Cres- cent, and he kept some of his seeds back for Doris every year. Although she loyally pretended these gifts were unnecessary, Barnaby guessed that Harold's dashing life- style left him little money to spare for what he would regard as inessentials. Now Harold's wife turned on Barnaby's companion a look of polite, slightly dazed inquiry.

'You remember my daughter?'

'*Cully.*' Last time Doris had met Barnaby's daughter the child had sported a green and silver crest of hair, was covered in black leather and hung with chains. Now she had on an acid-yellow evening dress, strapless with a puffball skirt caught in above her knees. Slender black silk-stockinged legs ended in high-heeled suede shoes with embroidered tongues. Her shoulders were draped with very old lace sparkling with brilliants and her hair, blue-black like hot-house grapes, was scraped into a tight coil on the top of her head and secured by an ivory comb. 'I hardly knew you, dear.'

'Hullo, Mrs Winstanley.' Cully shook hands. 'Hullo, Harold.' She was wondering how anyone could bring themselves to put that cardigan on even once, never mind year after year. Leaving his daughter after a stern warning glance had failed to connect, Barnaby pushed his way over to the door where a youngish man accompanied by a vapidly pretty girl was entering the foyer.

'You made it then, Gavin?'

'We did, sir.' Detective Sergeant Troy pulled down the cuffs of his sports jacket nervously. 'This is my wife Maure.' Mrs Troy moved her `foot. 'Ooh. Sorry. Maureen.'

'Pleased to meet you.' Maureen shook hands. She didn't seem especially pleased. Barnaby guessed she was about as fed up as Doris Winstanley but without the necessity to conceal the fact. He always put a CADS poster in the staff canteen without ever making a point of his connection with the company but his sergeant, hearing him mention Joyce's rehearsals, had put two and two together and tickets had been purchased. Barnaby could imagine the conversation in the Troy household. Gavin believing that keeping in with the old man couldn't be bad; Maureen picturing just what sort of draggy old time she was letting herself in for. She smiled now, a glum restrained smile, and she said she couldn't half get outside a lager and lime. Embarrassed, her husband eased her nearer the auditorium steps. As he did so he caught sight of Cully who was making her way towards the swing door opening on to the corridor which led backstage. After a few moments Maureen set him in motion again with a savage poke in the small of his back.

'It's a pity you didn't bring a knife and fork,' she said as they took their seats.

'What?' He stared at her blindly.

'You could have eaten her in the interval.'

Mr Tibbs was late and Dierdre was in a ferment of agitation. She was already regretting that she had accepted, even encouraged his wish to attend the first night. It seemed to her now the height of foolishness. If he had a bad turn or became frightened there would be no one to help him. She wished now she had thought of putting him next to Tom, but a gangway seat on the back row had seemed the better idea. She had been afraid he might feel threatened, surrounded by rows and rows of strangers. She clutched a programme, painfully aware of the insignificant position of her own name, and of Harold's which could not have been bolder unless burning with letters of fire.

She glanced at her watch. Where on earth could he be? She had booked a taxi for a quarter to eight and the journey was a few minutes at the most. Then she saw a cab drawing up at the kerb and hurried out into the cold night air. Mr Tibbs alighted.

'Oh, Daddy,' she cried, 'I was so worried –' She broke off, gaping. Her father was wearing a short-sleeved summer shirt and cream cotton trousers and carrying a linen jacket over his arm. She had left him wearing a thick tweed suit with a cardigan for extra warmth and five pounds tucked in the breast pocket. At least, she thought, watching him hand over the note, he had remembered to switch the money. As the driver wound up the window Dierdre tapped on it and said: 'Isn't there any change?'

'Do me a favour,' said the man. 'I had to sit ticking over for ten minutes while he changed all his clobber!'

Dierdre took her father's arm, ice-cold and slightly damp, and led him through the now almost deserted foyer to his seat in Row P. Fortunately the auditorium was warm and she would make sure he got a hot drink in the interval. She left him sitting up very straight and staring with febrile intensity at the rich red curtains.

In the foyer Barnaby nodded to Ernest and followed his daughter towards the wings, easing himself past

Harold who was being gracious to a heavyweight couple in full evening fig.

The ladies' dressing room was only being used by four people and, the actress playing Katherina Cavalieri also being part of the stage staff, now held only three. Joyce Barnaby in a puritan-grey dress and snowy white fichu was pressing powder on her nose. Kitty twitched and twirled about in her seat, clattering her bottles and jars and mumbling her opening lines with so much fervour they might have been a rosary. Rosa sat, apparently serene, in the chair nearest the electric fire. She had dressed and made up with sublime disregard as to the requirements of her character. Far from appearing plain and severe her face, splendidly orchidaceous, could have been that of a turn of the century *poule de luxe*. Eyelids shimmered like the inside of a mussel shell and her plummy lips glistened. She wore a large hat from which a bunch of cherries depended, lying against her damask cheek. Perfect speckled crimson ovoids, they could have been the eggs of some fabulous bird. There were two magnificent bouquets from Harold for his leading ladies. Joyce (small parts/wardrobe) had a bunch of wintersweet and hellebores tied with a velvet ribbon from her husband. On the back of a chair between Rosa and Joyce hung Kitty's baby.

The door opened. Cully put her head round briefly, said 'Neck and leg break', and vanished. Barnaby was close behind. 'Good luck, everyone.' Joyce slipped out into the corridor and hugged him. He kissed her cheek. 'Good luck Citizen of Vienna, Maker of the Cakes and Noises Off.'

'I've forgotten where you are.'

'Row C in the middle.'

'I'll know where not to look, then. Is Cully behaving herself?'

'So far.'

Barnaby found the men's dressing room charged with emotion. Only Esslyn, wearing the memories of past first nights like invisible gongs, appeared calm. Other actors were laughing insecurely or prowling about or wringing their hands or (in the case of Orsini-Rosenberg) all three at once. Colin called: 'Beginners: act one,' and pressed the buzzer. The Emperor Joseph shouted: 'The bells! The bells!' and let forth screams of maniacal laughter. Barnaby mumbled, 'The best of British,' and withdrew, backing into Harold who then leapt into the centre of the room with a clarion call of ill-reasoned confidence.

'Well, my darlings – I know you're all going to be superb . . .'

Barnaby melted away. Passing through the wings he saw Dierdre already in position in the prompt corner. In the light from the anglepoise he thought she appeared distressed. Colin stood by her side. Barnaby gave them both the thumbs up. He spotted Nicholas waiting behind the archway through which he would make his first entrance. The boy's face looked grey in the dim working light and was pearled with transparent beads of sweat. He bent down, picked up a glass of water and drank, then he clutched the struts of the archway with shaking hands. Better you than me, mate, thought the Chief Inspector. He had just made his way to Row C and settled next to his daughter when Harold followed, flinging open the pass door to the left of the front row with a quite unnecessary flourish then turning to face the audience as if expecting a round of applause simply on the ground of his existence. Then he sat in the centre of the row and the play began.

Things went wrong from the word go and everyone as they came off blamed the lighting. Tim and Avery, now sweating in the box, had been so totally wrapped up in their daringness and so entranced by the fact that they were, at long last, going to do their very own thing, that they had taken no account of the effect a whole new spectrum of light and colour might have on the cast. Actors became slow and muddled, as well they might. Even Nicholas who was prepared for the change was thrown badly and found it hard to recover. And his first

120

scene, full of four-letter words, nearly brought him to a standstill.

At first the residents of Causton, determined to show that they were as avant-garde as the next man, boldly took this profanity in their stride but when Mozart said he wanted to lick his wife's arse one honest burgher, muttering loudly about 'toilet humour', got up and stomped out, his good lady bringing up the rear. Nicholas hesitated, wondering whether to wait until they had disappeared or carry straight on. His indecision was not helped by hearing Harold clearly call 'Peasants!' after the departing couple. As Nicholas stumbled again into speech all the Rabelaisian relish had vanished from his voice. He felt morbidly self-conscious, almost apologetic as if he had no right to be on a stage at all. He was sharply aware of Kitty, floundering unsupported by his side, proving the truth of Esslyn's snide predictions. After his first exit he stood in the wings sick with disappointment, listening to Salieri, word perfect, roll smoothly and woodenly on.

For the first time ever Nicholas asked himself what the hell a grown man was doing standing drenched in nervous sweat, wearing ludicrous clothes, his face covered with make-up and a daft wig on his head, waiting to step through a canvas door into a world having only the most tenuous connection with reality. (Had he but known, these thoughts were to be repeated a thousand times in future years. And frequently in the most illustrious company.)

Act one did not improve. The tape of Salieri's march of welcome as reworked by Mozart started too soon. Fortunately the lid of the pianoforte hid the fact that Nicholas had not had time to actually reach the keys. At least, he thought as he sat down, I haven't fallen over my sword.

In the Seraglio scene Kitty, rushing across the stage crying: 'Well done, pussy-wussy' to her Wolfgang caught her foot in a rug and ended up hanging on to the Emperor's arm in an effort to remain upright. Franz

Joseph laughed and corpsed everyone else. Only Esslyn and Nicholas remained in character and straight faced.

On Barnaby's right Cully slid slowly downwards, her shoulders beneath the black lace trembling slightly, and covered her face with her hands. Three seats in front and to the left he saw Doris Winstanley glance anxiously at her husband. Harold's profile was rigid, his lips clamped tightly together. Then a light, so brilliant it seemed impossible the stage and four walls could contain it, shone. This was accompanied by a stellar explosion of glorious sound from the C Minor Mass, then everything faded to a pre-dawn grey. Esslyn finished his final speech, crammed his mouth with sweetmeats and strode off.

Barnaby watched Harold propel himself up the aisle two steps at a time, then rose himself and turned to his daughter. 'Would you like a drink?'

'Oh Dad,' she got up slowly. 'I wouldn't have missed that for the world. What's my eye make-up like?'

'Runny.'

'I'm not surprised. We did a cod panto at the Footlights last year but it wasn't a patch on tonight.' She followed him up the aisle. 'It must be some sort of record when you go to the theatre and the best thing on stage is the lighting. Oh . . . oh . . .'

'Don't start gurgling again.'

'I'm not . . .' She snuffled into her hanky. 'Honestly.'

As they drew level with the back row of seats and the exit doors Barnaby saw Mr Tibbs. He was leaning forward holding the back of the seat before him. He looked grubby and abstracted like a saint at his devotions. Barnaby, who hadn't seen him for nearly two years, was shocked at his physical deterioration. His skin was like tissue paper and salt white. Blue corded veins pulsed on his forehead. Barnaby greeted him and received a smile of singular sweetness in reply, although he was convinced the old man had no idea who it was that spoke to him. Three young people sitting between Mr Tibbs and the wall kept saying 'Excuse me' very politely but he did not seem to either hear or understand and eventually they climbed over the row of seats in front and got out that way.

The clubroom was packed. Cully dug out a wisp of lace and a mirror from her jet-encrusted reticule, spat in the hanky and wiped away a runnel of mascara. When Barnaby brought her wine she nodded across at the lighting box on which Harold was tapping more and more urgently. Then he put his lips to the door jamb and hissed. The door remained closed. Clamping his successful impresario's smile into position, Harold backed away and moved once more into the centre of the room where Cully caught his arm.

'Wonderful lighting, Harold,' she said. 'Brilliant. Tell Tim I thought so.'

'. . . There's . . . there's no need for that . . .' cried Harold putt putting like a faulty two-stroke. 'Tim is simply a technician. No more, no less. *I* design the lighting for my productions.'

'Oh. Really?' Cully's tone, though exquisitely polite, positively curdled with disbelief. Barnaby took her arm and hustled her away.

'I shan't bring you out again.'

'You used to say that when I was five.'

'You don't improve. Drink up.' Barnaby made an irritated tck as Cully lowered her delightful nose into the glass and sniffed. 'What's wrong with it?'

'Nothing. If you like paraquat and crushed bananas.'

Sergeant Troy approached trailing his resentful wife and Barnaby forced a smile. 'Enjoying yourself, Gavin?'

'Not bad, is it, sir?' He spoke to Barnaby but his eyes were on Barnaby's companion. 'I mean for amateurs.' He continued to stare until the chief inspector was forced to introduce them.

'*Your daughter*.' Barnaby appreciated Troy's poleaxed demeanour. Each time Cully returned home he was newly amazed that such an elegant, high-stepping creature should be the fruit of his loins. 'I'm surprised we haven't run into each other before, Cully.'

'I'm at Cambridge. Final year.'

Yes, you would be, thought Mrs Troy, reflecting tartly on the unequal distribution of gifts come christening time.

'Oh – this is my wife Maure,' said Troy and the two girls touched hands.

'More what?' said Cully.

'Troy,' said Maureen with a flinty spark in her eye.

Once more Barnaby led his daughter out of trouble. As they backed away he nearly stepped on Tim who nipped out of the box, looked quickly around the room and hurried down the stairs. Meanwhile Harold had stormed through the wings shooting glances of disgust at the stage staff who alone, during the disastrous first half, had hardly put a foot wrong, and was now in the men's dressing room impresairing like mad to powerful effect.

'Never . . . *never* in all my years in the business,' bawled Harold, 'have I seen such a grotesque display of mind-boggling incompetence. Not to mention complete lack of verismo. All of you were corpsing. Except Salieri.'

'Do you mind?' said Nicholas angrily. 'I certainly wasn't.'

'We were thrown by the lighting,' said the Emperor Joseph. Unfortunately adding, 'Fabulous though it was.'

'You should be used to my lighting by now,' squawked Harold, puce with rage.

Nicholas, jaws agape, stared at his director. He had wondered how Harold would react to Tim's defiant behaviour. He had visualized everything from freezing instant dismissal to temper tantrums and violent exhibitionism. What he had never considered, would never have considered in a hundred years, was that Harold would calmly annexe the new plot and re-present it as his own.

'All you'll catch that way is flies, Nicholas,' said Harold. 'I shall say nothing more now. You all know you've let me down. Yes – you too, Mozart. There's no need to look at me like that. Where is your sword?'

'Oh.' Tardily Nicholas realized why he had not fallen over it at the piano. 'Sorry.'

'Sorry is not enough. I want an improvement – no I

want a transformation – from everyone here in act two. You can do it. I've seen you all turn in marvellous work. So go back out there and show them what you're made of.' He spun around and a moment later they heard him haranguing the distaff side next door.

'That's all we need,' murmured Van Swieten. 'A little touch of Harry on the night.'

'That man's his own worst enemy.'

'And when you think of the competition.'

Boris made some tea in polystyrene cups, asking as he wielded the kettle, 'D'you think I should make some for Esslyn and his crapulous cronies?'

'Where are they anyway?'

'Last I saw he was in the wings rubbishing Joycey yet again about the cakes. God, David – you messy devil –'

'Sorry.' David Smy seized a paper towel roll and mopped up his tea. 'I didn't know it was there.'

'I saw them all go into the bog.'

'Ooo . . .' Boris waved a limp wrist. 'Troilism, is it? Bags I Cressida.'

'Never. You can say all sorts about Esslyn but I don't think anyone seriously thinks he's bent.'

Just then the three subjects of their conversation appeared in the doorway. They stood very still, their shadows taking a dark precedence, and the overheated, stuffy place suddenly seemed chilly. It was immediately obvious that something was very wrong. The Everards wore looks of sly anticipation and Esslyn, eyes glittering, darted his head forward in an avid, searching way. The head seemed to Nicholas to have become elongated and slightly flattened. A snake's head. Then he chided himself for such exaggerated speculations. A trick of the light, surely, that was all. Pure fantasy. As must be the idea that Esslyn was looking at him. Searching *him* out. Nevertheless Nicholas' throat was dry and he sipped his tea gratefully.

Esslyn sat down and started to re-tie his stock. Always self-contained, he now appeared almost clinically remote. But the over-careful movements of his hands, the tremor

125

of his jaw only partially controlled by his clenched lips and that terrible soulless glitter in his eye told their own tale. No one in the dressing room remained unaware that the company's leading man was boiling with suppressed rage.

Boris collected the cups in painstaking silence and the odd remark, uneasily passed, shrivelled as soon as uttered. When the buzzer went there was an immediate exodus with everyone easing their way cautiously around Esslyn's chair. As he left Nicholas looked back and caught a following glance so malign he felt his stomach kick. Convinced now that his earlier perceptions were not merely imagination, he turned hurriedly away but not before he noticed that Esslyn had removed all his rings.

Why this should strike him as ominous Nicholas could not understand. Perhaps it was simply that, given the man's present volcanic mein, any slight deviation from the norm gave cause for concern. Nicholas joined the other actors in the wings and stood quietly, a little apart, running over his next scene and forcing his mind to re-enter the eighteenth century.

With seconds to go Dierdre peeped out into the auditorium. She had taken her father a cup of coffee and had toyed with the idea of putting a little brandy in it (he had seemed so tense and still quite cold) but, not knowing how it might interact with his tablets, had decided against the idea. Now she watched him, staring eyes unnaturally bright, perched on the very edge of his seat as if preparing for imminent departure. What a terrible mistake it had been to allow him to come. She had almost called a taxi in the interval to take him home but feared for his safety if he was left alone in the house until eleven o'clock.

Colin touched her arm and she nodded, her attention now all on the opening of act two. Esslyn was already in position, a grey shape humped over the back of his chair. As she prepared to raise the curtain he lifted his head and looked into the wings and there was on his face an expression of such controlled ferocity that Dierdre, in spite of the distance between them, automatically stepped back, bumping into Kitty. Then she cued Tim's box, the house lights went down and the play began.

Esslyn turned to the audience and said: 'I have been listening to the cats in the courtyard. They are all singing Rossini.'

Silence. Not just lack of laughter. Or a stretch of time punctuated only by the odd cough or rustle or movement of feet but absolute total silence. Esslyn stepped down to the footlights. His eyes, glittering pinpoints of fire, raked the audience, mesmerizing them, gathering them close. He spoke of death and hatred with a terrible, thrilling purpose. In the back row Mr Tibbs whimpered softly. His hair seemed to stir softly on his neck although there was not the slightest breeze. In the wings knots of actors and stage hands stood still as statues and Dierdre rang the bell for Constanza's entrance.

Most actors love a good row on stage and the argument between Mozart's wife and Salieri had always gone well. Now Kitty screamed: 'You rotten shit!' and belaboured her husband with her fists. She had her back to Dierdre who was thus facing Esslyn and watched in mounting horror as he seized his wife by the shoulders and shook her, not with the simulated fury that he had shown in rehearsals but in a wild rage, his lips drawn back in a snarl. Kitty's screams too became real as she was whirled round and round, her hair a golden stream whipping across her face, her head on its slender support snapping back and forth with such force it seemed impossible her neck would not break. Then he flung her so violently from him that she staggered across the stage and was only halted by smacking straight into the proscenium arch.

Dierdre, appalled, looked at Colin. Her hand hovered near the curtain release but he shook his head. Kitty stood for a moment, winded, fighting for breath, then she sucked in air like a drowning man, took two steps and fell into Dierdre's arms. Dierdre led her to the only space in the crowded wings (next to the props table) and pulled up one of the little gilt chairs. She lowered the girl gently into it, handed her clipboard to Colin and took Kitty's hand in hers.

'Is she all right?' Nicholas came up and whispered. 'What the hell's going on?'

'It's Esslyn. I don't know . . . he seems to have had some sort of brainstorm. He just started throwing her about.'

'Christ . . .'

'Can you sit with her while I get some aspirin?'

'I'm on in two secs.'

'Get one of the ASMs then. Kitty . . . I shan't be a minute, OK?'

'. . . *My back* . . . ahh . . . God . . .'

Dierdre ran to the ladies' dressing room. The first-aid box kept always on the window sill in the far corner behind the costume rail was not there. Frantically she started searching, pulling the actors' day clothes – Rosa's fur coat, Joyce's looped grey wool, flinging various dresses and skirts aside. She knelt down, hurling shoes and boots out of the way. Nothing. And then she saw it. Sticking out from behind Rosa's wig stand. She grabbed the box and then the aspirin and struggled with the screw top. It seemed impossibly stiff. Then she realized it was a 'child proof' cap that you needed to push down first. Even as she shook out three tablets she recognized the futility of what she was doing. Aspirins were for trivial ailments. A headache, a rise in temperature. What if Kitty's spine was damaged? What if every second's delay increased the dreadful danger of paralysis? Dierdre suddenly felt afraid. She should have ignored Colin and stopped the play. Asked if there was a doctor in the house. It would be her fault if Kitty never walked again. She forced this dreadful possibility from her mind and murmured, 'Water . . . water.' There were various mugs and polystyrene beakers scattered about, all with dirty brown puddles in the bottom. Dierdre seized the nearest mug, rinsed it out, half filled it with cold water and ran back to the wings.

The first thing she heard was Nicholas' voice from the stage. This meant the first scene was over, the set change effected and scene two well under way. She had been longer than she thought. She hurried over to the props table but the chair where she had left Kitty was empty. Dierdre crossed to Colin who, on her mouthed 'Where is she?' mouthed back 'Toilet'.

Kitty was walking up and down the tiled floor when Dierdre entered. Walking stiffly, stopping every few steps to ease her shoulders but still, thank God, walking. Dierdre proffered the aspirin and the mug only to be met with a flood of invective the like of which she'd never heard in her life. The fact that it was aimed at Kitty's husband and Dierdre just happened to be in the firing line hardly lessened the shock. The language left her face burning and she 'sshhd' in vain. Some of the words were familiar from the text of *Amadeus* and one or two more from the odd occasion when Dierdre had been compelled to use a public lavatory, the rest were totally unfamiliar. And they had a newly minted ring as if normal run of the mill abuse could not even begin to do justice to Kitty's fury and she had been compelled to create powerfully primed adjectives of her own.

'*Please* . . .' cried Dierdre in an urgent whisper. 'The audience will hear you.'

Kitty stopped then, adding just one more sentence in a very quiet voice. 'If he lays a finger on me again,' she said, 'I'll fucking kill him.'

Then, still moving slowly and stiffly, she went, leaving Dierdre staring after her open-mouthed, the three aspirins, already sweatily crumbling, in the palm of her hand.

Barnaby and Troy, like the rest of the audience, were aware of the extraordinary change that had come over *Amadeus* in the second half. It seemed to them at the time that this was entirely due to the actor playing Salieri.

In act one he had given a capable if rather stolid performance. In act two his whole body seemed alive with explosive energy which it seemed to barely contain. You would not have been surprised, thought Barnaby, if sparks had flown when he clapped his hands or struck the boards with his heel. The very air through which he stalked, trailing clouds of inchoate rage, seemed charged. Maureen Troy thought she might not have missed *Coronation Street* for nothing, and Barnaby became aware that his daughter was now sitting up and leaning forward in her seat.

Salieri's startling transformation did not help the play as a whole. The rest of the cast, instead of interacting with him as they had done previously (albeit with varying degrees of convincingness) now seemed to have become quite disengaged, moving cautiously within his orbit and avoiding eye contact even when indulging in direct speech.

Nicholas waited for his cue, gazing into the brilliantly lit arena. He was tense but not alarmed. He responded to the crackling energy which, even in the wings, he could feel emanating from Esslyn in a very positive way. He felt his own blood surge in response. He knew he could match, even overmatch, the other man's power. His mind was clear; his body trembled pleasingly with anticipation. He stepped on stage and did not hear the Emperor Joseph whisper as he drifted by: 'Watch him.'

And if he had heard, Nicholas would have paid no mind. He had no intention of pussyfooting about. For him, always, the play came first. So he stepped boldly up to Salieri and when Esslyn said: 'I commiserate with the loser' and held out his hand, Nicholas gladly offered his own. Esslyn immediately stepped in front of the boy, masking him from the audience, gripped Nicholas' hand in his own and squeezed. And squeezed. Harder. And harder.

Nicholas' mouth stretched involuntarily wide in silent pain. His hand felt as if it were being wrapped in a bunch of savagely sharp thorns. Esslyn was smiling at him, a broad jackal grin. Then, just as Nicholas thought he might faint with agony, Esslyn suddenly let go and sauntered to the back of the stage. Nicholas gasped out a reasonable approximation of his next few lines and managed to get across to the piano and sit down. The Venticelli entered and Mozart, who had no more to say, took this opportunity to examine his hand. It was already puffing up. He straightened the fingers gently one at a time. The back of the hand was worse than the palm. Covered in tiny blue bruises with the skin actually broken in several places. The whole hand looked and felt as if someone had been trying to hammer tin tacks into it. At the end of the scene he made his exit. Colin approached him in the wings.

'Dierdre thinks we ought to stop it.'

Nicholas shook his head. 'I can cope. Now I know.'

'Let's have a look.' Colin stared at the hand and drew in his breath sharply. 'You can't go on like that.'

'Of course I can.' Nicholas, having got over the immediate shock of the attack, was now, despite the pain, rather relishing this opportunity to display his cool professionalism. He was a trouper. And troupers trooped no matter what.

Dierdre touched his arm and whispered, 'What happened?'

'His rings.' Nicholas held out his hand. 'I thought he'd taken them off but he'd just turned them round.'

'Bloody hell,' muttered Boris, peering over Dierdre's shoulder. 'You won't play the violin again in a hurry.'

'But why?' asked Dierdre, and Nicholas shrugged his ignorance.

On stage Salieri shouted his triumph. '*I filled my head with golden opinions yes! And this house with golden furniture,*' and the whole set was suffused with soft rich amber light. Gilded chairs and tables were carried on. Beside Nicholas Joyce Barnaby stood holding a three-tier cake stand painted yellow. Like everyone else she looked anxiously at him.

Nicholas nodded reassuringly back, attempting to appear both calm and brave. In fact he was neither. He felt intensely excited, rather alarmed and very angry. He strove to suppress the anger. The time to let that rip would be afterwards. Now he had to face the challenge of the next half hour. He would have more scenes alone with Salieri but only one where they had physical contact (another handshake) and that handshake he would make sure to avoid. And the man could hardly do him any serious physical harm in front of a hundred people.

In the audience, his exquisite daughter raptly attentive by his side, Barnaby's nostrils widened and twitched. The smell in the theatre was a smell he recognized. And so he should. It had been under his nose for a large part of his working life. A hot, burnt smell, ferocious and stifling. The whole place stank of it. The smell of violence. He withdrew the larger part of his attention from the play and glanced about him. Everyone was still and quiet. He could see Harold's profile, bulging with pleasure mixed with disbelief. His wife looked simply frightened. Others sat eyes wide, unblinking. One woman savaged her bottom lip, another had both fists knuckling her cheeks. Barnaby turned his head slightly. Not every gaze was out front. Sergeant Troy, alert – even wary – was also looking about him.

Behind them in the back row an old man gripped the back of the seat in front of him and pushed away from it so hard that it seemed his backbone must impress the wall behind. His face showed terrible anticipation mixed with a craven appeal for mercy. He looked like a child, innocent of wrongdoing, who awaits harsh punishment.

Barnaby redirected his attention to the stage and the source of his unease. Esslyn was like a man possessed. He seemed to be never still. Even when he withdrew to the back of the stage and rested in the shadows energy seemed to pulse through and around him as if he stood on a magnetic field. Barnaby would be glad when the play was over. Although he could think of no reason why Joyce should be at risk he would be happy to see *Amadeus* concluded, when whatever raging grievance Esslyn had could be sorted out in the proper manner. It was obviously something to do with Kitty.

She re-entered now, bulkily pregnant, leaning heavily on Mozart's arm. She looked neither crushed nor beaten. Her curtsey to Salieri was a mere ironic sketch, her mouth a hard line, and her eyes flashed. When she said 'I never

132

dream sir. Things are unpleasant enough to me awake'
her voice, though raw and bruised, surged with acrimony.
Barnaby glanced at his watch, (about twenty minutes to
go) and attempted to relax, giving himself up to the
ravishing music of *The Magic Flute*. How entrenched, how
impregnable must Esslyn's malice be that it could remain
undiminished in the presence of such glorious sound.

Now, clad in a long grey cloak and hat, the top half of
his face concealed by a mask, Salieri, harbinger of doom,
moved stealthily across the stage to where Mozart, madly
scribbling over sheets of paper was working, literally, to
a deadline, composing his own requiem.

Nicholas worked in a cold fever of exhilaration. Even
though he had spent the evening in a more or less constant
state of anxiety there had been enough luminous moments
to convince him that, as far as Mozart was concerned he
was on the right track. Whole sections had almost played
themselves and seemed to be newly created, moment by
moment as if the whole grinding discipline of rehearsal
had never been. I can do it! Nicholas thought, dazed with
jubilation. A dark figure moved in the doorway of his
pathetic apartment and came to stand behind him.

Afterwards, recounting the scene for Barnaby's benefit,
Nicholas found it impossible to describe precisely the
exact moment when the simulated terror with which he
had acknowledged Salieri's phantasmagoric appearance
fled and the real thing took its place. Perhaps it was
when Esslyn first laid a bony hand upon his shoulder
and breathed searing, rancorous breath over his cheek.
Perhaps it was when the other man cut their first move
and flung aside a chair that Nicholas had cunningly re-
sited as a possible barrier between them. Or was it when
he whispered: 'Die, Amadeus . . . *die*.'

Automatically at this point Nicholas, as he had done
at each rehearsal, dropped to all fours and crawled underneath the shrouded table that doubled as a writing desk
and bed. The table was permanently set flush to the
proscenium arch and Colin had stapled the heavy felt
cover to the floor on either side. So when Esslyn crouched

at the entrance and his cloak blotted out the opening like great grey wings, Nicholas was trapped.

He crawled back as far as he was able in the dark tiny space. He felt suffocated. What air there was was thick with the fusty staleness of the cloth and the reek of jackal breath. Esslyn curled back his lips in a hideous parody of a smile. And Nicholas realized that his earlier conviction (that he could come to no harm under the gaze of a hundred assorted souls) was a false one. He believed now that Esslyn would not be bound by the normal man's rational fear of discovery. Because Esslyn, Nicholas decided, was stark staring bonkers.

Now the other man's hand, knuckle-dustered with silver spikes and hard, violating stones, reached for Nicholas' throat. And Nicholas, cutting the rest of the scene, yelled Kitty's cue: '*Oragna figata fa! Marina gamina fa!*' He heard her footsteps the other side of the cloth and her first line, 'Wolfie?' Esslyn withdrew his hand, his arm, his shoulders and, finally, his vile grimace. By the time Nicholas crawled out Salieri had retreated once more to the shadows.

'Stanzerl . . .' Nicholas clung on to Kitty. She supported him, helping him to climb on to the table, arranging his pillows. His death scene (his marvellous death scene on which he had worked so hard) went for nothing. He gabbled the lines, his eyes constantly straying over Kitty's shoulder to the figure, furled all in grey, waiting in the dark. When Nicholas had died and been thrown without ceremony into his pauper's grave (a mattress concealed behind the fireplace) he lay there for a few moments then crawled off into the wings. He found his way to the chair by the props table and fell into it, resting his head against the wall.

Expecting instant attention and sympathy, he was surprised when no one paid him any mind, then realized that they could hardly have known what was going on beneath a covered table. Time enough to tell them afterwards. He became aware that his other hand, or at least the thumb, was hurting like hell. He held it up but the light was so dim that he could see only the outline. He hurried downstairs, passing Dierdre on the way up who cried 'Mind out!' and held a kettle of steaming water out of his way.

In the bright lights of the men's dressing room he discovered a great splinter rammed down the side of his nail. The surrounding flesh already had a gathered, angry look. He held it under the hot tap for a few moments then looked around for a pair of tweezers. Occasionally an actor would have some for applying wisps of false hair or eyebrows. But he had no success. He tried next door, knocking first.

'Ohh . . .' Rosa exuded kind concern. 'You poor lamb. I've got some twizzies. Hang on.' She rootled in her box. 'Have you put anything on it?'

'No. Just given it a rinse.'

'Here we are.' Rosa picked up some tweezers smeared with greasepaint. 'Let's have a look then.'

Nicholas handed over his thumb whilst eyeing the surgical appliance with some disquiet. 'Shouldn't we sterilize them or something?'

'Good lord, Nicholas. You want to enter the profession you'll have to learn to take something like this in your stride.'

Nicholas, who had never seen the willingness to embrace septicaemia as one of the more obvious qualities a young actor might find useful, jibbed at this robust assertion.

'There.' Rosa extracted the splinter with surprising gentleness then rummaged in her handbag, produced a grubby pink plaster and peeled off the shiny backing. 'How did you come to pick it up, anyway?' Nicholas told her. 'Ohhh . . . how you exaggerate.'

'I do not. He went straight for the jugular.' But even as he spoke Nicholas was aware of a watering down of his conviction. The fact was that the cosy air of normality in the dressing room and the fact that no one in the wings had noticed anything untoward were encouraging a slight feeling of unreality about his recollections. But there was one thing that was true and very real. Nicholas said, 'And he shook the living daylights out of Kitty.'

'Did he?' Rosa smiled and wrapped the plaster extra tenderly around her companion's thumb. 'Naughty boy.' Nicholas rightly assumed that this reproof was intended for Esslyn rather than himself although it seemed astonishingly mild under the circumstances. 'I expect he discovered,' continued Rosa creamily, 'that she was having an affair.'

'Bloody hell! How did you know that?'

'Common knowledge, darling.'

Nicholas, swamped by guilt, sat contemplating his throbbing hand. This was all his fault. If he hadn't told Avery and Tim it would never have got out. So much for Avery's promises. And for all he knew Tim had blabbed as well. They were both as bad as the other. 'Pair of gossipy old queens,' he muttered.

'Sorry?'

'Tim and Avery.'

'Well really, darling,' continued Rosa, 'if you feel like that about homosexuals you may just be entering the wrong profession. I understand there's at least one in every company.'

Nicholas stared at her severely, no longer grateful for the plaster. How would she know what there was in every company? Swathed in her nylon wrapper with its collar of moulting cerise ostrich feathers. Playing the leading lady, regurgitating chunks of past performances, trailing shreds of ersatz glamour as false and tawdry as last year's tinsel. The Latimer, thought Nicholas savagely, was the perfect place for her along with all the other poseurs and has-beens and never-would-be's and dead weights. Conveniently he forgot past kindnesses. The patience and encouragement shown to a neophyte who hadn't known a claw hammer from a codpiece. The support and refuge offered when he had suddenly left home. He only knew that he was sick of the whole narcissistic bunch. He jumped up, startling Rosa.

'I'm going to watch the end. Coming?'

'I don't think so, angel,' replied Rosa, batting her false lashes, gluey with mascara. 'I have seen it all before.'

In the wings actors were gathering for the call. Nicholas, last in the queue (Esslyn being already *in situ*), fetched up by the Emperor Joseph and said: 'What a night.'

'Carry on up the Şchönbrunn, lover.'

David Smy passed them carrying his valet's tray with the razor, wooden dish of soap, folded towel and china bowl complete with rising steam. One of the ASMs pushed Salieri's wheelchair on and David followed. He put his tray down on a little round table, took his master's will as instructed and retired to the back of the stage to amend his signature. Salieri picked up the razor, stepped down to the footlights and spoke, directly and passionately to the audience.

'*Amici cari*. I was born a pair of ears. It is only through hearing music that I know God exists. Only through writing music that I could worship . . .'

In the wings Joyce prepared to step forward. Behind her the Venticelli hovered ready for their final entrance.

'. . . To be owned . . . ordered . . . exhausted by an *Absolute* . . . And with it all meaning . . .'

Maureen Troy, although not actually sorry the end was nigh, found herself experiencing a shade of disappointment. Because she definitely fancied that bloke playing the wop. Just her mark. Tall dark and handsome, and old enough to have a grown-up daughter in the cast if Maureen's programme was anything to go by. Maybe the evening wasn't going to be a total bust after all. Her husband's shifty glances in Cully Barnaby's direction had not gone unnoticed, and two could play at that game. Maybe she could wangle an invite round the back and introduce herself.

'. . . Now I go to become a ghost myself. I will stand in the shadows, when you come to this earth here in your turn . . .'

Cully, on the other hand, had been impressed by Mozart. Obviously inexperienced and somewhat all over the place he had still given an energetic and very sensitive performance with touches of real pathos. She found herself wondering about the actor. How old he was. How serious about the theatre.

'And when you feel the dreadful bite of your failures – and hear the taunting of unachievable uncaring God – I will whisper my name to you. Salieri: Patron Saint of Mediocrities!'

Tim in his box said: 'Truth will out.' Avery smiled and Harold ran over his first-night speech. Tom Barnaby still sensed a slide towards misrule and sat upright and unrelaxed. In the back row Mr Tibbs had lost the theatre entirely and wandered in a dark wood pursued by demons and the howling of wolves.

'And in the depths of your downcastness you can pray to me. And I will forgive you. *Vi saluto.*'

Esslyn lifted the razor and, with one dramatic sweep, drew it across his throat. It left a bright red line. He stood for a moment frowning down at the blade, unexpectedly scarlet. He swayed forwards then jerked himself upright as if with great effort. The Keeper of the Cakes bustled cheerfully on with the breakfast tray. Salieri took a step to meet her. She stared at him, her mouth shaped to a silent O, then she dropped the tray and caught him as he fell. Then she screamed. Shrieks of pure terror. Over and over again. Whilst the bright blood flowed over her snowy fichu and dove-grey skirt on to the boards beneath.

ENTER THE BROKER'S MEN

Barnaby was out of his seat and on to the stage within seconds. Troy followed hard on his heels.

'Get the curtain down!' Dierdre looked blindly at and through him. '*Get it down.*'

There was a sweep of velvet plush as Colin released the holding mechanism, cutting off the grisly tableau from the audience's startled and excited gaze. Barnaby looked to his wife. She was standing absolutely rigid, her face blank, her eyes tightly closed. Esslyn, his life ebbing, hung around her neck with almost balletic grace like a dying swan.

Troy slipped his hands under the man's armpits and lowered him with infinite pointless care to the floor. Barnaby stepped outside the curtain. No need to say 'Could I have your attention please?' The conversation ceased as if by magic.

'I'm afraid there's been an accident,' he said calmly. 'If you'd remain in your seats for a few moments, please. Do we have a doctor present?'

No one spoke. Tim had put up the house lights and Barnaby noticed Harold's empty space and the swinging door by Row A. Cully's seat was also unoccupied. He stepped back on to the stage where Sergeant Troy, knife-creased trousers stained crimson, was kneeling, his head turned to one side, his ear almost touching Esslyn's lips. The sergeant's mouth was pursed and his brow pleated with the effort of concentration. He felt an exhalation – cold, infinitely frail – and heard one exhausted sound. The narrow red line was now a gaping incision and Esslyn's eyes were glazed. A moment later his life was over. A great crack of thunder, ludicrously apt, was heard, then the patter of rain on the roof. Troy stood up.

'Hear anything?'

'Bungled, sir. As near as I could get.'

'Right. Take the stage door, would you? Colin – over there in the check shirt – will show you where it is. No one in or out.'

The sergeant disappeared. Barnaby looked round. In the wings next to a clutch of fifth formers huddled together for comfort in a suddenly alien landscape Rosa's husband held her hand. The chief inspector crossed to them.

'Ernest, I need some temporary help. Would you go to the foyer, please. Notify the station what's happened on the pay phone. Don't let anyone leave. Won't be for long.'

'I would, Tom, but I feel I should stay with Rosa.'

'No, no. Do as Tom says.' Rosa wore a clown face, make-up crudely drawn on a chalky background. 'I'll be all right, really.'

'Shall I ask them to send help?'

'They'll know what to do.'

Ernest, still looking rather uncertain, left them both. By now the wings were full of actors and the stage deserted. Barnaby noticed with some relief that his wife had lost her terrible frozen stillness and was weeping in their daughter's arms. Colin returned and Barnaby asked him for a box or carrier bag and something to cover the body. Colin tipped some flex and electrical connections out of a shoe box and gave it to Barnaby who placed it over the razor which was lying near Esslyn's right hand. A curtain was found and Barnaby covered the corpse, stepping carefully around the blood which was still seeping outwards. It had made a large stain, pear shaped with an extra bulge on one side, like an inverted map of Africa. The curtain was hideously inappropriate, being covered with rainbows and balloons and teddy bears having a grand time. Barnaby took the key to the men's dressing room from the board, ran downstairs (closely shadowed by Harold) locked it and returned the key to Colin.

'You seem to be taking a lot upon yourself,' said Harold. Alone amongst the shocked and haggard faces his shone with lively indignation.

'What's it all for, Tom . . . all this . . .' said Colin,

gesturing with the key. 'I mean – a terrible thing has happened but it was an accident . . .'

'You're probably right,' answered Barnaby. 'But until I get a clearer picture there are certain precautions it's only sensible to take.'

'I must say I don't see why,' retorted Harold. 'All this showing off. Ordering people about, barging here and there, locking the place up. Who the hell do you think you are?'

'I'm just going to have a word with the audience,' continued Barnaby. 'Explain what is going on. We shouldn't have to keep them too long.'

'You most certainly will not have a word with the audience!' cried Harold. 'Any words to be had will be had by me. This is my theatre. I'm in charge here.'

'On the contrary, Harold,' replied Barnaby, and his voice made him a stranger to them all, 'until further notice I shall be in charge here.'

Half an hour had passed. Reinforcements had arrived. The audience had their names and telephone numbers taken and, with a single exception, had gone off to spread the news to family and friends considerably more excited than when they arrived which, as one elderly gentleman said whilst buttoning up his overcoat, made the evening a first in more ways than one.

One of the half dozen worried parents waiting outside to take the fifth formers home had been allowed to enter and was now acting as chaperone in the women's dressing room whilst they were being gently questioned. Registration numbers in the car park and adjacent streets had been noted and a constable was positioned in the pouring rain outside the main door. Another sat on stage on the Emperor Joseph's throne with the humped gay curtain.

In the clubroom Dierdre was trying to persuade her father to drink some coffee. When she had first fled up the aisle to him just after the curtain fell she had been horrified to see his staring eyes and wildly gesturing hands. His legs too had been shaking and twisting and he drummed his feet like a runaway horse. People sitting nearby were either ignoring him, looking sympathetic or, in the case of the teenagers in the same row, cracking their sides. Dierdre, tears of pity pouring down cheeks still pale with shock, gradually managed to soothe him into some sort of quiescence. Now he jiggled and joggled his beaker and splashed coffee all over the settee. Dierdre spoke softly, reassuringly to him while he stared over her shoulder. He had just started to make a toneless droning sound when the door opened and a young man with bristly red hair and a sharp narrow face entered. He wore a sports jacket and his trousers were marked with dreadful stains.

'You Miss Tibbs? The DCI would like a word.'

'I'm sorry,' said Dierdre. 'I don't think I can leave my father.'

'I'm not offering you a choice, miss.'

'Oh.' Dierdre got hesitantly to her feet. She wondered if she could be talked to in the clubroom then quickly realized what a stupid idea that was. The last thing she wanted, now her father was calming down a little, were questions which might recall the climax of the play.

'Could you . . . perhaps stay with him?'

'Sorry.' Troy held the door open, adding glibly, 'He'll be OK. Right as rain.' He closed the door and led her firmly downstairs.

Dierdre felt a little better when she entered the ladies' dressing room and realized the DCI was going to be Tom. She asked if he'd be very long as she was anxious to get her father safely home.

'No longer than I can help, Dierdre. But the quicker we can sort this business out the better. I'm sure you'll want to help us all you can.'

'Ohhh . . . of course I do, Tom. But I just don't understand how anything like this could have happened. It worked perfectly well at rehearsals.'

'When did you actually check the props this evening?'

'Just before the half. About twenty past seven, I suppose.'

'And the tape was in place then?'

'Of course. Otherwise I would have –' She broke off then, her eyes widening. 'Oh my God . . . you don't mean . . . ?' Her stare was a mixture of horror and disbelief. 'You can't . . .'

'What did you think had happened?'

'Well . . . I assumed it had rubbed thin. Or got torn.'

'I'm afraid not. Completely removed.'

Dierdre said 'My God' again and buried her head in her hands. After a few moments she looked up and said, 'Who on earth could have done such a terrible thing?'

Barnaby gave her a moment more then said: 'Where was the tray with the razor kept?'

'On the props table. At the back, out of the way. It only goes on once, you see. Right at the end.'

'And it's fairly dark in the wings?'

'Yes. A certain amount of light spills out from the stage, of course, although the flats cut off a lot. And I've got an anglepoise in my corner. For tape and lighting cues. Not that I needed to give any of those. Tim was doing his own thing. He's been threatening to for years but no one thought he ever would.'

'Did you see anyone touch the tray or anything on it during the evening?' Dierdre shook her head. 'Or anyone hovering about in that area who shouldn't have been?'

'No. But then I wouldn't, Tom. *Amadeus* has nearly thirty scenes. We don't have a second to think. Oh, there was Kitty, of course. And Nicholas. He sat down there for a minute after his last exit.'

'Tell me about Kitty first.'

'Well . . . you must have seen what happened in act two. I don't know what it looked like from the front . . .'

'Pretty savage.'

'I wanted to stop the whole thing but Colin disagreed. When Kitty came off she could hardly stand. I sat her down next to the table.' Noticing an intensification of watchfulness in Barnaby's expression, Dierdre added quickly, 'But she didn't stay. I went down to the dressing room to get her a drink and an aspirin –'

'How long do you think you were away?'

'Several minutes. First I couldn't find the aspirin . . . then I couldn't get the top off . . . then I had to wash a mug. Then I panicked. You can imagine.' Barnaby nodded, imagining very well. 'When I got back Kitty had gone and I found her in the toilet.'

'How did she react to what had happened?'

'She was terribly angry. Furious. She . . . well, she cursed a lot. Then she said, "If he touches me again I'll —" ' Dierdre broke off. She looked around the room at the bottles and jars and showy bouquets and at a Good Luck card sporting a large black cat who had obviously completely failed to get the hang of its required function. 'Sorry, Tom . . . I don't remember what she said after that.'

'Dierdre.' Dierdre made eye contact with a coffee jar, a tin of artificial sweetener and one of powdered milk. 'Look at me.' She managed a quick glance, timorous, almost pleading. 'This isn't a practical joke we're investigating.'

'. . . No . . .'

'So what did Mrs Carmichael say?'

Dierdre swallowed and took a deep breath. ' "If he touches me again . . ." ' The rest of the sentence was smothered in a whisper.

'Speak up.'

' "I'll kill him." But she didn't mean it.' Dierdre rushed on, 'I know she didn't. People say that all the time, don't they? Mothers to their children in the street. You're always hearing them. It doesn't mean anything, Tom. And she was probably worried about the baby. She hit the pros arch with a terrible smack.'

'Where did she go when she left the toilet?'

'Back to the wings. Joycey was standing by to put her padding on. And I followed. She didn't go near the table again, I'm positive.'

'Do you have any idea why Esslyn should have acted as he did?'

'No — I can't understand it. He was perfectly all right till the interval.'

'You haven't heard any gossip?'

'Gossip? What about?'

'Perhaps . . . another man?'

'Oh no, I shouldn't think so. Kitty was pregnant, you see.'

He was certainly meeting them tonight, thought Sergeant Troy, resting his Biro against the pad borrowed from the constable on pavement duty. First the old gaffer upstairs singing his cracked old song halfway up Delilah Street, now the floppy-bottomed daughter who apparently believed that once you'd got one in the oven you hung a NO TRESPASS sign round your neck. In fact, as Troy knew to his philandering benefit, it was the one time you could hold open house with nobody having to foot the bill. He covered his mouth with the back of his hand to conceal an involuntary twitch of derision.

'Now you know the tape was deliberately removed do you have any idea how this could have been done?' Dierdre's features seemed to gather themselves together in the centre of her face, so great were her efforts at concentration. Barnaby said, 'No hurry.'

'I just can't think, Tom. The risk . . . it was so sharp.' Suddenly she saw David's fingers, quick and deft, wrapping the razor.

'What is it?'

'Nothing.' Before he could persist Dierdre improvised. 'I mean — it was so dangerous it couldn't have been done in the dark. And although the wings and stage were brightly lit till curtain-up it couldn't have been done then either because of the chance they might have been seen.'

'Who was the first to arrive after you?'

'Colin and David.'

'Did you tell them you'd done the check?'

'I told Colin.'

'But if they were together that means you told them both.' Dierdre reconnected with the powdered milk. 'Do you remember who came next?'

'Not really, Tom. Half a dozen people arrived together. Rosa and the Everards . . . and Boris. All the ASMs were in on the half.'

'Did anyone ask if you'd done your check?' Barnaby knew this question to be rather futile. The last thing the person who doctored the razor would wish to do was draw attention to themselves. But he felt it still had to be put. Dierdre shook her head. 'Did you leave the stage area at any time?'

'Yes. I went to the dressing rooms to call the quarter. Then I fetched my ASMs from the clubroom and I went to meet my father. This was just before eight o'clock. He was late.' Reminded, she half rose, saying, 'Is that all, Tom? He's waiting, you see . . .'

'In a moment.' Reluctantly Dierdre re-seated herself. 'Did you like Esslyn, Dierdre?'

She hesitated for a minute then said, 'No.'

'Do you have any idea at all who might have done this?'

This time there was no hesitation. 'Not at all, Tom. To be honest I don't think anyone liked him very much but you don't kill someone just because of that. Do you?'

The question was not lightly put. It was flooded with such intense appeal that Dierdre seemed to be seeking reassurance that the police had perpetrated a shocking misconstruction and that the Sellotape had managed to fly away of its own accord. Barnaby's unconsoling reply was never made. There was a knock at the door and the constable who had been sitting with the body popped his head round and said: 'Doctor Bullard's arrived, sir.'

Meanwhile next door in the scene dock the company, whilst still shocked, was starting to bounce back. Some more than others, naturally. But hushed whispers had already gone the way of solemn looks and reverential head shakings. Now ideas and suggestions were being mooted but in tones of bashful solemnity out of respect for Kitty's grief.

Not that this was much in evidence. She sat on a workbench staring crossly at Rosa and tapping her foot with irritation. The first Mrs Carmichael, her mouth loose and frilly, wept continuously. Her make-up now resembled a Turner sunset. You would have thought that she not Kitty was the widow albeit, as Clive whispered in an aside to Donald, more of a Widow Twankey. Ernest, who could have gone home ages ago, remained by her side. Joyce, her bloodsoaked clothes hidden behind a screen with Cully's ruined dress, sat holding her daughter's hand and wearing her husband's top coat. Cully was wrapped in several yards of butter muslin that she had found in a skip. Nicholas, who could not take his eyes off her, thought she looked like an exquisite reincarnation of Nefertiti.

All of them had been searched quickly and efficiently and although it had been no more than the brisk impersonal going over anyone gets at an airport Harold had taken umbrage and threatened to write to his MP.

'If a man's been stupid enough to cut his own throat,' he had cried indignantly, 'I don't know what on earth the politburo expect to gain by subjecting my people to this humiliating procedure.'

None of his people had minded really but they had all been equally puzzled by the need for such a step.

'I really don't see,' said Bill Last (lately Van Swieten), 'why they've locked up the men's dressing room. My car keys are in there. And my wallet. Everything.'

'Right,' said Boris, who chain smoked and was desperate for a ciggie.

'I don't see why they want to talk to us at all,' complained Clive Everard. 'We're not responsible for checking the props. It's obviously Dreary's fault. Took the tape off for some reason. Forgot to put it back again.'

'Typical,' said his brother.

'It is not at all typical,' said David Smy angrily. 'Dierdre's very capable.'

'Hear, hear,' from Nicholas.

Kitty, who had caught sight of Dierdre being escorted by Troy, said: 'She's been in there a hell of a time, though. I'd say it looks quite promising.'

'What an unkind thing to say,' protested Avery. 'Honestly. I thought adversity was supposed to bring out the best in us.'

'You can't bring out what isn't there,' said an Everard.

'Bitch,' said Kitty.

Still the same thought struck them all, save one. It would be nice if Dierdre had just been careless. Problem solved. And in a not too uncomfortable manner. Quite neat and tidy, really. Then they could all get changed and go home to bed.

But it was not to be. Harold bustled in, quite unsubdued by his forced incarceration, all asimmer with tendentious self-esteem. 'I've just been questioning the uniformed halfwit in the foyer,' he began, 'as to why we are all being treated in this tyrannical fashion and why half my theatre seems to be out of bounds, and he was totally unforthcoming. Mumbled something about protecting the scene in a case like this and when I said "a case like what" he said I should have a word with the DCI. "Easier said than done, my man," I replied. Tom is on the stage at the moment,' he continued, looking accusingly at the chief inspector's wife, 'with a complete and utter stranger who is cutting away – *cutting away* at that magnificent blue brocade coat. What with that and Joyce messing up her costume you can imagine what my bill will be like.'

'That's show business,' murmured Tim. 'Start the evening with Mozart, end up with Gotterdammerung.'

'And when I tried to ask Tom what he thought he was playing at he told me to come down here and wait with the others. And an obnoxious youth with red hair practically strong armed me down the stairs. If there is one thing I cannot stand it's high-handedness.'

Harold gazed at the ring of incredulous faces and was struck by one showing a remarkably uncontrolled use of colour. 'And what on *earth*,' he concluded, 'is the matter with Rosa?'

Above their heads Jim Bullard crouched beside the

148

body and Barnaby watched him as he had done more times than he cared to remember.

'Mmm . . . well . . . Cause of death's plain enough. Don't need a pathologist for this one.'

'Quite.'

'Extraordinary thing to do. Slash your throat in front of a theatre full of people. I know actors are exhibitionists but you'd think there'd be some limits. At least there's no argument as to the time of death. Was he on anything?'

'Not that I know of.'

'Well, the PM'll show that up. Right.' He rose, dusted his knees and repacked his bag. 'You can get him shifted.'

'I'm scratching around for some scene-of-crime people. Davidson's at his Masonic dinner. Fenton's gone to the Seychelles . . .'

'Oh?' Dr Bullard looked enquiring. 'Not as straightforward as it seems then? I wish you luck.'

'Before you go, Jim, I wonder if you'd have a look at Mr Tibbs. He's the father of the girl who just went through. Upstairs in the clubroom.'

'What's the matter with him?'

'He's mentally ill. I think what happened tonight might've . . . well . . . pushed him just that bit nearer the edge. He looked very wild.'

'I will of course, Tom, but I haven't got anything with me to give him. You'd be better getting in touch with his own – God! What on earth is that?'

A terrible cry. An awful, keening cry shot through with desolation and woe. Then rapid running and, through the open doors at the top of the aisle, they saw Dierdre fly past and disappear into the foyer below.

Outside it was still raining. Freezing needles of rain that could burrow through the warmest cloth never mind a thin summer shirt and cotton trousers. (He had left his linen jacket behind.) Rushing blindly on to the pavement carrying it over her arm, Dierdre bumped into a young policeman, caped and helmeted, getting soaked in the pursuance of his duty. He caught her arm.

'I'm sorry. No one's allowed to leave –'

'He's finished with me, Tom – the chief inspector, that is. Have you seen an old man?' A little crowd opposite glumly standing beneath a cluster of bright umbrellas perked up at this sign of activity. 'He's got white hair . . . *Please* . . .' She clutched at the constable frantically, rain and tears intermingling on her cheeks. 'He's ill.'

'Slipped through my fingers a few minutes ago – racing he was. No coat or anything.'

'*Oh God* –'

'He went up Carradine Road. Wait – if you hold on I'll get in touch . . .'

But he spoke to the night air for Dierdre had run away. He saw her a moment later racing across the shining wet tarmac, her dress already soaked, her face a livid green blur in the glow from the traffic lights. Then she was gone.

Rosa was interviewed next. Supported by Ernest as far as the dressing room door she subsided opposite Barnaby in an excitation of cerise fluff.

'You must ask me anything, Tom,' she cried and her voice, though brave, was a rill of sorrows. 'Anything at all.'

'Thank you,' said the chief inspector, who fully intended to. 'Can you think of anyone who might have wished to harm your ex-husband?'

'Absolutely not,' replied Rosa promptly. But the look which followed implied that the speed with which her interlocutor had approached the nub of the matter might be considered a bit short on finesse. 'Everyone liked Esslyn.'

Barnaby raised his shaggy eyebrows. His eyes shone with a gleam at once caustic and humorous. The gleam implied that he quite understood she felt she had to say things like that and now she'd said them perhaps they could cut the obsequies and get down to the nitty gritty. Maybe even flirt with the truth a little.

'That is,' continued Rosa, acknowledging the proposition, 'on the whole. Of course he was terribly unhappy.'

'Oh?'

'Kitty, you see.' She gave him a slightly suggestive yet shaded look, as if she were acknowledging Kitty's guilt from behind a veil. 'A *mariage de convenance* is never a good start, is it? And of course once she'd got him safely hooked she started to play around.'

'Who with?'

'That's not really for me to say.'

'I quite understand.'

'David Smy.'

'Goodness.'

'Of course it might just be a rumour.'

'It was Esslyn's child, though?'

'We all assumed so.' The verb's emphasis was beautifully judged. 'Poor little mite.'

Barnaby changed tack, deliberately hardening his voice. 'How did you feel, Rosa? After your divorce?'

Rosa's pose fell away. Her naked face showed plain through its rioting complexion. She looked cornered. And older. 'I . . . really don't see . . . what that has – Has to do with anything, Tom.' She took a deep breath and seemed to be fighting for control.

'Just background.'

'Background to what?'

'One never knows what might be helpful.'

Rosa hesitated and her feathers trembled. Barnaby appreciated her predicament. It was one which every person he interviewed would be in right up to their neck. For the first time in his life all the people connected with the case (for case he was sure there would prove to be) were known to him and the history of their present and past relationships even better known to his wife. Which made all the usual subterfuges, evasions, white lies, black lies, half truths and deliberate attempts to lead him round the gasworks rather dodgy. Advantage Barnaby. For once.

'To be absolutely honest, Tom . . .' She paused, resting a crimson nail against her nose as if checking it for rapid growth.

'Yes?' murmured Barnaby/Gepetto.

'I was angry at first. Very angry. I thought he was making a terrible mistake. But by the time the *decree nisi* came through I had changed. I realized that . . . for the first time in years . . . I was free.' She flung her arms wide, narrowly missing Harold's flowers. Her sailor's gaze raked the far horizon. 'Free!'

'And yet you remarried so quickly.'

'Ahh . . .' The gaze became wary, contracted from the hemispheric and swept the floor coyly. 'Love conquers all.'

They were back in fantasy land observed Barnaby to himself, but he let it ride. For now. And fantasies were not entirely unrevealing. He repeated his first question.

'Well, Tom, I don't know about anyone wanting to kill Esslyn but Nicholas came down here just before the final curtain with a splinter in his thumb and said that Esslyn had tried to kill him!' Barnaby received this dramatic pronouncement with irritating self-control. 'Under the table,' continued Rosa. 'In the requiem scene. And he'd already damaged Nicholas' hand.'

'Oh,' said Barnaby. Then, disappointing her, 'If we could return to the razor. Did you see anyone touching it or handling the tray who shouldn't have been?'

'No. And I'll tell you why.' She looked with deep solemnity at both men. 'When I'm acting . . . when I'm in that state of high concentration that we in the profession must be able to summon if the performance is going to work, I see nothing – but *nothing* that isn't immeasurably relevant to my part.'

'Even when you've no lines?' asked Barnaby, po-faced.

'Especially then. *Sans* words there's only the action of the drama to anchor the emotions.'

'I understand.' Barnaby nodded, matching her gravity. Troy, unimpressed, wrote on his borrowed pad, 'Saw nothing suspicious at props table'.

'What time did you arrive this evening, Rosa?'

'On the half. I went straight to my dressing room and didn't come out till my first entrance. About ten minutes into act one.'

Barnaby nodded again then sat, silent, drumming his fingers absently against the arm of his chair. As the moments passed Rosa shifted uneasily. Troy, long familiar with the chief's technique, simply anticipated.

'Rosa.' Barnaby gathered himself and leaned forward. 'It is my belief that, far from welcoming your freedom at the time of your divorce and wishing Esslyn well in his second marriage, you fought to keep your own going and have hated him ever since he left you.'

Rosa cried out then and covered her clown's mouth with her fingers. Her hands shook and sweat rolled down her face. Barnaby sat back and watched the actorish deceit evaporate leaving, oddly now that truth was present, doubt and childlike bewilderment.

'. . . You're right . . .' Having said this she sounded almost relieved. She paused for a long time then started to speak, stopping and starting. Feeling her way. 'I thought it would fade . . . especially after I remarried. And Ernest is so good. But it persisted . . . eating at me . . . I wanted a child, you see. He knew that . . . he denied me. Persuaded me against it. And then to give one to Kitty.' She produced a handkerchief and rubbed at her face. 'But the amazing thing, Tom – and I do mean this, I really do – is that all the hatred's gone. Isn't that extraordinary? Just as if someone somewhere pulled a plug and let it drain away. It doesn't seem possible, does it? That something so strong it was poisoning your life could simply disappear. Like magic.'

After a few moments' silence during which Barnaby mulled over Rosa's excellent motive for murder he indicated that she was free to go. She stood for a moment at the door looking, in spite of her cheap flamboyant robe and rampaging complexion, not entirely ridiculous. She seemed to be searching for some concluding remark, perhaps with the idea of ameliorating her former harshness. Eventually, almost as if memory had caught her by surprise, she said, 'We were young together once.'

Barnaby interviewed Boris next, who twitched and shook his way through the questions until Sergeant Troy, from pure pity, offered him a Benson's Silk Cut. Boris insisted that he had seen no one handle the razor all evening and could not imagine why anyone would want to kill Esslyn. All the other small-part actors came and went saying the same thing. As each one left the scene dock they were followed by a cry of fury as Harold protested against this disgraceful reversal of the natural order of precedence.

One scene-of-crime man arrived, closely followed by Colin Davidson, untimely wrenched from his Masonic maffickings. After a briefing they went about their business, working through the men's dressing room first and releasing it for occupation. Cully took her mother home, Esslyn left for the county morgue and Barnaby called for the Everards.

Clive and Donald came prancing in, their eyes aglow with anticipation, trailing clouds of *Schadenfreude*. They were still made up and their pointilliste complexions were the peculiar tea-rose pink of old-fashioned corsets. Barnaby chose to see them together, knowing their habit of egging each other on to ever more indiscreet and racy revelation. Now, preening and clucking like a couple of cassowaries, they circled the two chairs cautiously a couple of times before perching. They stared beady-eyed at Sergeant Troy and his notebook and he stared boldly but uneasily back.

The sergeant liked men to be men and women to be glad of it. Here was a pair he couldn't place at all. He always boasted he could tell an arse-bandit a mile off but he wasn't at all sure about this particular combo. He decided they had probably been neutered at an early age and, having pinned them down to his satisfaction, heard Barnaby ask if they could think of anyone who would wish to harm the dead man, and flipped over to a new page.

'Well, Tom,' said Clive Everard, taking a keen deep breath, 'quite honestly it'd take less time to tell you who wouldn't wish to harm him. I shouldn't think there's anyone in the company hasn't come up against Esslyn at some time and been the worse for it.'

'If you could be a little more specific.'

'Oh – if it's *specific* you want –' They exchanged glances sheeny with spite. 'Why not start with Dierdre. He was telling this wonderful story in the dressing room –'

' – Positively hilarious –'

'About her father –'

'Laughter and applause –'

'And suddenly there she was in the doorway. She must have overheard Esslyn call the old man senile –'

'Which of course he is.'

'But d'you think she'll admit it? Absentminded . . . disoriented . . . poorly . . .'

'*Poorly*,' cackled Donald. 'So what more natural than that she had a stab at getting her own back? Ooops . . . Freudian slip there. Sorry.' He didn't look sorry. His smile was as bright as ninepence as he added: 'And of course who would have a better opportunity?'

'This happened when she called the quarter?' asked Barnaby, recalling Dierdre's distressed appearance as he had passed through the wings.

'That's right. Would you care to hear the story?' added Clive politely.

'No,' said Barnaby. 'Anyone else?' Then, when they appeared to be savouring a multitude of possibilities, 'What about Nicholas?'

'Ahhh . . . you've sniffed out that little contretemps. Well . . . Esslyn'd just discovered that his little kitten was having an affair.'

'And I'm afraid,' murmured Donald, looking with shy regret at Sergeant Troy, 'that it was rather our fault.'

'Not that we thought he'd react anything like he did.'

'Heaven forfend.'

'I mean his complacency is legendary.'

'Undentable.'

'So who,' asked Barnaby, 'was she supposed to be having an affair with?'

'Well we heard from Rosa who got it from Boris who

got it from Avery who got it from Nicholas that it was David Smy.'

'And where did Nicholas get it from?'

'My dear – apparently he actually saw them,' cried Donald. 'Going at it like the clappers in Tim's lighting box.'

Barnaby supposed stranger things had happened. Himself he would not have thought that Kitty, whose winsome appearance masked, he felt sure, a self-serving duplicitous little nature, would have fancied the rather stolid David. Mind you if she was looking for a change no one could have been a greater contrast to Esslyn.

'And as he was our friend,' said Donald with an unctuous wriggle, 'we felt he ought to know.'

'So we told him.'

'*In the middle of a performance?*'

'Well you know what an old pro he is . . . was. Nothing fazed him.' No need to ask how Barnaby knew precisely when. Act two spoke for itself. 'Or so we thought.'

'But my God – the effect!'

'We didn't take his ego into account, you see. He's like Harold. Sees himself as a prince . . . or a king. And Kitty belonged to him. No one else was allowed to touch – '

'Lese-majesty.'

'He went white, didn't he, Clive?'

'Quite white.'

'And his eyes blazed. It was really frightening. Like being a messenger in one of those Greek plays.'

'Where you hand over the bad news then they take you outside and rearrange your innards with a toasting fork.'

'He got hold of my arm – I've still got the marks, look . . .' Donald rolled back his sleeve. 'And he said *who . . .?*'

'Just the one word, "*who?*" '

'And I looked at his face and I looked at my arm and I thought, well *I'm* not going to be the one to tell him who.'

'Friendship can be taken just so far.'

'Absolutely,' said Barnaby ignoring his nausea and giving an encouraging smile. 'So . . . ?'

'So I said,' continued Donald, 'better ask Nicholas. And before I could say another word –'

'Before either of us could say another word –'.

'He'd stormed off. And I never had a chance to add, "He's the one who knows." '

'And we'd realized once we'd got down to the dressing rooms that Esslyn'd got hold of the wrong end of the stick and thought that Nico was actually the man!'

'And you didn't feel like disabusing him?'

'The place was packed, Tom.' Clive sounded reproving if not scandalized. 'You don't want everyone knowing your business.'

Even Troy, so impassive in his role of bag-carrier that suspects occasionally thought he had entered a period of hibernation, choked back an astonished laugh at this astounding example of double think. The Everards turned and studied him carefully. Clive spoke.

'He's not writing all this down, is he?'

Dierdre ran on. And on. She seemed to have been running for hours. Her legs and feet ached and a savage wind repeatedly plastered strips of soaking wet hair over her eyes and mouth. She felt, from the soreness of her throat and totally clogged mucous membranes, that she must be crying, but so much water was pouring down her cheeks that it was impossible to be sure. Her father's now sodden coat, still clutched to her bosom, felt as heavy as lead. She peeled her hair away from her face for the hundredth time and staggered into the doorway of McAndrew's Pharmacy. Her heart leapt in her breast and she tried to take long, deep breaths to calm it down. She averaged about one in three, the rest being broken by deep juddering sobs.

She rested between the two main windows. On her left stacks of paper nappies and Tommy Tippee teething mugs all resting on a surge of polystyrene worms. On her right a display of carboys, cans of grape concentrate and coils of lemon plastic tubing like the intestines of a robot. (Be Your Own Fine Wine Merchant.)

Dierdre moved to the edge of the step and stared up at the arch of the black thundering sky, a soft anemone when she had first left home. The stars in their courses, never all that concerned with the welfare of the human race, tonight looked especially indifferent. Through the rivulets making their way down Dierdre's glasses individual stars became blurred then elongated into hard shining lances.

She had been running in circles. Starting in the High Street then working outwards in concentric rings. She had looked in all the shop entrances, and checked Adelaide's and the Jolly Cavalier although a public house was the last place she would normally expect to find her father. In both places bursts of laughter had followed her wild appearance and speedy withdrawal. She squelched round and round, obsessed by the idea that she was just missing him. She saw him, old and cold and drenched to the skin just one street ahead or a hundred yards behind or even in a directly parallel path concealed only by a house or dark gathering of trees.

Twice she had called in at home, checking every room and even the garden shed. The second time she had been terribly tempted by the still faintly glowing embers in the kitchen grate to take off her wet clothes and make some tea and just sit by the fire for a while. But, minutes later, she was driven out to the streets again, afraid she would never find him yet compelled by love and desperation to keep on trying.

So now she stood, her hand pressed against her pounding heart, her skin stinging under the arrowheads of rain, unable to take another step. Not knowing which way to turn. She tormented herself with pictures of her father lying in a gutter somewhere. Or huddled against a wall. No matter that, having covered every gutter and every wall, if he had been she would have long since discovered him. The ability to think rationally vanished the moment she had stepped into the clubroom and seen the empty chair and blind panic took its place. She pressed her face against the cold glass and stared into the window.

It is axiomatic that, when appalling national or personal disaster strikes, our occupations at that moment, however trivial or innocent, are invested with a terrible authenticity. And so it was that Dierdre could never look at any article connected with the making of home-made wine or read the words 'A White Wine from the Loire' to the end of her days without an immediate upswell of spontaneous dread.

Once more she turned her face towards the savage constellations of stars. God was up there, thought Dierdre. God with his all-seeing eye. He would know where her father was. He could direct her if he chose. She locked her fingers together and prayed, choking on half-remembered fragments of childhood incantations: 'Gentle Jesus . . . now I lay me down to sleep . . . in thee have I trusted . . . neither run into any kind of danger . . .' Numb with cold, her hands pressed against each other in an urgency of supplication as she stared beseechingly upwards.

The rain stopped but nothing else changed. If anything the great wash of iridescent stars looked even more distant and the milky radiance of the moon more inhumanly bright. On one of Dierdre's lenses a rivulet spread sideways; the lance became a stretched grin.

She recalled her father's years of pietistic devotion. His simple confidence that he was loved by his lord. Overlooked always by that luminous spirit and safe from all harm. Slowly anger began to course through her veins, unfreezing her blood, thawing out her frozen fingers. Was this to be his reward for years of devotion? To be allowed to slide into madness then abandoned and left to caper about in the howling wind and rain like some poor homeless elemental?

As Dierdre gazed with ever fiercer intensity into seemingly infinite reaches of space a terrible, traitorous thought entered her mind. What if there was no one there at all? No God. No Gabriel with golden footprints and twelve-foot fiercely protective wings. She shook her head (rat tails of hair went flying) as if to dislodge this heretical supposition, but without success. Having arrived the thought stuck, quivering in her mind like a poisoned dart, spreading its venom of doubt and disbelief. A wave of anguish swept over her. Followed by feelings of fury directed at a God she was no longer sure even existed. She stepped out of her shelter onto the wet pavement and shook her fist at the heavens.

'. . . You . . .' she screamed. '. . . You were supposed to be looking after him!'

The police Escort, alerted by the constable outside the Latimer, had just missed Dierdre several times. Now Policewoman Audrey Brierley gave her companion a nudge and said: 'Over there . . .'

Dierdre had stopped yelling by the time they had got out and just stood with sad resignation awaiting their approach. Very gently they persuaded her into the car and took her home.

After showing in Tim and Avery, Troy pointedly moved his chair several feet away. Then he sat, legs protectively crossed, giving off waves of macho fervour, his breathing ostentatiously shallow. One might have thought the air to be thick with potentially effeminate spores, a careless gulp of which might transform him from a sand-kicker supreme to a giggling, girlish wreck.

Avery, aware of the antagonism, typically became over-helpful, even ingratiating. Tim calmly shifted his chair so that his back was towards the sergeant and ignored him throughout the interview. In reply to Barnaby's opening question they agreed they had arrived on the half, gone up to the clubroom and had a glass of Condrieu accompanied by Nicholas who'd had a bitter lemon. Then they'd drifted around to the dressing rooms in what Tim called 'a whirl of insincere effusion and fake goodwill'. They did not touch the razor or notice anyone else doing so. They entered the box at ten to eight and stayed there.

'You came out at the interval, surely?'

'. . . Well . . . no . . .' said Avery.

'Not even for a drink?'

'We have our own wine. Tim won't drink Roo's Revenge.'

'I was perhaps mistaken then . . . ?' Barnaby's voice trailed off mildly.

'Oh! I did dash to the loo,' said Tim. 'Once the coast was clear.'

'Yes. Splendid lighting.'

'Our swan song.'

'Was that the actors' loo off the wings or the public?' asked Barnaby.

'The actors'. There was a queue in the clubroom.'

'Can you think of any reason,' continued Barnaby, 'why anyone would wish to harm Esslyn?'

Avery started to flutter, like a young bird trying to get off the ground. Fatally he glanced at Troy, receiving in return a look of such poisonous dislike that it took him a full five minutes to recover. Nervously he rushed into speech. 'He wasn't an easy person. Expected everyone to defer all the time, and most of us did. Except for Harold of course. I quite liked him myself –'

'Oh for heaven's sake, Avery!' interrupted Tim. 'We're both in the clear. We were in the box. There's no need to be such a bloody toady.'

'Ohhh . . .' Avery looked disconcerted, then relieved. 'I hadn't thought of that. "Phew!" as they say.' He mopped his forehead with an emerald green Paisley hanky. 'Well, if that's the way of it I don't mind admitting that I thought Esslyn was an absolute shit. And so did everyone else.'

Tim laughed and felt the blade of Troy's attention in the small of his back.

Barnaby said: 'Some more than others, perhaps?'

'Well . . . people often weren't bold enough to show it.'

'Or careless enough.'

'Pardon?' Avery looked puzzled but willing, like a puppy who hasn't quite got the point of a trick but is prepared to give it a try.

161

'He means,' said Tim drily, 'that this was probably some time in the planning.'

Troy resented the speed of this connection. His own thought processes, though he liked to think he got there in the end, were less wing footed. Queers were bad enough, he thought, stabbing at the page with his Biro, but clever queers . . .

'You wouldn't like to make a guess who is responsible?'

'Certainly not,' said Tim.

'Avery?'

'Ohhh . . .' As if called upon unexpectedly to make a speech Avery half rose in his seat then sank back again. 'Well . . . I'd have thought Kitty. I mean – she can't have enjoyed being married to Esslyn. He was over twice her age and about as much fun as a night out with the ton-ton macoutes. And of course they were heading for trouble as soon as the baby came.'

'Oh? Why was that?'

'Esslyn would have been so jealous. He couldn't bear not to be the centre of attention and babies need an awful lot of looking after. At least,' he added, it seemed to Barnaby a trifle wistfully, 'so I understand.'

'You knew she was having an affair?'

'So Nicholas told us.' Avery blushed and looked rather defiantly across at his partner. 'And I for one don't blame her.'

Neither of them could think of anything else at the moment that might be of help so Barnaby let them go, turning to his sergeant as the door closed and saying, 'Well, Troy. What do you think?'

Troy knew that it was not his opinion of homosexuals that was being solicited. There had been a particularly repulsive example of the species in a case the previous year at Badger's Drift and Troy's suggestions as to how the man's activities might be curtailed had been very frostily received. His chief was funny like that. Hard as iron in many ways. Harder than the iron men who thought they could never be broken and were now serving their time. Yet he had these peculiar soft spots. Wouldn't come out and condemn things that everyone knew to be rotten. Probably his age, thought Troy. You had to make allowances.

'Well, sir – I can't think of any reason why either of them should have been involved. Unless the dead man was bent and that's why his missus screwed around. But from what I've heard he seemed to have had a steady stream of tarts on the go.'

Barnaby nodded. 'Yes. I don't think his heterosexuality is in question.'

'And those Everards – well . . . just slimy little timeservers.'

'That seems to be the general opinion. Right – let's have Nicholas.'

The sergeant paused on his way out. 'What shall I tell that little fat geezer? Every time I go in and it's not for him he nearly wets himself.'

'Tell him,' Barnaby grinned, 'tell him the dame always comes down last.'

Scenes-of-crime had worked their way through the wings and were now tackling the stage. To save time Colin and David Smy had been released and told to present themselves at the station the next morning. Barnaby was interviewing Nicholas.

He had always liked the boy and had become quickly aware that Nicholas was enjoying the drama of the situation whilst feeling rather ashamed of himself for doing so. Which, thought Barnaby, was one up on certain other members of the company who had taken in the enjoyment whilst stopping well short of the shame. Having ascertained that Nicholas knew and saw nothing in relation to the tampering with the razor Barnaby asked if he could think of any reason why anyone would wish to harm Esslyn.

'You've never acted with him, have you?' said Nicholas, with a strained laugh. He was blushing with nerves and anxiety.

'I advise you to keep facetious remarks like that to yourself,' said Barnaby. 'A man has died here tonight.'

'Yes ... of course. I'm sorry, Tom. It was just nerves ... panic ... I suppose.'

'What have you got to be panicky about?'

'Nothing! ... nothing ...'

Barnaby paused for a moment, letting his impassive gaze rest on Nicholas. Then he exchanged a look with Sergeant Troy. Anything could have been read into that look. Nicholas, already a bundle of quivering apprehension, felt his spine turn to jelly.

Barnaby could not have seen what had happened to him on stage under the table. But if he had he would never believe the attack to be entirely unmotivated. Who would? And if Esslyn appeared to have a reason for attacking Nicholas might Nicholas not be supposed to have a reason for killing Esslyn? How airy-fairy now, thought Nicholas, did his reasoning seem that the other man was temporarily mad. Nicholas could see himself drawn into a whole area of emotional muddle and mess with questions and counter-questions all under that basilisk eye. (Could this be old Tom?) Thank God no one else had seen the confrontation. All he had to do was not get rattled and he'd be fine.

'What have you done to your hand?'

'What hand?'

'Let's have a look.' An irritated grunt. 'The other one, Nicholas.'

Nicholas held out his hand. Barnaby regarded it silently. Troy allowed himself a low whistle.

'Nasty,' said the chief inspector. 'How did you manage that?'

'... Stung ...'

'What by?'

'Wasp.'

'A wasps' nest in the wings? There's a novelty.'

'I did it yesterday.'

'Ah.' Barnaby smiled and nodded as if he found this arthropodally unsound explanation quite satisfactory, then said, 'I understand it was you who started the rumour of Kitty's infidelity.'

'It wasn't a rumour,' retorted Nicholas hotly. 'I know I was wrong to tell Avery and I'm very sorry, but it wasn't a rumour. I actually saw her in the lighting box with David Smy.'

'You're sure?'

'Yes. They were the only two people in the building.'

'Apart from yourself.'

'Well . . . of course . . .'

'So we only have your word for it that anyone was with Kitty.'

'She'd hardly have been reeling and writhing about up there on her own.'

'But she might have been there with you.'

'*Me.*'

'Why not? I'd have thought you were a much more likely contender than David.' Nicholas looked more trapped than flattered.

'Why on earth would I want to tell tales about myself? It doesn't make sense.'

'You might have wanted things out in the open.'

'That's nonsense –'

'What happened to your hand, Nicholas?'

'I *told* you.'

'Forget the wasps. It's November, not mid July. What happened to your hand?'

'. . . I . . . don't remember . . .'

'All right. What happened to your thumb?'

'A splinter.' Nicholas seized gladly at this opportunity to give a brief and truthful reply.

'When?'

'Tonight.'

'How?' Barnaby's look became more concentrated and Nicholas closed his eyes against the glare.

'I . . . um . . . I've forgotten . . .'

'Nicholas.'

Nicholas opened his eyes. The glare was muted now. Tom looked slightly more like his old self. Nicholas, who hadn't realized he was holding his breath, let it out gratefully; his backbone stiffened a little; his shoulders relaxed.

'Yes, Tom?'

'Why did you believe that Esslyn was trying to kill you?'

Nicholas gasped as if a pail of cold water had been thrown in his face. He struggled to regain his equilibrium and formulate a sensible reply. At the moment his brain seemed unravelled, nothing but kaleidoscopic fragments. All he could do was stall.

'What?' He tried a light laugh. It came out a strangled croak. 'Where on earth did you get that idea?' Rosa. Of course. He had forgotten Rosa. Tom had stopped looking like his old self. He spoke.

'I've been sitting in this chair for a very long time, Nicholas. And I'm getting very tired. You start messing me about and you'll find yourself in the slammer. Got that?'

Nicholas swallowed. 'Yes, Tom.'

'Right. The truth then.'

'Well . . . my hand . . . he did that with his rings. Turned them all facing inwards and squeezed tight. Then, near the end of the play, when I crawl under the table, he came after me. His cape cut all the light off . . . I was trapped. Then he tried to strangle me . . .' Nicholas trailed lamely off. Barnaby leaned forward and studied his lily-white throat. 'Oh – he didn't actually touch me.'

'I see,' said the chief inspector. 'He tried to strangle you. But he didn't actually touch you.'

Nicholas fell silent. How could he convey the feelings he had experienced during those dreadful minutes when, half paralysed with fear, he had shrunk away from Esslyn's jackal-breath and groping, bony fingers? He stumbled into speech, explaining about cutting a page and a half and bringing Kitty on.

'And you really believe that it was only her entrance that stopped him attacking you?'

'I did then . . . yes.'

'But temporarily?'

'I'm sorry?'

'Well obviously anyone really determined, balked at one attempt, will look for an opportunity to make a second.'

'That didn't occur to me. I just felt that if only I could get off stage I'd be safe.'

'You really expect me to believe that?'

'I know it sounds unlikely, Tom –'

'It sounds bloody ridiculous! How much more likely that you come off frightened and angry. Take the razor, nip off to the loo, remove the tape and bingo! You get him before he gets you. Problem solved.'

'*That's not true.*'

'Cop a plea of self-defence,' said Barnaby cheerfully, 'get off with three years.'

'No!'

'Why go straight to the props table?'

'I just sat down for a second. I felt shaken. I'd got this splinter. It hurt like hell. I went down to the men's dressing room.' Nicholas could hear the sentences clattering out through chattering teeth. Each one less convincing than the one before.

'Anyone see you?'

'. . . I don't know . . . yes . . . Rosa . . .'

'What on earth was Rosa doing in the men's dressing room?'

'She wasn't. I couldn't find any tweezers so I went next door.'

'Who was in the men's then?'

'No one.' Barnaby tutted. 'But . . . if I'd been messing with the razor I'd have taken the tape off then gone straight back, surely? To put it back before it was missed.'

'Oh I don't know. If I'd been messing with the razor I'd have made sure I had a good excuse to be downstairs and someone saw me going about my lawful business.'

'You don't think I rammed that splinter down my thumb on purpose? It was bloody agonizing.' Nicholas plucked at the square of grubby fabric. 'Do you want to have a look?'

Barnaby shook his head then slowly got to his feet. 'See if you can rustle up some tea, Sergeant. I'm parched . . .'

Nicholas waited for a moment and when Barnaby made no attempt to continue the conversation also got shakily to his feet. . . . 'Is that all then, Tom?'

'For now.'

'D'you think' – Nicholas appeared almost to gag on the words – 'I ought to find a solicitor?'

'Everyone should have a solicitor, Nicholas,' said Barnaby, with gently smiling jaws. 'You never know when they're going to come in handy.'

It was about ten minutes later when Nicholas was putting on his coat that the odd thing struck him. Barnaby had not asked the first question that even the most inexpert of investigators must surely have put. And the chief inspector, as Nicholas' still twitching nerve ends could testify, was far from inexpert. He had not asked Nicholas why Esslyn would wish to kill him. There must be a reason for this very basic omission. Nicholas did not believe for a moment it was either lack of care or forgetfulness. Perhaps Barnaby thought he already knew. In which case he knows a darn sight more than I do, thought Nicholas. He decided to look into this further and retraced his steps to the ladies' dressing room.

Long afterwards, when she was able to look back with some degree of equanimity on the first night of *Amadeus* and its shocking aftermath, Dierdre marvelled at the length of time it had taken her to realize that there was only one place where her father felt safe and cared for when she was absent. Only one place where he could possibly be.

The Day Centre (Laurel Lodge) was nearly a mile from the middle of town. Two custard-yellow mini buses, Phoenix One and Phoenix Two, collected the elderly and infirm at their homes and ferried them to and from the Centre each weekday. So Mr Tibbs knew the way. In fact it was not complicated. You just took the B416 as if you were going to Slough then tapered off on a side road towards Woodburn Common. The distance could be covered in about an hour. Or less if you were running your heart out and pacing yourself against dark unreasoned fears.

Dierdre remembered the Centre when she had been hunched over the electric fire in the kitchen being urged by the policewoman to swallow some hot, sweet tea and try not to worry. Now she sat once more in the back of the Escort, warmed by the drink and above all by the knowledge that the hopeless misdirected floundering was over and that they were definitely on their way to where her father would be waiting. She struggled to keep calm, knowing that her attitude was bound to affect the situation when they met.

She couldn't help worrying, of course. For instance the place was locked up and there was no caretaker on the premises so Mr Tibbs would not have been able to get in. This observation when first made had considerably threatened Dierdre's equilibrium. For the building thoughtfully, even lovingly designed so that its inhabitants would get the benefit of all the light and sunshine that was going, was made almost entirely of glass. And what if her father, frenziedly searching for Mrs Coolidge (or Nancy Banks who made such a fuss of him) harmed himself by hammering on those heavy slabs or, worse, seized a stone from the garden and tried to smash the doors. Suppose he then tried to squeeze through, gripping the jagged raw edges . . .

At this point Dierdre would wrench her mind away from such dreadful fancies and once more wrestle her way towards comparative tranquillity. But the idea would not easily be vanquished and when the car drew up outside Laurel Lodge and the dark glass structure loomed apparently undisturbed, she felt a great rush of relief.

The iron gates were locked, a token restraint merely as the grounds were surrounded by a brick wall barely a metre high. There was still a high howling wind. As Dierdre staggered across the gravel her coat streamed out behind her and her cries of 'Daddy – where are you? It's

Dierdre . . .' were blown back into her mouth as soon as uttered. Constable Watson had a torch in his hand and was testing all the doors and windows and bellowing 'Mr Tibbs?' in what seemed to Dierdre a very authoritative, even threatening manner. He disappeared around the side of the building, shining his light into each of the five transparent boxes; the workroom and kitchen, the rest room and office, the canteen. Then he came back shouting 'He's not here' and Dierdre, uncomprehending, yelled back 'Yes, yes . . . somewhere . . .'

She waved at the surrounding garden and the man followed the movement with his torch. The beam swept an arc of brilliant light over the surrounding lawns and shrubbery. A band of green-gold conifers, waving and soughing like the sea, leapt into sight then vanished as the torch moved on. The flowerbeds were empty brown sockets and the shrubs that gave the place its name creaked in the bitter whirling wind. (Dierdre had always hated the laurels. They were so coarse and melancholic and their leathery spotted leaves made her think of the plague.)

She seized PC Watson's arm, gasped 'We must search' and started pulling him towards the nearest dark mass of shrubbery. He resisted and Dierdre, turning back, was just about to redouble her efforts when the blistering roar of the wind ceased. The strife-torn trees rustled and groaned for a few moments more then settled into silence.

Surprisingly – for they were half a mile from the nearest habitation – a dog barked. This was followed by another sound which, although muffled by the belt of Leylandii, was unmistakably a human voice. It was calling out, not in any panic-stricken way but with a sonorous, tolling necessity like a town crier. Dierdre moaned 'The lake!' and flew in the general direction from which the recitations had come. Her companion followed, trying to light her with his torch, but she was running so fast and zigzagging so wildly back and forth that he kept losing her. Once she tripped, fell into a flowerbed and scrambled up, her hands and clothes plastered with mud.

In fact the lake was not a lake at all but a reservoir. A vast natural hollow which had been extended and shaped into a rectangle then edged with masonry and planted all about with reeds and other vegetation. People were allowed to sail on it in the summer and it was home to a large variety of birds and small mammals. Nearby was a concrete building surrounded by a high wire fence with a sign attached. It showed a yellow triangle with a jagged arrow and a man lying down and read: DANGER OF DEATH. KEEP OUT. Just as Dierdre arrived the moon, so white it appeared almost blue in the icy air, sailed serenely out from behind a bank of dark cloud. It illuminated an astonishing sight.

Mr Tibbs was standing rigidly upright in an oarless rowing boat in the very centre of the reservoir. His arms were flung wide and, as his fingers were almost precisely aligned with the perfect circle of the reflected moon, he seemed to be holding a new mysterious world in the palm of his hand. His trousers and shirt were torn, his hair stuck out wildly in all directions and his forearms and chest were scratched and bleeding. But his face as he stared upwards was stamped with such ecstatic bliss that it was as if he saw streams of celestial light pouring from the very gates of Paradise.

Mr Tibbs had an audience of one. A rough-haired rather shabby brown and white mongrel with a plumed tail. He sat bolt upright on the bank, his head cocked to one side in an attitude of strained attention, his ears pricked. He paid no attention when the others crashed into view but kept his eyes (brown and shiny as beech nuts) firmly fixed on the figure in the boat.

'I saw a mighty angel come down from heaven!' cried Mr Tibbs. 'Clothed with a cloud. And a rainbow was upon his head! And his face was as it were the sun . . . And his feet as pillars of fire!'

Whilst the constable used his radio to organize assistance Audrey Brierley was hanging on to a struggling Dierdre.

'We're getting reinforcements, love,' Audrey said

urgently. 'And an ambulance. They'll be here in no time. *Please* calm down. There's nothing you can do. If you get in there that'll be two people we'll have to pull out. Twice the trouble, twice the risk. Now you don't want that, do you?' Dierdre stood still then. 'Good girl. Try not to worry. He'll be cold and wet but he's in no real danger.'

'If any man have an ear let him hear,' clarioned Mr Tibbs. Then he flung out his arm in a wide sweep encompassing his human audience of three, the concrete hut and the scrupulously attentive canine, and fell into the water.

Dierdre screamed, Policewoman Brierley hung on anew and Constable Watson peeled off his heavy tunic, got rid of his boots and dived in. He kicked out with great difficulty (his trousers were immediately saturated), cursing the Fates that had put him on late turn. He attempted a strong crawl towards the dark outline of the boat and each time he turned his head a little of the water, freezing cold and tasting richly of mud and iron, slopped into his mouth. He grabbed what he thought was his quarry only to find himself clutching a huge skein of slimy weed. He swam further in. On his limited horizon the water lapped and bobbed against the sky. Mr Tibbs' descent had fractured the immaculate circle of the moon and it now lay in broken bars of silver around the policeman's head. He could hear wails from Dierdre interspersed with barks from the dog which, now that the declamation had ceased and the action had started, was running excitedly round in circles.

The policeman reached Mr Tibbs, hooked an arm around the old man's neck and turned him round. To the anguished Dierdre, wringing her hands on the bank, her father seemed to spin with graceful ease but to Jim Watson it was like hauling a hundredweight sack of potatoes. Thank God, he thought, feeling his arms wrenching in their sockets, the old man wasn't threshing about. Indeed Mr Tibbs seemed quite unaware that there was any danger in his position at all. He drifted beatifically, cruciformly on his back. With his rigid unnatural smile and

172

spreading white hair he looked like the corpse of a holy man floating in the Ganges. PC Watson plodded on. His arm was almost beating the water in his efforts to keep them both afloat.

Then Mr Tibbs decided he had had enough and announced his approach to the next world. 'We are coming, Lord,' he cried. He twisted himself out of the policeman's grasp and made the sign of the cross, poking PC Watson savagely in the eye.

'Christ!' exclaimed the unfortunate constable as an agonizing pain exploded behind his forehead. Mr Tibbs, no doubt encouraged by this sign of solidarity, placed both hands on his rescuer's shoulders and sank them both. Jim Watson held his breath, kicked his way violently to the surface, took a fresh lungful of air and dived again, bringing up Mr Tibbs.

'Ohhh . . .' wailed Dierdre. 'We must *do* something.'

'He'll be all right.' PW Brierley sounded more confident than she felt. The two pale faces were still a long way from the edge.

'Can't you go in and help?'

'Then there'd be two of us round his neck.'

'I thought everyone in the police had to be able to swim.'

'Well they don't,' snapped Audrey, unpleasantly aware that her uniform was wet and filthy, her hat lost somewhere in the bushes, her tights in shreds and that she was screamingly ragingly desperately dying for a pee. She moved slightly forward, extending her fingertips another inch. The inch that might make all the difference. She said, 'Hang on to my legs.'

The dog, as if sensing the situation was now completely out of his control, had crouched quietly down and was looking back and forth from the couple on the edge to the couple in the water with increasing degrees of anxiety.

PC Watson had been unable to seize Mr Tibbs with his former neat precision and, having awkwardly grabbed at his shoulder, was now lugging rather than towing him. The policeman's muscles ached almost beyond endurance with the double effort of trying to steer them both to the bank and keep Mr Tibbs' head above the water. Also the old man's benign attitude had become transformed, no doubt due to his being snatched from the jaws of death against his will, to one of extreme truculence. He flailed his arms and legs about and gave little wheezy hoots of crossness. Kevin Lampeter, the ambulance driver, said afterwards it was as if someone was trying to drown a set of bagpipes. He arrived just after the police reinforcements who had brought a coil of rope and drawn PC Watson and his burden to safety.

Dierdre immediately flung herself on her father, supporting him and calling his name over and over again. But he shrank away as if from an unkind stranger. The ambulance men persuaded him on to a stretcher and the bedraggled group limped, staggered or, in the case of the dog, trotted briskly towards the waiting vehicle. The wall was negotiated with far less ease than previously. PC Watson, a blanket around his shoulders, climbed heavily into the back of the ambulance and Mr Tibbs, all the light fled from his countenance, went next. The dog, attempting to follow, was sternly rebuffed.

'You'll have to take him up front.'

'Oh but he's not —' said Dierdre, bewildered. 'I mean . . . I don't know . . .'

'If you could hurry it up please, dear. The sooner we get the old man to a hospital the better.'

Dierdre climbed into the cab but the dog had got there first. When she sat down he bounded on to her lap, unfurled his plume-tail, wrapped it neatly around his hind quarters and stared intently out of the window all the way to Slough.

Kitty settled herself composedly. She inspected her pretty face, flirted her curls a bit and accepted a cup of tea from Sergeant Troy with a look that was as good as a wink and then some. Barnaby assumed her sang-froid to be genuine. Given her present position as suspect number one this argued either great cunning, absolute innocence

174

or absolute stupidity. Of the three Barnaby was inclined to favour the latter. He started with formal condolences.

'A terrible business this, Kitty. You must be dreadfully upset.'

'Yeah. Terrible. I am.' Kitty's sapphire glance slid sideways and fastened, sweet and predatory, on Troy's carrot-coloured crown. He looked up, met the glance, flushed, smirked and looked down again.

'Do you have any idea who might have wanted to harm your husband?'

'Could've been any number of people. He was an absolute pig.'

'I see.' He was obviously not going to have the same problem with the second Mrs Carmichael that he had had with the first. 'You would include yourself amongst that number?'

'Definitely.'

'But it wasn't you who removed the tape?'

'Only because I didn't think of it first.' Bold madam, thought Troy. And get a load of those sweet little oranges.

'Did you and Esslyn arrive together?'

'Yes. I went straight to the dressing room. Got dressed and made up. All of a twitch and a tremble I was. Ask Joycey.'

'That was a savage bit of business in act two,' said Barnaby, circling closer.

'Bastard. Nearly broke my back.'

'I understand he'd just discovered you'd been having an affair.'

'*An affair!*' Dismay, indignation and comprehension jostled for position on Kitty's foxy face. 'So that was what set him off. How the hell did that get out?'

'You were seen.'

'Charming. Nosy buggers.' She scowled. 'Where was I seen?'

'In the lighting box.'

'Oh no.' Kitty laughed then. A blowsy coarse chuckle. 'Poor old Tim. He'll be furious.'

'Would you care to tell me who the man is?'

175

'But –' She stopped. Her face, spontaneously surprised, became smooth and guarded. 'Not really. You seem to be doing very well on your own. I'm sure by this time tomorrow you'll know his name, what he has for breakfast and the size of his socks. Not to mention the length of –'

'Yes, all right, Kitty,' interrupted Barnaby, noticing his sergeant's look of rollicking appreciation.

'In any case it wasn't what you'd call an affair. Not a real steamer. More of a frolic . . . all very light-hearted really.'

'Did you expect your husband to see it like that?'

'I didn't expect my husband to find out, for God's sake!'

'Who do you suppose told him?'

'His little muckrakers, I should think. They're never happier than when they're turning over a nice big stone and mixing up the ooze. He relied on them for all the juicy bits.'

'I understand that after this violent scene on stage you rested for a while in the wings –'

'Hardly for a while.'

' – Next to the props table. In fact almost on top of the tray with the bowl of soap and the razor.'

'I was only there a second.'

'A second is all you would need,' said Barnaby. 'It's obvious that whoever messed with the razor took it away to do so. And almost the only place where it could have been tampered with undisturbed was a locked lavatory cubicle.' His voice tightened. 'I understand it was in the ladies' where Dierdre found you.'

'Where d'you expect her to find me? In the gents'?'

'And that you then said that if Esslyn touched you again you would kill him.'

Kitty stared, suddenly wheyfaced with shock. 'What a brilliant lot. Gossips. Spies. Peeping Toms. And now a bloody tipster. You wait till I see her. Little cow!'

'You mustn't blame Dierdre,' said the chief inspector, feeling that the least he could do was save the wretched girl from a further stream of opprobrium. 'You were overheard. In the wings.'

176

'. . . Well? So what?' Kitty was quickly regaining her balance. 'You saw what happened on stage. What d'you think I'd say? We must do this more often? In a pig's eye.'

Her voice was steely and laced with bravado. Barnaby, remembering the coquettish adoring glances directed at her husband and her other mimsy wriggling little ways, could only reflect wrily on the commonly held assumption that Kitty couldn't act for toffee.

'Anyway,' she continued, her eyes bright and astute, 'if I'd been in the loo taking the tape off I'd hardly start shouting to the world that I was thinking of killing him.'

'Stranger things have happened. You could have been perpetrating a double bluff. Assuming that we would think exactly that.'

'Oh come on, Tom. You know me. I'm not that clever.'

They stared each other out. Kitty, her periwinkle-blue eyes dark with anger, was thinking she'd find out who had spotted her in the lighting box and when she did they'd wish they'd never been born. Barnaby was wondering if she had genuinely not known the reason for Esslyn's sudden explosion of rage. Had she really been sitting in the scene dock for (he checked his watch) the best part of two hours with Nicholas, also the recipient of Esslyn's violence, without coming to any conclusions? They must surely have discussed it. He supposed if the Everards had kept their mouths shut this could be the case. Was Kitty a bored young wife playing around, he wondered? Or was she a calculating harpy who had snaffled a financially secure older husband and then wished to be rid of him? Was the removal of the tape an impulsive act? Or planned for some time? If so Barnaby asked himself (as he was to do over and over again in the coming days) why on earth should it be done on the first night? He became aware that Kitty was leaning forward in her seat.

'You're not sticking this on me, Tom,' she said firmly.

'I have no intention of "sticking" this on anyone, Kitty. But I intend to find out the truth. So be warned.'

177

'I don't know what you mean. I've nothing to hide.' But her cheeks bloomed suddenly and she did not look at him.

'Then you've nothing to fear.'

After a longish pause during which Kitty recollected herself to the extent that she was able to send a second slumbrous glance in Troy's direction she got to her feet and said: 'Well, if that's all, a person in my condition should have been in her lonely bed hours ago.'

'Quite a girl,' said Barnaby as the door closed behind her.

'Anybody's for a gin and tonic,' murmured the sergeant, hopefully memorizing the telephone number at the top of Kitty's statement. Then he added: 'Maybe they were in it together. Her and her bit of crackling.'

'The thought had occurred to me.'

Troy scanned his notes briefly then said, 'What now, sir?'

Barnaby got up and collected his coat. 'Let's go and find the big white chief.'

Barnaby had hardly set foot in the scene dock before Harold, incandescent with rage, sprang before them like a greyhound from the slips. 'So there you are!' he cried, as if to a pair of recalcitrant children. 'How dare you leave me whilst one and then the other of the company is interviewed? It's not as if you aren't aware of my position. How am I supposed to keep control when they see me constantly passed over like . . . like the boot boy!'

'I'm sorry you're upset, Harold,' said Barnaby soothingly. 'Please . . . sit down.' He indicated a rustic arbour on which dusty blue paper roses were impaled. Reluctantly, simmeringly, Harold lowered himself.

'You see,' continued the chief inspector, 'everyone has had a story to tell. Sometimes these are mutually supportive, sometimes they contradict each other, but what I need at the end of the day is the viewpoint of someone who knows the group through and through. Someone perceptive, intelligent and observant who can

178

help me to draw all the information together and perhaps see some underlying pattern in this dreadful affair. This is why I left you until the last.' He looked concernedly at Harold. 'I thought you'd understand that.'

'. . . Well . . . of course, Tom . . . I sensed that something like that was behind it all . . . But I would have appreciated a discreet word. To have been kept informed.'

Barnaby's look of regret deepened. Troy, sitting just to the side of Harold in a deckchair (Relatively Speaking), watched with proprietorial pleasure. You could almost hear the steam hissing out of the old geezer (or geyser, revised the sergeant wittily), and see self-importance taking its place. Next would come complacency, the most fertile ground for the forcing of revelation. (Not fear or anger as is commonly supposed.) Troy tried to catch his chief's eye to indicate his appreciation of the manoeuvre but without success. Barnaby's concentration was total.

Actors, thought the sergeant, wearing the shade of a contemptuous smile. You'd have to get up early to find one to match the DCI. He had as many expressions to his face and shades to his voice as a mangy dog had fleas. He could imitate the dove and the scorpion and even the donkey if he thought it would serve his ends. More than once Troy had seen him shaking his head in apparent dumb bewilderment whilst witnesses feeling secure in his incomprehension happily babbled on, quite missing the echo of the turnkey's tread. And he had a special smile seen only at the moment of closing in. Troy practised that smile sometimes at home in the bathroom mirror and frightened himself half to death. Now Barnaby was congratulating Harold on the excellence of his production.

'Thank you, Tom. Not an easy play but I pride myself on a challenge, as you know. I wasn't *altogether* delighted with act one but the second half was a great improvement. So intense. And then to end like that . . .' He clicked his tongue. 'And of course, any sort of cock-up people immediately blame the producer.'

'I'm afraid that's the case,' agreed Barnaby, marvelling

at Harold's grasp of the essentials. 'You were hardly back stage at all, I believe?'

'Not really. Went through on the five to wish them all *bonne chance* – well, you were directly behind me, I believe? Then again at the interval to tell them to pull themselves together.'

'And you saw no one acting suspiciously in the wings?'

'Of course not. If I had I would have stopped them. We had five more performances, after all. And Saturday's sold out.'

'Do you have any idea who might have tampered with the razor?'

Harold shook his head. 'I've thought and thought, Tom, as you can imagine. There might be someone in the company who's got it in for me but' – he gave a perplexed sigh – 'I can't possibly think why.'

'Or Esslyn.'

'Pardon?'

'It could be said that Esslyn had been sabotaged just as successfully as your production.'

'Ohhh . . . quite.' Harold pursed his lips judiciously, implying that although this was a completely new slant on the situation it was not one he was prepared to reject out of hand. 'You mean, Tom – it might have been something personal?'

'Very personal, I'd say.' Troy, almost alight with enjoyment, leaned back too hard in his deckchair and broke the strut. By the time he had sorted himself out Barnaby had reached the sixty-four-dollar question. 'Did you have any reason for wishing Esslyn Carmichael harm?'

'*Me?*' squeaked Harold. 'He was my leading man. My star! Now I shall have to start all over again training Nicholas.'

'What about his relationships with the rest of the company?'

'Esslyn didn't really have relationships. His position made that rather difficult. I have the same problem. To hold authority one must keep aloof. He always had a woman in tow, of course.'

'Not since his recent marriage, surely?'

'Perhaps not. I'm sure we'd all know. I'll say this in Esslyn's favour – he never attempted to conceal his infidelities. Not even during his years with Rosa.'

Quite right, thought Troy, flicking over his page. What's the point of having it if you don't flaunt it?

'She seemed very distressed, I thought.'

'Rosa could always weep to order.'

'In fact,' insinuated the chief inspector, 'far more so than the present incumbent.'

'Ahhh . . .' In an ecstasy of enlightenment Harold slapped himself about the jowls like S.Z. (Cuddles) Szakall. 'In other words, "*cherchez la femme*". Could be, could be. He was the sort to make enemies, mind you. Selfish to the core.'

Barnaby had always believed it was possible to judge the love and respect in which the newly deceased was held by the width of the gap between the immediate, almost inevitable reaction of shock and distress (even if only on the 'every man's death diminishes me' principle) and the point at which the dead party's failings could be discussed with something approaching relish. In Esslyn Carmichael's case the gap was so narrow it would have hardly accommodated one of Riley's whiskers.

'But in spite of that you got on with him?'

'I get on with everyone, Tom.'

'Personally and professionally?'

'They're intertwined. Esslyn didn't always accept my suggestions easily but there was never any question of compromise. There can only be one leader.'

Harold's disdain for accurate introspection and his airbrushed memory were certainly working overtime tonight, observed Barnaby. Or perhaps he genuinely believed that Esslyn had dutifully carried out the instructions of his imperator, which argued a hazy grip on reality to say the least.

'Returning to the question of motive, you have to remember,' continued Harold, borrowing the obituarist's subtle shorthand when describing arrogant insensitives,

181

'that he didn't suffer fools gladly. But then' – a smug smile peeped through the silvery boskage – 'neither do I.'

When Harold had been dismissed and left, apparently without noticing that he had neither given an overview nor pulled any threads together, Barnaby returned to the now scrupulously investigated and empty wings and took the reel of Sellotape from a box on Dierdre's table. He wound it twice round the handle of her microphone then removed it by slicing it through with a Stanley knife. He gave it to Troy. 'Chuck that down the toilet.' Then he stood listening to the repeated flushings and gushings till his sergeant returned.

'Can't be done, chief.'

'Tried the ladies' as well?'

'And upstairs. And the disabled.'

'Well, the search proved none of them were concealing it. Scene of crime didn't turn it up. So . . .'

'Out of the window?'

'Right. And with this wind it could be halfway to Uxbridge by now. Still – we might be lucky. It could've caught up somewhere. Have a look in the morning. I've had enough for one night.'

As they made their way up through the deserted auditorium Troy said: 'Why did you leave him till last, sir? Old fat'n'hairy?'

'I don't like the way he speaks to people.' Then, when Troy still looked inquiring, 'He thinks everyone's there to do his bidding. Takes them for granted, gives them no thanks and talks to them like dirt. I didn't think it would do him any harm to be at the end of the queue for once.'

'Think it'll do him any good?'

'No. Too far gone.'

'I think he's round the twist.'

'All theatricals are round the twist, Troy,' said Barnaby, tugging at the doors that led to the foyer. 'If they weren't they'd get out of the business and into real estate.'

It seemed to take for ever for Mr Tibbs to be seen by all

the people who had to have a look at him. Dierdre gave the few details that were to be entered on his admission card and was then told to wait in reception. She had been there over an hour when a nurse came and said she could see her father for a tick just to say goodnight.

Mr Tibbs lay, neatly swaddled, in the iron rectangle of his hospital bed. He did not respond to her greeting but stared straight ahead, humming something atonal. His cheeks were flushed bright red.

'Nurse!' called Dierdre, anxiety overcoming her innate wish not to be any trouble. 'I think he's got a fever.'

'We've given him something for that. He'll be asleep soon.' The nurse bustled up with a steel bedpan and started drawing the curtains of the bed next door. 'You'll have to go now.'

'Oh.' Dierdre backed away. 'Yes. I'm sorry. I'll ring in the morning.'

'Make it latish. The rounds will be over then and we can tell you how he's been and where he's going.'

'Won't he stay here, then?'

'No. This is just emergency admissions.'

'I see . . . well . . . goodnight then,' said Dierdre to some orange folds of fabric. 'And thank you.'

After a final look at her father, who already seemed to be part of another world, Dierdre drifted back to the reception area. A young man was in the middle of a conversation, phone clamped to his ear supported by his shoulder. He said 'Just a sec' to Dierdre and went on talking. 'Don't talk to me about Miss Never On Sunday,' he said. 'I saw her in the Boltons last night and she spent every other second in the john.' He listened for a moment, sucking his cheeks. 'If promises were piecrusts, dear, she'd be in crumbs up to her armpits.' He was very dark. Dierdre wondered if he could possibly be Italian. After he had hung up she explained that she was now ready to go home.

'No can do, I'm afraid. Transport's for emergencies only.'

'B . . . b . . . but . . .' Dierdre stammered in her distress. 'I live miles away.'

'That's as may be, love. What would we do if there was a pile-up on the motorway and you were out joyriding in the ambulance?'

'. . . you've got more than one, surely . . .'

'Sorry. Those are the rules.'

Dierdre stared blankly at him. In the close hot air of the vestibule her still damp clothes started to steam. She was swaying from exhaustion. Now that her father was being safely cared for all her emotions – fear, love, terror, despair – tumbled away. She was benumbed almost to the point of non-existence.

'The buses start up at seven . . . you could have a little doss down . . .' He felt sorry for her, no doubt about that. She looked really zonked out. 'If it was up to me, dear . . .' He always said that, it made them feel better. Made him feel better, come to that. 'Or I could call you a taxi.'

'A taxi.' It wasn't a question. She just repeated it like a child learning a lesson. Dierdre struggled to think. The machinery of memory, like all her other psychological and physiological functions, seemed to have ground to a halt. A taxi meant money. She put her hands carefully into each of her pockets. She had no money. With great effort she forced herself to print a memory on the blank screen of her mind. She saw herself running from the Latimer. She was wearing her coat and her hands were empty. That meant her bag must still be at the theatre. So (her brows fretted with the effort of working out the next step) if she took a cab there the driver could wait while she picked up her bag then she could pay him and he could drive her home. Dierdre, her face grey with exhaustion, laboured over the details of this simple plan but could find no flaw.

'Yes,' she said, 'a taxi.'

'Be double time,' said reception, cheerfully dialling. 'After twelve, you see.'

Dierdre declined the offer to relax on a settee whilst she was waiting, feeling that once she sat down she would simply keel over and never get up. As it was she could not understand how her legs supported her body. They felt as if they were made of broken pieces of china insecurely glued together. The car came almost immediately. The driver, a middle-aged man, regarded Dierdre with some alarm.

And indeed she was an alarming sight. Her face was deathly pale, her eyes – dull and staring – were black ringed. Her damp clothes showed patches of mud and somewhere during the course of the evening she had lost a shoe. She was also (the cabbie could not help noticing) minus a handbag. This fact, combined with her bizarre appearance – he had already decided she was some sort of hippy – gave rise to the quite natural apprehension that his fare might not be forthcoming. Once reassured on this point he offered his arm, which she did not ignore as much as not seem to see, and they left the building together.

'Animals is extra,' he said when they reached the car.

'What?'

'He is yours, ain't he?' The man nodded at a small dog who had been patiently waiting outside the main doors and was now trotting alongside.

'Oh . . .' Dierdre hesitated, looking down at the creature. The gargantuan task of trying to explain her lack of comprehension as to his background, ownership and reasons for being there was quite beyond her. 'Yes.'

The roads were almost deserted and they covered the twelve miles to Causton in under twenty minutes. It was not until they drew up outside the Latimer that the large snag in Dierdre's plan became apparent. There was no sign of life. The building was dark, the policeman outside had gone. Dierdre stood on the pavement, having realized that not only were her house keys in her bag. So also were her keys to the Latimer.

The cabby, all his suspicions reawakened, tooted his horn. Dierdre moved towards the theatre, noticing as she did so a tall gangling scarecrow of a figure with wild spiralling hair suddenly reflected in the glass. She pushed on one of the doors. It didn't move. She leaned on it then with both hands, more for support than anything else, and felt it shift slightly. Then she pushed with all her might. It was like trying to roll a giant boulder up a hill. Dierdre stepped into the darkened foyer. Surely, she thought, there must be someone still here or why would the door be unlocked? Perhaps, with all the kerfuffle (light years ago it now seemed) they'd just been forgotten. At least she would be able to get her bag. She regarded the dim outline of the steps leading, like a cliff face, to the auditorium and the immense reaches of carpet to be covered before she could start to climb.

She took the first step. And tottered two more. Then light flooded the foyer as the auditorium doors swung open and two figures emerged. Dazzled, Dierdre saw the still-moving doors fly slowly up into the air. The steps followed. Then she felt the sudden hard thud of the floor against the back of her head.

EXIT, PURSUED BY A BEAR

The Barnabys were at breakfast. Cully was enjoying some fresh pineapple and Greek yogurt. Barnaby was squaring up to the wobbly challenge of a half cooked egg and Joyce was putting two sprigs of *Viburnum bodnantense* in a glass vase on a tray.

'I bet,' said Cully, 'absolutely everybody who was in the theatre yesterday will be chewing over the drama with their bacon and egg.' They had been doing so themselves until a moment ago when Cully had remarked that at least Harold couldn't complain about lack of verismo and been severely criticized for her insensitivity. But she soon returned to the subject. 'Do you think it's the merry widow in cahoots?'

'Possibly.'

'I bet it is. Like in film noir. *The Milkman Always Comes Twice.*'

'Don't be rude, Cully.'

'Alternatively,' said Barnaby, shaking out a tablet, 'it seems to be even-stevens on Dierdre.'

'Poor Dierdre,' said Joyce automatically. Then she tutted at her husband's pill-taking, which she insisted on regarding as an amusing affectation.

'You ought to stop saying that. Everybody ought.'

'What do you mean, dear?' asked her mother.

'This persistent attitude towards her as an object of pathos.'

'It's understandable,' argued Joyce. 'She's had a very sad life. You've had all the advantages. You should be kinder.'

'Since when does having all the advantages make you kind? You and Dad are sorry for her. That's awful – so patronizing. Pitying people isn't a kindness. It makes them supine. And those who seek it don't deserve respect.'

187

Barnaby looked at his bright beautiful clever daughter as she continued: 'Last time I was home Mum was going on about her losing some weight and getting contact lenses. I mean – it's so sentimental. The Cinderella bit. Dierdre's quite interesting and intelligent enough as she is. I should think she could wipe the floor with the lot of them at the Latimer, given half a chance. She's got a grasp of stage management that would put Cardinal Wolsey to shame.' She added, as her mother took down a jar of instant coffee, 'Don't give her that, for God's sake. It's going to be hard enough waking up this morning as it is. Give her one of my filters.'

Joyce took one of the Marks and Spencer individual coffee filters out of its box and set it on a cup. Cully always brought what she called protective rations home with her. One of the reasons her father looked forward to her visits so much. Now she said: 'Could I have the vegetable lasagne tonight? It's in the freezer.'

'I'm doing a *bouillabaisse*.'

'Oh Ma – don't be silly.'

'It's all in here.' Joyce indicated a book lying open near the breadboard. 'Very plainly explained. I'm sure I shall cope perfectly.'

Cully finished her pineapple, crossed to her mother and picked up the book. '*Floyd on Fish?* It's not like you to be seduced by the telly.'

'Oh, I didn't buy it. Harold gave it to me.'

'*Harold?*' said her husband. 'Harold wouldn't give you the fluff from his navel.'

'He didn't buy it either. It turned up at the theatre anonymously. *Toast* . . .'

Cully snatched the bread from the jaws of the toaster in the nick of time, saying: 'What a peculiar thing to give to a place that doesn't sell food.'

'I don't think it was for the theatre. It was addressed to him personally.'

'When did it arrive?' asked Barnaby.

'Ohh . . . I don't know . . .' Joyce put some butter in a saucer. 'Couple of weeks ago.' The coffee drip-dripped through the fine-meshed gauze, its fragrance mingling with the scent of the viburnum.

'Let's have a look.' Cully brought the book over, hissing 'Burn it' in Barnaby's ear as she put it close to the egg, which had now congealed almost to the stage where he might just feel able to put a little in his mouth. He opened the book. There was no inscription.

'Did it come through the post?'

'No. Pushed through the letter box. So Dierdre said.'

'Fancy.' Barnaby slipped the book in his pocket.

'Tom! What about the *bouillabaisse?*'

'A delight I fear we shall have to postpone, my love.' Barnaby got up. 'I'm off.'

As he left he heard his daughter say, 'Have you got the phone number of that boy who played Mozart?' and Joyce reply, 'Open the door, Cully.'

Joyce bore the tray upstairs, put it down outside the spare room and knocked gently.

Dierdre had slept and slept. Even now, hours after she had been helped to bed after drinking a hot rum and lemon toddy, she was barely conscious. Sometimes she heard a voice but very distantly, and occasionally chinking and chiming sounds that seemed to be part of a dream. She resisted wakefulness, already faintly aware that it was pregnant with such dismay that reaching it would make her long for oblivion again.

Joyce opened the door and crept in. She had already looked in twice and found the girl so deeply asleep she had not had the heart to disturb her.

When Tom had brought Dierdre home at two o'clock that morning she had been in a terrible state. Soaking wet and covered in mud, her face scratched and tear-stained. Joyce had taken her temperature and between them they had decided that she was simply distressed and exhausted and that there was no need to call out a doctor. Tom, when paying off the taxi, had discovered the starting point of Dierdre's journey and Joyce had already rung the hospital before breakfast, hoping to have some cheerful news with which to wake the girl. But they had been very cagey (always a bad sign) and, when she admitted she was not a close relative, simply said he was as well as could be expected.

Now she crossed to the side of the bed and watched consciousness wipe the look of sleepy confusion from Dierdre's face.

Once awake Dierdre sat up immediately and cried: 'I must go to the hospital.'

'I've rung them. And the gas office. I just said you were a bit off colour and wouldn't be coming in for a couple of days.'

'What did they say? The hospital?'

'He's doing . . . reasonably well. You can ring as soon as you've had breakfast. It's nothing too complicated.' Joyce laid the tray across Dierdre's knees. 'Just a little bit of toast and some coffee. Oh – and you're not to worry about your dog. He's being looked after at the station.'

'Joyce . . . you're so kind . . . you and Tom. I don't know what I would have done last night . . . if . . . if –'

'There, there.' Joyce took Dierdre's hand, thought the hell with being patronizing, and gave her a hug. 'We were very glad to have the chance to take care of you.'

'What lovely flowers . . . everything's so nice.' Dierdre lifted her cup. 'And delicious coffee.'

'You've Cully to thank for that. She didn't think the instant was good enough. The nightie too.'

'Oh.' Dierdre's face darkened. She looked down at her voluminous scarlet-flannelled arms. She had forgotten Cully was home. She had known the Barnabys' daughter since the child was nine years old and was well aware of Cully's opinion of the CADS, having heard it fruitily bruited during her early teens. Now she was acting at Cambridge no doubt she would be even more scathing. 'I don't think I can manage any toast.'

'Don't worry – you have only just woken up after all. But I expect you would like a bath?' Joyce had done no more previously than sponge Dierdre's face and hands whilst the girl had stood in front of the basin swaying like a zombie.

'. . . Please . . . I feel disgusting.'

'I've looked out some clothes for you. And some warm tights. I'm afraid my shoes'll be too small. But you could probably squeeze into my wellies.' Joyce got up. 'I'll go and run your bath.'

'Thank you. Oh, Joyce – did they find out after I'd gone . . . the police I mean . . . who had . . . ?' Joyce shook her head. 'I still can't believe it.' Dierdre's face quivered. 'What a terrible night. I'll never forget it as long as I live.'

'I don't think anyone of us will,' replied Joyce. 'You might like to ring the hospital while you're waiting for your bath. I've left the number by the phone.'

After Joyce had gone Dierdre found her glasses, put them on and sat on the edge of the bed staring into the dressing table mirror. Cully's gown billowed around her like a scarlet parachute. It was the red of wounds and freshly killed meat. Hearing the water start to gush reminded Dierdre of the reservoir. She gripped the edge of the bed. In her mind the two images juxtaposed: Esslyn's throat gaped anew. Blood came – a trickle, a stream, a torrent, pouring into the reservoir, turning the water crimson. Her father fell again from his boat, disappeared and surfaced, his face shining, incarnadined. He did this over and over like a mechanical doll. Oh God, thought Dierdre, I'm going to see those two things for the rest of my life. Every time I stop being busy. Every time I close my eyes. Every time I try to sleep. For the rest of my life. Futilely she covered her eyes with her hands.

'Hi.' Dierdre jumped up. Cully stood in the doorway, elver-slim, an eel in blue jeans. She also wore a T shirt enscribed '*Merde! J'ai oublié d'éteindre le gaz!*' 'You look much nicer than I ever did in that thing, Dierdre. Do keep it.'

That's a dig at my size if ever I heard one, observed Dierdre to herself. She replied primly, 'No thank you. I have several pairs of pyjamas at home.' Then she thought, what if Cully was simply trying to be kind? How brusque and ungrateful I must sound.

191

'OK.' Cully smiled, unoffended. She had perfect teeth, even and brilliantly white like a film star's. Dierdre had read once that very white teeth were chalky and crumbled easily. It seemed a small price to pay. 'I just came to say that I got some super bath oil for my birthday from France. Celandine and Marshmallow – and it's on the bathroom window sill. Use lots – it really makes you feel nice.' Cully turned to go, turned back and hesitated.

'Terrible business last night. I'm so sorry. About your father, I mean.'

'He'll be all right,' said Dierdre quickly.

'I'm sure he will. I just wanted to say.'

'Thank you.'

'Not sorry about Esslyn, though. He was an outbreak of rabies and no mistake. If I were queen I'd order dancing in the streets.'

When Cully had gone Dierdre rang the hospital and was told that her father was resting, that he was being seen that afternoon by a specialist and they would prefer her not to visit until the following day. On receiving the assurance that he would be told she had rung and given her love, Dierdre made her way to the bathroom, rather guiltily relieved that she had a whole day to rest and recover before the stress of a visit.

She measured out a careful thimbleful of Essence de Guimauve et Chélidoine, tipped it in then stepped into the faintly scented water. Then, as she lay back letting go, floating away, sliding away, vanishing, her mind emptied itself of ghastly memories and a new idea gradually, timidly drifted to the surface. It was an idea too appalling really to be given house room yet Dierdre, tensing a little with not unpleasurable alarm, braced herself to consider it.

Cully's intemperate phrases when referring to the previous night's disaster had shocked Dierdre deeply. She had been brought up to believe that you never spoke ill of the dead. As a child she had assumed that this was because, given half a chance, the dead would come back and savage you. Later she modified this apprehension to include the understanding that a) if you only said nice things about them they might put in a good word for you when your turn came and b) it just wasn't honourable to attack people who couldn't answer back.

Now, hesitant and half fearful, she prepared to examine – even acknowledge – an emotion she had always prayed would be for ever absent from her heart. She recalled Esslyn's behaviour to his fellow actors. His condescension and spite; his indifference to their feelings, his impregnable self-esteem and swaggering coxcombry. His laughter and sneers against her father. Holding her breath, lying rigidly fists clenched in the perfumed bath, Dierdre faced, more or less boldly, a terrible new perception about herself. She had *hated* Esslyn. Yes. Hated him. And, even worse, *she was glad that he was dead*.

White faced she opened her eyes and stared at the ceiling. Waiting for a sign of God's displeasure. For the thunderbolt. When told as a child that every time she told a lie he got one out and it was only his all-forgiving love that stopped him firing it off pretty smartish, she had tried to picture this celestial weapon of retribution but all her young mind could come up with was the bolt on the kitchen door magnified a thousand times and painted shining bronze. Nothing even remotely similar crashed punitively through the Barnabys' bathroom ceiling.

At the recognition that it never would and that she could be glad without fear of divine retribution that Esslyn was no longer in a position to cause anyone pain or distress, a tremendous wave of something far too powerful to be called relief broke over Dierdre. She lay dazed, still faintly incredulous at this new truth. She felt as if someone had removed a great yoke from her shoulders or heavy chains from her legs and feet. Any minute now she might drift up to the unriven ceiling. She felt weak but far from helpless. She felt weak in the way the strong must sometimes do. Not chronically but accepting the need of occasional rest and refreshment. She wished now she had eaten her toast.

After a few somnolent minutes more she turned on the

hot tap and reached for the Celandine and Marshmallow elixir. If a thimbleful had this effect, reasoned Dierdre, what could half a cupful do?

Barnaby, having perused his scenes-of-crime reports and witnesses' statements, sat gazing at his office wall, lips pursed, gaze vacant, to a casual observer miles away. Troy, having seen all this before, was not deceived. The sergeant sat on one of the visitors' chairs (chrome tubes and tweed cushions) and stared out of the window at the dark rain bouncing off the panes.

He was dying for a ciggie but did not need the restraint of the NO SMOKING sign on the back of the door to stop him lighting up. He was used to being closeted all day with a clean-air freak. What really bugged him was that the DCI had been a fifty-a-day high-tar merchant in his time. Reformed smokers (like reformed sinners) were the worst. Not content, thought Troy, with the shining perfection of their own lives they were determined to sort out the unregenerate. And with no thought at all as to the possible side effects of their actions. When Troy thought of all that fresh cold air rushing into poor little lungs denied their protective coating of nicotine he positively trembled. Pneumonia at the very least must be waiting round the corner. He insured himself against this eventuality by lighting up in the outer office, in the toilet and anywhere at all the second his chief was off the premises. As a sop to all the haranguing he had changed from Capstan to Benson's Silk Cut, flirting with Gitane Caporal along the way. He admired the idea of a French cigarette more than the things themselves and when Maureen had told him they stank like a polecat on the razzle he had not been sorry to give them up.

Troy had read through the statements but not the scene-of-crime reports. He had also been present an hour ago when the Smys were interviewed. David had arrived first and stated, in an even and unflurried manner, that he had not removed the tape from the razor nor seen anyone else do so. His father had said the same but much less calmly. He had blushed and blustered and stared all over the place. This did not mean that he was culpable. Troy was aware that many innocent people, finding themselves being formally questioned in a police station, become overwhelmed by feelings of quite unfounded guilt. Still . . . Smy senior had been in a state. Troy became aware that Barnaby was making a vague rumbling sound. He gathered his wits about him.

'That last word, sergeant . . .'

'Sir.'

'Bungled . . . Odd, wouldn't you say?'

'Yes. I've been thinking about that.' Troy waited politely for a nod of encouragement, then continued, 'Was someone supposed to do something and they bungled? And was the throat-cutting the result? Or was it Carmichael who bungled? I mean – I assume he was doing what he should have been doing? What he did when they all . . . practised?'

'Rehearsed. Yes. Everyone seems to agree the last scene ran as usual . . .'

'So what could the bungle have been? I did wonder actually if he took the tape off himself –'

'No. He was the last person to commit suicide.'

'– What I meant is if he took it off for some cockeyed reason of his own. Maybe to get someone into trouble. Then, in the heat of the moment – acting away with all that music and everything – just forgot. Maybe he was trying to say "I've bungled".'

'A bit unlikely.' Troy looked so crestfallen that Barnaby added, 'I haven't come up with anything either. But he struggled to tell us something with his dying breath. It must have a point. And a very important one, I'd say. We'll just have to poke away at it. This' – he slapped his scene-of-crimes report sheets – 'has one or two surprises. For a start the razor, supposedly checked by Dierdre and further handled by Sweeney whoever it was, only has one set of prints. We'll check it out of course but they must be those of the murdered man. We all saw him pick it up and use it. Now – as Dierdre would have no reason for wiping her own off –'

'Unless, sir, she could see we'd think that. And wiped them for that reason?'

'I doubt it.' Barnaby shook his head. 'That argues a degree of cunning that I just don't think Dierdre has. And I've known her for ten years. Apart from anything else she has very strict ideas of right and wrong. Quite old-fashioned for someone her age.'

'Well – that still leaves us plenty to play with.'

Barnaby was not so sure. In spite of the large amount of people milling around both on and off the set he believed the razor renovator would be found within the handful of people intimately known to the dead man. He thought it highly unlikely, for instance, that an evil prankster would be discovered amongst the youthful ASMs although he had their statements on file should he wish to follow up the idea. Nor did he feel he was in with much of a chance with the small-part actors, three of whom had no previous knowledge of the dead man, having only joined the company for *Amadeus*. Although keeping an open mind on both these available options Barnaby actually chose to cleave tightly to his core of hard-line suspects. Chief of whom, he surmised aloud, must be the widow.

'An armful of spontaneous combustion there, sir.'

'So they say.'

'And I wouldn't be surprised if the current bun might not be the husband's. Women are a faithless lot.' Troy spoke with some bitterness. He had been laying none too subtle siege to Policewoman Brierley for about two years, only to see her fall the previous week to a new recruit, hardly out of his rompers before he was into hers. 'And as for these actors – well . . . you just don't know where you stand.'

'Can you expand that a bit?'

'The thing is,' Troy continued, 'when you usually talk to suspects they either tell you the truth or, if they've got something to hide, they tell you lies. And on the whole you know what you're dealing with. But this lot . . . they're all exaggerating and swanking and displaying themselves. I mean – look at that woman he used to be married to. Getting her to answer questions was like watching Joan of Arc going to the stake. Almost impossible to know what she really felt.'

'You think she wasn't genuinely distressed?'

'I just couldn't decide. I'm damn glad you knew them all beforehand.'

'Just because someone displays an emotion in the most effective or even stylish manner of which they're capable doesn't mean it isn't genuine. Remember that.'

'Right, chief.'

'And in any case, with the exception of Joyce and Nicholas, you should be able to see through them. They're all dreadful actors.'

'Oh.' Troy kept his counsel. Actually he had thought the show was rather good. His disappointment had been in looking at the scenery close to. All old stuff cobbled together, painted over and held up by what looked like old clothes props. Marvellous what a bit of illumination could do. Which reminded him. 'I take it Doris and Daphne are definitely out, sir? Airy and fairy in the lighting box?'

'I'm inclined to think so. Apart from the fact there's no discernible motive, they were in the wings and dressing rooms so briefly – as these statements from the actors confirm' – he tapped the pile of forms with his hand – 'and also so near to the first curtain that there would simply have been no time for tinkering. The same goes for Harold. I happened to arrive at the theatre when he and his wife did. He hung up his coat and started swanning around in the foyer doing his Ziegfeld number. He was there when Cully and I went to wish the cast good-luck –'

'Beautiful girl that, chief. Fantastic.'

' – And came down himself a minute or two later. And we all left virtually at the same time to take our seats.'

'He didn't slip into the bog?' Barnaby shook his head.

'What about the interval?'

'Same problem with time, really. He was up in the clubroom for a bit then went backstage to give them hell for lack of verismo, so my wife says. Then went back to his seat with the rest of the audience. And anyway, not only did Harold have no discernible motive for wanting Esslyn out of the way, he had very positive reasons for wanting him to stay alive. He was the only person in the group who could tackle leading roles in a moderately competent manner. He was doing Uncle Vanya next.'

'Who's he, sir, when he's buying a round?'

'It's a Russian play.'

Troy's nod was distant. It seemed to him that you could go on for a very long time indeed before you ran out of decent English plays without putting on foreign rubbish. And communist rubbish at that. He tuned back into the chief inspector's gist.

'. . . I think the next thing is to give Carmichael's house the once-over. There might be something in his effects that will give us a lead. Organize some transport, will you? I'll sort out a warrant.'

Rosa had a plan. She had not revealed it to Ernest despite the fact that, if the plan came off, his life would never be the same again. Time enough to spring it on him if it proved to be workable. Really it all hinged on whether Rosa had read Kitty's character correctly. And Rosa was sure she had. Kitty had always struck her as a vapid silly little thing, frankly on the make. A good-time girl. Now she was free, rich (unless Esslyn had been singularly spiteful in drawing up his will) and still only nineteen. What on earth, reasoned Rosa, would someone in that position want with a child?

Kitty had been in the company for two years. Never during this time had she been heard to express the slightest interest in children. Dressing room conversation, when touching on family matters, produced only yawns. Various offspring of CADS members backstage from time to time hardly merited a glance, let alone a kindly word.

So, given this lack of interest, Rosa, like the majority of people at the Latimer, assumed that Kitty had got herself deliberately pregnant to ensnare Esslyn. Now that he was so conveniently despatched, surely the means of ensnarement would be nothing but a hindrance? Of course there were those with no concern for other people's children who still, when their own arrived, found them a never-ending source of wonder and delight, but Rosa believed (or had persuaded herself to the belief), that Kitty was not of that number. And it was this persuasion that had instigated her grand design.

Since Esslyn's death Rosa had been whirling around in a veritable hodgepodge of emotions and troubled thoughts. Beneath her affected public manner she was increasingly aware of an aching pulse of sorrow. She recalled constantly the early days of her marriage and mourned the passing of what she now believed to be a tender and passionate love. And, as she dwelt on those happier days, it was as if her imagination, newly refurbished by the recent tragedy, wiped out in one blessed amnesiac stroke the years of disillusionment, leaving her with a wholesome if slightly inaccurate picture of Esslyn as sensitive, benevolent and quite unspoiled.

It was this sentimental sleight of memory that had led her first to covet Kitty's baby. A child, Esslyn's child, alive and growing in his wife's womb, would transform her (Rosa's) barren life, making it fresh and green again. Over the past two days the idea of adoption had flickered through her mind, returned, settled, taken root and flowered with such intensity that she had now reached the point where she was practically regarding it as a *fait accompli*.

Until she picked up the telephone. Then her previous sanguinity was swamped by a flood of doubts. Prominent among these was the idea that Kitty might decide to have an abortion. Having dialled the first three digits of White Wings, Rosa replaced the receiver and pondered this alarming notion. Common sense forced her to admit that it must appear to Kitty the obvious solution. And she would have the money to go privately, so there would be no hold-ups. The whole thing would be simplicity itself. In and out: problem solved. The baby, vulnerable as an egg shell, all gone. She might even now be making the arrangements! Rosa snatched up the receiver again and re-dialled. When Kitty answered Rosa asked if she might call in for a chat and Kitty, as laconic as if such a request was an everyday occurrence, said: 'Sure. Come when you like.'

Backing the Panda out of the garage and crashing the gears with nervousness, Rosa struggled to plan out the strategy which would shape the argument she would have to present to Kitty. If it was going to be successful she must look at the whole situation from the younger girl's point of view. Why, Kitty might well and understandably ask, should she lumber around for the next few months, getting heavier and heavier, less and less able to circulate and enjoy life, then go through the lengthy and perhaps extremely painful ordeal of giving birth only to hand over the result of all this travail to another woman? What (Rosa could just see her sharp, calculating little eyes scanning the odds) was in it for her?

During the ten-minute drive over to White Wings Rosa made herself answer that question to what she hoped would be Kitty's satisfaction. First she would point out the psychological as well as the physical damage which might result from an abortion. Then she would ask Kitty if she had thought of the expense involved in rearing a child. A child cost thousands. They weren't off your hands until they were eighteen and even then, if Ernest's sister's complaints were anything to go by, you had to cough up for three more years while they went to university. 'But you will have none of that financial burden,' Rosa heard herself saying, 'I will take care of everything.'

On the other hand, once the adoption was legally formalized, she would make it clear that Kitty could continue to see the child whenever she wished. Surely, Rosa thought as she drove, far too fast, down Carradine Street the triple thrust of her argument (huge savings, no responsibility, ease of access) must win the day. She had already forgotten her previous assumption – that Kitty's maternal instinct was minus nil – which made immediate nonsense of prong number three.

And, as things turned out, none of the previous dialectic was of use anyway. Because at the moment of pressing the bell at the house and hearing it jangle in that so familiar way in the sitting room, all Rosa's careful reasoning evaporated and she was left, trembling with the urgency of her appeal, on the doorstep. And when Kitty opened the door and said 'Hi' and clicked back to the kitchen in her feathered mules Rosa followed, mouth desert dry and floundering with uncertainty.

The kitchen was just the same. This was both a surprise and a comfort. She had been sure that Esslyn must have changed things around. That Kitty must have wanted new furniture, wallpaper, tiles. Apparently not. Rosa looked at the eggy, fat-smeared plate and the frying pan on the hob and noted the lingering fragrance of the full English breakfast. All this grease couldn't be doing the baby much good, she thought proprietorially. Which brought her back to her reasons for being there. As Kitty removed a butter dish, its contents liberally garnished with burnt toast crumbs and smears of marmalade, Rosa reviewed the situation.

Momentarily she wondered if she should throw herself on Kitty's mercy. Reveal how she'd always longed for a child and that this might be her last chance. Almost immediately this idea was rejected. Kitty would just give the thumbs down. She would enjoy that. Seeing Rosa on her bed of nails. The thing to do – why hadn't she thought of it before? – was to offer money. Rosa had five thousand pounds in the bank and some jewellery she could sell. That was the way. Not to let Kitty see that she was desperate but to remain calm, even casual. Just to slip the subject almost light-heartedly into the conversation. Won't be much fun coping with a child by yourself. Or, I expect you feel differently about having a baby now that Esslyn's gone. Kitty removed more crumbs from the table by the simple expedient of sweeping them on to the floor with the sleeve of her negligee, and asked Rosa to take the weight off her feet.

As soon as she did so Rosa felt the move was a mistake. She felt uneasy and at a disadvantage. Kitty put the frying pan on top of the dishes already in the sink and turned on the hot tap. The water hit the handle of the pan and sprayed upwards and all over the tiles. Over her shoulder Kitty said: 'And how's dear old Ernest?'

She always referred to Ernest in this manner, as if he was a shambling family pet on the verge of extinction. An ancient sheepdog perhaps. Or elderly spaniel with rapidly stiffening joints. The point of such remarks, Rosa knew, had always been to force a comparison between her husband and Kitty's, the man Rosa had loved and lost. Normally it evoked a response of irritation shot through with bitterness. Now, noticing these dual emotions twitching into life, Rosa made a determined effort to repress them. Apart from not wishing to give Kitty the satisfaction of knowing she'd drawn blood, any feelings of antagonism would assuredly work against a successful outcome to the mission. And, Rosa comforted herself, whatever Ernest's shortcomings in the youth and glamour stakes, he did have the undeniable advantage of still being alive. That should give him some sort of edge if nothing else.

She settled back a little more easily in her chair. Outside, the waxen dark green leaves and scarlet berries of a cotoneaster framed the kitchen window through which the winter sun streamed, further gilding Kitty's already extremely honeyed curls. It was intensely hot. The central heating was full on as was the Aga, and Rosa sweltered in her heavy cape. Kitty was wearing a shortie cream satin nightie styled like a toga, slit almost to the waist on one side and a spotted blue chiffon cover-up with little knots of silver ribbons. And not a knicker leg in sight, observed Rosa sourly. And her stomach still almost as flat as a pancake. She noticed with some satisfaction that, without her armoury of blushers and shaders and pencils and lipsticks, Kitty's face looked almost plain.

Kitty dried her hands on the tea cloth and, leaning against the bar of the Aga for extra warmth, turned to face her visitor. She had no intention of offering coffee or tea. Nor any other form of sustenance. Kitty did not go in for female friendships at the best of times and certainly not with women old enough to be her mother and with a hefty axe to grind. Now, watching Rosa's greasy, large-pored nose which seemed to Kitty to be positively quivering under the urge to poke itself into matters which were none of its business, she braced herself against what she was sure would be a great slobbery wash of false sympathy and sickly reminiscence.

Rosa took a deep breath and shuddered under her heather-mixture bivouac. She felt immobilized by the complexity of her thoughts. She saw now that she should have blurted out the reason for her visit, no matter in what garbled and emotional form, the minute she entered the house. The longer she sat in the untidy, homely kitchen (only a high chair needed to complete the picture) the more bizarre did her request appear. And Kitty was no help. She had made no welcoming gesture; not even the one regarded as virtually mandatory in any English home when a visitor calls. Realizing she had missed the boat on the instant clarification front, Rosa had just decided to approach the subject snakily, starting with a formal expression of sympathy, when Kitty spoke.

'What's on your mind, then?'

Rosa took a huge lungful of air and, not daring to look at Kitty, said: 'I was thinking now that Esslyn's dead maybe you wouldn't feel able to keep the baby and was wondering if I could adopt it.'

Silence. Timidly Rosa looked up. As she did so Kitty lowered her head and covered her face with her hands. She made a small sound, a little plaintive moan, and her shoulders trembled. At this Rosa, who was basically a kind-hearted person, experienced a spontaneous welling up of sympathy. How callous, how imperceptive she had been to assume that, just because Kitty made no public display of sorrow, she was unmoved by the shocking fact and manner of her husband's death. Now, observing the thin shoulders shaking in despair, Rosa pushed her chair back and, awkwardly holding out her arms, made a tentative somewhat clumsy move to comfort the sobbing figure. But Kitty shook off such consolation and crossed to the open door where, her back to Rosa, she started to make terrible jackdaw squawks and cries.

Rooted to the spot, impotent, distressed and self-castigating, Rosa could only wait, her hands held beseechingly palms upward, continuing to offer solace should it be eventually required. At last the dreadful noises stopped and Kitty turned, her face puffy and red, traces of tears on her cheeks, her shoulders still feebly vibrating. And it was then Rosa realized, with a tremendous shock of outrage and indignation, that Kitty had been *laughing*.

Now, shaking her head, apparently with disbelief at the pricelessness of the situation, Kitty pulled a crumpled tissue from the pocket of her negligee, mopped her streaming eyes and dropped it on the floor. Her shoulders finally at rest and her breathing quietened, she stared across at Rosa and Rosa, still mortified but starting to get healthily angry, stared back.

Everything became very still. And quiet. A tap dripped making a dull, soft spreading sound. Already, only seconds into this embarrassing and faintly ridiculous confrontation, it was getting on Rosa's nerves. She stood (she would have said stood her ground) and could think of nothing to say. In any case she felt it was not up to her to speak. She had described why she was there and invoked in Kitty an explosion of grotesque mirth. Now it was up to Kitty to either explain her behaviour or bring the interview to an end.

Rosa forced herself to meet that deep sapphire gaze. No merriment there. Indeed, now she came to think of it, there had not been much humour in those raucous hoots in the first place. They had been run through with an almost . . . almost *crowing* aggression. Yes! that was it. There had been triumph in those sounds. As if Kitty, with the battle lines hardly sketched out, was already victorious. But why was she crowing? Probably, thought Rosa with a stab of humiliation, about the fact that she had Esslyn's first wife in a begging position. What a tale that would make to pass around the dressing rooms. Rosa could just hear it. 'You'll never guess. Poor old Mrs Ern came round the other day wanting to bring up the baby. Talk about an absolute scream. Left it too late to have any of her own. Silly old fool.'

Ah well, observed Rosa, she'd brought it on herself. Imagining Kitty's phantom gibes made her now wonder how she had ever entertained the ridiculous misbegotten idea of adoption for a minute, never mind letting herself get to the stage where she'd actually visited the house and put the question. What in the world, queried Rosa, now devil's advocate, did she want with a child at her time of life? And dear Ernest, who had brought up three and, whilst doting on his grandchildren, found a half hour a week romp and dandle with each a contact of ample sufficiency. How would he have coped? But there was no point in railing, she thought doughtily. What was done was done. Now the only course open was to withdraw with as much dignity as she could muster. And she was about to do just that when Kitty closed the door.

The click sounded very loud. And rather final. Having shut the door Kitty didn't move away but leaned back against it in what seemed to Rosa a rather threatening manner. And then she smiled. It was a terrible smile. Her narrow top lip with its exaggerated lascivious arch did not spread sideways. It lifted in the manner of an unfriendly animal revealing pointed sharp incisors. The light glinted on them. They looked dangerously sharp and bright. Then she stopped smiling and that was worse. Because Rosa, distracted briefly by the sight of those alarming pale fangs, made the mistake of looking into Kitty's eyes. Brilliant azure ice. Inhuman. Suddenly the air in the room was thick and fearful. And Rosa knew. She knew that all the joshings and suppositions and half-serious theories bandied about in the clubroom were no more than simple facts. And that Kitty had truly got rid of her husband for his money and her freedom. And that she, Rosa, was now alone with a murderess.

Rosa realized she had been holding her breath and let it out now with great care, as if the gentle purling might snatch Kitty's attention and activate some quiescent impulse to destroy. Rosa tried to think but all her cerebral processes seemed to have ground to a halt. She tried to move as well and found to her horror that, far from simply standing on the floor as she had supposed, she seemed to be rooted in it like a tree. Her heart thudded and the drop of water plashed and spread. And it seemed to Rosa that the long long space between one splash of water and the next and one thud of her heart and the next was alive with the pulsating obscene hum of evil.

What could she do? First look away. Look away from those guileless cruel eyes. Then have a go at tautening her sagging mental faculties. If only she had told someone – anyone – that she was going to White Wings. But then, thought Rosa sluggishly, ticking over again at last, Kitty didn't know that. Bluff! That was the thing. She would bluff her way out. She would say that she had told Ernest where she was coming and that he was driving over to pick her up any minute now. Quaveringly she got the information across.

'But Rosa – how can he be? The car's out there in the drive.'

Oh but she was cunning! All that was in her voice was simple puzzlement. Rosa joined Barnaby in wondering how the hell they had all come to believe that Kitty couldn't act. Well, that was bluff down the sluice. What next? Kitty moved away from the door and Rosa's brain, now miraculously freed from its former coagulate state, leapt into protective action feeding dozens of combative images across the screen of her mind.

She floored Kitty with a kung fu kick or a straight upper cut. She pressed her to the ground and held a knife to her throat. With one immaculate Frisbee spin of a plate she stunned her into insensibility. As the last of these comforting pictures faded she realized that Kitty was slowly walking towards her.

Oh God, prayed Rosa. Help me . . . *please*.

She felt huge and stifled, hippo sluggish in the heat. Runnels of sweat ran over her scalp and down between her breasts yet her upper lip and forehead prickled with chill and her blood felt thick and unmoving. She stared at Kitty, young, Amazonian, slim as a whip with strong sinewy arms and legs, and thought again – what chance will I have?

Kitty was smiling as she came on. Not her genuine weaselly smile but a false one, painted on her lips. A simulacrum of concern. So might she have smiled at Esslyn, thought Rosa, as she wished him luck on the first night before unsheathing the means of his destruction. And then, recalling her first husband, she had a sudden vivid impression of Ernest arriving home as he would be just now and wanting his lunch. At the thought of never seeing his dear face again Rosa felt her blood stir and start to flow. Anger chased out fear. She went up on the balls of her feet (now miraculously unstuck) and felt her calf muscles tense. She would not go down without a fight.

Kitty was barely a foot away. It was now or never. Rosa hooded her eyes in what she hoped was a menacing fashion. And sprang.

Colin Smy sat alone in his workshop. He was cold but could not be bothered to light the heater. He held a smooth blond piece of maple in his hands but the beauty and grain of the wood, once a certain stimulus to feelings of the deepest contentment and an amulet against despair, this morning had lost the power to move. Next to him was a cedarwood cradle commissioned by a neighbour. Only two days ago he had been delicately chiselling a border of leaves and flowers around the name BEN. He pushed the cradle with his finger and it rocked on its bed of fragrant rust-coloured shavings. He got up then and moved a little stiffly around the room, touching and stroking various artefacts, pressing the outlines hungrily and devouring the detail of line and marking as a man might who was on the point of going blind.

Colin picked up his chisel. The varnish on the handle had long since worn away and it fitted the palm of his hand to such perfection that the word familiar was totally inadequate to describe the sensation. Colin always felt vaguely ill at ease away from his workshop and the beloved tools of his trade. Now, believing that it might be months or even years before he saw or touched any of them again, he felt a great, gaping prescient sense of loss.

He stilled the cradle and stood looking round for a moment more. Although his emotions were chaotic his thoughts were crystal clear. Paramount was the vow he had made to Glenda when she lay dying. 'Promise me,' she had cried, over and over again, 'that you will look after David.' And he had reassured her, over and over again. Almost her last words (before 'such a short while' and 'goodbye, my darling') were, 'you won't let any harm come to him?'

Colin had kept his promise. Since her death David had been his world. He had given up everything, and gladly, for the boy. His welding job had been the first to go. So that he could take David to and from school and be available at the weekends and holidays, Colin had taken up freelance woodwork and carpentry, at first with scant success. In material terms they'd had very little but they had each other and Colin had been overwhelmed with pride when his son had shown a talent far surpassing his own for carving. Two of David's sculptures stood now on his workbench. A grave old man, a sower of seed, a shallow basket in the crook of his arm; and a kneeling heifer, a present for Ben, most tenderly carved, its head bowed, the horns tipped at such an eloquent angle.

After Glenda had left them Colin put thoughts of remarriage aside. At first, grieving for his wife, this had not been difficult. Later, when occasionally meeting women he might normally have been tempted to pursue, the thought that they might not love David as he deserved or, worse, come to resent him had stopped the chase before it started. But now David was grown up and had even brought home one or two girls of his own, but the affairs had petered out and Colin had been glad at the time. The girls had seemed a touch over-confident (one of them was almost domineering) for David. Now of course Colin wished to God his son had married one of them. But even then, he had to admit, if David had continued helping out at the Latimer, he would still have met Kitty.

Colin sat down again and held his aching head in his hands. When he had first heard the rumour about David and Esslyn's wife he had been unalarmed if a little disappointed in his son. But Kitty was an attractive young woman and, like everyone else in the company, Colin was not averse to the idea of Esslyn's eye being put out. But to think it could lead to this . . .

Last night, sick at heart, he had tried to talk to David but when it came to the sticking point he had lacked the courage to put his feelings of dread into plain words. Instead he had mumbled, 'Now she's free . . . I suppose . . . well . . . you'll be . . .'

'Yes dad.' David had spoken calmly. 'She's free. Although I wouldn't have wanted it to happen like this, of course.'

Colin had listened, struggling with feelings of amazed disbelief. That David could speak in such a manner. In such a detached *heartless* manner. David, who had never harmed a living thing. Who would carry spiders carefully out into the garden rather than kill them. Who, when he was ten and his hamster died, had wept for three days. When he added: 'I shall have to go very carefully at first . . .' Colin, not trusting himself to reply, had left the house and spent the ensuing hours walking round and round Causton trying desperately to come to some decision. Knowing what the right thing to do was, realizing simultaneously that he could never do it, and struggling to alight on an alternative course of action.

Because he must do something. He had experienced great alarm during his interview with Tom at the station on Tuesday morning. More alarm than David apparently who, when asked at one o'clock how it had all gone, had just said 'Fine' and continued with his dinner. Although Colin's time at the station had been short it had also been deeply disturbing. He had never thought of old Tom as being specially clever but the sharp piercing quality of the chief inspector's gaze – quite absent from their cosy sessions in the scene dock – had caused him to think again. Now, having got a glimpse of the measure of the man, Colin realized that Barnaby was a hunter. He would pursue; questioning, checking, re-checking, perceiving, concluding, closing in. And how well would David be able to stand up to that sort of treatment?

Before going back to work he had told his father that he had simply denied any knowledge of razor tampering and this had been accepted, but already Colin was seeing this supposed acceptance as a clever ploy. David was so guileless. He would not see that Barnaby was only pretending to believe him. That, even now, they were probably questioning Kitty. Making her admit complicity. And she would, too. She would tell them everything to get herself off the hook.

Colin snatched up his mac. One of the sleeves had got tangled and he almost growled with impatience as he tried to force his arm in. What the hell was he doing sitting here brooding, going round and round the situation while perhaps any minute . . .

He ran out, not even stopping to lock his shed, skidding on the icy pavement. He cursed his previous indecision. He had known hours ago; had known when he was walking the streets at three a.m. that there was only one course of action he could possibly take. Because of what he had sworn to Glenda all those years ago. ('You won't let any harm come to him? Promise me?') Oh! Why had he waited? Now Colin became convinced as he slid and skittered towards the police station, that he was already too late. That some time during the afternoon the police had fetched David from his place of work and were even now working on him, trying to break him down.

At last he hauled himself up the station steps, searing his hands on the freezing metal rail, and asked at the desk to see Detective Chief Inspector Barnaby. A pretty dark-haired policewoman told him that the inspector was out and showed him to a small room, acrid with stale cigarette smoke, where he could wait. Noticing his white face and trembling hands she asked if he would like to talk to anyone else. Then if he would like some tea. But Colin declined both these offers and was then left in peace studying an anti-theft poster and waiting to confess to the murder of Esslyn Carmichael.

'How the other half lives, eh, chief?' muttered Troy snidely as he drove up the graceful curve of the drive to White Wings and swanked into a semicircular pre-parking spin, throwing up several pounds of gravel in the process. Troy drove fast, skilfully and with care but could not resist the flourish of a zig-zag or curlicue when coming to a halt. Occasionally Barnaby felt it sensible to restrain this flamboyant behaviour and then Troy, with a piqued almost disconsolate air, would park with such funereal exactitude that it was all his superior could do to keep a straight face. This usually lasted a few days then exuber-ance gradually sneaked back in. Troy regarded this pzazz as part of his style. He was very hot on style and despised those dullards who didn't know a Cordobian reversal from an uphill start. Right now, feeling a lecture coming on, he snapped his belt and started to climb out before the chief could really get into the swing of it.

As he did so a piercing yell came from the house. Then a series of screams. Troy raced to the baronial front door, tried it, found it locked and pounded on it with his fists shouting: 'Open up! This is the police!' Barnaby had just joined him when a key was turned and the door swung inwards. Kitty stood in the opening in a pretty blue house-coat with the most extraordinary expression on her face. She looked in a state. A bit fearful, a bit angry but shift-ingly so, as if she didn't know whether to laugh or cry.

She stood in the centre of the hall patting her curls and pulling a mock-horrified face.

'What's wrong?' demanded Barnaby. 'Who was that screaming?'

'. . . Me actually . . .'

'Why?' An icy wind was blowing into the house. Troy shut the front door but the blast continued. Barnaby strode into the kitchen. The back door was wide open. 'Who else is here?'

'No one.' She tittuped across to the garden door and closed it. 'Brrr.'

'Whose car is that outside?'

'I'm going to make some coffee to calm my nerves. D'you want some?'

'Kitty.' Barnaby stopped her. 'What the devil's going on?'

'Well . . . you won't believe this, Tom, but I think I've found your murderer.'

'Perhaps I can make some coffee, Mrs Carmichael?' said Troy with his most winning smile. 'You sound as if you could do with some.'

'Oh how sweet.' Kitty's unpainted lips returned the smile. Troy noticed with an uprush of excitement that beneath the lusciously lipsticked Cupid's bow he had so admired the other evening was a real one. Just as luscious and twice as sexy. 'But I'd better do it,' she continued. 'It's all Eyetalian, the equipment . . . it might blow up in inexperienced hands.' Although her voice barely changed it managed to imply that she was sure Sergeant Troy's hands were anything but inexperienced and, given the opportunity, would be more than prepared to put her theory to the test. 'Shan't be a mo.'

'I assume you can talk, Kitty, while you're getting to grips with that contraption.'

'Course I can,' replied Kitty, juggling with water, coffee, twists of chrome and a couple of retorts. 'To put it in a nutshell Rosa just came round here and *attacked* me.'

'Just like that?' asked the chief inspector, shaking his

212

head at Troy who seemed quite prepared to hare off and make an instant arrest.

'Just like that.' She set the contraption on a low gas, clopped to the Aga and nestled against the rail. 'Warm me bottie. Otherwise I'll get goose bumps.' She pulled the blue wrapper very tight and at least two of the bumps leapt into prominence.

'Any idea why?'

'Jealousy. What else? She killed Esslyn because she couldn't bear to see him happy. Then she came round after me.'

'But they'd been divorced for over two years. Surely if she couldn't bear to see him happy she'd have done something about it before now.'

'Ahhh . . .' Kitty shook a cigarette out of a packet. Troy's nostrils twitched in anticipation. 'Before, there wasn't the baby.'

'Perhaps you'd better tell us from the beginning.'

'OK.' Kitty, having lit her cigarette and dragged deep, coughed and said: 'It's hard to credit, I know, but she had the bloody cheek to come round here and ask me when the baby was born if I'd hand it over to her and ancient Ernie.'

'And what did you say?'

'I didn't actually *say* anything. To tell you the truth it was so funny I had to laugh. And then once I started I couldn't stop. You know how you get . . .' She winked at Troy who, tormented enough already by the smoke from her Chesterfield, nearly collapsed under the extra strain.

'And why was it so funny?'

'Because there wasn't any baby.'

There was a pause whilst the apparatus gurgled and googled and backfired. Then Barnaby said: 'Can I just get this clear, Kitty. Are you saying that you've had a miscarriage? Or that there was never a child in the first place?'

'Never one in the first place.'

'And I assume Esslyn was not aware of this?'

'Do me a favour. D'you think he'd have married me if

213

he had been?' The smile was almost voluptuously satisfied. It said, 'Aren't I clever? Don't you wish you were as smart as me?'

Tricky little tart, thought Troy. He looked at Kitty, torn between admiration and resentment. He understood her class and stamp (he often picked up her less fortunate sisters round the bus station trying to turn a trick) without recognizing how close it was to his own. So her nerve and determination earned his grudging respect. On the other hand she had definitely made a monkey out of one of the superior sex and he couldn't go along with that. He couldn't go along with that at all.

'And what did you plan to do,' asked Barnaby, 'when your condition – or rather lack of one – became obvious?'

'Oh – I thought a tiny tumble down the step. Nothing too drastic. Poor little precious' – her sorrowful sigh went ill with her saucy grin – 'wouldn't have had a chance.'

'So your husband's death could hardly be more opportune.'

'Right.' Kitty poured the coffee into three opalescent beakers. 'Men on the job like lots of sugar, don't they? For energy?'

'None for me, thank you.'

Troy asked for two sugars and plenty of milk.

Barnaby accepted his drink and took a sip. In spite of the baroque extravagance of the Eyetalian ganglia the coffee was absolutely disgusting. Worse even than Joyce's and that was saying something. For some odd reason he found this rather a comfort. He was about to re-start the conversation at the point where it had broken off when Kitty did it for him.

'And when you discover who carried out the dirty deed I shall go and thank him personally.'

As Kitty drank her coffee she stared at Barnaby over the rim of her beaker. The stare was so sassy he wondered if she was aware of just how precarious her situation actually was. He returned the stare in a manner that made the weather outside seem positively summery. 'You've been seemingly very frank with us, Kitty. And

214

your refusal to pretend to any grief you do not feel does you credit. But if your belief that the world was well shot of your husband has given you any ideas about protecting his killer, or hindering our investigation in any way, I advise you to think again. Because you'll find yourself in very serious trouble.'

'I wouldn't do that, Tom,' said Kitty soberly, stubbing out her cigarette on top of the Aga. 'Honestly.'

'As long as we've got that straight. Now – to return to this business with Rosa. She'd asked for the baby, you'd had a fit of giggles. Then what happened?'

'It was really weird. There was a terrible draught from that door' – she nodded towards the hall – 'and me being only in my naughties and feeling the pinch I went over and closed it. Then when I turned round she was staring at me – her eyes were positively *bulging*. Then she started shaking. She looked as if she was going to have a fit. So I thought I'd get her some water . . . I didn't know what to do . . . I mean – it's not the sort of thing that happens to you every day, is it? So I went to the sink, which meant I had to cross the room and I was just in front of her when she jumped at me. I yelled and started to scream . . . and she ran away –'

'Just a minute. Was that when Sergeant Troy started banging on the door?'

'Is his name Troy? How romantic. No – that was the funny thing. She ran off the second I started shouting. Before we knew you were here at all.'

'It doesn't sound much like a serious attempt to do you harm.'

'That's a nice attitude for the police to take, I must say. I shall sue her for assault.'

'That's up to you, of course.'

'Actually – why are you here? With all the excitement I never asked.'

'We're continuing our inquiries, Kitty.'

'Ohhh Tom.' She smiled delightedly. 'Do you really say that? I thought it was just on the movies.' She crossed to the littered pine table and pulled out two wheelback chairs. 'Park yourselves then if you're stopping.'

The two men sat at the table and Kitty joined them. She sat quite close to Troy and he was aware that she had not yet bathed. She gave off a warm intimate faintly gamy scent redolent of night-time retreats and assignations.

'I'd like first to ask you, Kitty,' continued the chief inspector, 'if you noticed anything – anything at all in the weeks leading up to your husband's death that might assist us?'

'What sort of thing?'

'Did he talk of any plans? Any special difficulties? Problems with relationships?'

'Esslyn didn't have relationships. There was nothing of him to relate to.'

'What about a break in his usual routine?'

'Well . . . he did pop into the office on Saturday morning. Said he had to call . . . something in . . . and oh! Yes – his costume. He brought his costume home. I've never known him do that before.'

'Did he say why?'

'Didn't want to risk leaving it in the dressing room. He really fancied himself in that coat. Course in the play he starts off in a grotty old shawl and dressing gown then flings them off and ends up looking like the Queen of Sheba and we're all supposed to go "ooh" and "aaah". He tried the whole thing on on Saturday, prancing about looking in the glass. Practically hugging himself to death, he was. Then he said what a coo . . . coody . . . something . . .'

'*Coup de théâtre.*'

'. . . Yeah . . . whatever that is . . .'

'A staggering theatrical effect.'

'He made that all right,' giggled Kitty, then catching Barnaby's eye had the grace to blush. 'Sorry, Tom. Bad taste. Sorry.'

'Can I pin you down on this, Kitty? It may be

important. Can you remember precisely what it was he said?'

'No more than I've just told you.'

'What a *coup de théâtre* it'll be.'

'Yes.'

'You're sure by "it" he meant this transformation in act one?'

'Well . . . that's what he was talking about just before.'

Barnaby, watching Kitty closely, then said: 'Your husband did speak once before he died.' No flicker of fear there. No spark of alarm. Just straightforward curiosity. Damn, thought the chief inspector. And my favourite suspect too.

'What did he say?'

'My sergeant got the sound of the word "bungled". That mean anything to you?'

Kitty shook her head. 'Except . . .' Under Barnaby's look of encouragement she stumbled on. '. . . Well . . . that something had gone wrong. That's what bungled means, isn't it? And it had. For Esslyn anyway.'

'Perhaps his grand *coup de théâtre*.'

'No – that's at the beginning of the play. He pulled that off all right. This was right at the end.' Sharp little cookie, thought Troy, wincing as she shook out another fag and lit up. Catching his greedy eye she held out the pack.

'Not on duty, Mrs Carmichael, thank you.'

'Gosh. I thought that was just hard liquor and . . . er . . . what was the other?'

'I have a warrant with me, Kitty.' Barnaby got up abruptly. 'I'd like to look through Esslyn's effects before I go. Especially any correspondence and personal papers.'

'Help yourself. I'd better slip into something tight.' They followed her into the hall and she nodded towards a door on the left. 'That's his study. See you in two ticks.'

Troy watched her long tanned legs disappear up the thickly carpeted stairs. He thought she looked like a delectable slave girl in one of those telly comedies set in ancient Rome. Where all the birds pranced around in shortie nighties and the men had brushes growing out of their helmets. He wouldn't mind chasing her round the Forum. Whu-hoo.

'Forget it, Troy.'

'I'm off duty at seven, chief. Might find out something.'

'The only thing you'll find out is how to stunt your growth. Now come on – let's get cracking.'

They entered a small room sparsely furnished with a kneehole desk, bookshelves and a couple of armchairs. Troy said, 'What are we looking for?'

'Anything. Everything. Especially personal.'

No section of the desk was locked but the contents proved to be meagre and unexciting. Insurance. Documents for the BMW. Mortgage and a few bills. Bank statements which showed regular standing orders and moderate monthly transfers from a deposit account. Barnaby put these aside. There were also a couple of holiday brochures. They checked the shelves of books (all on accountancy apart from a set of Dickens which looked as if it had never been opened, let alone read) and shook them but no sinister letter or revealing *billet doux* fell out.

Esslyn's wardrobe and the rest of the house were equally unrevealing. By the time they were ready to leave, Kitty, in a black track suit, was racing away on her exercise cycle. She came down to the hall to see them out. She had brushed her hair and it lay like pale satin against her velvet shoulders.

'Beautiful house,' said Troy, putting a friendly smile in the bank for future use.

'Miles too big for little me,' replied Kitty, opening the front door. 'I'm putting it on the market tomorrow.'

'I should make sure it belongs to you first,' said Barnaby.

'What do you mean? Everything comes to me as next of kin.'

'A commonly held misconception, Kitty.' Then, looking at her suddenly frozen features, Barnaby patted her arm sympathetically. 'I'm sure Esslyn left things in order but

I'd pop into the solicitor if I were you. Just to make absolutely sure.'

He left then and his sergeant was about to follow when Kitty laid her hand on his sleeve.

'Funny you being called Troy, isn't it?'

'Why's that, Mrs Carmichael?' Even through the thickness of his overcoat he could feel the warmth of her fingers.

''Cause my second name's Helen,' she said with a wicked smile.

'Hold it . . . hold it.'

Barnaby stopped Colin on line one, asked for some tea and talked vague generalities until it turned up. He waited while Colin had dissolved his three sugars with a lot of active stirring, then pulled a pad and pencil towards him.

'Tea OK?'

'Ohhh . . . yes . . . thank you.' Colin had been in such a state waiting for the chief inspector that he hadn't really got much past picturing his own declaration of guilt. If he had he'd certainly have envisioned a slightly more excitable reception than he had received so far.

'What did you expect, Colin?' asked Barnaby. 'That I'd clap you in irons?'

Colin flushed. And felt a deep stab of alarm that the other man could read his mind so easily. He struggled to compose his expression. To set it in a mask of unconcern. 'Course not.' He swallowed nervously. 'I knew there'd be tea. Seen it all often enough on the box.'

'Ah yes. They only got bread and water before Z Cars.'

Colin felt he should laugh or at least crack a smile. There was a long pause. What were they waiting for? Colin scraped his throat nervously and drank some more tea. Perhaps this was the way it worked. How they broke people down. Ordeal by silence. But what was there to break down? He'd come in to make a confession, hadn't he? Why the hell couldn't he just get on with it? The continuing quiet stampeded him into speech.

'It's been preying on my mind, Tom –'

'Messing with the razor?'

'Yes. I felt I couldn't . . . um . . . live with myself so . . . I came to confess . . .'

'I see.' Barnaby nodded seriously but without, Colin noticed, writing anything on his pad. 'And why exactly did you do it?'

'Why?'

'Not an unreasonable question surely?'

'No . . . of course not.' *Why?* Oh God, Colin! You great fool. You haven't thought any further than the end of your bloody nose. 'Because . . . he was awful to David . . . sneering and laughing at him at rehearsals. Humiliating him. I . . . decided he should be taught a lesson.'

'Rather a savage lesson.'

'. . . Yes . . .'

'Disproportionately harsh, one might say.' Barnaby picked up his pen.

'I didn't expect –' Colin's voice strengthened. 'He was an absolute bastard to David.'

'He was an absolute bastard to everyone.' When Colin did not reply Barnaby continued: 'Well, what didn't you expect?'

'That he'd . . . die.'

'Oh come *on*, Colin. Why do you think there were two thicknesses of tape on the thing? What did you think would happen when they were removed and he dragged it across his throat? If you've got the guts to come and confess at least have the guts to admit you knew what you were doing.' Although Barnaby had hardly raised his voice at all it seemed to Colin to positively boom, bouncing off each wall in turn, belabouring his ear drums. 'So when did you take the tape off?'

'After Dierdre checked it.'

'Obviously. But when precisely?'

'Do you mean the time?'

'Of course I mean the time!'

'. . . Um . . . after she'd called the half, I think . . . yes. That's right. So between seven thirty and forty.'

'Bit dodgy, wasn't it? Must've been quite a few people about.'

220

'No. Dierdre had gone to collect her ASMs from upstairs. All the actors were still in their dressing rooms.'

'And where did you do it?'

'Pardon?'

'*Where?*'

'. . . Well . . . the scene dock.'

'You'd have to be quick. What did you use?'

'A Stanley knife.'

'The same one that was in the wings?'

Colin hesitated. Fingerprints, he thought. His should be all over the one in the wings but you never knew. 'No. I used my own.'

'Got it with you?'

'It's in my workshop.'

'And what did you do with the Sellotape?'

'Just . . . scrumpled it up.'

'And left it there?'

'Yes.'

'So if we went over now you could produce it?'

'No! Afterwards . . . when I realized how terrible everything was . . . I threw it away. Down the bog.'

Barnaby said, 'I see,' and nodded. Then he leaned back in his chair and gazed out of the window at the black and grey scudding clouds. Colin leaned back a little too. His breathing returned to near normal; his heart stopped thundering. That hadn't been too bad. All he had to do now was remember precisely what it was he'd said (for Barnaby's pad now seemed to be quite covered with lines and squiggles) and stick to it. And that shouldn't be too difficult.

Colin glanced at the clock. To his amazement barely ten minutes had passed since he had entered the room. The delusion that he had been shut up here blabbing away for hours must be simply down to stretched nerves. Barnaby drained his tea, 'Some more, Colin?' When the other man declined, Barnaby said: 'I think I will,' and disappeared.

Left alone Colin gathered his wits. He was bound to be asked all the foregoing questions again and probably

221

many more (although he could not imagine what they might be), but now he had got the time, method and motive firmly tethered he felt a lot more confident. After all, those were the basics. The crucial underpinnings to the case. And no one could prove that he wasn't telling the truth. He would stand up in court and swear. He would swear the rest of his life away if need be.

Barnaby was a long time. Colin wondered why he hadn't just pressed the buzzer as he had before if he wanted more tea. Colin inclined his ear towards the door but he could hear nothing but the distant rattle of a typewriter. Perhaps Barnaby was finding someone to take down a proper statement. Colin listened again then, hearing no approaching footsteps, leaned over the desk and turned the chief inspector's pad around. It was covered with beautifully drawn flowers. Harebells and primroses. And ferns.

Alarmed, Colin slumped back in his seat. Tom had not written down a single thing! Following this realization came another more terrible. The only reason for this must be that Tom had not believed a word that he, Colin, had said. He had been sitting there, nodding, scribbling, asking questions and all the time he had just been play-acting. Only pretending to take things seriously. Colin's leg started to tremble and his foot to jounce on the linoleum floor. He pressed his leg hard against the chair to keep it still then felt his mouth brim with bile. He was going to be sick. Or faint. Before he could do either Barnaby returned, sat behind his desk and gave Colin a concerned glance.

'You look a bit green. Are you sure you don't want another drink?'

'. . . Some water. . .'

'Can we have a glass of water,' said Barnaby into his intercom. 'And I'd like some more tea.'

The drinks arrived. Colin sipped his slowly. He said, 'Didn't you go out for some more tea, Tom?'

'No. To arrange some transport.'

'Ah.' Colin put his glass on the desk. He desperately

needed time to think. Struggling to apply his attention to the matter Colin, almost immediately, saw where he had gone wrong. It was in the murder motive. No wonder Tom had been disbelieving. Colin, in the chief inspector's shoes, would have felt the same. How ridiculous – to kill someone because they had been unkind to your son. And him a grown man. If only, Colin chided himself, he had prepared what he had come to say more carefully. But it was not too late. He saw now how he could put things right. And what he should have said in the first place.

'The truth is, Tom,' he blurted out clumsily, 'David is in love with Kitty. You've seen . . . you were in the audience . . . how violent Esslyn was towards her. He found out, you see. And I was afraid. Afraid for her and for David. He was fiendish, Esslyn. I really thought he might harm them both.'

'So you spiked his guns?'

'Yes.'

'Well . . . that sounds a bit more likely.'

'Yes. I didn't say that at first because I thought if I could keep them out of it I would.'

'Such delicacy does you credit.' Barnaby drank deep of his breakfast blend. 'There's only one little snag in that scenario. Esslyn believed his wife was having an affair with Nicholas.'

'*Nicholas.*'

'But of course you weren't to know that.'

'Was it true?' Colin turned an eager look upon the chief inspector.

'No. The general consensus seems to be that David was indeed the man. By the way – where was he while you were carrying out all this jiggery-pokery?'

Colin's breath stopped in his throat. He gazed at Barnaby; the rabbit and the stoat. He felt the skin on his face prickle and knew it must be stained crimson. He opened his mouth but no sound came. He couldn't think. His brains were stewed. Where *was* David while all this was going on? *Where was David?* Not in the wings or (obviously) the scene dock. Not upstairs. In the dressing room! Of course.

'In the dressing room. Anyone will vouch for him.'

'Why should anyone need to vouch for him?'

'Oh – no reason. Just . . . if you wanted to check.'

'I see.' Barnaby completed to perfection the tight curled tip of the *Asplenium trichomanes*. 'I feel I should tell you that we tried to flush Sellotape down every loo in the theatre and were completely unsuccessful.'

'. . . Ohh . . . did you? . . . yes . . . sorry . . . my memory . . . I threw it out of the window . . .'

'Well, Colin,' Barnaby put down his pen and smiled rather severely at his companion. 'I've sat at this desk and listened to some sorry liars in my time but if I gave a prize for the worst I think you'd cop it.'

He watched Colin's face which had already shown every aspect of alarm and apprehension further suffuse with emotion. It seemed to blow up like a balloon. The skin stretched tight across his cheekbones and jaw and his eyes darted around like tiny trapped wild creatures. He seemed to have no control over his mouth and his lips worked in little push-pull convulsions. He swayed in his chair as if giddy.

And giddy was what he felt. For Colin was reeling under the force of a double-edged blow. He now saw with icy clarity that coming to the station and making a false confession was the worst thing he could possibly have done. Not only had he failed to save his son but the slightest pause for reflection must have shown him that David would never stand silently by whilst his father, innocent of any crime, was arrested, perhaps imprisoned. In trying to protect the boy Colin now saw that he had stupidly thrust him into the very heart of the crime where all the danger lay. He covered his face with his hands and moaned.

Barnaby shifted from his chair, came round to the front of the desk and perched on the edge. Then he touched Colin on the shoulder and said: 'You could be wrong, you know.'

'No, Tom!' Colin turned a desolate seeking look upon the chief inspector. The look was wild with unfounded expectation. It begged Barnaby, even at this late stage when a traitorous admission, though still unspoken, lay as solid as a rock between them, to perform a magical conjuring trick. To say it wasn't so. When Barnaby remained silent Colin gave one terrible dry sob, wracked from his gut, and cried: 'You see . . . I saw him do it. *I actually saw him do it.*'

Ten minutes later, having accepted more tea and, to some degree, composed himself, Colin told Barnaby what he had observed in the wings at the first night of *Amadeus*. He spoke in an emotionless voice, hanging his head as if deeply ashamed to be speaking at all. Barnaby received the information impassively and when Colin had finished said: 'Are you positive he was tinkering with the razor?'

'What else could he have been doing, Tom? Looking round so furtively to make sure that no one was watching. Bending over the props table. And he actually went into the toilet, came out and went back again.'

'But you didn't see him touch it?'

'Well . . . no. I was over the other side of the stage, behind the fireplace. And of course he'd got his back to me . . .' Colin looked up then and a tiny wisp of hope touched his voice. 'Do you think . . . Oh, Tom . . . d'you think I've got it wrong?'

'I certainly think we'd better not leap to any more conclusions. One's enough to be going on with. We'll see what David has to say when he gets here.'

'*David . . . here* . . . Oh God!' Horrified, Colin rose from his seat.

'Sit down,' said Barnaby, irritated. 'You come in here and make a false confession. As you're not a head case it's clear that you're protecting someone. There's only one person you'd go to those lengths for. Obviously we need to speak to that person. And here' – the buzzer sounded – 'I should imagine, he is.'

As the door opened Colin quickly bowed his shoulders

and buried his face once more in his hands. He did not look up as David almost ran across the room and knelt beside him.

'Dad – what is it? What are you doing here?' Getting no response he turned to Barnaby. 'Tom, what the hell's going on?'

'Your father has just confessed to the murder of Esslyn Carmichael.'

'*He's done what?*' David Smy, absolutely dumbfounded, stared at Barnaby then turned again to the figure crouched in the chair. He tried to move his father's head so that his face was visible but Colin gave a fierce animal cry and burrowed ever more firmly in the wedge of his arms.

David stood up and said: 'I don't believe it. I simply don't believe it.'

'No,' replied Barnaby drily. 'I don't believe it either.'

'But then . . . why? What's the point? *Dad.*' He shook his father's arm. 'Look at me!'

'He's shielding someone. Or thinks he is.'

'You stupid . . . What do you think you're playing at?' Panic streamed through David's voice. 'But . . . if you know he's lying, Tom . . . that's all right, isn't it? I mean . . . that's all right?'

'Up to a point.'

'How "up to a point"?'

'Who do you think he would be prepared to go to prison for?'

David frowned and Barnaby watched his face move through incomprehension, dawning apprehension and incredulity. Incredulity lingered longest. 'You mean . . . *he thought it was me?*'

'That's right.'

'But why on earth would I want to kill Esslyn?'

Barnaby had heard that phrase (give or take a change in nomenclature) a good many times in his career. He had heard it ringing with guilty bluster and innocent inquiry; spoken in high and low dudgeon, afire with self-righteous indignation and shot through with fear. But he

226

had never before been faced with the quality of complete and utter stupefaction that was now stamped on David Smy's bovine features.

'Well,' answered the chief inspector, 'the general consensus seems to be because of your affair with Kitty.' David's expression of disbelief now deepened to the point where he looked positively pole-axed. He shook his head from side to side slowly as if to clear it from the effects of a blow. Barnaby said, 'I should sit down if I were you.'

David collapsed into the second of the tweedy chairs and said: 'I think there's been some mistake.' Colin raised his head then, the disturbed agony of his gaze quietened, transmuted.

'You were seen acting suspiciously in the wings,' said Barnaby. 'Around the quarter.'

David went very pale. 'Who by?'

'We had an anonymous tip. These things have to be followed up.'

'Of course.' David sat silently for a moment then said, 'I was sure there was no one around.'

'You don't have to say anything else!' cried Colin. 'You have all sorts of rights. I'll get you a solicitor –'

'I don't need a solicitor, Dad. I haven't done anything all that dreadful.'

'Do you think we could get down to exactly what you have done?' said Barnaby brusquely. 'My patience is rapidly running out.'

David took a deep breath. 'Esslyn told this unkind story about Dierdre's father. It was so cruel. Everyone laughed and I knew she'd overheard. She was just on the stairs outside. Then I saw her afterwards checking the sound deck, and she was crying. I got so angry. When she went upstairs to collect the ASMs I got some Vim from the gents' and I shook it all over those little cakes he eats in act one. I know it was silly. And I know it was spiteful and childish and I don't care. I'd do it again.'

Barnaby stared at David's stubborn face then shifted his glance to the boy's father. Before his eyes Colin's countenance was rinsed clean of misery and despair and brightly transformed as is a child's face when a smile is 'wiped' on by the back of its hand. Now Colin was expressing a delight so intense it made him appear quite ridiculous.

'I didn't know you fancied the girl,' he cried joyously.

'I don't "fancy" her, Dad. I care deeply for her and have for some time. I told you.'

'What?'

'We were talking about her last week. I told you that I cared for someone but she wasn't free. And we discussed it yesterday as well.'

'You meant *Dierdre?*'

'Who else?' David looked from his father to Barnaby and back again. His expression was stern. He had the air of a man who was being trifled with and could do without the experience. 'I don't know who got this idea off the ground that I'd got something going with Kitty.' Barnaby shrugged and smiled and David continued indignantly: 'It's no laughing matter, Tom. What if it got back to Dierdre? I don't want her thinking I'm some sort of Don Juan.' The thought of David with his shining countenance and straight blue eyes and simple heart in the role of Don Juan caused Barnaby's lips to twitch once more and he faked a cough to cover it. 'As for you, Dad . . .' Colin, looking discomfited, shamefaced and radiant with happiness, shuffled his feet. 'How did you get to know about all this anyway?'

'We called at the house,' cut in Barnaby before Colin could reply. Not that he looked capable. 'I'm afraid your father drew his own conclusions from the form our questions took.'

'You silly sod,' said David affectionately. 'I don't know how you could have been so daft.'

'No,' said Colin. 'I don't either, now. Well . . .' He got up. 'Could we . . . is it all right to go now?'

'Can't wait to see the back of you.'

'Actually, Tom,' said David hesitantly, 'there's something I'd half meant to tell you. It seemed so vague that's

228

why I didn't mention it yesterday but I've been thinking it over and . . . as I'm here . . .'

'Fire away.'

'It's very slight. So I hope you won't be cross.'

'I shall be extremely cross any minute now if you don't hurry up and get on with it.'

'Yes. Right. Well, you know I take the tray with all the shaving things on at the end of the play. There was something odd about it on the first night.'

'Yes?'

'That's it, I'm afraid. I told you it was vague.'

'Very vague indeed.'

'I knew you'd be cross.'

'I am not cross,' said Barnaby with an ogreish grin. 'All the usual things were there, I take it?'

'Yes. Soap in wooden dish. Pewter bowl with hot water. Shaving brush. Closed razor. Towel.'

'Placed any differently?' David shook his head. 'Different soap perhaps?'

'No. It's never used actually so we've kept the same piece, Imperial Leather, all the way through rehearsals.'

'In that case, David,' said Barnaby rather tersely, 'I'm at a bit of a loss to see what was so odd about it.'

'I know. That's why I hesitated to tell you. But when I picked the tray up from the props table I definitely got that feeling.'

'Perhaps then it was something *on* the table?' asked Barnaby, his interest quickening. 'In the wrong position. Or maybe something that shouldn't have been there at all?'

David shook his head. 'No. It was to do with the tray.'

'Well.' Barnaby got to his feet dismissively. 'Keep mulling it over. It could be important. Ring me if anything clicks.'

Colin thrust out his hand and the strength of his gratitude for Barnaby's white lies could be felt in the firm grip. 'I'm very, very sorry, Tom, to have been so much bother.'

They left then and Barnaby stood at his office door and watched them, David striding forward looking straight ahead, Colin loping alongside in a cloud of relief so dense it was almost tangible. As they went through the exit Colin, careful not to sound incredulous said: 'But why Dierdre?'

And Barnaby heard David reply, 'Because she needs me more than anyone else ever will. And because I love her.'

Dierdre walked up the drive towards the Walker Memorial Hospital for Psychiatric Disorders, the dog trotting at her heels. On being informed by Barnaby that he was being kept in one of the police kennels until she claimed him, Dierdre had called there on her way to the hospital to put the record straight. The nice blonde policewoman was in reception and asked how Dierdre was feeling. Dierdre asked in her turn after the constable who rescued her father, then the policewoman lifted the counter flap, said, 'Through here,' and disappeared.

Dierdre, murmuring, 'The trouble is, you see . . .' followed.

The kennels were really large cages and held three dogs. Two lay mopingly on the earthen floor, the third leapt to its paws and moved eagerly forward. Dierdre, repeating, 'The trouble is, you see . . .' looked down at the questing black nose and soft muzzle pressed against the wire mesh. The tail was wagging so fast it was just a brown blur. Policewoman Brierley was unfastening the padlock. Now was the time to explain. Afterwards, trying to understand why she hadn't, Dierdre decided it was all the dog's fault.

If he had whined or complained or yapped or reacted in any other way but the way that he had she was sure her heart could have been hardened. But what she couldn't handle was his simple confidence. There was no doubt at all in his eyes. Here she was at last and off they would be going. And didn't she owe him something? reasoned Dierdre, recalling the terrible night when he had been her father's only companion.

'Got his lead?'

'Oh . . . no . . . I came straight from the Barnabys'. I haven't been home yet.'

'Shouldn't really take him without a lead.' She was replacing the lock. Dierdre looked at the dog. His expression of dawning dismay was terrible to behold.

'It'll be all right,' she said hurriedly. 'He's very well trained. He's a good dog.'

PW Brierley shrugged. 'OK. If you say so . . .' she said, and opened the cage. The dog ran out, jumped up at Dierdre and started licking her hands. She signed a form for his release and they left the station together and entered the High Street. The cobblers had some brightly coloured leads and collars and Dierdre chose one of scarlet leather with a little bell. As she bent down to put it on, the man behind the counter said: 'D'you want a disc for him? In case he gets lost? Do one while you wait.'

'Oh yes – please.' Already, barely minutes into dog ownership, Dierdre could not bear the thought of him getting lost. She gave her address and telephone number.

'And his name?'

'His name?' She thought frantically as the man stood with the drill buzzing ready. All sorts of common or garden dogs' names came to mind, none of them suitable. He was certainly no Fido or Rover. Nor even a Gyp or Bob. Then she remembered the Day Centre where she had first seen him, and the name came. 'Sunny!' she cried. 'He's called Sunny.' The man engraved 'Sonny', added the other details and Dierdre fixed the disc to the collar.

Now, arriving at the main hospital entrance she wondered what to do with him, 'You can't come inside,' she said. 'You'll have to wait.' He listened closely. She tied his lead around an iron foot-scraper and said, '. . . Um . . . sit . . .' To her surprise he immediately lowered his ginger rump to the floor and sat. She patted him, said, 'Good dog,' and went indoors.

She was immediately engulfed in a series of labyrinthine corridors and started walking with a heavy heart. When she had been told, on ringing the general hospital to inquire when she could visit, that her father had been transferred to 'the Walker', she had been horrified. The brooding soot-encrusted Victorian pile of bricks had always been known locally as the fruit and nut house and, as a child, she had luridly imagined it inhabited by chained people in white robes, raving and shrieking, like poor Mrs Rochester.

The reality was very different. So quiet. As Dierdre continued on past several pairs of swing doors looking for the Alice Kennedy Baker Ward you could have believed the place to be deserted. Thick, shiny linoleum the colour of cooked veal muffled every footfall. The walls were dirty yellow, the paint cracked and peeling and the radiators, though giving out powerful blasts of heat, were scabbed with rust.

But all these things, though depressing, were as naught compared to the deadening pall of despair that permeated the atmosphere. Dierdre felt it choking her lungs like noisome fog. It smelt of stale old vegetables and stale old people. Of urine and fish and, most profusely, of the sickly synthetic lavender that had been aerosoled everywhere in a futile attempt at apeing normal domesticity. A sister, crackling by in white and sugar-bag blue, asked her if she was lost then pointed her in the right direction.

The Kennedy Baker Ward appeared to be empty but for a West Indian nurse sitting at a small table in the centre by a telephone. She got up as Dierdre entered and said the patients were in the sun lounge. She explained why Dierdre had not been consulted over the decision to transfer her father. Apparently there was no question of permission being sought. He was being admitted to the Walker for his own safety and that of others. If Dierdre wished to speak to the doctor in charge of his case an appointment could be made.

'Your father's feeling very well though, dear,' she added as she led Dierdre to the sun lounge, a bulbous growth on the far end of the ward. 'Quite tip-top.'

The lounge had a grey stained haircord carpet, assorted shabby chairs and an ill-conceived and poorly executed oil painting of its benefactress in true electric blue gazing munificently down at the assembled company. There were five people in the room: three elderly women, a young man and Mr Tibbs who was sitting by the window wearing alien pyjamas and a violently patterned dressing gown surely designed to stimulate rather than to soothe.

'Your daughter's come to see you, Mr Tibbs. Isn't that nice?' said the nurse very firmly as if expecting some denial.

Dierdre pulled up a low chair with scratched wooden arms and sat down saying, 'Hullo, Daddy. How are you feeling?'

Mr Tibbs continued to gaze out of the window. He didn't look very tip-top. His jaw gaped in a sad loose way and was covered in greyish white stubble and snail trails of dried saliva. Dierdre said, 'I've brought you some things.'

She unpacked her bag and laid his toilet articles, some soap and arrowroot biscuits on his lap, keeping back his special treat, a box of Turkish Delight, until the last moment to ease the pain of parting. He looked at the little pile with fierce puzzlement then picked the things up one at a time, handling them very carefully as if they were made of glass. He obviously had no idea what they were and tried to put the soap in his mouth. Dierdre took them all away again and put them on the floor.

'Well, Daddy,' she said brightly, struggling to keep her voice on an even keel, 'how are you –' Oh God, she thought, I've asked that already. What could she say next? And what an incredible question to be asking herself. She who had spent years quietly and contentedly talking and listening to the old man in the basket chair who bore such a strange resemblance to her father. She couldn't even tell him about the dog in case it brought back memories of that shocking night at the lake. So she just held his hand and looked around the room.

The young man in baggy flannel trousers was drumming on his knees with the tips of his fingers at tremendous speed. He sat next to an elderly woman with the hooded gorged glance of a satisfied bird of prey. Then there was a dumpy, bald woman with warts like purple Rice Krispies who was stretching out her arms, palms inward, holding an invisible skein of wool. The third woman was just a bundle of clothing, (checks and spots and stripes and concertinaed lisle stockings) with a tube disappearing up the skirt from which depended a plastic bag of yellow liquid. There they sat, each sealed in an impenetrable bubble of drugs and dreams. They could not even be said to be waiting since the act of waiting acknowledged the possibility that life might be about to change. Dierdre eased back her sleeve and looked at her watch. She had been in the sunshine lounge for three minutes.

'If there's anything else you want, Daddy, I'll be happy to bring it next time I come.'

Mr Tibbs perked up at this then capped her remark quickly with: 'Look alive, nurse. Two and six.' He sat, poised on the edge of his chair, as if they were playing some sort of game. Suddenly he had the spry twinkling look that people have who boast that you'd have to get up early to catch *them* out. His false teeth snapped as if they had a life of their own and his face creased into a goblin slyness. Dierdre covered her face with her hands for a long moment then brought out his box of Turkish Delight. Immediately his face changed. It lost its 'gotcha!' expression and became red and angry. He darted a fierce almost beleaguered glance at the round, fragile container as if it were about to attack him. Then, as his daughter tentatively held it out, he took a mighty up and under swing with his closed fist and knocked it high into the air and halfway across the room. Powdered sugar flew about in little puffs like gunsmoke. Rose pink and not quite white squares of scented jelly tumbled all over the floor. With a shrill squall the assorted bundle of clothes ran forward, seized one, rubbed it on the leg of her half-mast bloomers and popped it, whole, into her mouth. The warty old lady gathered up most of the rest, squeezing them savagely into one great gelatinous lump which she then proceeded to nibble, holding it between cupped paws like a squirrel with a nut. The young man had now started to slap and scratch himself furiously as though he were being eaten alive.

Dierdre could stand no more. She fastened her coat and started to pull on her gloves. Her father had retreated to position one and was once more gazing blindly out of the window. I can do nothing here, she thought. I am no help. No use. 'I'll come again soon, Daddy . . . on Sunday . . .'

She stumbled out into the ward proper. Before she had reached the swing doors she heard her father's voice raised in song to the tune of his favourite hymn, 'The Old Rugged Cross'. But the words were strange and garbled and some of them obscene.

Nicholas, invited to dinner, had arrived bursting with excitement, brandishing his letter of acceptance to Central and sporting a cauliflower nose. He had been at the house half an hour and hadn't stopped going on about the letter although, as far as Avery was concerned, you could have covered the subject adequately in two minutes flat and still had time for a lengthy reading from the Koran.

'Isn't it absolutely marvellous?' Nicholas was saying yet again.

'Enough to bring stars to your eyes,' smiled Tim. 'Drink up.'

Avery, egg-shell brown tonsure gleaming under the spotlights, was slicing a tenderloin of pork into shives so thin they fell into soft rosy curls on the marble slab. Peanuts and chillies stood by. The real tomato soup was keeping warm in the double boiler. Basil, picked the previous summer and immediately frozen into an ice cube, thawed in a cup. Avery moved purposefully amongst his culinary arcana and drank a little Doisy Däene sec, almost content. Almost, not quite. A cloud, no bigger than a man's lie, would keep drifting across his horizon. And a tiny scene – hardly a scene even, a vignette – was stamped on his memory.

Tim and Esslyn, standing together in the clubroom, heads close, two tall dark blades. Esslyn talking quietly.

When Avery had entered they moved apart not guiltily (Tim never did anything guiltily) but quickly nonetheless. Avery had let several days drag by before he had casually asked what the fascinating conversation had been about. Tim had said he couldn't recall the time in question. The lie oblique. Bad enough. Avery let the matter slide. What else could he do? But then, much worse, came the lie direct.

Whilst they were all huddling frailly in the wings, whilst Esslyn's life blood seeped into the boards and Harold stormed, Avery had whispered: 'This will put the lighting out of his mind. P'raps we won't have to leave after all.'

And Tim had said, 'No. We'll definitely have to go now.'

'What do you mean *now?*'

'What?'

'You said, "We'll definitely have to go *now*." '

'No I didn't. You're imagining things.'

'But I distinctly heard —'

'Oh for Christ's sake! Stop nitpicking.'

So, of course, Avery had stopped. Now, not quite content, he watched his love through the yellow mottled screen of mother-in-law's tongue relaxing, toasting Nicholas.

'I must say,' Avery called, making a special effort to put his fears aside, 'I do miss not being able to badmouth Esslyn.'

'I don't see why you shouldn't,' replied Tim. 'When he was alive you never stopped.'

'Mmm . . .' Avery took a heavy iron pan down, poured in some sesame oil and added a pinch of anise. 'Half the pleasure then was the chance that it would somehow get back to him.'

'Tom said I ought to get a solicitor,' said Nicholas suddenly. 'I'm sure he thinks it was me.'

'If he thought it was you, dear boy,' said Tim, 'you wouldn't be sitting there.'

Nicholas cheered up then and, for the third time of asking, wondered if they thought he would have any problem getting a grant for drama school. Avery reached for his chillies and threw a couple in. He shook and rattled his pan a little more loudly than was strictly necessary. He often did this when visitors came. Childlike, he was afraid both that they might forget he was there behind the monstera and philodendron or that, if they did remember, might not appreciate just how hard he was working on their behalf.

Nicholas leaned back on a raspberry satin sofa seamed and scalloped like a great shell and drank deep of his apéritif. He loved Tim's and Avery's sitting room. It was an extraordinary mixture of downy delights such as the sofa and austere pieces of donnish severity like Tim's Oscar Woollen armchair, two low black glass Italian tables and a stunning heavy bronze helmet lying on its side near the bookshelves. He said: 'What's on the menu today, Avery?'

'Satay.'

'I thought that was a method of doing yourself in.' Nicholas slithered about on the shiny cushions. 'Whoops! Can I have some more of this marvellous wine, Tim?'

'No. You're already all over the place. And there's some Tignanello with the meat.'

'Shame!' cried Nicholas. Then, 'Did you see Joycey's daughter on the first night? Wasn't she the most breathtaking thing?'

'Very lovely,' said Tim.

'Those legs . . . and that long neck . . . and eyelashes . . . and those spectacular bones . . .'

'Well, you may not be the most sober person in the room, Nicholas,' said Avery. 'But my God you know how to take an inventory.'

'Will you come and see me in my end of term shows?'

'How the boy leaps about.'

'If asked,' said Tim.

'Maybe in my last year I shall win the Gielgud medal?'

'Nicholas, you really must at least pretend to be a bit more modest otherwise the rest of the students will positively loathe you.' Avery turned his attention back to his cooking. He frazzled the pork a little, sipped some more wine, checked the soup and peeped at his little sugar baskets with iced cherries keeping cool in the larder. Then he took hot brown twists of bread from the oven, poured the soup into a warm tureen and tuned once more into the conversation.

Nicholas was saying that he would come back and see them in the holidays. Personally Avery believed that, once the lad hit the smoke, neither of them would see or hear from him again. In this he was only partially correct. Although Nicholas never returned for a visit or invited them to any of his increasingly prestigious first nights they were to receive Christmas cards from him, jointly addressed, for many years to come.

Avery called, 'From me to you', and took in the tureen, the bread and an earthenware bowl of Greek yogurt and sour cream. The talk was still of the theatre.

'I don't know whether to stay on for *Vanya* or shoot off now,' Nicholas was saying.

'You won't start at Central for months,' said Tim.

'But I could get some sort of job and see all the plays and join a movement class or something.'

'There are three marvellous parts in it,' continued Tim. 'And now that Esslyn's gone you could take your pick.'

'Mmm.' Nicholas spooned in some more soup. 'This isn't very tomatoey, Avery.'

'Miss Ungrateful,' retorted his host. 'Still, if your taste buds are punch drunk on monosodium glutamate, what can one expect?'

'I don't know the play,' said Nicholas. 'What's it like?'

'Twice as long as *Little Eyeolf* but without the laughs,' said Avery. 'And the tap routines.'

'It's wonderful. A Russian classic.'

'I don't think I fancy being directed by Harold in a Russian classic. He'll have us all swinging from the samovars. I think I'll go.'

'You may not be allowed to go,' said Tim, 'while the investigation's still going on.'

'Blimey.' Nicholas scraped his bowl clean and held it

out for more. 'I hadn't thought of that. I suppose we're all under suspicion. Present company excepted.'

'We've guessed and guessed at the possible culprit,' said Avery, wielding the ladle, '– you don't deserve this – but answer came there none.'

'The present odds-on favourite is the Everards.'

'Don't talk to me about the Everards,' said Nicholas, tenderly touching his swollen nose.

'That was wicked of Tom to tell you,' said Tim. 'I didn't think the police did that sort of thing. I thought statements were in confidence.'

'What have they got?' asked Avery.

'A black eye each and one cut lip.'

'Don't swagger, Nicholas.'

'He asked me! Anyway – why are they top of the list? They were the court toadies.'

'Nasty position, court toady,' said Avery, passing the still warm twists. 'You must get to hate the person you're sucking up to.'

'Not necessarily,' said Nicholas. 'Weak people often respect those much stronger than themselves. They feel safe getting carried along on their coat tails.'

'You surely don't see the Everards as weak, Nico?' said Tim.

'Well . . . yes . . . don't you?'

'Not at all.'

'I can see him wanting to get rid of *them*,' continued Nicholas, 'nasty little parasites. But not vice versa. I still favour Kitty.'

'What about Harold?' suggested Avery.

'Of course, along with everybody else, I'd just love it to be Harold. In fact, apart from him having neither motive nor opportunity, I see Harold as the perfect candidate.' Nicholas slurped his last spoonful. 'This soup really grows on you, Avery.'

'Well you're not having any more,' cried Avery, bearing away the empties. 'Or you'll have no room for the nice bits.'

Avery scraped the sauce, smelling of butter and

peanuts, into a boat and took his shallow Chinese dishes from the oven. He loved using these. They had a shaggy bronze chrysanthemum painted on the bottom and small blue/green figures touched with gold around the sides going about their wily oriental business in a world of tiny trees and short square white rivers, tightly corrugated, like milky squibs. Avery got much pleasure from causing all this exquisite artificiality to vanish then, as he supped, gradually exposing it again. They were the only things in the kitchen that never went into the dishwasher and only Avery was allowed to clean them. They had been an anniversary present from Tim bought during a holiday at Redruth and so doubly treasured. Now he brought the bowls with their curls of crispy pork and scurried round the table, placing them before the others.

Tim said, 'I do wish you wouldn't romp,' and Nicholas sniffed and murmured, 'Aahhh. . . . Bisto.' Avery bowed his head for a moment, more in relief over a job well done than in thanks for benisons received, and they all tucked in. Avery passed the sauce to Nicholas, lifting it high over the candle flames.

'There's no need to elevate it,' said Tim. 'It's not the host.'

The Tignanello was opened and poured and Tim lifted his glass. 'To Nicholas. And Central.'

'Ohh yes . . .' Avery toasted Nicholas who grinned a little awkwardly. 'R and F before you're twenty-five or I shall want to know the reason why. And don't forget – we believed in you first.'

'I won't.' Nicholas gave a slightly slugged smile. 'And I'm so grateful for everything. The room . . . your friendship . . . everything . . .'

'Don't be grateful,' said Tim. 'Just send seats in the front row of the dress circle for all your first nights.'

'Do you think then . . . the gods will reward me by answering my prayers?' The heavy attempt at sarcasm was only partially successful. Nicholas' voice trembled.

'Nico – you're so naïve,' smiled Tim. 'That's the way the gods punish us – by answering our prayers.'

'Oh my – it's not going to be one of your world-weary evenings, is it? I don't think I could stand that.'

But Avery's response was jocular and he appeared the picture of contentment. He beamed and his little blue eyes twinkled. He started to relax. He had been tiptoeing about very carefully all day because his morning horoscope, though fairly jolly on the whole, had ended: 'There may be friction in the home, however.' But surely, reasoned Avery, by nine thirty any respectable bird of ill omen must be safely tucked up in its nest, reading the runes for the following day.

'Is it all right?' he asked, mock anxious.

'My love – it's absolutely marvellous.' Tim reached out and his slim El Greco fingers rested briefly, lightly on Avery's arm. Avery's face burned with the intensity of his pleasure and his heart pounded. Tim *never* used an endearment or touched him when other people were present and Avery had quickly learned that he must behave with the same propriety. Of course it was only Nico, but even so . . .

Avery breathed slowly and deeply, experiencing the spicy scents of the meat, the delicate fragrance of the jasmine in its hooped basket, the aroma of the wine and the slightly acrid drip of the candles, not just briefly in the membranes of his nose but pervasively, as if they had been injected into his bloodstream and were spreading languorously through his body. He broke a piece of bread and popped it into his mouth and it was like the bread of angels.

The phone rang. Everyone groaned. Avery, who was nearest, pushed back his chair and, carrying his glass, went to answer it.

'Hullo? . . . Oh hullo, darling.'

'Who is it?' mouthed Tim silently.

Avery pressed the secrecy button. 'The wicked witch of the north.'

'My condolences.'

'Tim sends his love, Rosa.'

'And mine.'

'And Nicholas. We've been having the most divine – Oh all right. I'll be quiet. There's no need to be rude. One must go through these opening civilities otherwise one might just as well take to the hills . . . Shut up yourself if it comes to that.' He switched again. 'Evil-tempered old crone.'

The two men at the table exchanged glances. Tim's faintly humorous, rather resigned. Nicholas' wry, even a touch patronizing. A look that would never have graced his features when their friendship had first begun. They turned their attention back to Avery whose face was avidity personified. His soft lips, delicately tinted toffee brown from the satay, were pushed forward into a thrilled marshmallow O.

'. . . My dear . . . !' he cried, 'but didn't we always say? Well I certainly always said . . . are you sure . . . well, that clinches it then . . . Of course I will . . . and *you* keep *me* posted.' He hung up, took a deep swallow of his wine and hurried back to the table. Bursting with information he looked from Tim to Nicholas and back again. 'You'll never guess.'

'If there are three more irritating words in the English language,' said Tim, 'I've yet to hear them.'

'Oh come on,' said Nicholas, rather slurrily, 'what she say?'

'The police have arrested David Smy.'

Avery sat back more than satisfied with the effect of his pronouncement. Nicholas gaped foolishly in disbelief. Tim's face, golden and ivory in the candle's flame, became bleached, white and grey. He said: 'How does she know?'

'Saw him. She was going to the library when a police car drew up outside the station and two rozzers marched him inside.'

'Did he have a blanket over his head?'

'Don't be so bloody silly, Nicholas. How on earth could she have known it was David if he'd had a blanket over his head?'

'Only they do,' persisted Nicholas with stolid determination. 'If they're guilty.'

'Well, really. Sometimes I think your thought processes should be in a medical mysteries museum.'

'Leave the boy alone.' Tim's voice laid a great chill over the lately so festive company. 'He's had too much to drink.'

'Oh . . . yes . . . sorry.' Avery picked up his glass then nervously put it down again. His exhilaration was draining away fast. Almost as he entertained this thought the last couple of wisps evaporated. He looked across at Tim who was not looking at him, Avery, but through him as if he didn't exist. Avery looked down at the glistening puddle of peanut sauce, picked up his spoon which clatterd against the gilded rim of the bowl, and tasted a little. It was nearly cold. 'Shall I warm this up, Tim . . . do you think? Or bring in the pudding?'

Tim did not reply. He had withdrawn into himself as he occasionally did in a way that Avery dreaded. He knew Tim didn't mean this behaviour as any sort of punishment. The action was so undeliberate as to appear almost involuntary yet Avery inevitably felt responsible. He turned to their guest. 'Are you ready for some pudding, Nico?'

Nicholas smiled briefly and shrugged. He looked a little sulky and deeply abashed, as if guilty of some social misdemeanour. Yet, Avery thought, it is I who have committed the solecism. How unpleasant now, how *crass*, his reception of Rosa's news appeared. With what salacious relish had he rushed to the table to relay the information as if it were some edible goody he couldn't wait to share. If he had stopped to think, even for a moment, he must have behaved differently. After all this was a friend they were talking about. They all liked David and his kind unhurried ways. And now he might be going to prison. For years. No wonder Tim, extremely fastidious at the best of times, had removed his attention from such a lubricious, blubbery display.

So poor Avery reasoned and argued, unaware that there was a far more alarming reason for his friend's silence. Or that his small world which, in spite of constant little heart murmurs of alarm and frettings of worry, he felt to be a basically secure one, was about to be savagely ruptured.

'Well . . .' he said, forcing cheeriness into his voice. 'It doesn't do to get depressed. OK . . . Rosa saw him going in . . . what does that mean? He might have just been asked to help clear up one or two points. Help them with their inquiries.' Avery wished he hadn't said that. He was sure he'd read somewhere that was the official way of announcing that the police had got the guilty party but weren't legally supposed to say so. 'Just because he was the man in the lighting box doesn't mean . . . well . . . what else have they got to go on after all?' (Only that he had ample opportunity. Only that he was the man who took the razor on. Only that his mistress was now a rich widow.) Tim was getting up.

'What . . . what's happening?' said Avery. 'We haven't finished.'

'I've finished.'

'Oh but you must have some cherries, Tim! You know how you love them. I made them especially. In little sugar baskets.'

'Sorry.'

I could kill Rosa, thought Avery. Malicious scandal-mongering interfering old bitch! If it weren't for her this would never have happened. And we were having such a lovely time. Tears of disappointment and frustration sprang to his eyes. When they cleared Tim, wearing his overcoat and Borsalino hat, was at the sitting room door. Avery leapt to his feet.

'Where are you going?'

'Just out.'

'But *where*, Tim?' Avery hurried across and hung on Tim's arm. His voice trembled as he continued, 'You must tell me!'

'I've got to go to the station.'

'. . . The . . . the police station?' When Tim nodded Avery cried: 'What on earth for?'

But even as he asked Avery's heart was squeezed with

the terrible cold foreknowledge of what would be Tim's reply.

'Because,' said Tim, gently removing Avery's hand from his sleeve, 'I was the man in the lighting box.'

Tim was sorry he had come. Barnaby had vouchsafed the information (it seemed to Tim with a certain amount of wry pleasure) that David Smy, far from being arrested, was as free as a bird and likely to remain so. Still, Tim's confession had been made and he could hardly take it back. He had assumed that once his simple statement had been completed he would be free to go, but Barnaby seemed keen to question him further. To add to the charm of these unwelcome proceedings the poisonous youth with the carroty hair was also present at his scrivenings.

'. . . Just background, you understand, Tim,' Barnaby was saying. 'Tell me how you got on with Esslyn.'

'As well and as badly as anyone else. There was nothing to get on with, really. He was always posing. You never knew what he truly felt.'

'Even so it's unusual for someone to belong to a group for over fourteen years and not have a single relationship of any depth or complexity.'

'Oh, I don't know. Lots of men don't have close friendships. As long as Esslyn was much admired and had plenty of sex he was content.' Tim smiled. 'The advertiser's dream made manifest.'

'No more than human.' Barnaby sounded indulgent. 'Which of us can't say the same?'

Bang on target, thought Troy. Don't knock it till you've had enough. Like when you're stepping into your coffin. Troy was feeling very put out. He just couldn't cope with the revelation that the man he thought of (apparently only too appropriately) as the cocky bugger in the executive suit had had it off with Kitty. Paradoxically his resentment against Tim was now doubled. And the way he sauntered about . . . Look at him now . . . completely at home, mildly interested, cool as a cornet. The dregs of society, thought Troy, should know their place and not come floating to the surface mingling with the good honest brew.

'He was never short of female company, then?' Barnaby was asking.

'Oh no. Nothing that lasted long, though. They soon drifted off.'

'You don't know of anyone in the past that he had rejected? Who might be suffering from unrequited love?'

'Anyone involved with Esslyn, whether rejected or not, suffered from unrequited love. And no, I don't.'

'You must realize, I'm sure, that Kitty is our number-one suspect. Did you assist her in doing away with her husband?'

'Certainly not. There would have been no reason for me to do so. Our affair was trivial. I was already tired of it.'

'Did she let anything slip while you were together that might give us some insight into this matter?'

'Not that I recall.'

'Or hint at any other man?'

'No.'

'To get on to Monday night –'

'I've really nothing to add there, Tom.'

'Well,' said Barnaby easily, 'you never know. Try this: Why did the murder happen then? Why not for instance at one of the early rehearsals? Less people hanging around. No coppers present.'

'The wings are never dark at rehearsal. And there's always someone there prompting. Or wanting to do a scene change.'

'They're not dark at the run-through, surely. Or the dress rehearsal?' When Tim did not reply Barnaby added: 'By the way – did I congratulate you on your splendid lighting?'

'I really don't remember.'

It was like touching a snail on the horns, thought Barnaby, sensing the quick (protective?) folding in of the other man's attention.

'Harold seemed quite put out.'

'Did he?'

'I noticed him thumping away in the interval on the door of your box.'

Tim shrugged. 'He runs on a short fuse.'

'Might've been less alarming if you'd sprung these splendid illuminations before the first night.'

'If I'd done that they'd never have reached the first night.'

'So Harold didn't know?'

The snail disappeared completely. Although Tim's expression remained laconic, even a tinge scornful, his eyes were disturbed and the skin seemed to tighten over his patrician nose. 'That's right.'

'So he got two shocks for the price of one?'

'As things turned out.'

'Quite a coincidence.'

'They happen all the time.'

Not this time, thought Barnaby. He did not know how he knew, but he knew. Somewhere way back in the murk of his mind, so faint as to be hardly apprehended, he heard a warning rattle. This man, who could not possibly have murdered Esslyn Carmichael, knew something. But he met Barnaby's gaze frankly, almost dauntingly, nor did he look away.

'You're probably not aware,' said Barnaby, 'that Harold is claiming the new lighting plot as his own.'

'Hah!' Tim laughed harshly, strainedly. His face flushed. 'So that –' The laughter cracked. 'So that was all we had to do. Say "Yes, Harold" to everything. And go our own way. Just like Esslyn.'

'So it seems.'

'All these years.' He was still laughing in a rasping irascible way when the chief inspector let him go a few minutes later.

Barnaby had seen no point in keeping Tim there or in applying pressure at this stage. Tim was not the sort to wilt under generalized bullish cajoling. But Barnaby knew now where the pressure point was and could apply a little leverage if or when it became necessary. He turned to his sergeant.

'Well, Troy?'

'A worried man, sir,' replied Troy quickly. 'All right till you touched on his lights, then shut up like balls in an ice bucket. He might have been hard put to it to have done the murder but he knows something.'

'I believe you're right.'

'How would it be if I had a word with his friend?' Troy arched his wrist limply. 'Little Miss Roly Poly. On her tod like.' He winked. 'She'd soon crumble.' He received in exchange for the wink a stare so icy that he all but crumbled himself.

'First thing tomorrow I want to visit Carmichael's office. And his solicitor. Get on the phone and fix it.'

Nicholas had left fairly quickly after Tim, thanking Avery for the dinner then saying on the doorstep with absolute clarity: 'I'm not as think as you drunk I am.'

Now Avery sat alone. He had finished the Tignanello, pouring and gulping, pouring and gulping at first in shock and then, steadily, in bitter loneliness and despair. After emptying the bottle he had, in a confused state of aggressive misery jumbled up with vague ideas of retaliation, opened some Clos St Denis, Grand Cru that he knew Tim was keeping for his birthday. He wrestled savagely with the cork, breaking bits off and sloshing the wine about.

The candles in their Mexican silver rose holders guttered and Avery blew them out. But even in the dark the room was full of memories of Tim. Avery flinched at the word memories and chided himself for being melodramatic. After all, Tim was coming back. But no sooner had this thought, which should have been a comfort, struck him than it was swamped by a hundred others all permeated with the fervour of self-righteousness. Oh yes, observed Avery to himself with a miserable snigger, no doubt he'll be coming back. He won't find anyone else like me in a hurry. Who else would cook and iron and

248

clean and care for him with just the odd kind word for wages? And that tossed so casually into the conversation it might have been a bone to a mangy cur. Who but me would have bought a bookshop and given – *yes given*, fulminated Avery – half of it away? Whose money had furnished the house? And paid for the holidays? And he asked so little in return. Just to be allowed to love and look after Tim. And to be offered in exchange a modicum of affection. Immensely moved by this revelatory glimpse into the nobility of his soul, Avery shed a disconsolate tear.

But the tear had no sooner dried on his cushiony cheek than the cold finger of reason pointed out that, for a reasonable sum, people could be found to cook and iron and clean and that Tim had once earned an excellent living teaching Latin and French in a public school and no doubt could do so again. And that if Avery poured out all the tiger words which, at this moment, were prowling round his heart when Tim came back he might put on his Crombie overcoat and Borsalino hat and leave again, this time for always. And in fact (Avery felt sick with apprehension) even if he made the most tremendous superhuman efforts at self-control and behaved with calmness and understanding when his lover returned, it was probably too late. Because Tim had already met someone else.

Avery stood up silently and put the light on. He felt he must move. Walk about. He thought of going down to the station to meet Tim, to know the worst straight away, and had seized his coat and opened the front door before he recognized what a foolish thing that would be to do. For Tim hated it when Avery 'trailed around' after him. Also (Avery dropped his coat on to the raspberry bouffant sofa) his quick dash to the door had revealed him to be intensely, dizzily nauseous. He moved to the table and sat upright with difficulty, holding on to the edge. He felt as if he were trapped in a revolving door of the emotions. Having whipped rapidly and passionately through jealousy, rage, yearning fear and concupiscence he now seemed to be meeting them all on the way back.

Avery made a huge effort to fight free of this soggy swamp of wretchedness. He drank several large glasses of Perrier and sat quietly struggling to compose himself. He tried to think as Tim would think. After all what was done could not be undone. Perhaps, thought Avery tremulously, I am blowing it up out of all proportion. Also getting into this state is just what Tim would expect. Poor Tim. Sitting down there for hours at the police station and then coming home to face a raging screaming row. How remarkable, how truly amazing it would be if he were welcomed by a tranquil, smiling, naturally slightly distant but ultimately *forgiving* friend. Let him without sin, decided Avery, and all that jazz. What would be the point after all of railing at Tim because he was not doggedly faithful? It's because he's so completely unlike me, realized Avery, now quite moony with sentiment, that I love him so. And how proud he will be when he sees just how well I can actually handle things. How mature and wise, how detached he will find me in the face of this, our first real catastrophe. Avery's chest had just swelled to a pouter pigeon prominence when he heard a key in the door and a moment later Tim was standing before him.

Avery yelled, 'You faithless bastard!' and threw one of the Chinese bowls. Tim ducked and the bowl hit the architrave and shattered into small pieces. When Tim bent to pick them up Avery shouted: 'Leave it! I don't want it. I don't want any of them. They're all going in the dustbin!'

Ignoring him, Tim picked up the pieces and put them on the table. Then he got a clean glass from the kitchen and poured some of the Clos St Denis. He sniffed at it and made an irritated sound, picking out a few cork crumbs.

'I was laying this down.'

'Seems to be your favourite occupation.'

'If you wanted to get tanked up why on earth didn't

you use the Dao? There's half a dozen bottles in the larder.'

'Oh yes – the Dao! Any old rubbish will do for me, won't it? I haven't got your exquisite palate. Your celebrated *je ne sais quoi*.'

'Don't be silly.' Tim took a thoughtful swallow. 'Wonderful fruit. A lot of style. Not as big as I expected.'

'Well hoity fucking toity.'

'I'm tired.' Tim removed his muffler and coat. 'I'm going to bed.'

'You most certainly are not going to bed. You are going to leave my house. And you are going to leave it now!'

'I'm not going anywhere at this hour of the night, Avery.' Tim hung up his coat. 'We'll talk in the morning when you've sobered up.'

'We'll talk now!' Avery leapt up from the table and stumbled over to the hall where he stood at the bottom of the staircase barring the way. Tim turned then, made his way to the kitchen and started filling up the cafetiére. Avery followed, crying: 'What do you think you're doing?' And 'Leave my things alone.'

'If I'm going to stay awake I need some strong coffee. And so, by the look of things, do you.'

'What did you expect? To come home and find me all sweet reason? Clearing up after the last supper? Counting out your thirty pieces of silver?'

'Why are you being so dramatic?' Tim spooned the Costa Rica out lavishly. 'And come and sit down before you fall down.'

'You'd like that, wouldn't you? You'd love it if I fell and hit my head and died. Then you'd get the shop and the house and you'd be able to move that bloody little tart in here. Well you can think again because first thing tomorrow I shall go to the solicitor's and change my will.'

'You can do what you like tomorrow. For now I should concentrate on parking your bum on something and getting this coffee down you.'

Avery, allowing a moment for a disdainful pause, thus making it clear that any move he might be inclined to make would be entirely of his own choosing, made his erratic way over the kitchen floor and contemplated the north face of the bentwood stool. Somehow he managed to clamber up and hang on, swaying like an aerial mast in a high wind.

The rich homely smell of coffee filled his nostrils, cruelly recalling a thousand shared starts to happy days and as many intimate and gossipy after-dinner exchanges. All gone now. All ruined. He and Tim would never be happy again. Avery's eyes filled with sorrow as the utter terribleness of the situation struck him anew and a thrill of pain stabbed clean through the deadening haze of alcohol. A needle to the heart.

As Tim passed the coffee he folded Avery's limp unresisting fingers around the cup and this gesture of concern was the last straw breaking the back of Avery's anger and releasing a great gush of tears. And with the release of tears came an overwhelming need for contact and solace. He cried: 'I *trusted* you . . .'

Tim sighed, put down his drink, pulled up a second stool and sat next to Avery. 'Listen, love,' he said, 'if we are going to have a heart to heart at this ridiculous hour of the morning let's not start with a false premise. You have never trusted me. Ever since we started living together I've known that whenever we're apart you do nothing but worry and fret over whether I'm meeting someone else or that I might one day meet someone else. Or that I've already met someone else and I'm concealing it. That is not trust.'

'And you can see why now, can't you? How right I was. You said you were going to the post office.'

'I went there first. Don't worry. All the books went off.'

'*I didn't mean that!*' screamed Avery. 'You know I didn't.'

'It was of no importance,' said Tim quietly. 'Not compared to us.'

'Then *why*? Why risk you and me . . . all this . . .' Avery gestured at the cosy sitting room with such vigour that he slid off his perch.

'God – you're pixilated,' said Tim, helping him back up.

'I am not pissilated,' wept Avery. 'I mean . . . if it wasn't David in the box I thought it might be Nico . . . or Boris. I never in a million years thought it could be you.'

'I don't see why not. You know my sexual history.'

'But I thought you'd turned your back on all that,' said Avery. Then: *'Don't laugh.'*

'Sorry.'

'And why Kitty of all people?'

Tim shrugged, remembering the combination of fragile bones and tough, sly cherubical smile that had briefly excited him. 'She was pretty, and lean . . . quite boyish really . . .'

'She won't be boyish for long,' cut in Avery. 'Very unlean and unpretty she'll be.'

'I wouldn't have wanted her for long,' said Tim. And for a second he looked so desolate that Avery forgot who was the guilty party and almost made a move to comfort him as he would have done before the betrayal. 'If it makes you feel any better,' continued Tim, 'it was Kitty who made the running. I think she regarded me as some sort of challenge.'

'Some people don't seem to know the difference between a challenge and a bloody pushover.' Avery braced himself. 'How long . . . how many . . .'

'Half a dozen times. At the most.'

'Oh God!' Avery gasped as if from a body blow and covered his face with his hands. 'And was she . . . I mean . . . has there been . . .'

'No. No one else.'

'What shall I do?' Avery rocked from side to side on his stool. 'I don't know what to do.'

'Why should you do anything? It seems to me more than enough's been done already. And don't blubber.'

'I'm not.' Avery took his little butterball fists, shiny with moisture, from his teary eyes. His pale yellow curls, limp with sorrow, looked like a ring of scrambled egg. He choked out the next words. 'I don't know how you can be so heartless.'

'I'm not heartless but you know how I hate these honky-tonk emotions.' Tim tore a piece off the paper towel roll and mopped Avery's face which was criss-crossed with rivulets of tears and mucous and sweat. 'And give me that cup before it's all over the floor.'

'Everything's soiled . . . and . . . spoiled . . . I just can't bear any more . . .'

'I don't see how you can possibly know that until you try.' This cold sinewy reasoning brought Avery to a fresh pitch of misery. 'I mean it, Tim!' he cried. 'You must promise me faithfully that you'll never ever *ever* again –'

'I can't do that. And you wouldn't believe me if I did. Oh – you might now because you're desperate but tomorrow you'd start to wonder. And by the day after that . . .'

'But you *must* promise. I can't go on with all this insecurity.'

'Why not? Everyone else has to. Your trouble is you expect too much. Why can't we just muddle along like Mr and Mrs Average? You know . . . doing our best . . . picking each other up if we fall . . . making allowances . . . Cloud nine's for retarded adolescents.' Tim paused. ' "I never promised you a rose garden." '

'Well,' said Avery, with a flash of the old asperity. 'If I'm not going to have a rose garden I shan't want all this shit, shall I?' Then, when Tim smiled his shadowy, introspective smile Avery suddenly cried: 'It'd be all right if I didn't love you so much!'

'But if you didn't love me so much what on earth reason would I have for staying?'

Avery pondered this. Was such a remark a consolation? It seemed to imply that what he had to offer (the shop, the house, the meticulous and affectionate concern with which he went about his daily tasks) was not, after all, the reason why Tim stayed. Yet what else, worried Avery, did he have to offer? He turned the thought over. It seemed to him that the question had a catch in it some-where and he said so.

'There's always a catch.' Tim moved back to the sitting room and collected the pieces of the Chinese bowl. 'I must get some stuff tomorrow to fix this.'

'That's right. Put the boot in.' But Avery felt his woozy unhappiness touched by a flicker of warmth. Perhaps Tim would not be packing his bags after all. Perhaps in the morning they could open up the shop and check the till and tidy the books and carefully, like the walking wounded that they were, reach out to each other for comfort. Tim came back and put the painted fragments on the kitchen table.

'I'm sorry about the dish.'

'No, no. It's what I've always wanted,' said Tim kindly. 'An Araldited home.'

'. . . Do you remember Cornwall?'

'To my dying day. I thought I'd never get you away from that Redruth fisherman.'

'Ohhh . . .' Avery turned a guilty countenance towards his lover. 'I'd forgotten all about that.'

'I hadn't. But . . . as you can see . . . I'm still here.'

'Yes. D'you think' – Avery held out his hand – 'we'll ever be really happy again?'

'Stop living in some mythical future. You can't invent happiness. It's just a by-product of day-to-day plodding along. If you're lucky.'

'We have been lucky, haven't we, Tim?'

'We are lucky, you old tosspot. Best not to talk any more now. I'm wacked.'

Tim went upstairs then, leaving Avery to finish his coffee.

Avery felt like a punchball once the belabouring had ceased. Still vibrating with the memory and bruised. Then, because the first terror had passed and because Tim had come home and was going to stay, the concen-tration of despondency that had obscured Avery's fear lifted and the cloud no bigger than a man's lie returned.

Tim's remark, which he had first denied making then

255

shrugged aside, appeared suddenly to have developed an ominous gloss. For it seemed to Avery that to say 'We shall certainly have to leave *now*' indicated some secret knowledge. Surely it implied that, if Esslyn had not been killed, Avery and Tim, in spite of the lighting conspiracy, would have been able to stay? Now, to add to Avery's alarm, was the information that Tim had been Kitty's lover. And it was Tim who had supplied the razor. Had he really gone down to the loo in the interval of the play? And why go downstairs at all when there were two lavatories in the clubroom?

Tim called down, 'What's keeping you? Come on . . .'

But for the first time ever Avery, even whilst experiencing the usual sting in the flesh, did not get up and hurry towards the source of his delight. He sat on in his disordered kitchen getting colder and colder. And feeling more and more afraid.

It was the following day and Harold was making one of his rare appearances at the lunch table. Usually he dined out and Mrs Harold, who put up the sandwiches, was quite thrown by this sudden change of plan. Her household budget was tiny and any incursion at one point meant immediate retrenchment at another. She had found a Fray Bentos tinned individual steak and kidney pudding at the back of the cupboard and had rushed out and bought some carrots out of her flower seed money. But Harold had eaten so abstractedly that she felt she could well have given him her own lunch (boiled potatoes and two slices of luncheon meat) without him being any the wiser.

Now, as he scraped up the last smear of gravy, she said: 'It's not like you to come home midday, Harold.'

'I'm taking the afternoon off. It's Nicholas' half day and we have to have a serious talk about his future.'

'Does he know you're coming?' Harold looked blank. 'I mean . . . have you made some arrangement?'

'Don't be silly, Doris. I don't make arrangements with junior members of the company.'

256

'Then he might not be in.'

'I can't imagine where else he would be on a dreadful day like this.'

Doris looked out at the black rods of rain hammering against the kitchen window. She said, 'There's a piece of cake for sweet, Harold. If you'd like it.'

Harold did not reply. He stared at his wife but did not see her yellowish grey hair and shabby skirt and cardigan. His mind was full of his future leading man. He saw Nicholas striding the stage as Vanya and perhaps later as Tartuffe and later still as Othello or even Lear. Why not? Under Harold's expert guidance the boy could develop into a fine actor. Every bit as good as Esslyn. Perhaps even better.

Harold had not come to this decision easily. He had toyed with Boris and even the Everards who gave, in their quirky posturing way, quite interesting performances. But he was aware that the potential of all three put together was still nowhere near that of Nicholas. The only reason Harold had considered, even briefly, an alternative was because of a certain wilfulness, an antic disposition, that he had sensed strongly in the boy during rehearsals for *Amadeus*. Several times he had felt Nicholas getting away from him and glimpsed flashes of prowling energy that were disturbing to say the least. And of course Nicholas was very saucy. But Harold was confident that he could handle it. After all he had always managed to handle Esslyn.

'What are you going to see him about?' asked Doris.

'I'd have thought that was obvious. I have to find a replacement for Esslyn.'

Mrs Harold dutifully saw her husband off the premises and waved as he squeezed his paunch into position behind the wheel of the Morgan and backed out of the carport. A replacement for Esslyn indeed, she thought as she put the plates and cutlery in the sink. Anyone'd think he was a door handle. Or a broken teapot.

She had been deeply shocked by the reaction of Harold and the rest of the CADS to the death of their leading actor. She knew he wasn't popular (she hadn't liked him much herself) but some tears should be shed somewhere by someone. She decided to go to the funeral and left the dishes to soak whilst she went upstairs to sort out something dark and respectable.

Meanwhile Harold zipped up Causton High Street and parked outside the Blackbird. He planned to kill two birds and was pleased to see that Avery, who returned his greeting in a very subdued manner, and his partner were both in the shop. Harold beckoned Tim grandly to the cubbyhole and said: 'I'm holding auditions for *Vanya* on Friday evening. Dashing around and notifying everyone. Is Nico in?'

'Yes but he's –'

'Good. Now – I'd be very interested to see any ideas you might have on lighting the play.' Ignoring Tim's surprised and ironical glance he continued, 'Technically you're very capable and I think it's high time you were given a chance to branch out.'

'Thank you, Harold.'

'Nothing too fancy. It's Russia, don't forget.' On this enigmatical note Harold whisked aside the chenille curtain and heaved himself up the wooden stairs.

Nicholas was sitting on the floor declaiming. The gas fire was on and the room was warm and cosy. Cully Barnaby was curled up on the bed drinking coffee. Play scripts littered the floor and Nicholas was reading from the Harrison translation of the *Aeschylus*: 'Down, down, down he goes, and falling knows nothing, nothing. A smother of madness clouds round the victim. The groans of old –' As Harold appeared in the doorway Nicholas broke off and he and Cully looked at the intruder rather coolly.

'Ah,' said Harold, missing the coolness but spotting the apellation. 'I'd have expected to see you reading *Uncle Vanya*?'

'Why, Harold?'

'The auditions are on Friday.' Harold would have preferred this conversation without Tom Barnaby's daughter sitting in. She had been, in his opinion, although quite a good actress a nasty self-opinionated little girl and she didn't improve with age. Harold cleared his throat.

'I'm sure you will be very proud . . . very excited to hear that I have chosen you out of all the company to succeed Esslyn as my leading man.' Harold could see from the expression on Nicholas' face that he should perhaps have led up to this revelation more subtly. The boy looked deeply alarmed. Reassuringly Harold added: 'You're too young for Vanya, of course, but if you work hard, with my help I know you'll be a great success.'

'I see.'

So overwhelmed was Nicholas with emotion that he choked out the words. Then he added something else but the girl chose that precise moment to indulge in a fit of coughing and Harold had to ask Nicholas to repeat himself. When he did so Harold, open-mouthed with dismay, tottered to the nearest chair and fell into it.

'*Leaving?*'

'I'm going to Central.'

'Central what?'

'Central School of Speech and Drama. I want to go into the theatre.'

'But . . . you're *in* the theatre.'

'I mean the real theatre.'

The force of Harold's response lifted him clean from his seat. He gave a great cry in which rage and incredulity and horror were equally intermingled. Nicholas paled and climbed hurriedly to his feet. Cully stopped coughing.

'How dare you.' Harold walked across to Nicholas who stood his ground, but only just. 'How dare you! My theatre is as real . . . as true . . . as fine as any in the country. *In the world.* Do you have any idea who you're talking to? What my background is? I have heard the sort of applause for my work in what you are pleased to call the real theatre that actors would sell their souls to achieve. Stars have clamoured to work for me. Yes – stars! If it weren't for circumstances completely beyond my control do you think I'd be working in this place? With people like you!'

The final sentence was a tormented shout then Harold stood, panting. He appeared bewildered and ridiculous yet there was about him the tatters of an almost heroic dignity. He looked like a great man grown overnight too old. Or a warrior on whose head children have placed a paper crown.

'I'm . . . I'm sorry . . .' Nicholas stumbled into speech. 'If you like I could stay for *Vanya* . . . I don't have to go to London immediately –'

'No, Nicholas.' Harold stayed the boy's words by a simple gesture. 'I would not wish to work with anyone who did not appreciate and respect my directorial gifts.'

'Oh. Right. I might come along and audition anyway . . . if that's OK?'

'Anyone,' replied Harold, magisterially breaking upstage right, 'can audition.'

After he had left the two young people smiled at each other; celebrating their meeting and mutual admiration.

'Will you go on Friday?' asked Cully.

'I think so. He might've calmed down by then.'

'Then I shall, too.'

'You wouldn't.'

'Why not? I'm not due back till the end of January. And I'd give anything to play Yeliena. We can always work our own way.'

'Gosh – that'd be fantastic.'

Cully parted her lovely lips and smiled again. 'Wouldn't it though?' she said.

Barnaby and Troy were in the office of Hartshorn, Weatherwax and Tetzloff. Their Mr Ounce, who handled Esslyn Carmichael's affairs, was being affable if slightly condescending. Entertaining the police, his manner implied, was not what he was used to but he hoped if it was thrust upon him he could behave as well as the next man.

But if Barnaby had hoped to discover some sinister

undertow to the murdered man's life in his solicitor's office he was unlucky. Mr Ounce could reveal little more than did the arid contents in the desk at White Wings. Barnaby had been unlucky at the bank as well. No suspiciously large sums of money ever leaked in or out of the Carmichael account, all was depressingly well ordered, the balances no more and no less than one would have expected. The only thing remaining was the will which he was about to hear read. (He had offered to apply in the proper manner and go to a magistrate but Mr Ounce had graciously waived the necessity, saying he was sure time was of the essence.)

The document was brief and to the point. His widow would get the house and a comfortable allowance for herself and the child as long as she carried out her maternal duties in a proper manner. Carmichael junior would get the full dibs on reaching twenty-one, and in the event of the child's demise everything, including White Wings, went to the brother in Ottawa. Mr Ounce replaced the stiff ivory parchment folds in a metal deeds box and snapped the lock.

'Neatly tied up,' said Barnaby.

'I must confess my own fine Italian hand was somewhat to the fore there, Chief Inspector.' He rose from his old leather swivellor. 'We can't let the ladies have it all their own way, can we?'

'Blimey,' said Troy, when they were back in the station and warming themselves up with some strong coffee. 'I wouldn't mind being a fly on the wall when Kitty hears that.'

Barnaby did not respond. He sat behind his desk tapping his nails against each other. A habit to which he was prone when deep in thought. It drove Troy mad. He was just wondering if he could sneak out for a quick drag when his chief gave voice.

'What I can't get, Sergeant, is the timing . . .' Troy sat up. 'There are dozens of ways to kill a man. Why set it up in front of a hundred witnesses . . . taking risks back stage . . . tinkering with a razor when all you have to do is wait and catch him on some dark night on his tod?'

'I feel that's rather a strike against Kitty myself, chief. Trying it at home she'd be the first person we'd suspect.'

'A good point.'

'And now we've flushed the lover out,' Troy bounded on, encouraged, '*and* discovered that he was the one who supplied the razor in the first place. I bet he even suggested the Sellotape —'

'I think not. I've asked a lot of people about that. The general consensus seems to be that it was Dierdre.'

'Anyway — there he is with the perfect alibi, leaving Kitty to carry the can. That sort always do.'

'I don't know. It's a bit obvious.'

'But . . . excuse me, sir . . . the times you've said the obvious is so often the truth.'

Barnaby nodded. The observation was a fair one. As was Troy's implication that the familiar unheavenly twins lust and greed were once again probably the motivating power behind a sudden death. So why did Barnaby feel this case was different? He didn't welcome this perception, which seemed to him at the moment to lead absolutely nowhere, but it would not be denied. He saw now too that his previous knowledge of the suspects which he had regarded from the first as an advantage could also work against him. It was proving well nigh impossible to make his mind the objective mirror it should be if he were to appreciate what was really going on. His understanding of Kitty's character, his liking for Tim and the Smys, his sympathy for Dierdre all were gradually forcing him into a corner. At this rate, he observed sourly to himself, I'll hardly have a suspect left.

And then there was *Floyd on Fish*. He picked it out of his tray and fanned the pages yet again. The thing had been through the works at the lab. It was no more and no less than what it purported to be, and smothered with dozens of assorted prints. Now why the hell should someone send Harold, who had not the slightest interest in cooking, a recipe book? Why was it given anonymously?

Troy, asked for his ideas, had been worse than useles[s].
Just given one of his excruciating winks and said: 'Ver[y]
fishy, chief.' Joyce said Harold had seemed to be genuinely
puzzled by its arrival, assumed it to be a gift from an
unknown admirer and promptly given it away. Barnaby
couldn't see a single way in which it might be connected
with the case, but it was certainly odd. A loose end. And
he didn't care for loose ends although, as the case looked
at the moment like a bundle of cooked spaghetti, he
supposed another one more or less didn't much signify.

Troy was clearing his throat, and Barnaby retrieved his
wandering thoughts and raised his eyebrows. 'If we're
leaving sex and cash out, chief, I suppose the other big
one would be that he'd got something on somebody and
they wanted to keep him quiet.' Barnaby nodded. 'I know
we didn't find any surprises in his account but it could
have been blackmail. He could've been stashing it
abroad.'

'Mmm . . . it's an appealing idea. The trouble is it
doesn't fit the nature of the beast.'

'Sorry, sir . . . I'm not quite with you on that one.' Troy
was frowning; a little anxious about being found wanting
but determined to have each step quite clear before
proceeding to the next. He never pretended that he understood what Barnaby was getting at when he didn't, and
the chief inspector, knowing how his sergeant longed to
give the impression of keeping up or even leaping ahead,
respected this veracity.

'I just don't think Carmichael was the type. It's not
that he was a nice man – far from it – but he was
completely self-absorbed. He had no interest in other
people's affairs or the sheer energetic nastiness a successful
blackmailer needs.'

'Jealousy then, chief? Him being the leading light and
all that. Maybe somebody else wanted a go?' Even as he
voiced this suggestion Troy thought it was probably a
non-starter. Although he had quite enjoyed *Amadeus* he
thought the actors a load of poncy show-offs. Personally
he wouldn't have thought any of them had the guts to

skin a rabbit never mind putting somebody in the way of cutting their own throat. Still, he had been wrong before (Troy saw his willingness to admit to possessing this almost universal human weakness as a sign of real maturity) and might well be so again. 'Perhaps they were all in it together, sir? Like that film on the train . . . where everybody had a stab at the victim. A conspiracy.'

Barnaby raised his head at this and looked interested. Interested but glum. Troy remembered a phrase from the early morning news and essayed one of his witticisms.

'A putsch-up job, sir?'

'What?'

'P-u-t-s-c-h — it's a joke, chief. A sort of play on words . . . Putsch up — put up . . .'

Barnaby was silent for a minute then spoke slowly: 'My God, Troy. You might just be right.'

Gratified the sergeant continued, 'It was in one of these banana republics —'

'It's so near . . .'

'That's what I said. Put and —'

'No, no. I'm not talking about that. Perhaps . . . let me think . . .'

Barnaby sat very still. A nebulous possibility, no more than a glimmer, flickered into his mind. Flickered and was gone. Came back, solidified a bit, was gently tested.

'I wonder . . .' continued Barnaby '. . . perhaps . . . Esslyn gave us the reason for the murder . . . at least . . .' He groped towards the next words slowly. 'He gave it to Kitty. She didn't have the wit to see the implication behind what he said, but I should have done. There's no excuse for me.'

Troy, appreciating that he also hadn't had the wit and that there was no excuse for him either, regarded his boots sulkily. Barnaby got up and started to pace around, then sent his sergeant for some more coffee. Troy disappeared into the outer office and helped himself from the Cona.

When he returned to the inner sanctum the DCI was gazing out of the window. Troy put the mugs on the desk and returned to his seat. When Barnaby turned he was struck by the paleness of the chief inspector's countenance. Pale but lively. No sooner had one expression, hopeful elation, registered than it was chased away by disbelief which in turn gave way to a jauntiness that was almost debonair dissolving into puzzlement.

'You've . . . got something then, sir?' asked Troy.

'I don't know . . . it's all out of whack . . . but it must be. I just can't see *how.*'

Fat lot of good that is then, opined Troy silently. The old sod always did this when he believed a case was shifting towards a conclusion. He would say that all the information so far obtained was as available to Troy as it was to him and that the sergeant should be perfectly capable of coming to his own assessment. The fact that this remark was a perfectly valid one in no way lessened the sergeant's chagrin every time he heard it. Now he noticed Barnaby was looking at him rather oddly. Then, to his alarm, the chief walked around the desk, came up to Troy's chair, bent down and brought his lips close to the younger man's ear. Bloody hell, thought Troy, preparing to leap for the door. Who'd have thought it? Barnaby moved his mouth, breathed faintly and returned to his seat. Troy produced a hankerchief and mopped his face.

'Well, Sergeant,' said Barnaby, in a blessedly masculine and unseductive manner. 'What did I say?'

'Bungled, sir.'

'Aaahhh . . .' It was a long slow hiss of satisfaction. 'Nearly, Troy. A good guess. Nearly . . . but not quite.'

Bangles? thought the sergeant. Burgled? Boggled? Buggered? (Back to Doris and Daphne.) Or how about bon-bons? Heyy . . . how *about* bon-bons? The bloke was eating sweets all through the play. Or there was borrowed. That fitted. The razor was borrowed. All the dead man's clothes were hired. Wasn't much like bungled, though. *Fumbled.* Something had been fumbled. That was more like it. Meant practically the same thing after all. As no revelation appeared to be forthcoming from the horse's mouth Troy decided to settle for fumbled. He looked across at Barnaby who seemed to have gone into a trance. He was staring over Troy's left shoulder, the light of intelligence quite absent from his eyes.

But his mind was whirring. Like a chess player he moved his figures around. On the black squares (the wings, the stage, the dressing rooms) and on the white (the lighting box, the clubroom, the auditorium). He forged likely and unlikely alliances and guessed at possible repercussions. He imagined mirrored reflections of his suspects, hoping that way to surprise a familiar face in secret revelatory relaxation. And gradually, by way of improbable juxtaposition, glancing insights and hard-won recall of certain conversations, he arrived at an eminently workable hypothesis. It fitted very well. It made perfect sense and was psychologically sound. It explained (almost) everything. There was only one slight snag. The way things stood at the moment what it hypothesized (who had murdered Esslyn Carmichael and why) could not possibly be anywhere near the truth. He muttered that fact aloud.

Fat lot of good that is then, thought Troy, still smarting over his inability to suss out Barnaby's earlier insights. Now the chief was rumbling again. Rumble, rumble. Mutter, mutter.

'There *had* to be an audience, Troy. We've been looking at things from quite the wrong angle. It wasn't a hazard – it was an essential. So that everyone could see what he was doing . . .'

'What, Carmichael?'

'No, of course not. Use your nous.' Barnaby picked up a Biro and started scribbling. 'And don't look so affronted,' he continued, not looking up. 'Think, man!'

Whilst Troy thought Barnaby reflected minutely on the times and the names and the positions he had jotted down. If everyone was where they said they were at the times they said they were, doing what they said they were doing, then he was up a gum tree. So someone was lying. Fair enough. You expected murderers to lie. But when you had a theatre full of people prepared to stand by what was after all the evidence of their own eyes and back him up, then you were in real schtuck. Especially when two of the eyes were your own.

But he knew he was right. He knew in his blood and in his bones. Over the years he had come to this point in a case too many times to be mistaken. Details might be unclear, practicalities elusive, methodology right up the Swanee, but he knew. The backs of his hands prickled, his neck in the stuffy overheated office crawled with cold. He knew and could do nothing.

'Oh fuck it, Troy!' The sergeant jumped as Barnaby's fist hit the desk. 'I'm bloody hemmed in. Nobody can be in two places at once . . . can they?'

'No, sir,' replied Troy, feeling for once on pretty safe ground. He was not displeased to see Barnaby foxed. You could put up with just so much swanking about. Now there were two of them without a bloody clue. He watched his chief's fierce frown and tightly clamped jaw. Any minute now the little brown bottle would appear. And here it was. The chief inspector shook out two indigestion tablets and chased them down with cold coffee. Then he sat and stared at his piece of paper for so long that the neat black letters became meaningless.

'This is where,' he said to Troy, 'if I were a religious man I should start praying for a miracle.'

And, such is the wickedly unfair tilt of things in a world where a monk can spend his life on his knees and never get a nibble, for Tom Barnaby, sometimes profane, moderately decent, frequent faller by the wayside, the miracle occurred. Buzz, buzz. He picked up the phone. It was David Smy. Barnaby listened for a moment, responded: 'You're quite sure?' and replaced the receiver.

'Troy,' he said, presenting an awesome countenance. 'When all this is over, remind me to send a hefty cheque to a worthwhile cause.'

'Why's that then, chief?'

'Strokes of luck like this must be paid for, Sergeant. Otherwise whoever's sending them gets shirty.'

'So what did they say? Whoever it was.'

'If you remember,' said Barnaby, with a smile so broad it seemed to touch his ears, 'David thought there was something odd about the tray he took on.'

'But he described it all and there wasn't.'

'Quite right. But you'll recall from his statement that as it was a personal prop he gave the tray a quick suss round about the five. Now – the razor that Young supplied and that the murdered man used to cut his throat had a mother-of-pearl design of flowers and leaves on one side of the handle and a little line of silver rivets on the reverse. The reason David Smy thought there was something odd when he entered the wings with it laying sunny-side-down on his tray was because he noticed the rivets.'

'So?'

'When he gave the tray the once-over before eight *the rivets were not there*.'

'Then . . .' Troy picked up the inspector's excitement '. . . there were two?'

'There were two.'

'So . . . all our problems with the time . . . ?'

'Gone. The whole thing's wide open. It could have been tinkered with any time between when Dierdre checked it and ten o'clock when David took it on.'

'So . . . whoever it was left the substitute, took the tape off and slipped the original back in his or her own good time.'

'Precisely. I'd thought of that option, of course, but assumed no one would dare risk leaving the tray on the props table minus the razor for more than a few minutes, even with the wings dark. But, as we now see, they didn't have to.'

'So you're no longer boxed in, sir?' Troy struggled hard not to sound peevish. He didn't wish to appear mean spirited but really, the way information fell into some people's laps was beyond a joke. Then he recalled that some of the kudos at the end of a successful case always fell on the bag carrier, and cheered up. 'So we've got a full house then? Anybody could have done it?'

'I think we'll have to except Avery Phillips. He didn't

come out of the box till after the murder. But apart from him, yes . . . anybody.' He got up, suddenly full of zip and vigour, and grabbed his coat. 'I'm going to sort out a warrant. Get the car round.'

'We looking for the other razor, sir?'

'Yes. I expect whoever it is has had the sense to chuck it by now, but you never know. We might strike lucky.'

By the time Barnaby returned from Superintendent Penrose's office Troy, sub-Burberry tightly belted, had brought the car round.

'Where to first, sir?'

'Might as well start at the top and work our way down.'

'Chief Uncle Bulgaria is it then?'

Barnaby laughed. 'My daughter used to love the Wombles.'

'So did I,' replied Troy, and Barnaby winced.

Dierdre opened the front door of the house and stepped inside. It was eerily quiet. She had always thought of her father's presence as a silent one; now she realized it had instigated many subtle sounds. The creak of his armchair, the soft rub of his clothes against the furniture, the snatched papery rustle of his breath. She took off her coat and Sunny's lead and hung them in the dingy hall then walked to the kitchen where she stood uncertainly, looking at the dishes that had been sitting in the sink, gravied and custard streaked, for the past four days. They looked as much a fixture as the spotted chrome taps and grubby roller towel. Best to keep busy, the medical social worker had said, and Dierdre knew this was good advice. Even as she stood there she saw herself sweeping and polishing and dusting. Hanging gay new curtains, placing a bright geranium on the window sill. But, vivid as these pictures were, they paled beside a concomitant weight of ennui so great that, after a few more minutes attached to the hearth rug, she began to believe she would never move again.

Sunny, who had gone in for the most dashing leaps and runs when they were out, had already sensed the situation and now sat quietly at her feet. Dierdre picked up her copy of *Uncle Vanya*, interleaved and crammed with production ideas and sketches for the set. One of the nicest things during her stay with the Barnabys had happened on Wednesday morning when she had discussed the theatre for hours with Cully – at first tentatively then, as her companion responded with great interest, more and more enthusiastically. They had talked through lunch (extraordinarily inedible) and well into the afternoon, in fact right up to the time Dierdre had had to leave for the hospital. She couldn't understand now why she had ever thought Cully sneering and standoffish.

Sunny made a hopeful sound, stretching his lips in that strange manner that dogs have; half yawn, half grin. Dierdre started guiltily. He had not eaten all day and had made no complaint till now. There were three tins of meat and a large bag of Winalot in her bag and she put some food on a plate then filled his stone dish marked DOG with clean water. She left the sound of steady lapping behind as she climbed the stairs.

In her father's room she started automatically to make his bed then stopped, sharply recalled to the complete pointlessness of her task. She looked around, a fall of green blanket in her arms, taking in the bottle of medicine and little jars of pills on the bamboo table; the Bible open at the first book of Kings showing an engraving of Elijah being delicately fed by ravens; two pieces of Turkish Delight in a saucer.

Gradually and with the deepest apprehension she absorbed the full enormity of what had happened. Her father was not poorly or a little unstable or susceptible to queer turns. He was senile and a danger to himself and others; the balance of his mind disturbed. Dierdre had a sudden vision of some old-fashioned scales and an impersonal hand dishing out wholesome grains of sanity with a little brass scoop. They were white and clean like virgin sand. Into the other shallow metal saucer was poured a hot dark flux of irrationality until the saucer overflowed and the chaste pale granules were first swamped then quite washed away in the black froth of madness.

Dierdre bowed her head. She swayed and, momentarily, fought for breath. But she did not sit down. And she did not cry. She stood for five full minutes in a tumult of misery and sorrow then started to strip the bed and fold up the sheets and blankets. She opened the window and, as the cold air rushed in, realized for the first time how stuffy the room was. Fearful of her father's health, once October had arrived she had kept the window tightly closed. 'That'll blow the cobwebs away,' he would say when she opened it again in May. Having put the bedding in a neat pile Dierdre picked up the waste basket and swept all the jars and bottles into it together with his carafe and glass. The Bible she snapped shut and replaced on the bookshelf.

She worked mechanically, under no illusion that her activities could even begin to ease let alone transform her situation. But (the social worker had been right in this respect) as she continued to go briskly from one simple task to the next, generating her own momentum, she became aware that the procedure did offer some slight degree of comfort. And, even more important, was getting her through the period she had dreaded most, her first time alone in Mortimer Street.

She shook the two rugs in the back yard and noticed how threadbare the dark red and blue Turkish one was. She rolled it up and pushed it in the bin. Then she carried the bedding downstairs and put it by the front door. She would have the sheets washed, the blankets cleaned, and give the lot to the Salvation Army. She cleaned and polished for the next hour until the room shone and smelt fragrantly of beeswax and Windowlene. She replaced the single mat and put Mr Tibbs' tortoiseshell hair brush and comb and leather stud box away in the chest of drawers. Then she leaned against the window sill and sighed with something like satisfaction.

The room looked clean and neat, and would have appeared to a casual visitor quite impersonal. Dierdre completed her task by dusting the pictures. Two Corot reproductions, a text (TRUST IN THE LORD) garlanded with pansies and ears of wheat and framed in burnt pokerwood, and *The Light of the World*. Dierdre flicked the dust from the first three whilst they were *in situ* then took down the Holman Hunt and studied it pensively. The figure that had given comfort to her childish hurts and sorrows and had seemed to stand loving guard when she slept now appeared nothing more than a sentimental dreamer, a paper saviour impotent and unreal, standing in his flood of insipid yellow light. She fought against the pity that always gripped her at the sight of the crown of thorns; she fought against insidious false comfort.

Running downstairs again, holding the picture away from her almost at arm's length, Dierdre hurried through the kitchen to the back garden and once more lifted the lid of the dustbin. She dropped *The Light of the World* inside. Replacing the cover she turned away immediately, as if that sad calm forgiving gaze might pierce the metal and catch her own. And she had no sooner gone back upstairs than the upbeat energy, the essential driving feeling that she was tackling a job well done, drained away. Now, looking at the poor denuded room with all traces of her father so firmly erased, Dierdre was appalled. She was behaving as if he were dead. And as if his memory must always bring pain and never solace. She apologized aloud as if he could hear, and brought out his brush and comb and stud box and replaced them on the bamboo table. Then she returned to the back yard and retrieved the painting.

She stood, indecisive and shivering in the cold air, with it in her hands. She did not want to take it back inside but felt now that it was out of the question that it should be destroyed. In the end she put it in the shed, placing it carefully on an old enamel-topped table beside the earth-encrusted flowerpots, balls of green twine and seed trays. She closed the door gently as she left, not wishing to advertise her presence and invoke Mrs Higgins.

Dierdre had only seen her neighbour once since Monday evening, when she had called in briefly to collect any post. Mrs Higgins had been all agog with many a 'fancy' and 'poor Mr Tibbs – out of the blue like that'. Dierdre had reacted tersely. Out of the blue had seemed to her an especially fatuous remark. Terrible things surely came out of the grey, or out of a deep transforming black. At the realization that there would be no more little envelopes or lugubrious sighs and miserable forecasts when she arrived home from the Latimer, Dierdre's spirits lifted once more.

She returned to the kitchen where Sunny, curled up in front of an empty grate, immediately got up and ran to meet her. She crouched down and buried her face in his sparkling cream and ginger ruff. Glancing at the mantelpiece she realized there were three hours before she needed to leave for the Chekov auditions. How slowly the clock seemed to be ticking. Of course there was plenty to do. All those dishes for a start. Perhaps Sunny might like another walk. And she still hadn't unpacked her case. It occurred to Dierdre suddenly how much *time* there seemed to be when you were unhappy. Perhaps this leaden comprehension, that each minute must last for at least an hour, was what people meant by loneliness. Time turning inwards and then standing still. Well – she'd just have to get used to it and soldier on. She was turning the hot tap when the doorbell rang.

She decided not to go. It was probably one of her father's so-called friends who had heard the news and, after cutting him dead for the past eighteen months, was now calling to see if there was anything they could do. Or Mrs Higgins, dewlaps aquiver with curiosity. It wouldn't be the Barnabys. Although warmly pressing her to stay Joyce had left it that Dierdre would get in touch if she wanted any further help. The bell rang again and Sunny started to bark. Dierdre dried her hands. Whoever it was was not going away. She opened the front door. David Smy stood on the step clutching a bunch of flowers.

'Oh!' Dierdre stepped back awkwardly. 'David . . . what a - Come in . . . that is . . . come in. What a surprise . . . I mean . . . what a nice surprise . . .' She chattered nervously (no one from the company had ever visited her at home before) as she led him to the kitchen. On the threshold she remembered the state of the place, backed away and opened the door of the sitting room.

'Please . . . sit down . . . how nice . . . how lovely to see you. Um . . . can I get you anything . . . some tea?'

'No thank you, Dierdre. Not at the moment.'

David sat, as slowly and calmly as he did everything, on the Victorian button-backed nursing chair, and removed his corduroy cap. He had on a beautiful dark green soft tweed suit that Dierdre had never seen before and looked very smart. She wondered where on earth he was going. Then he stood up again and Dierdre fluttered to a halt somewhere between the piano and the walnut tallboy.

David's flowers were long-stemmed apricot roses, the flowers shaped like immaculate candle flames. The florist had assured him that, in spite of being scentless and unnaturally uniform they were the finest in the shop and had been flown in from the Canaries only yesterday. David, starting as he meant to go on, had bought every bloom in the bucket (seventeen) at a cost of thirty-four pounds. Now he held them out to Dierdre and she closed the gap between them, reaching out hesitantly.

'Thank you . . . that is kind . . . Actually I've already been to the hospital but I'll be going again on Sunday. I'm sure my father will love them. I'll get a vase.'

'I don't think you quite understand, Dierdre.' David stopped her as she turned away. 'The flowers are not for your father. They're for you.'

'For . . . for *me*? But . . . I'm not ill . . .'

David smiled at this. He further narrowed the gap between them and bent upon her a look of such loving kindness that she all but burst into tears. Then he stretched out his green tweedy arm and drew her to him.

'Ohhh . . .' breathed Dierdre, hope and disbelief shining, fifty-fifty, in her eyes. 'I didn't . . . I didn't know . . . I didn't understand . . .'

She did weep then; little sobs of joy. Sunny, much

concerned, started to whimper. 'It's all right.' She bent down and patted him. 'Everything's all right.'

'I didn't know you had a dog.'

'It's a long story. Shall I tell you? Perhaps while we have some tea –' She turned towards the door but David drew her back.

'In a moment. I've been waiting a long time to do this. And we have the rest of our lives to have some tea.' And then he kissed her.

She nestled once more against his shoulder and his arm tightened. It was not a white feathered arm and it was certainly not twelve feet tall yet, such was the feeling of exhilarating comfort, for a moment it seemed to Dierdre that she might have been enclosed in a tightly furled wing.

Rosa sat in the middle of Row D feeling disappointed. She had been convinced there would be an 'atmosphere' at the audition for *Vanya*. Surely the unseemly departure of the company's previous leading man would mark the proceedings in some way? Slightly lowered tones, perhaps; a nice hesitancy in putting oneself forward for an unexpectedly vacant title role. But no, everything was proceeding as usual. Actors striding on and off the stage, Harold pontificating, Dierdre at her table. David Smy was in the back row next to his father with an oddly assorted dog on his knee and Kitty, who had had quite a bit of fun running away from Rosa with mock squeals of fright, was now leaning against the pros arch and sulking. She had come down not to read but to have a nice cosy chat with Nicholas, only to find him deep in conversation with Joycey's showy daughter.

Joyce herself, hoping for the part of Maria the elderly nurse, was waiting in the wings with Donald Everard. Clive, to everyone's surprise, had cheekily taken to the stage to try for Telyeghin. Boris, having just given Astrov's 'idle life' speech, was drinking the house white, and Riley rested on Avery's bosom darting many a snappy glance over his shoulder at the dog in the back row, suspecting some planned territorial infringement.

When Clive had finished, Cully Barnaby stepped forward to read for Yeliena Andreyevna and Rosa sat up. No reason why the child shouldn't make an attempt, of course. There was no denying that she was marginally nearer to the character's age (twenty-six) than Rosa or that, as a youngster, she'd had quite a little way with her on stage. Still . . . Rosa half settled back and waited, uneasy.

'You're standing by the window,' called Harold. 'You open it and talk half looking out. From "my dear – don't you understand" . . . Page two one five.'

Then Cully moved, not towards the window at the back of the set (still in place from *Amadeus*) as Rosa had expected but right down to the footlights where she pushed against an imaginary casement and leaned out, her lovely face stamped with irritated melancholy. She began to speak in a rich, sharp voice, vivid as an ache and not at all in the musical 'Chekovian' manner the CADS thought proper. Her anger flowed into the auditorium, powerful and bitter. Rosa, chilled to the marrow, felt her heart tumble out of its place and bounce against her ribs.

But Cully was hardly into the speech when two men appeared at the swing doors under the exit sign and walked, with measured tread, down the aisle. So unflurried and even was their stride (neither fast nor slow), so closely did the younger man emulate the bearing of his companion that there was something almost comic in their sudden appearance. They might have been making an entrance in a musical comedy. Until you looked at the first one's face.

Cully faltered, read one more line, stopped and said: 'Hello, Dad.'

'Well *really*, Tom . . .' Harold got up. 'Of all the times. We're auditioning here. I hope this is important.'

'Extremely. Where are you going?' Tim had climbed out of his seat.

'To open some wine.'

'If you'd sit down, please. What I have to say won't

276

take long.' Tim sat down. 'Perhaps everyone on stage and in the wings could come to the stalls. Save me screwing my neck round.'

Nicholas, Dierdre, Joyce and Cully clambered down from the stage. Donald Everard followed and slid into the seat next to his twin. The young detective in the raincoat sat on the steps leading from the stage and Barnaby walked to the pass door at the end of Row A, turned and surveyed them all. Even Harold fell silent, though not for long, and Nicholas, innocent though he might be, thought, 'this is it', and experienced a thrill of alarm so strong it made him feel almost sick.

Barnaby began by saying: 'I felt it only fair to keep you abreast with the current investigations pertaining to the Carmichael case.' What a tease, thought Boris. As if the police ever kept a suspect abreast of anything. Tom's setting something up. 'And I'd like to talk for a moment if I may about the character of the murdered man. It has always been my belief that an accurate assessment of the victim's personality is the first step in an inquiry of this kind. Random killing apart, a man or woman is usually done away with because of what they think or believe or say or do. In other words, because of the sort of person they are.'

'Well, I hope we're not going to waste much time going over that,' interrupted Harold. 'We all know what sort of person Esslyn was.'

'Do we? I know what the general opinion was. I went along with it myself – why not? Until now I'd no reason to go into the matter in any detail. Oh yes, we all knew what sort of person Esslyn was. Eminently fanciable, vain, strong-willed, solipsistic, a wow with the ladies. But when I tried to get to grips with this character I found he simply wasn't there. There were outward signs, of course. Certain narcissistic posturings, and Casanovian pursuits, but beyond this . . . nothing. Now why should this be?'

'He was shallow,' said Avery. 'Some people just are.'

'Perhaps. But there is always more to any one person than what they choose to reveal. So I asked questions and listened to the answers and examined my own perceptions a bit more closely and gradually a very different picture began to emerge. First perhaps we can look into the question of women. There is no doubt that he was loved, and very truly loved, by one.' His glance fell on Rosa and her mouth folded tightly into a controlled line. 'She accepted him for what he was. Or what she thought he was.'

'There's no thought about it,' cried Rosa, her voice raw. '*I knew him.*'

'But who else ever cared? When I tried to pin this down I got varying replies. Esslyn himself naturally fostered the illusion that they all cared. That, like Don Juan, he had no sooner had his way with one blossom than he moved on to pluck the next, leaving a trail of broken hearts. But I could find no actual proof of this. It was all hearsay, very vague. I did however come across one or two interesting comments. "Nothing ever lasted very long for Esslyn" and "They used to get fed up and drift off". *They*, you'll notice – not he. Certainly when he finally did break up his marriage for a pretty girl she'd left him within the month. And his second wife had no love for him at all.'

Kitty's eyes, already quite tarnished with crossness, glowered. Barnaby guessed at a recent visit to Mr Ounce.

'And why was it such a piece of cake for her to lead this man, who supposedly had the pick of the bunch, to the altar by simply lying about a pregnancy?'

There was an audible intake of breath at this revelation from several people, and Rosa made a thick choking sound. The Everards whickered like excited horses.

'To move on to his position as an actor. In this company he was top dog. A big fish in a little pond –'

'I beg leave to take issue there, Tom. This theatre is –'

'*Please.*' Harold subsided reluctantly. 'A little pond. True he had leading roles but he did not have the talent, the perception or the humility to make anything of them. Neither did he have the ambition to look for pastures new. There are bigger groups in Slough or Uxbridge where he might have stretched himself but he never showed the

278

slightest inclination to do so. Perhaps because he may not have found another director quite so amenable.'

'Amenable!' cried Harold. 'Me?'

'There are many people I know who regarded his refusal to take direction as revealing supreme confidence. I disagree. It is putting yourself in a producer's hands, trying different ways of working, taking risks that shows an actor's confidence. And I gradually came to the conclusion that ambition and self-assurance were two things that Esslyn Carmichael had very little of.'

He got a lot of puzzled looks at that but none of actual disbelief. More than one person seemed to find the idea feasible. Rosa, whilst looking a little mystified, also nodded.

'And yet . . .' Barnaby left his position at the pass door and walked slowly up the aisle. Every head followed. 'There were certain signs that this aspect of his personality was undergoing some sort of change. The feeling I picked up during questioning was that, over the last few months, he had become openly argumentative, querying or defying Harold and castigating the only other actor in the company who was any serious threat.' Nicholas looked rather pleased at that remark and gave Cully a wide smile. 'Now,' continued Barnaby, 'why should that be?'

The company recognized the question as purely rhetorical. No one spoke. In fact two people looked so deeply disturbed you could have been forgiven for thinking that they might never speak again. 'I believe that once we know the answer to that we shall know why he was murdered. And once we know why we shall know who.'

Troy found his mouth was dry. At first guarded and resentful of his chief's deductive progress, he had sat outside the circle with a slightly defiant air, knowing his place, showing his detachment sniffily. Now, in spite of himself, totally gripped by the thrust of Barnaby's narrative, he leaned forward caught in the story teller's net.

'I'd like to jump to the first night of *Amadeus* and the drama within the drama. I'm sure you all know by now that rumour and misinformation were running rife and that Kitty and Nicholas were both attacked by Esslyn during the course of the evening.' At this indication that his previous declaration had been validated Nicholas looked even more pleased. 'This naturally put them high on the list of suspects. In any case I'm afraid the widow of a murdered man is usually thrust into this unenviable position. Kitty had the motive – he'd discovered she was unfaithful and, once the baby had "disappeared", would perhaps have turned her out. And she had the perfect opportunity –'

'I didn't kill him!' shouted Kitty. 'With all the witnessess I'd got to physical cruelty I could've got a divorce. And maintenance.'

'That sort of procedure can take a long time, Kitty. And not always end to your advantage.'

'I never touched the bloody thing.'

'Certainly your prints were not on the razor but then neither were anyone else's until the dead man picked it up. But then the most inept delinquent knows enough to wipe the handle of a murder weapon clean. Even so all my instincts set themselves against this simple solution.'

Rosa and Kitty engaged glances. Disappointment and triumph sizzled back and forth.

'I also decided that David, Colin and Dierdre were in the clear and for pretty much the same reasons. I've known them all a long time and although I'd never be foolish enough to say that none of them are capable of murder I very much doubt if they were capable of this *particular* murder. But of course they did have the opportunity. And this was my real stumbling block. Because, until earlier this evening all the wrong people had the opportunity and all the right people had none.'

'What happened earlier this evening, then?' asked Harold, who had been quieter for longer than anyone present could ever remember.

'I discovered there were two razors.'

The remark fell into the silence like a stone. Ripples of emotion spread and spread. Some faces looked eager, some were flushed and serious, one turned ghastly pale. Avery, noticing, thought, Oh God – he knows something. I was right. Then, not caring whether or not he was publicly rebuffed, he took his lover's hand and squeezed it; once for comfort and twice for luck. Tim didn't even notice.

'This of course opened up the whole thing. Almost anyone could have taken it, left the substitute, removed the tape when it was convenient and then slipped the original back.'

'Who's the almost, Tom?' asked Nicholas.

'Avery. He didn't return to the wings till the play was over. Now I knew how,' continued Barnaby, 'I was left with the two whys. Why should anyone wish to murder Esslyn in the first place and, much more puzzling, why choose to do it in front of over a hundred people? Frankly I still haven't understood the second but I have become quite sure about the first.'

Now he retraced his steps and, once again, every head, as if yoked together on one invisible string, turned. He leaned back against the thrust of the stage hands in pockets, and paused. The old ham, observed Cully admiringly. And I thought I got it all from me mum.

'Putting aside the motives we first thought of – namely passion and money – we are left with a third, equally powerful and, I believe, the correct one. Esslyn Carmichael was killed *because of something he knew*. Now, our investigation has proved that, unless he's been ordering his affairs with special cunning, there have been no large sums of money coming his way and that seems to rule out using this knowledge for financial coercion. But a blackmailer's demands can be other than monetary. He can put sexual pressure on people or he can use his secret to obtain power. I thought the first, as he was so newly married and, according to his imperceptive lights, quite satisfied, was unlikely. Yet, how much more unlikely, given my understanding of his character as lacking ambition and confidence, was the latter. And yet I became more and more certain that it was in this area of investigation that my solution lay.

'Like all of you, I'm sure, I have thought of this murder as a theatrical one. Although on this dreadful evening reality crept upon the stage in certain unpleasant ways, we all knew, until the very last minute, that we were watching a play. Esslyn wore make-up and costume, he spoke lines and executed moves that he had rehearsed. Whoever killed him was a member of the company. It seemed so plain that everything centred on the Latimer that I hardly took into account the rest of Esslyn's life – the larger part of it after all. It was Kitty who reminded me that from nine till five Monday to Friday Esslyn Carmichael *was an accountant.*'

At this point Tim covered his chalk-white countenance with his hands and lowered his head. Avery put an arm around his shoulders. As he did so his mind became crowded with bathetic images. He saw himself visiting Tim in prison every week even if that meant for years. He would bake a cake with a file in. Or wear a rope beneath his woolly. At the thought of the food Avery felt a colly definitely start to wobble. How would Tim survive?

'If you remember, Kitty . . .' Avery forced his attention back to what Tom was saying. '. . . I asked you if you had noticed any change recently in your husband's routine and you said he had gone to work the Saturday morning before he died. I don't know, Rosa, if you recall . . . ?'

'Never.' The first Mrs Carmichael shook her head. 'He was quite firm on that. Said he had enough of facts and figures during the week.'

'He had gone to the office, Kitty told me, to "call something in". A strange phrase, surely. One you'd be more likely to hear from the lips of a gambler than an accountant. Or a debt collector. Because that's what the phrase means. You "call in" a debt. And I believe this is what Esslyn was about to do. What was owed and for how long we don't know. But he had apparently decided that it had gone on long enough.'

'But Tom,' interrupted Joyce, 'you said he was killed because he knew something.'

'And also,' Nicholas took advantage of the breach, 'owing someone money isn't much fun but it's not the end of the world. Certainly not worth killing for. I mean – the worst that can happen is you get taken to court.'

'Oh, there was much more than that at stake. To discover precisely what, we have to go back to the point I reached earlier and ask again what happened several months ago – six to be exact – to give Esslyn the confidence to start throwing his weight about?'

Barnaby paused then and the silence lay ripe with suspicion and stabbed by startled looks. At first dense it slowly became more lightsome, gathering point and clarity. Barnaby was never sure who first fingered the Everards. Certainly it was not him. But, as if telepathically, first one head then another pointed in their direction. Nicholas spoke.

'He got himself a pair of toadies.'

'I see nothing wrong –' rushed in Clive Everard.

'– neither do I –' said Donald.

'– in becoming friendly with –'

'– in *devotedly* admiring –'

'– even venerating –'

'– someone of Esslyn's undoubted talents –'

'– and remarkable skills –'

'You bloody hypocrites.' Barnaby's voice was so quiet that for a moment people glanced around uncertain from where that damning indictment had arisen. Troy knew and his adrenalin shot up. Barnaby walked to the edge of the row in which the brothers were sitting and said, still softly: 'You malicious wicked meddling evil-minded bastards.'

Pasty-faced, their nostrils pinched in tight with alarm, the Everards shrank closer together. Kitty gazed at them with dawning horror, Cully, unaware that she was gripping Nicholas' arm very tight, half rose from her seat. Avery's expression of misery was suddenly touched with a glow of hope. Joyce felt she would choke on the suspense, and Harold was nodding. His head wagged back and forth as if it were loose on his shoulders like the head on those gross Chinese buddhas found sometimes in antique shops.

'You've no call to speak to us like that,' cried one of the Everards, recovering fast.

'Since when has it been against the law to admire an actor?'

'*Admire.*' Barnaby almost spat out the word and the volume of his voice increased tenfold. He pushed his angry face close to theirs. 'You didn't admire him. You *despised* him. You laughed at him. You sported with him. You led him around like a bear with a ring through its nose. And he, poor bugger, never having had a friend in his life, thought no doubt that this was what friendship was. Court toadies? Quite the reverse. Whatever that might be.'

'*Eminences grises?*' suggested Boris.

'And directly responsible for his death.'

At this Donald Everard flew out of his seat. 'You heard that!' he screamed, flapping his arms at the rest of the gathering. 'That's libel!'

'We shall sue,' shrieked his brother. 'You can't go around saying we killed Esslyn and get away with it!'

'We've got witnesses!'

'All these people!'

'I didn't say you had killed him,' said Barnaby, stepping back from these hysterics with an expression of deep distaste. 'I said I believed you were responsible for his death.'

'It's the same thing.'

'Not quite. As you'll realize if you'll stop flinging yourselves about and settle down to think about it.' When they had reluctantly, with many an injured cluck and toss of a gel-stiffened crest, reseated themselves, Barnaby carried on. 'So we now have a puppet, a hollow man with someone pulling his strings. And what do they do, oh so subtly, so slyly, these puppeteers? At first they encourage intransigence. I can just hear it . . . "You're not going to take that, are you? You're the leading man . . . don't you realize how powerful you are? They couldn't do anything without you." But after a few weeks that rather modest mischief starts to pall. They've gone about as far as they can go with that one. So they look around for something more interesting and I suspect it was about this time that Esslyn shared with them the information that was to instigate their grand design and lead directly to his death.

'In fact it was something my sergeant said in the office today that pointed me in the right direction.' His sergeant, suddenly in the spotlight, attempted to look intelligent, modest and invaluable. He also managed a surreptitious wink at Kitty who promptly winked back. 'He's given to making feeble, atrociously unfunny jokes,' continued Barnaby (Troy immediately looked less intelligent), 'the latest being a play on the word "putsch" but, as these things sometimes do, it reminded me of something very similar from a recent interview. I don't know if you remember, Kitty . . . ?'

Suddenly addressed, Kitty, who was still ogling Troy, blushed and said, 'Sorry?'

'You told me that Esslyn spoke to you of the dramatic effect he intended to make on the first night.'

'That's right, he did.'

'And because he was admiring himself in his costume you assumed that he referred to his own transformation.'

'No – you said that, Tom. When you explained that funny French bit.' Barnaby almost repeated the phrase, making it a question, and Kitty said, 'That's right.'

'Are you sure?'

Kitty looked around. Something was amiss. People were staring at her. She suddenly felt cold. What had she done that they should stare so?

'Yes, Tom, quite sure. Why?'

'Because what I just said was not quite the same phrase.' So near though, and it had taken him two days to get it. 'What I said – what *Esslyn* said was "*coup d'état*". A seizing of power.'

'Oh God –' The fragment of sound from Dierdre was

almost inaudible but David immediately handed the dog to his father and took her hand.

'Twice a phrase was misheard or misinterpreted. And in both instances the correct readings would have provided vital clues.'

'What was the other, Tom?' asked Boris, the only member of the group who seemed relaxed enough to speak.

'Esslyn tried to tell us with his dying breath of the plan that had undone him. Only one word and that word was thought to be "bungled". But I performed a simple experiment earlier today and I'm now quite sure the word in fact was "uncle". And that if time had been granted him the next word would have been Vanya. Isn't that right, Harold?' Harold's head continued to nod.

'Did you not pick up the razor as you went through the wings, remove the tape in the interval, wipe the handle with your yellow silk handkerchief and put it back on the tray? And while you had it in your pocket did you not put this in its place?' He produced an old-fashioned razor from his pocket and held it aloft.

'Yes, that's right, Tom,' said Harold pleasantly.

'And with an audience prepared to swear you never left your seat you would be in the clear.'

'Certainly that's how I envisaged it. And it all seemed to work terribly well. I can't imagine how you spotted the substitution.' Barnaby told him. 'Imagine that,' continued Harold ruefully. 'And I always thought David rather a slow-witted boy.'

David did not seem to take offence at this but his father glared at the back of Harold's head and Dierdre flushed angrily.

'I shall have to have a firm word with Doris about letting you root amongst my private possessions.'

'She had no choice in the matter. We served a warrant.'

'Hmn. We'll see about that. Well, Tom, I expect now you know how you'd like to know why?' Barnaby indicated that he would indeed and Harold rose from his seat and started pacing in his turn, thumbs hooked into his waistcoat pockets, the DA making his closing speech.

'To elucidate this rather annoying matter we have to go back some considerable time. In fact fifteen years to the building of the Latimer and the formation of my present company. Money was short. We had a grant from the council but not nearly enough for something that was to become the jewel in Causton's crown. And when that drunken old sot Latimer dropped dead his successor was not nearly so sympathetic – I believe he had leftish tendencies – and cut our grant. No doubt he would have preferred to see a bingo hall. So, almost from the beginning, we had cash-flow problems. And naturally one had to keep up a certain lifestyle. An impresario can't go round in a Ford Escort dressed like a shop assistant.' Harold broke here, having reached the top of the stairs, wheeled dramatically, took a deep breath and continued.

'I have an import/export business as you may know, and flatter myself that the hours I worked yielded very satisfactory returns. I kept my domestic expenses to a minimum and put my profits where they showed, that is about my person and into the Latimer productions. However, healthy as these profits usually were, a huge percentage of them went to the Customs and Excise sharks for the VAT and import duty, and another great slice to the Inland Revenue. Obviously I resented this, especially when the scrap I got back in the form of a grant was slashed. So I decided to even the situation out a little. Of course I intended to pay *some* tax and a proportion of the VAT required, after all I'm not a criminal, but a judicious rearrangement of the figures saved me, in that first year, several hundred pounds – most of which went into *The Wizard of Oz*, our opening production. I don't know if you remember it, Tom?'

'A splendid show.'

'Of course when Esslyn prepared my accounts I expected him to recognize my sleight of hand but I was sure, as the company's star, he would appreciate the necessity for such a procedure. However, to my amazement, he said nothing. Just submitted them as usual. Naturally I had mixed feelings about this. On the one hand no one wants an accountant so incompetent he can't spot a necessary juggle or two. On the other it augured very well for the future. And so it proved. I kept back a little more every year – several thousand when I bought the Morgan – and every year no comment was made. But do you know what, Tom . . . ?'

Harold had come to rest near Barnaby. His head, which had been doing no more than gently bob in time to his movements, now began to jiggle and shake alarmingly. '*He had known what I was doing all the time.* He had known and said nothing. Can you imagine anything more deceitful?'

Barnaby, facing the murderer of Esslyn Carmichael, thought yes he could imagine one or two things more deceitful actually, but just said: 'When did you discover this?'

'Last Saturday afternoon. I'd just got in from being interviewed at the theatre. He rang and asked if he could come over. Doris was out shopping so we had the place to ourselves. He didn't beat about the bush. Just said he was taking over direction at the Latimer starting with *Uncle Vanya* and making an announcement to that effect after the curtain call Monday night. I said it was out of the question, and he produced all these figures and said I could either step down or go to prison. I immediately spotted a third alternative which I lost no time in carrying out. I got the duplicate razor from a shop in Uxbridge on the Monday morning. I knew Dierdre's routine and that everything would have been checked long before the five. Esslyn never touched props so I knew he wouldn't be likely to spot the substitution. I simply picked up the original as I went through the wings and, in the interval, took off the tape –'

'Where was this?'

'Well, I popped into the actors' loo but Esslyn and his cronies were there. So I just stepped outside the stage door for a minute on my way to the dressing rooms to give them all a rollocking. Then, going back I made the switch again. It only took a second. I used Doris' flower knife, it's very sharp. Simple.'

Harold gave everyone a delighted smile, squinting at each face in turn and gobbling a little in his cleverness. His beard had lost its clean sculptural outline and now had a disordered, almost herbaceous air.

'I knew of course Esslyn hadn't worked it out all by himself, especially when he owned up to sending that silly book. It was supposed to be a hint, he said. I was involved in "fishy" business, you see. And a cook book because I was "cooking the books". Well really, he could never have thought of anything so subtle to save his life. I knew where that had come from all right. And all the fifth-column work at rehearsals to make me seem incompetent so the takeover would be more acceptable.'

The Everards, trying to register self-righteousness and lofty detachment, merely looked as if they wished they were a thousand miles away. The rest of the company expressed surprised disgust, excitement, amusement and, in two cases (Dierdre and Joyce Barnaby) shades of pity. Troy got up from his position on the steps and crossed the stage. Harold started to speak again.

'You do understand, don't you, that I had no choice? This' – he made a great open-armed gesture gathering in his actors, the theatre, all of the past and triumphs yet to come – 'is my life.'

'Yes,' said Barnaby, 'I do see that.'

'Well, I must congratulate you, Tom.' Harold held out his hand briskly. 'And I can't say I'm sorry that all this has been cleared up. No doubt it would have come out sooner or later but it's nice to start a new season with a clean slate. And I can assure you no hard feelings – at least on my part. And now I'm afraid I must ask you to excuse me' – the hand returned, unshaken, to his side – 'I must get on. We've an awful lot to get through tonight. Come along, Dierdre. Chop, chop.'

No one moved. Tom Barnaby stood, irresolute, opened his mouth to speak and closed it again. He had arrested

289

many criminals in his time, quite a few of them for murder, but he had never been faced with one who had confessed, offered to shake hands, then turned to go about his business. Or one who was so obviously mad.

'Harold . . .'

Harold turned, frowning. 'You can see I'm tied up here, Barnaby. I've been reasonable so far, I'm sure you'll agree –'

'I want you to come with us.'

'What – *now?*'

'That's right, Harold.'

'Out of the question, I'm afraid. I must get *Vanya* cast tonight.'

Barnaby felt Troy move and put a restraining hand on the sergeant's arm. Apart from Barnaby's own sensibilities which made dragging a demented possibly screaming man out of a building and into a car a task he would hardly relish, there was the fact that his wife and daughter were present. Not to mention Dierdre who must have had more than enough of this sort of thing already. Harold was now standing waving his arms about urgently in the centre of the stage. No one laughed. Barnaby prayed for inspiration.

'Harold,' he repeated, moving towards the director then gently touching his arm. 'The press are waiting.'

'. . . The *press* . . .' Harold repeated the honeyed words then his brow darkened. 'That pot-bellied idiot from the *Echo* . . .'

'No, no. The real press. *The Times, The Independent, The Guardian*. Michael Billington.'

'*Michael Billington*.' The blaze of hope in Harold's eyes dazzled. 'Ohh Tom . . .' Harold placed his hand on the chief inspector's arm and Barnaby felt the weight of his exultation. 'Is it really true?'

'Yes,' said Barnaby, his voice rough.

'At last! I knew it would come . . . I knew they'd remember me . . .' Harold gazed wildly round. His face was white with triumph, and saliva, like a bunch of tiny crystal grapes, hung on his lips. He allowed Barnaby to take his arm and guide him down the steps leading from the stage. Halfway up the aisle he stopped. 'Will there be pictures, Tom?'

'I . . . expect so . . .'

'Do I look all right?'

Barnaby looked away from the shining countenance disfigured by lunacy. 'You look fine.'

'I should have my hat!'

Avery got up and collected Harold's succubus and silently handed it to him. Harold put on the hat at a grotesque angle with the tail hanging over one ear then, satisfied, continued his progress to the exit.

Troy, a few steps ahead, opened and hooked back one of the double doors and held aside the heavy crimson curtain. Harold paused on the threshold then turned and stood for a moment to take a last look at his kingdom. He held his head a little to one side and appeared to be listening intently. On his face memory stirred and an expression of the most intense longing appeared in his crazed eyes. He seemed to hear, from far away, a trumpet call. Then, still touched by the magic of death and dreams, he walked away. The heavy crimson curtain fell and the rest was silence.

ANOTHER OPENING,
ANOTHER SHOW

Christmas had come and gone and the weather was far
from clement. The woman who climbed out of the shiny
blue Metro was wearing a full-length fur coat (beaver
lamb) and a silk-lined fur hood. She made her way across
the wet pavements to the Far Horizons Travel Agency
and gratefully hurried into the warm. She pushed back
the hood as she waited at the counter revealing soft, grey-
blue curls, and also removed her gloves. She asked for
some cruise brochures and, at the sound of her voice, the
agency's only other customer, a slender girl in black,
turned and spoke in some surprise.

'Doris . . . ?'

'Kitty – hullo.' Doris Winstanley's response was a spontaneous smile, then, remembering past circumstances, an
embarrassed silence. Kitty was far from embarrassed. She
smiled back and asked Doris where on earth she was
planning to sail away to.

'I'm not sure. It's just that all my life I've dreamed of
going on a cruise. Of course I never thought I'd have the
opportunity.'

'Don't blame you, Doris. Weather like this. You want
to be careful, though.'

'I'm sorry? I'm not sure . . .'

'Lounge lizards. All those charmers looking round for
unattached wealthy ladies.'

'Oh I'm not at all wealthy,' Doris said quickly. 'But I
have had a little windfall. So I thought I'd treat myself.'

'Super. Are you going to stay in Causton when you
come back?'

'Oh yes. I have quite a few friends here.' (Indeed it
had surprised her how many people had visited and

shown genuine concern and support over the last few weeks. People who had never shown their faces when Harold was at home.) 'And I'm going to let my two spare rooms to students when I come back. I've already contacted Brunel. It'll be lovely to have young people around the place again. My own children are so far away.'

Doris talked on for a few minutes more. She didn't mind at all Kitty asking questions or the brazen flavour to her advice. Doris was only grateful that Esslyn's widow was able to meet her and chat with some degree of kindness. Kitty looked very attractive and had made no concessions to the weather. Her black suit had a miniskirt and she seemed to be wearing neither blouse nor jumper beneath the tight-fitting jacket. She was beautifully made up and had on a little pillbox hat with a black veil which came just to the bridge of her pretty nose and through which her pearly skin gleamed. Doris concluded her ramblings by asking Kitty what she was doing in Far Horizons.

'I'm picking up my plane tickets. I fly to Ottawa on Tuesday. To visit my brother-in-law.' She adjusted the veil with rosy-tipped fingers. 'He's been *so* kind. They're very anxious to console me.'

'Oh,' said Doris. There didn't seem to be much else she could say except, 'Have a nice trip.'

'You too. And watch out for those lizards.' Kitty pushed her ticket into her bag. 'Now I must rush. I've got a friend coming at seven and I want to have a bath. See you.'

Doris reflected for a moment on the unlikeliness of this assurance ever coming to pass, then she collected her pile of brochures and made her way to the Soft Shoe Café where she ordered tea and cakes. It was much more comfortable there than at home. There was hardly a stick of furniture in the place a⁺ the moment. All the tired stained hateful old rubbish of a lifetime had gone to the knacker's yard and she would take her time replacing it. She would buy some new things and hunt for some little treasures in junk shops. There would be plenty of time for this. And plenty of money. She had got an awful lot for the Morgan and, to her surprise, a very capable solicitor that Tom Barnaby recommended had sold the business for what seemed to Doris an enormous sum. And of course the house was in her name.

The cakes arrived. Doris selected a praline choux bun with coffee icing, oozing fresh cream, and opened the first of her brochures. It was for a cruise to the Canaries and straightaway Doris knew it was for her. She could almost feel the warm breeze ruffling her hair and see the flying fish leaping from the waves while seabirds called over-head. She would laze the winter away and then sail home in the spring just in time to receive her delivery of shrubs and roses ordered the previous week. And she would get a greenhouse. All her life she had longed for a greenhouse. Doris saw herself pottering amongst the compost and potted plants and tomatoes in gro-bags, and picked up her little silver fork, quite overwhelmed by happiness.

Avery was cooking supper. They were eating in the kitchen as the surface of the dining room table had almost disappeared under a large and beautiful working model of the set for *Uncle Vanya*. Tim had spent the last hour with a torch and cuttings of gelatine experimenting with lighting and making notes. Personally he thought the main room in the composite set looked as if it belonged to a villa in New Orleans rather than one in turn of the century Russia, but there was no denying the close, enervating feel of the place especially when the jalousies were closed and the light seeped through them and fell in dusty bars across the furniture.

'I hope you understand it's just a scratch.'

'So you keep saying.' Tim transferred his attention to Avery's garden, wonderfully light and airy, and pictured it under a bright blue sky. Then he went to the larder, chose a bottle of 86 Mercurey, Clos du Roy and wielded the corkscrew. 'What are you scratching, then?'

'Skate.'

Tim poured two glasses of wine and put one by the

cooker. Then he picked up *Floyd on Fish*. 'I thought you said he wasn't sound.'

'One mustn't be too purist in these matters. Joycey didn't want to keep it – understandable under the circs – so I took it off her hands. In fact' – he tasted the juices in the pan – 'I think this is going to be rather good.'

Silently Avery cursed himself for leaving the book out (it was usually at the back of the tea towel drawer). The last thing he wanted was to remind Tim of the occasion of Esslyn's death. For Tim had confessed to Avery (and Barnaby too) that he had known about the plan to unseat Harold from its very emergence – although not about the blackmail. Assured by Esslyn that, once he had taken charge, there would be no interference in the area of lighting or design, Tim had seen no reason why his original plot should not be used on the first night.

Now, of course, he blamed himself for the outcome. If he had not kept the secret, if he had only told Avery – i.e. the entire company – Esslyn would probably be alive today. For weeks after Harold's arrest Tim sat around the house melancholic and racked with guilt. He hardly ate and took no interest in the shop which, in the pre-Christmas rush, nearly had Avery demented, even though Nicholas gave up his job at the supermarket to help.

On top of this Avery had his own feelings to cope with. A certain disappointment for instance at the realization that Tim's seemingly brave and generous offer over the lighting had actually carried no risk at all if he knew Harold was to be deposed. But Avery nobly struggled to live with the fact that one small bubble had burst and continued to cook ravishing meals when he wasn't belting round the shop and catching up on orders till midnight. But now Tim was getting better. Almost his old self. Avery drained his glass and smiled across at his companion.

'Don't slosh it down like that. It's a premier cru.'

'How you do go on.' Avery lifted the skate on to an oval dish and Riley, who had been curled on top of the bentwood stool like a piebald cushion, leapt (or rather thudded) to the ground. Since Sunny had started visiting the theatre on a regular basis Riley had refused to enter the building and had skulked, wet, shivering and martyred, in the yard by the dustbins. Avery had not been able to bear this for long and the cat was now ensconced in the house, stout, comfortable and living the life to which, in his most far reaching and secret dreams, he had always believed his name entitled him. Now he padded over to his plate and attacked the fish with gusto. It was not up to the *pheasant Périgord* he had had last night but he was certainly prepared to give it eight out of ten for succulence.

'I've made some brown bread ice cream for pudding.'

'My favourite.'

Avery chopped some parsley over the vegetables. 'But I didn't have time to shop today so I'm afraid the baby carrots are frozen.'

'My God!' Tim banged down the knife with which he had been chopping a baguette. 'And I understood this place had five stars.'

'Not for the food, duckie.' Tim laughed then. The first real laugh Avery had heard for weeks. They started to eat. 'How is it?'

'Delicious.'

'What do you think . . .' mumbled Avery.

'Don't speak with your mouth full.'

Avery swallowed and drank some more wine. 'It's ambrosial, this stuff. What do you think we ought to give Nico for a going away present?'

'We've already given him *The Year of the King.*'

'But that was weeks ago. Now he's staying on for *Vanya* shouldn't we give him something else?'

'I don't see why. We hardly see him what with rehearsals. And Cully.'

'There's talent if you like.'

'Terrifying. I thought Nico was good but she lights up the stage.'

'Tim . . . you're not sorry . . . Kitty's gone?'

'Of course not . . . don't start.'

'I'm not. Truly.'

And, truly, he wasn't. Avery, having weathered the first really shattering blow to the relationship that was the cornerstone of his existence now experienced, somewhere unreachably deep within his heart, a safe abiding peace. He didn't quite understand this. It wasn't that he thought that Tim would never stray again. Or even that he might not, on some future occasion, stray himself (although this struck him as incredibly unlikely). Rather it seemed that his personality had somehow developed an extra dimension where hurts or sharp surprises could be absorbed or even neutralized. Gratitude for this unexpected and surprising state of affairs, and for the very fact of his continuing existence, struck him anew and he smiled.

'What are you beaming at in that fatuous manner?'

'I'm not.'

'You look ridiculous.'

'Ohhh . . . I was just thinking how nice it was that the good ended happily and the bad unhappily.'

'I thought that was only in fiction.'

'Not always,' said Avery and poured some more wine.

'Can you drop me off?'

Barnaby and Troy were about to leave the office. Troy, trench coat tightly belted, a shiny packet of Silk Cut to hand, was already anticipating that first cloudy cool lungful. Barnaby shrugged on his greatcoat, adding: 'It's on your way home.' When his sergeant still did not reply the chief inspector added, 'You can smoke if you like.'

Blimey. In my own car. In my own time. Thanks a bloody million. Troy noticed his boss's eyebrows, which today looked more like used-up shreds of Brillo pads than ever, lift inquiringly.

'. . . Um . . . where's the Orion, sir?'

'Joyce took it in for an MOT.'

'Only I'm not going straight home . . . calling at the golden swans.' More waggling. 'It's a free house,' explained Troy. 'Out on the Uxbridge Road.'

'That's all right by me. I could do with something wet and warm on a night like this.'

'Well . . .' Red-faced, hanging on to the door handle, Troy elucidated further. 'It's not really a pub . . . that was just a joke . . . they're on the bath . . . you see . . .'

Barnaby looked at his sergeant. And saw. 'Ah. Sorry, Troy. I'm not usually so slow on the uptake. It's been a long day.'

'Yes, sir.' The younger man made it halfway through the door then turned and squared up to Barnaby in a manner both awkward and defiant. 'I mean the case *is* over.'

'Oh yes, yes. What you do off duty's your own affair.' Then, when Troy still hovered: 'If you're waiting for my approval you'll stand there till daisies grow out of your arse.'

'Goodnight then, sir.'

'Goodnight, Sergeant.' As the door closed Barnaby called, 'Give my regards to Maureen.'

That reminded him of the song about Broadway which reminded him of theatres which reminded him of the Latimer which reminded him of Harold who he was trying to forget which he did most of the time especially once he got into the business of the day. After all he told himself (yet again) it was just another arrest. A bit out of the ordinary in that it was someone he knew. Also slightly out of the ordinary in that, once Harold had realized that the *crème de la crème* of British journalism had not gathered to honour him, it had taken three men to hold him down and get him into a cell. Barnaby, for the first time that he could remember in working hours, took the coward's way out and left them to it. But, even in the canteen, he could still hear Harold screaming.

'Oh Christ!' Barnaby slammed the office door and decided to walk home. A brisk trot through the snapping air should cool his blood. And calm his recollections. He strode down Causton High Street, darkness by his side. Naturally he had never expected, even as a naïve young constable in the early fifties, that his policeman's lot would be an entirely happy one. He had been prepared for foulness galore and the preparation had not been in vain.

298

But there were occasions when all the foulnesses memory held seemed to join together and become one great dark malodorous scab blotting out the good times, the bright times.

He strode on, crossing the road before he got to the Latimer even though it meant he would have to cross back further on. He didn't want to go near the place. Neither did he have any intention of helping to paint the set for their next production, 'heavenly' though his daughter had asserted it to be. She and Joyce would be in there now – he glanced at his watch – carrying on. He knew he'd probably feel quite differently in a few days' time, perhaps even tomorrow, but just at the moment he was sick of actors. Sick to death of their ramshackle emotions and dissembling hearts. Of their posturing ways and secret gossipy gatherings.

Then, on the principle that spiteful coincidence always seeks out those who can least be doing with it, as he moved out on to the pelican crossing the car that had stopped gave a friendly hoot and, glancing across, Barnaby saw the Everards. Their faces were grubby yellow under the sodium street lamps. Clive wound his window down and called: 'Hello.o.' and Donald, who was driving, tootled again. Barnaby carried on walking.

There must be something he grimly thought, as he grimly plodded on, still in a welter of miserable recall, to turn this sorry tide of introspection. Then, felicitously outside the Jolly Cavalier, he stopped. The scene at that morning's breakfast table popped into his mind. Joyce had said would he mind terribly, as she had a packed day and had to be at the theatre by seven, getting something from the Indian or Chinese for his supper? So Barnaby pushed open the door of the Cavalier and went in.

Moving with the times the pub offered a Family/No Smoking room at the back. They also did all their own cooking. Barnaby obtained a large helping of meat pie – rich steak and kidney and flaky pastry – buttered broccoli, roast potatoes and steamed treacle pudding for afters. He added a pint of real ale and took his tray through.

The Family room, living up to its name, held one small family. A thin young woman nursing a baby and a youngish man, heavily tattooed, who was crouching in front of a cardboard box filled with much used toys and showing them to his three-year-old daughter. He was speaking quietly and offering first a shabby animal then a doll. Their table was littered with crisp packets and beer bottles. Barnaby nodded curtly (he would much rather have had the place to himself), and sat down.

The hot savoury food was soothing and gradually he started to relax. The little girl eventually chose a woolly lamb, took it back to their table and offered it to her brother. He took and dropped it on the floor. She reclaimed it and gave it back. He threw it down again. They both seemed to think this was a great joke.

Barnaby started on his pudding. He no longer wished he had the place to himself. The family about which, perhaps fortuitously, he knew nothing seemed to offer, in a muddled way he could not be bothered to define, a kind of solace. He drained his glass and, deciding to make an evening of it, went to get another pint.

The Latimer caravan rolled on. Right now there was a rehearsal for *Uncle Vanya*. Rosa, who had seriously thought about getting off for good and all when she had been offered the measly part of the old nurse, was now glad that she hadn't. It had been a near thing though, more than once. Especially when she'd been told there was no such thing as a small part, only small actors. She'd flounced out then but had sidled back after Joycey had made her some coffee and talked about how exciting it would all be. And Rosa had to admit that it was. Exhilarating in fact. But frightening too.

All the little technical tricks she had accumulated over the years had had to go. And that romantic husky voice the audience loved. All very well being told to use her imagination, search for the truth and follow the syntax. Armourless, Rosa frequently felt she had never been on a stage before in her life. It was like stepping out over an abyss on a thin wire. And *tired*. She had never been so tired. When she looked back at all the leading roles that she had played, all on technique, without even getting out of breath, she marvelled at her present exhaustion. Thank goodness for dear Ernest. He was such a comfort; warming her slippers by the fire, cocoa freshly made as soon as she tottered in. Rosa gathered her wits. It was nearly time for her entrance; opening act four.

Nicholas and Joyce sat together halfway up the stalls. They were both thinking of Cully. Nicholas, madly in love, wondered if she meant it when she said they would meet in London and, if he was in anything at Central, he was to let her know and she'd come along to cheer and shout.

Joyce, observing the sad splendour in which her daughter moved as Yeliena Andreyevna, marvelled and was afraid. What a business she was going into. Cully knew all about theatrical uncertainties of course, her mother had made sure of that. All about the resting and the unanswered letters and the auditions where they would let you know and never did. But, like all young hopefuls, she didn't really think they would apply much to her. Joyce turned her attention to the stage where Boris as Telyeghin was holding out his arms which were draped with a skein of wool. The ancient nurse, Marina, wound the ball slowly, holding it with great care in arthritic fingers. Her face and humped shoulders were old but there was a robust peasant merriment in her cackling voice.

'Who'd ever have thought,' whispered Nicholas, 'that Rosa could turn in a performance like that . . .'

Joyce smiled. All of them were thinking – and feeling – on their feet, alive, alive-o, re-creating moment to moment. Her ideas on her own character (Maryia Voinitskaia) had met with pretty short shrift. Cully had got off lightest. Not that any of them minded. Because what was happening on stage made it all worthwhile.

In the scene dock David Smy was re-covering a chaise longue with olive-green patterned velvet. Sunny lay yawning by the portable gas fire. There seemed to be a lot going on at the moment, he thought, and certainly his walks were getting shorter and shorter but he was not a dog to complain. Perhaps when the nice weather came things would perk up.

Colin worked on a huge armoire, painting it with a walnut stain. Phoebe Glover, the ASM, would pop down and tell them when it was OK to saw and bang and generally make a racket. Colin wasn't too worried. The set was almost finished. There hadn't been any flats to paint or rostrums to drag about, it all looked so simple yet seemed to work very well. He glanced across at David's bent head. Colin was neither a fanciful nor a religious man but, just at the moment, found himself wondering if Glenda knew of their son's present happiness. Why not? Stranger things must have happened. He smiled at the thought. David looked up.

'What is it, Dad?'

'I'm parched, that's what. I'm popping up to the clubroom for a drink. Coming?'

'No. I want to get this done.'

'Henpecked.'

David gave a broad grin. 'You want to bet?'

Upstairs they were taking a break. The cast had gathered together and were sitting, standing or lying about on the stage. Their director rose from her seat in the back row, a tall slim figure in a white boiler suit, and came down to the footlights, clipboard in hand.

'That wasn't bad at all. We've a long way to go yet. Don't look like that, Rosa – what you got in act four was marvellous. Really very good.'

There was a murmur of genuine agreement and Rosa, proud but inexplicably shy, studied the carpet.

'I'm sure we could all do with some coffee. Phoebe?' The ASM hurried out from the wings. 'Put the kettle on, there's a good girl.'

'I'm just painting the candlesticks . . .'

'Leave those for now. Go on, then . . .' said Dierdre, and she smiled. A smile with all the zing and glitter of a bold young Samurai. Then she clapped her hands and cried: 'Chop, chop!'

A selection of bestsellers from Headline

APPOINTED TO DIE	Kate Charles	£4.99	☐
SIX FOOT UNDER	Katherine John	£4.99	☐
TAKEOUT DOUBLE	Susan Moody	£4.99	☐
POISON FOR THE PRINCE	Elizabeth Eyre	£4.99	☐
THE HORSE YOU CAME IN ON	Martha Grimes	£5.99	☐
DEADLY ADMIRER	Christine Green	£4.99	☐
A SUDDEN FEARFUL DEATH	Anne Perry	£5.99	☐
THE ASSASSIN IN THE GREENWOOD	P C Doherty	£4.99	☐
KATWALK	Karen Kijewski	£4.50	☐
THE ENVY OF THE STRANGER	Caroline Graham	£4.99	☐
WHERE OLD BONES LIE	Ann Granger	£4.99	☐
BONE IDLE	Staynes & Storey	£4.99	☐
MISSING PERSON	Frances Ferguson	£4.99	☐

All Headline books are available at your local bookshop or newsagent, or can be ordered direct from the publisher. Just tick the titles you want and fill in the form below. Prices and availability subject to change without notice.

Headline Book Publishing, Cash Sales Department, Bookpoint, 39 Milton Park, Abingdon, OXON, OX14 4TD, UK. If you have a credit card you may order by telephone – 0235 400400.

Please enclose a cheque or postal order made payable to Bookpoint Ltd to the value of the cover price and allow the following for postage and packing:
UK & BFPO: £1.00 for the first book, 50p for the second book and 30p for each additional book ordered up to a maximum charge of £3.00.
OVERSEAS & EIRE: £2.00 for the first book, £1.00 for the second book and 50p for each additional book.

Name ....

Address ....

....

....

If you would prefer to pay by credit card, please complete:
Please debit my Visa/Access/Diner's Card/American Express (delete as applicable) card no:

Signature .... Expiry Date ....